T0146428

THE
DRAGON'S
REVOLUTION

CODY GOGGINS

THE DRAGON'S REVOLUTION

Copyright © 2018 Cody Goggins.

All rights reserved. No part of this book may be used or reproduced by any means, graphic, electronic, or mechanical, including photocopying, recording, taping or by any information storage retrieval system without the written permission of the author except in the case of brief quotations embodied in critical articles and reviews.

If all of the places mentioned in the book are fictitious, then insert "places" as follows: This is a work of fiction. All of the characters, names, incidents, places, organizations, and dialogue in this novel are either the products of the author's imagination or are used fictitiously.If all places are real with the exception of only one or more locations, the author can identify them:This is a work of fiction. All of the characters, names, incidents, organizations, and dialogue as well as [location] in this novel are either the products of the author's imagination or are used fictitiously. For example: "… the town of Pleasantville"

iUniverse books may be ordered through booksellers or by contacting:

iUniverse
1663 Liberty Drive
Bloomington, IN 47403
www.iuniverse.com
1-800-Authors (1-800-288-4677)

Because of the dynamic nature of the Internet, any web addresses or links contained in this book may have changed since publication and may no longer be valid. The views expressed in this work are solely those of the author and do not necessarily reflect the views of the publisher, and the publisher hereby disclaims any responsibility for them.

Any people depicted in stock imagery provided by Getty Images are models, and such images are being used for illustrative purposes only.
Certain stock imagery © Getty Images.

ISBN: 978-1-5320-5032-9 (sc)
ISBN: 978-1-5320-5033-6 (e)

Library of Congress Control Number: 2018907779

Print information available on the last page.

iUniverse rev. date: 08/07/2018

PROLOGUE

I n the beginning, there was only one wandering creature amid the nothingness. He wandered for an incredible amount of time but could not find anything until he came across a material about which even he would soon forget. However, when he touched it, life came forth, and the multiverse began. This creature then set out to create more, and the first things that he created were six beings that he called the Original Creatures. These six creatures held incredible strength, and each of them represented several fundamental ideas. Once he finished creating them, he created both heaven and hell and the angels that would guard them.

After they were created, God started building universes at an immeasurable pace. These universes varied in strength, but all of them would eventually access enough power to thrive. The creator, or God, would eventually become bored with this process and want to be replaced or die, but he would only allow another being to replace him on the throne if that being could fight against him and win.

None of the angels could best him, and neither could Lucifer, his right-hand man. After that, God started inspecting all his universes, looking for someone to beat him, but nothing surfaced. Eventually, he sent the six Original Creatures down to a new planet that he'd created and ordered them to fight. The winner would have the honor of fighting him. While they fought, God continued his search.

These creatures fought for billions of years with no clear victor emerging, except for one who always refused, for some unknown reason, to finish off the others. It got to the point where that creature bested the four of the other five in combat but still refused to kill any of them. Lucifer, who had been watching them fight the entire time, grew far past his patience and fell to the planet to fight and kill all of them. He was accompanied by most of heaven's angels who believed him to be a better person than their creator. Some of the angels believed that their creator had influenced Lucifer's decision so that he could find a worthy successor faster.

It didn't matter, as all six of the creatures banded together and were able to defeat Lucifer and all the angels. They did this by the skin of their teeth, though, and knowing that the angels couldn't die, they began to prepare their world for their inevitable return, each one then cultivating its part of the world to its own liking, creating the most powerful world in the multiverse.

Now, things took their natural course, and many beings evolved within that world, including humans. The creatures would then choose one person per generation of humans to be their host in case Lucifer came back during that time. They would do anything to protect their worlds.

This is the story of the Devil Dragon's host and his friends.

CHAPTER

1

S ame dream. Same one for the umpteenth day in a row. Me just floating in a sea of absolute nothingness for hours until a gigantic pearly-white dragon appears out of nowhere. With it a sense that I should—no, needed to—ask a question, but I wake up every time before it can be asked. This time was no different. After shooting up in my bed, it took me a second to relax, get up, and get ready for the day.

I went to the bathroom, started the shower, and brushed my teeth while the water heated up. The hotel room that my airline had provided me for canceling my flight was terrible, but it was better than nothing. I showered quickly after brushing my teeth. Once done, I grabbed the clothes from yesterday—a plain white T-shirt and jeans—and put them on. Doing a once-over in the mirror, I didn't look too bad. With short brownish hair with a fade up and brown eyes, I could pull off almost anything. It helped that I had a well-built body and what my mom said was the face of a hard worker. I could wear generic clothes, but I was anything but generic.

Being a mixed martial artist since the age of ten already put me far beyond generic. Then came the work ethic people described as near suicidal. Finally came what was inside of me—not some indomitable will or great leadership that could lead a nation but what was in less than one-billionth of the world's population. It was magic. And because of my stardom, my magic powers were well known. The amount of magic inside me would be able to power the entirety of the world for well over a million years. I don't know how I've been able to control it my entire life, but I've kept it in check the entire time. Losing control of it all has been only one minor slipup away. With one stray emotion, everyone dies—not just everyone around me either. Everyone in the world goes. And people wondered why I stayed away from girls.

Sitting down on the edge of the bed, I began to scroll through my phone. Time passed so fast that I had only ten minutes to get to my gate. Grabbing my earbuds, phone, and wallet, I ran out of the room and made my way to my gate. Thankfully, the hotel was inside the airport, so that made getting to the gate easy. When I got there, they were already in the process of boarding, so I just got into the line, scanned my ticket without the stewardess noticing, and boarded the plane. It took me less than two minutes to fall asleep after getting to my seat. I didn't wake up until we landed, and some old lady woke me up with a smile on her face. I got off the plane and made my way to luggage claim to get my bags. That's when something started to not feel right.

Every single person was giving me a wide berth, as if I were poison to them. Looking around, I saw people eyeing me with immense suspicion. A cold chill went up my spine, but nothing immediately happened. Looking around once again, I caught a couple of soldiers dressed in full tactical gear looking at me, one of whom was talking into his radio. Not taking any chances, I headed toward the closest exit and walked out to see two soldiers waiting for me with their guns raised.

It was a split-second decision by them, but it cost them. One of the two soldiers fired his rifle at me, and it got caught by my scale-covered hand. Looking at the soldiers now, I made up my mind and attacked. Both my hands went clean through their chests before they could even react. I pulled out my hands, which were more like claws with scales, out of their backs, and they fell flat on their faces dead. Killing them didn't really affect me, to my surprise. I had no remorse or sympathy. They had tried to kill me. But I realized that if they were attacking me, then something big was going down, and it wasn't just me.

I made the decision to go to my parents' house. Whatever was going on, they would know, and they should be safe. The run would be about three miles to their house—nothing special, but I'd have to go undetected, and that wouldn't be easy in any way, especially with the soldiers crawling around.

Here's a little update on what exactly is going on here. Some background information is needed. In my world, there are people born with magic powers. These special people didn't appear until about eighty years ago. For close to fifty years there was no hate or prejudice. People with magic developed higher IQs than most people because they were given a unique education, and as a result every single one of them was either a prodigy or a master. This gained them a lot of popularity around the world. Most of them became high-ranking people in the world. Some even became politicians, and they controlled a lot of the world—that is, until twenty-seven years ago.

That was when MO showed up. No one knew where they came from or whether it was a group or just one person. Either way they destroyed ten military bases, along with anything in their way in between the bases. There was total chaos, and no one knows why they started their rampage, but it had severe ramifications. Once their rampage was over, they disappeared into the wind, and there hasn't been a single peep out of them since. It didn't help that absolutely no one knew what they looked like. This left everyone taking out their fear on every magic user out there. We went from loved to hated and despised within a month. It was worse for me, specifically, because I had the same type of power as MO, called Devil's Anger.

Devil's Anger was the strongest type of magic out there. It was volatile and dangerous to everyone around when activated. Not only was I covered in impenetrable scales, but I radiated heat like none other. As a comparison, when I killed those soldiers, the air around me became superheated to about one thousand degrees Fahrenheit. Thankfully it was so quick that it didn't destroy my clothes, as it usually did. Still, because I had Devil's Anger magic, I was in the top 1 percent of all magic users in the world in terms of power. There's no doubt in my mind that no one is stronger than me. However, strength and power don't matter if you don't have control over them, and control has never been my strong suit. My record for controlling power for over five minutes was 1.0×10^{-500} percent of what was available in me. That little amount was enough for me to run at speeds far exceeding supersonic and to be able to punch with enough force and precision to put a clean hole through a mountain. I really wonder what I could do at 100 percent.

But it wasn't like that was going to happen anytime soon, especially considering that my entire town was crawling with soldiers. I don't know why, but they were looking for me. Fortunately, living in the same town all my life helped me learn every corner of the area. That's what my parents taught me to do. It sure as hell helped now. Especially in the city, the soldiers had no choice but to go street by street, and it was easy to avoid them. Still I didn't know why they were here or what they were doing, but it couldn't be good. The only reason I could think of was that they were coming after magic users.

It didn't take long to get out of the city and to my house in the suburbs. That was when it started to get tricky; the soldiers there had trackers. Those things always found me no matter the circumstances. Deciding to just fight them instead, I walked outside and stood in the middle of the street for them to see. It wasn't just them there. Turning the corner four Humvees screeched to a halt, all with .50-caliber machine guns on them. The soldiers and I looked at each other for what seemed like forever, but the moment ended when they opened fire. The caliber of the gun didn't matter, as it wasn't going to be enough to hurt me with scales on. While they were firing at me, a soldier picked up a rocket launcher and fired it at me. Catching the rocket before it hit me, I squeezed it in my hand, causing it to explode, creating a smoke screen. Through that smoke screen I exploded, easily killing each and every soldier in an assortment of ways.

I finished that up, sprinted to my house, and saw that the front was suspiciously empty of all soldiers, but that didn't matter to me. I ran into the house after breaking down the door and yelled for my parents, but no response came. Running to the backyard, I saw my parents on their knees with their hands behind their heads. That's when all the soldiers appeared. I never thought the rumors were true about someone being able to cloak others, but it looked to be true. I was about to move to kill all the soldiers, but I was hit with something from behind, and all my energy was sapped from me.

Falling to the ground on my hands and knees, I was furious. I turned around, and my scaled hand ripped right through the soldier's chest. A few more soldiers fell to the same fate before they could subdue me. I don't know how, but my energy was being absolutely sapped, and that's how they were able to subdue me. It wasn't pleasant. Plenty of rifle butts, along with batons, slammed against my body. I kind of had it coming, though, so I just dealt with it. When the soldiers were done, they dragged me up to look at my parents.

"Bryce, become their leader. They will need one, and you can do it." Those were the last words my mom ever said to me.

As soon as the bullets went through their heads, I lost control. At least a fiftieth of my power came out before I got it back under control, but it was far too late by that time. All the soldiers were incinerated by the pure heat that came off me, as a result of my power.

The next thing I knew, hundreds of soldiers and close to a hundred attack helicopters were surrounding me. I felt like my head was being hit with a jackhammer as they surrounded me. My vision started to fade until I couldn't see anything. The last thing I remember before losing consciousness was going onto all fours and growing.

I woke up with chains around my wrists and ankles that connected to walls close to fifty feet away from me. The chains had me spread eagle in midair, and I was left in only my underwear. I couldn't believe this was happening to me. I had gotten careless and let my power take over, causing me to go on a rampage and be as vulnerable as a newborn baby. It was probably why I was tied up right now too, with no access to my powers. I looked about the room and saw a man dressed in all black walk into the room. He was followed by a TV on a roller, similar to what you would see in a classroom. The man didn't say anything but took the controller for the TV, turned it on, and turned it to one of the many news channels.

What was on the TV horrified me. It was a bird's-eye view of my city from a helicopter. It was completely in ruins, and the headline on the TV was "Omaha Devastated." The news anchor began to speak, and the news was worse than I could've ever expected.

"As you can see, the city of Omaha has been completely devastated by a Devil's Anger user named Bryce Ceribri, who as a lot of people know was an MMA prodigy. Out of the 3.2 million people here in Omaha, there have been no reported survivors. It is still possible that there are survivors out here, but out of the 3.2 million, 2.9 have been confirmed dead. This is possibly the greatest tragedy to happen to the world since the

MO attacks. This is but a prime example of why the law banning magic and condemning anyone who uses it is possibly the best law passed in the last one hundred years."

The man in black shut off the TV and looked at me. He didn't say anything as he left the way he'd come. A couple of minutes later, another man in a tailored suit came in with an assortment of tools on a roller table. On the roller table were a scalpel, a spiked whip, salt, alcohol, a jagged knife, and a blowtorch. That was all that I saw before he blindfolded me. There I heard even more roller tables rolling in after that. After a couple of minutes and countless roller tables, the sound stopped and the door closed.

"You obviously know why you're here, but here's a little extra. You officially don't exist in the real world. The only people who even know you're alive are me, my superiors, and the other prisoners. That means that until you die, you will become someone who will be used as a scapegoat to destroy the hope of all magic users. This isn't meant to get you to cooperate or to get any information out of you. It is meant to kill you in the most painful and slowest way possible."

What was he saying? Was I basically his guinea pig until death? Just what exactly was going on here? Were they going to torture me until they killed me? I had so many questions, and I planned on getting them answered, but my power wouldn't come out. I looked around to determine how this was possible. A blue substance was being pumped into me. My best guess was that was the cause. All my questions were answered as the man cut two one-inch cuts on my left pec and then made a long cut from the base of my hip on the right all the way to my kneecap. Then he put the scalpel back and grabbed another object. He put what felt like a serrated knife on my left shoulder blade. There he made a zigzag pattern with it all the way to my butt, continuing over my butt and all the way down to my calf. It hurt like you wouldn't believe, but I refused to yell or cry in pain. Just because they held me prisoner didn't mean that I had to act like one.

Then one of them doused me in water and began to electrically shock me with jumper cables for a solid hour. Once they were done, they again took the scalpel and cut me, but this time they started it from my elbow and went along the inside of my arm to my armpit and all the way down to my hip. They did this on both sides. After that, they took a whip and began to furiously beat me with it until most of my body was cut open. This went on for hours, and just when I thought it would be endless, they stopped, removed the blindfold, and then put an IV for a blood transfusion into my arm. They left the room, and as soon as they did, the room got ice-cold. I heard a song playing above me. It was one of those Russian techno songs that was just one beat, and it kept going the entire night. Sleep was nonexistent, and I'm not ashamed to say I cried that night.

After almost twelve hours of the song, it ended, but as soon as it was over, the door opened. It started the same way it had yesterday, but they put in the IV first. They reopened the two cuts on my chest and made two new ones right next to them. Then they reopened every cut they made yesterday. Afterward, they took salt and poured it into every cut and then doused all the cuts in alcohol and blasted the wounds with a high-powered hose of water, opening the cuts even farther.

Once they were done with all that, they started up a blowtorch, pointed it at the bottom of my feet, and used it to the point where blisters started to form—not enough to destroy the nerves, making it as painful as possible. As the blisters finished forming, they popped every one of them, and they again threw salt into them. Then they took close to one hundred short nails and stuck them two centimeters into my legs, arms, shoulders, calves, and forearms. As soon as all the nails were in, they turned each of them ninety degrees and then pulled them all out, leaving one hundred small holes all over my body.

After pulling out all the nails, they told me to turn my scales, which I did but that's all the power that was available to me otherwise they would be dead. They then started hitting me all over with what felt like baseball bats. This went on for what felt like an eternity. Once they were done, they told me to take off my scales, which I did. As that happened, there was a collective "Huh" from everyone in front of me, followed by the scratch of pen on paper. That was it for the day too, as they took the blindfold off, left, and turned on the same music they had played yesterday.

Looking down at myself after they left, I realized their "Huh" was well earned. There was no blood on me even though they had reopened all my cuts, and they were all healed—not completely, but they all had scabs. It looked as if my scales increased the natural healing of my body. That wasn't the only note I had made from today's torture. My power was still there, but it was being suppressed by something unknown to me, probably the blue stuff. Eventually my immunity would build to the point where it wouldn't work anymore. Now it was all about making it to that milestone.

They brought out everything for me, from waterboarding to sleep deprivation. They just loved to torture me, or at least that's how it felt. I don't know how long it had been either. The days synced together. Every day the blue stuff was losing its potency in me. Still, it was nowhere near the point it needed to be for an escape, but at least there was a silver lining here. Today was slightly different. The three torturers came into the room but with only chairs for them to sit on and no torture tools. The smallest one sat on the left, while the woman sat in the middle, and the tallest of the three sat on the right. I couldn't make out any of their faces, as they were covered from head to foot. However, once they were seated, none of them said anything for what felt like ten minutes. Then the woman spoke.

"What is your name?" she asked.

"Huh?" was my response, as the question caught me off guard. They were probably just checking to see if I was still sane.

"What is your name?" the woman repeated but in a slightly agitated voice.

"My name is Bryce Ceribri. I was born on October 28, eighteen years ago. My parents' names are Xavier Ceribri and Madelyn Ceribri, whose maiden name is Madelyn Argentum. Good enough? I'm still sane," I said smugly.

The woman shifted in her chair, as if she was agitated. The smallest one on the left did nothing, but the man on the right whispered to her. She quickly regained herself and continued to question me.

"Do you know why you're here?" she asked.

"Apparently I killed 3.2 million people," I said.

After a short silence, they began questioning me again, but the questions were not normal, at least in my mind.

"What does the tattoo on your back mean, and how long have you had it?" the woman asked.

"It's a birthmark, and it means nothing to me. I was born with it," I said.

"Has this been painful so far?" she asked.

"Yes," I responded.

"Then how have you never even so much as grimaced during this time?" she asked.

"Because it doesn't hurt enough." In truth, everything they'd done hurt so bad I wanted to cry for my mom, but I wouldn't let them have that satisfaction, ever.

"Okay then. We're done here," she said.

"Wait." The woman stopped herself from getting up and looked at me. "What's your name?" I asked the woman. Hey, I might as well know who was torturing me.

"Captain Julie."

I saw a look in her eyes, and I don't know how or why, but I knew that she was like me: a magic user.

"Why do you work for them? They're taking our freedom away, and you're helping them."

I should've been angrier, but I wasn't. I don't know why.

"My cooperation for my family. It was an easy trade to make."

"Even when the rest of us suffer?"

"Makes it easier when it's people like you who kill innocents."

That shut me up and got me to look down in shame. I couldn't control what happened, but I had still done it.

Their footsteps echoed throughout the room as they left, but they came back quickly with all of their tools for the day. They started out as usual, putting a blood transfusion needle in my arm and running, blindfolding me, and then reopening the six cuts on my chest and making two more next to them. However, today they didn't reopen any of the other cuts on my body. Instead, they took the scalpel and cut a perpendicular line through every cut.

Once that was over, the chains that held me began to stretch, pulling me both downward and upward at the same time. This stretched every inch of my body. After close to an hour of this, the chains went slack and brought me back to my original position. They wasted no time. As soon as my body was within their reach, they started putting the nails one centimeter in all over my body but in different spots than last time. Once they were all in, they did what they had done the last time and turned them all ninety degrees before they pulled them out.

That was only the beginning of the day.

CHAPTER

2

"I'm impressed with his resolve so far," General Summers said to me.

"I am too, considering he's just a civilian," I said.

I wasn't lying either. I had been the warden of this prison, along with many others in my life span—all military ones allowing torture—and never had I seen someone with this much resolve.

Looking over at the general next to me, I had personally never heard about him, but his résumé was legitimate and impressive. He was young for a general, but to me that just meant he was ambitious. He was about six feet tall, with jet-black hair in a crew cut, and he held himself in good form. What set me on edge around him, though, were his eyes. They held an unparalleled intelligence. It was frightening. He also had one gloved hand—I assumed it was from a war wound, but still, he set me on edge.

"What about any of the other prisoners here? Are any of them showing signs that they would work for the military?" the general asked as we walked past the door to the prisoner's room.

"The answer is no, two tops right now," I answered.

"Out of three thousand, only two look like they would help the military?" he asked in mild shock.

"You can't expect much after everything that's happened. It's only been a week. Give it time," I said. There was no way anyone we held was going to ever work for anything affiliated with the government.

"Okay, show me some of the strongest ones you have then," the general said.

I took him back toward the way we had come, past the prisoner Bryce's cell. Once we passed the cell, we saw glass boxes piled on top of each other, where only the strongest were put. They didn't go through the same torture as Bryce did. They were only isolated, but they could move freely in the general population once a week. Having talked to most of these people over the last week, I knew the oldest one among them was twenty-two, and all of them were nice people, just born in the wrong time, I guess.

"Explain to me how you ranked each individual on their strength," demanded the general.

"Well, all magic users are in a ranked system, but these fifty people are separated from that ranking system and put into the *s* category. There are only forty-six regular s-class people, as the top four are ranked as zeros, ranging from s0 to s0000. Bryce is of course the s0000, and the woman who oversees his torture is the s000. The other two s0s are Heaven's Justice users, but they're both psychopaths and have been heavily sedated so as not to harm anyone," I said. That should explain it rather well.

The general then opened the file that he still had on him and flipped through it until he found what he wanted. "Please show me Connor Zmiana. I want to speak with him," he said.

I turned toward the closest guard and asked him to take us to the second floor, where Connor was. He was the s10. Connor was a tall, skinny boy topping out at 170 pounds and about six feet four inches in height. He had black wavy hair that stayed close to his head. Other than that, he was an average kid—except for the fact that he could go undetected anywhere and escape from anything like it was his job to do so. There was currently a pool among the staff about who would escape first, and the smart money was on Connor; mine was on Bryce.

The platform the general and I stood on went up one story and then to the right about fifty feet. We stopped in front of a glass room identical to the ones around it, with the prisoner chained up inside. As soon as the door was opened by the same guard who had taken us there, General Summers went in and sat down in front of the young man who was one of the younger ones here, being only eighteen. As soon as the general sat down in front of Connor, his questions began.

"Exactly how long have you known Bryce Ceribri?" General Summers asked.

"About fifteen and a half years," Connor said without missing a beat and in a very polite manner.

"Would you say that you are best friends?"

"Yes."

"Do you know what Bryce did?"

"Yes."

"Do you forgive him for what he's done?"

"Yes," Connor said with extreme conviction.

"Why?"

"Because he probably lost control and couldn't control himself. And if I had to wager, he probably lost himself because his parents were killed in front of him. But, hey, that's just me," he said, never breaking eye contact with the general.

"If given the chance, would you help him escape or escape with him?"

"Why wouldn't I? Ya really think that I wouldn't leave this place?" he asked, shaking the chains that bound both his feet and hands.

"Would you ever consider killing as an option to escape?"

"I already killed enough, and I still got caught. Next time I'll just be smarter about it," he said, staring me down this time.

It was time to cut this off. I was getting an uneasy feeling about all this. As soon as we were out the door and it closed, I turned to see the prisoner standing and the chains on the ground, not on him. All he did was smile and sit back down and put the chains back on before we went back down. He was taunting us, saying that he could leave and escape whenever he wanted, but why was he waiting?

"So what can he do?" the general asked as we were leaving. He saw the prisoner out of the chains too.

"He can turn his body into anything he touches. He can quite literally be made of anything from steel to sand. He's ranked s10 because of his power numbers we got from the scanners, but in pure terms of body count, he's third only to Bryce and the s2. He killed five thousand soldiers while trying to escape capture," I said as the elevator-like floor took us back to where we started.

"5,000. How?"

"Got onto a ship, killing everyone on it, and then figured out the missile system. I'm sure you can figure it out from there." It got quiet between us for a couple of seconds before he continued.

"Who's the s2? I'd like to meet him," he said.

"The s2 is a she, sir. Her name is Annabeth, no known last name. She's only sixteen and will only talk to women," I said.

The reason she didn't talk to men wasn't that she was scared of them. That girl was the definition of a Casanova, only she was a lesbian. In fact, after the first two times she seduced the guards, no one even dared to go near her cell. She was a very pretty girl with wavy dirty-blonde hair and sparkling gray eyes. She was quite tall for her age too, sizing up to about five feet eleven inches, which was taller than Bryce, who was only five feet ten inches.

"Take me to her, please," the general said even after hearing that she'd only talk to women.

I signaled to the guard who was guiding the floor to take us to s2. He gave an inquisitive look for a second but then started hitting the control panel, taking us to s2.

We got there after about a minute of traveling. Her cell was on the complete opposite side of where the s10's cell was, and it didn't help that the floor elevator, as I liked to call it, was really slow. The conversation that these two were about to have would be either short or funny, hopefully. I needed to laugh today.

As we arrived, she looked at us with her sparkling gray eyes and a hint of excitement that quickly faded away once she noticed that there were no women with us. She quickly turned her head away from us after noticing this and didn't budge a single inch even when the general came into the room. She stayed curled up in a ball, facing the corner of her cage, while the general just sat there and waited for her to turn toward him. This continued for almost five minutes, with no talking whatsoever. I was just about to take the general out when she spoke.

"Why won't you leave? I don't want to see either of you," she said, still not turning to face us.

"I won't leave until you talk to me," the general said.

With that, she finally turned to face him and sat up. With the way she was now, it was easy to see how she was so good at what she did. She had pure gray eyes that seemed to sparkle when you looked at them, accompanied by dirty-blonde hair that was cut short, only reaching midway down her neck, which framed her face in a very pretty way. Even with the white garments she wore and the chains on her body, it was easy to tell she had a nice figure. She was pretty. *When this is over, I'm calling my wife. I need a bit of reassurance now.*

"Hi," she said. "Now leave. We talked."

The general chuckled at that but showed no signs of moving.

"You really want to talk, don't you?" she said to him after a minute. He nodded his head, and then she said, "Ask away then."

"Do you know how many you've killed?" he asked.

"Close to thirty thousand. My sister and I lived in the suburbs of the city Bryce destroyed. The people where we lived didn't like magic users in the slightest, and we were constantly beaten without remorse. My parents threw us away as soon as they found out about our magic, and we lived day to day finding new places to stay and food to steal to eat. We were never helped by anyone until we came to that city where Bryce and Connor found us rummaging for food outside of a fast-food place almost seven years ago. At first I thought they were going to beat us up, but then Bryce showed me his scales, and Connor showed me how he changed when he touched his hand to the brick building. We were relieved. They essentially took us in after that and cared for us in every way possible. They always hid us at either one of their houses and would give us food every day. They even found places for us to stay once they went to boarding school. I owe both of them a lot," she said. Both the general and myself were not expecting that outburst.

I never knew she had a sister. She must still be at large.

"Okay ... but how is your body count so high when you were near the city Bryce destroyed?" the general asked.

"I cleaned up. Everyone he didn't kill I killed. I know it sounds merciless, but, well, far more than half of my kills were mercy kills. People who had either lost everything or begged me to kill them or, more abundantly, the people who already had fatal wounds. The rest of my kills were from soldiers trying to capture my sister and me."

"General, we should really get going. You have to leave and get to your meeting," I said before the general could say anything to continue the conversation.

After a couple of seconds, the general nodded his head in agreement. He then bid farewell to the s2, and we were transported back to where we had started. I proceeded to walk him out of the prison. We didn't speak at all on the way out, and that usually wouldn't have seemed unusual, but something seemed different about the general as we were walking out. As we arrived at the gates where his car was waiting, he turned to me and bid farewell.

CHAPTER

3

What day was it? At this point, everything had gotten so hazy that it was hard to tell what was up and what was down. This mostly had to do with the fact that the torture hadn't stopped since they interviewed me. The only time they weren't torturing me was when they were doing what they had already done and changing the blood bags that kept me alive. I didn't know how many they'd already gone through, but the number was high enough that the number escaped me. At this point, it was impressive that they were still going and a miracle that I was still alive. It wouldn't be that much longer until my immunity to whatever they were pumping into me was high enough to escape—maybe another week until that was possible.

There was a way to tell how many days it had been. At the beginning of each day's torture session, before this marathon started, they would always make two vertical cuts in my chest, stretching about one and half centimeters. Now it was only a matter of counting them and seeing how many there were. *Shouldn't be that hard.*

It turned out that it would be really hard to do that. There was so much blood on my chest and cuts from other things that it was hard to find those specific cuts. Also, my dizziness didn't show any signs of disappearing soon, as they were still torturing me with a lot of vigor. That just meant that I would have to wait it out before finding out how many days it had been.

The torture continued after my short inner dialogue. It was hard to stay awake during that time, and I refused to let them win, but eventually the continual torture became too much for my body, and my mind finally went dark. I didn't know how much time passed after that, but every now and again the door would open, and someone would come in. The person would add two new cuts to my chest and then replace the bandages that covered my entire body. The individual never stayed long but sometimes would talk to me. It was impossible for me to determine what the person was talking about, but the individual was probably just using me to vent daily frustrations.

Toward the end of all this, a guy who looked to be in his early forties, appeared. He was wearing what looked like army pants and boots but had a regular T-shirt on. He had jet-black hair and seemed to be a couple of inches taller than me. Also, his body was skinnier than mine, but it lacked nothing in tone, as was evident from his bare arms. However, on his left hand was a white glove. What stood out most about him to me were his eyes; they were sharp and calculating and held an unimaginable intelligence behind them.

He did practically nothing but smile and pace around the room. This continued for what felt like ten minutes, but at certain points he would start either twiddling his thumbs or snapping his fingers, but neither lasted long. His pace slowed until he came to a complete stop right next to me. There he stood looking at me for a solid minute, sizing me up. At the end of that minute, he tilted his head to my right, smiled, and then disappeared. Once he was gone, I saw hundreds upon hundreds of flashes of dead bodies. All were torn, smashed, ripped apart, slashed, or just simply dead. One at the end looked particularly horrifying; she was still alive and begging for help before the life finally left her, and she lay dead surrounded by tons of debris.

As soon as her body disappeared, I shot up awake, drenched in sweat and screaming in the dark room in which they had tortured me. Looking over my body quickly, I saw what must have been hundreds of cuts and marks all over my body, but the most uniform ones were those they made every day. Those went over and through other marks, and since they did two every day, I quickly counted how many there were. The total came out to roughly 364 cuts, which meant that they had been torturing me for roughly six months.

At that moment, the door opened, and two people walked in. The light behind them made it impossible for me to tell who they were until they stepped out of the doorway. I stood up to face them head-on, but as soon as our eyes met, my guard softened; it was Annabeth and Connor. We all stood there for a couple of seconds just looking at each other before we rushed forward into a three-way bear hug. I was overjoyed to see that they were still alive, and they seemed to feel the same way about me, but once they saw my scars, they became furious with me.

"Why are you letting them do that to you!" yelled Annabeth.

"It's not like I have much of a choice, but it won't be long until we escape," I said, wiggling the needle in my arm that was connected to the IV bag full of the blue stuff.

Connor subsequently smacked me upside the head and pulled out the needle.

"You can't just let them get away with anything anymore. They started a war, so now we're allowed to do anything. You know that, right, Bryce?" Connor asked.

"Of course, I do. Annabeth, where's Lucy?" I asked, hoping to steer the conversation away from me and to Annabeth's twin.

"She took advantage of the soldiers being focused on me and escaped while I was fighting them," she said.

"So she's still out there? Once your sister gets here or we hear from her, we'll escape. That good?"

"Why do that when we could escape now? Escaping from this place for us would be like walking out of a fast-food place," she said.

She wasn't wrong. At least the top one hundred here could walk out of here like it was no problem.

"For one, if we escape now, we'll have no idea where your sister could be. It'll be better to wait. She'll come to us eventually."

"I hope you know that the reason no one's escaped yet is that they're waiting on you. No matter what you've said about leading us in the past, it doesn't matter. You are our leader now. Plus, it helps that everyone will be gunning to stop you and not the others if there's a mass escape. Also,

Charlie and Marie are here," Connor said before putting a syringe in my hand and leaving me to my own devices.

Charlie and Marie were there. It never crossed my mind that they would've been caught. They were the smartest people I knew. They must've been caught when they were sleeping or when they were having sex. Those were the only two ways they got caught. It was also entirely possible that they had no idea what was going on and walked into a trap without knowing it.

I wasn't given much time to dwell on that, as only three minutes after Connor and Annabeth had left, over twenty soldiers came into the room with their guns raised. They were probably looking for Connor, because there was no way they would let him and Annabeth visit me. As soon as they entered the room, however, I felt someone poke at the edge of my mind. Lucy was nearby. Maybe now was a better time than any to escape. It was obvious that the soldiers wanted me to lock myself back up into the chains that hung in the middle of the room. This wasn't really a problem, but if I continued to let them push me around even after they started all this, it might become a problem. It was time to show them that I was just letting them do this to me. Pushing the syringe Connor had given me into my butt and injecting whatever was in it, I simply smiled at the soldiers, feeling my magic rush back into me.

In an instant, I was covered in scales and attacking the soldiers. They were taken aback for half a second before the bullets started flying at me. I must have been little more than a blur to them. They were too easy to dodge, and before they were even halfway through their first magazine, five of them had already been killed by slashes from my claws to their necks and arteries. After that, the soldiers became so reckless that they started firing every which direction, trying to hit me, but the bullets were still much too slow to even get close to me.

In the next twenty seconds, they were all dead by my hand. I gave the last one alive a special treat. I had grabbed him by the neck and raised him up above my head. He looked at me with pure horror as he tried to loosen my grip on his neck, but it was no use. Once he gave up and looked at me with a pleading gaze, I crushed his neck in my hand, leaving only the skin intact; even the upper part of his spine was crushed to dust.

He dropped to the ground with a slight thud that echoed throughout the room. I then proceeded to pick up every body and throw them into a pile right outside the door. I went back to the cot and waited for more to come. I looked down at my body. It seemed to be covered in blood, but it wasn't all theirs. Almost every cut on my body that they had made was now open. The cot was soon stained red with blood after only a minute of waiting. Before I started to get dizzy, I covered and uncovered myself in scales getting my wounds to scab over.

After about ten more minutes of waiting, someone walked into the room. It was Julie. She looked furious, and I could feel the power coming from her as she stood ten feet away from me. She was a Devil's Anger user just like me. She stood there emanating enough power to incinerate normal people until she finally changed and was fully covered in scales with flames billowing out from her.

Getting up from the cot, I turned to face her directly. She attacked me as soon as my body was in position. Her speed easily exceeded Mach 3. However, my magic was activated and ready, which made dodging her punches easy. Even though we had the same magic, our power levels were too far apart for her to be a serious threat. She was still much faster than I was, as she was pumping more magic into herself than I could, but it didn't matter. Every move she made was telegraphed, making it easy to dodge and counter. Every punch she threw ended up just hitting air, and every time, she ended up with one of my fists in her face, rib cage, or back. Even her kicks were easy to see coming. I dodged easily and hit the back of her legs every time. She never stood a chance.

She thrust with her left arm toward my stomach. Dodging it, I grabbed her arm and threw her toward the wall. She spun in midair, planted her feet on the wall, and boomed back toward me. Again she spun in the air; her right leg came for my head. Blocking it with my hands, I grabbed her foot and slammed her down onto the ground, creating a shock wave that shook the entire room to the point of almost collapsing. While the room was still shaking, I rotated her ankle until there was a resounding crack loud enough to be heard over the shaking of the room. She became immobile, and I got on top of her and started punching her at an incredible rate, hitting every part of her upper body and completely breaking her arms and defense, leaving her face wide open. By the time it was over, the ground had been indented a couple of feet. She was still alive, however, but that was a good thing. I had a gut feeling that eventually she would be useful to me and my friends.

As I did with the soldiers, I picked her up and dragged her to the door by her hair, as she had no clothes left, thanks to her fire. Just as I was about to toss her out of the room, she grabbed my hand, but hers was really weak, and she was in no condition to fight. She was able to speak, and she asked, "Why ... you not ... kill ... me?"

It was easy to tell that she was still broken and probably had a severe concussion along with a lot of broken bones, but there was no reason not to answer her question. "Because I think you could be a help to me in the future."

"Were you ... even ... tryin'?"

"No."

It didn't take them long to send another twenty-plus soldiers to the room where they found the previous group all dead and their strongest magic user on the verge of death. They were probably scared out of their minds when they went into the room, expecting to find me lying in wait to kill them. What they didn't expect to find was me sitting peacefully on the floor, cross-legged, waiting patiently for them. All their guns were raised immediately, and they were poised to attack at any moment—not like it would do them any good. It would have been easy to kill all of them without even moving, but there wasn't a need to do so.

As I started moving to get out of my cross-legged position, one of the soldiers fired a shot that bounced off my scales. They knew immediately that they had just made a grave mistake. They probably didn't even feel anything; their deaths were so quick. The only one who was left standing was the one who had fired the shot. He looked absolutely horrified at what had just happened. He even had blood from his teammates all over his face. Looking at the bodies of his dead teammates, he realized that this was all his fault. He reached down to grab his pistol and brought it up to his head. My hand was on his gun before he could pull the trigger.

"We all make mistakes and have to live with them. Don't take the easy way. Redeem yourself in some way," I said to him while my hand was on his gun. He pulled away from me but left the gun in my hands as he ran out of the room and down the hall. It would be another twenty minutes before there was any contact with me; this time it wasn't through soldiers but through the intercom.

"Hello, Bryce, this is the head of the Släve. There are twenty-four people outside your room right now who come from various criminal backgrounds from yakuza to street gang head to even a disgraced special operations sergeant. All of whom are armed with various weapons of their choice, from knives to clubs. The only thing they weren't allowed to have was guns. Now the rules of this fight are very simple. You can't use your powers, and if you do, your friends, along with half the people here, will be killed. The rewards for this fight are also very simple. You win, and your friends and others live. You lose, and you die. Just so you know too, there are cameras in there, broadcasting throughout the whole prison, and everyone will know if you betrayed them. Now fight."

When he finished those words, the door blasted open, through which came men dressed in various assortments of clothes. The man from the speaker wasn't lying either. They were armed to the teeth, and if what he said about freeing them was true, there was no way any argument would work with them. The only two out of the twenty-four whom I noticed who didn't want to be here as they were circling me were the yakuza and the special ops sergeant. Their clothes and weapon choice showed who they were. They probably would rather die than be allowed to live dishonorably. There was no honor in this fight. The other twenty-two looked hungry to kill and had probably been killing their entire lives. This was not going to be easy without magic.

I needed a weapon; otherwise, there was no chance without powers. I surveyed the people, and one guy looked promising. He was black, standing about six feet five inches, and was wearing clothes that suggested that he was a smuggler from Africa or South America. His weapon was a machete, which would be perfect for this, but there was no way he was going down without a weapon or time. I turned around to see if anyone had a suitable weapon to take him down, and someone dressed like he was part of the Mafia attacked me with a wooden bat. He swung at my head, and I dodged just in time. As he followed through with the swing, my body jolted back up, and I gave him three quick but powerful jabs into his side and one up under his right shoulder, dislocating it. When his arm flopped to his side, he swung the bat again at my head with his other arm, but it was slow. I grabbed the bat, twisted it until he let go of it, and then swung it up and made contact with his jaw, popping his head straight up and back, eliciting a sickening crack.

When he fell, my head whipped back toward the smuggler, and I charged him, sliding into his legs as he swung his machete. He fell face-first onto the ground. As he was pushing himself up, my bat contacted his head and shattered. He was either knocked out or dead. It was hard to tell, but his machete just lay there in his hand. Without skipping a beat, I took the machete and raised it in front of me, and my body instinctively went into a fighting stance. That was when everyone else charged. Thank God they weren't organized and didn't attack all at once. They probably would have killed me if they had done that.

The next couple of minutes were a blur of slashing, dodging, parrying, and blood. At the end of the haze, only two of the twenty-four were still standing, and they were the yakuza and the special ops sergeant. The yakuza held a short katana, and the sergeant held a combat knife but also had some throwing knives on his side. I was already cut up, bleeding a lot and beginning to bruise from the others' attacks, and these guys were more trained than the rest, so this wasn't going to be easy by any means. Additionally, the machete was now on its last legs and looked as if it was going to break soon.

The first one to move was the yakuza member, who dashed forward with his sword raised. As he charged, the sergeant threw his knives at me, forcing me to block and dodge the knives while the yakuza got closer and closer. Just as he brought down his sword, I blocked the last throwing knife and dodged, but it was too late. The sword made a large gash from my right shoulder all the way down and across my back to the opposite side of my hip, ripping through and opening other scars. The pain was enough to make me yell, but the yell was a precaution so that my scales wouldn't instinctively activate.

The yakuza soldier didn't wait after the attack and immediately came after me with a downward swing while I was getting up from partially dodging his previous attack. I raised my machete, and our weapons collided, and they stayed there until his sword slid off mine to the left. As soon as the sword hit the ground, I grabbed his hands over the hilt with my free hand, and he knew it was over. The machete went straight through his neck, leaving a hole all the way through his neck. He was dead before his body hit the ground.

The sergeant picked up all his knives and was completely ready to both attack and defend. I slowly got up from my kneeling position, discarding the machete in favor of the katana to face him head-on. We stared at each other for the longest time as we began to circle each other, me with the short katana held out front and him with his throwing knives in one hand and his combat knife in the other. He would make the first move.

He threw his knives as he ran at me with his combat knife. He was faster than I had expected, and when I had dodged the final knife, he was already on me with his knife going for my leg. At the last instant, I was able to twitch just enough so that his knife didn't cut my artery, but it still ripped my leg open. He tried to follow this attack with one to my back leg, but my sword was there before he could finish it. We were at a standstill, and he began to move his other hand to hit the back of my left leg to unbalance me, but my right leg was faster than his arm, kicking him in the chest and pushing him away from me. As he staggered back, I spun around and swung the katana at him at an angle from right to left. It made a perfect cut from his left shoulder all the way to his right hip, and he fell onto his back, barely breathing. He would cease to breathe a minute later. The fight had ended but not really.

As soon as the soldier died, someone poked inside my mind. Someone was trying to worm their way in, and I would have resisted if the consciousness wasn't one that I recognized. It was Lucy. She had arrived, so the time to escape had now begun. Connor or Annabeth had probably told her that the escape would begin when she got here. She said nothing but just poked my consciousness, telling me that she was there. Without skipping a beat, I covered myself in scales and said to the supposed people watching, "Now." This statement was followed by tremendous amounts of crashing and breaking of glass, bars, chains, and all other kinds of restraints. The escape had begun, and now I only had to find clean clothes that fit me.

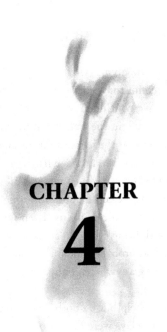

CHAPTER

4

I walked out of the room to see Connor and Annabeth waiting for me, surrounded by dead bodies—most of which were from me, but a lot weren't. Connor took the lead of the three of us and took us along the medium-sized steel hallway for what felt like a mile on feet that hadn't really walked in half a year. Eventually, after skipping five turns, he turned right, and we saw a giant steel wall. Connor turned toward me and gestured for me to take the lead. Annabeth could have easily done this too, but he knew that I would want to get back into things as quickly as possible.

Walking up to the wall, I turned on my scales and flicked the wall. For a split second, nothing happened, but then it exploded outward like out of a cannon. The power seemed to still be there even in my weakest state, but there was still a lot to improve on. What lay beyond the steel wall was a paradise for us: canned foods, supplies for survival, clothes, sleeping bags, blankets, tents, and even rucksacks to carry all of it. Most importantly, they had clothes that fit me.

We practically stormed the supplies, and by the time we were all done, we had five rucksacks in total filled to the brim with supplies. As we headed out of the room, about twenty soldiers fired at us. A gigantic wall of thick ice appeared in front of us, courtesy of Annabeth, who could create and control ice. We continued to hear them fire at the ice, but it quickly ended as Annabeth sent the wall down the hall with a flick of her wrist. The shooting stopped as the ice wall hit the end of the hallway. The soldiers weren't there anymore, and the ice had started to change colors.

We continued down the way we came, and all around fighting was going on. We helped where we could, and our group gradually got bigger until there were a few hundred behind us. Even with that vast number, there was still plenty of fighting going on as we were leaving. Connor was leading the way, as he had probably taken this path many times. He had always been good at going anywhere at any time without detection. The man was practically a ninja.

As we ran I couldn't help but be bothered by our slow pace, as time was of the essence. Our delays were due to our helping others, however, so it was worth it. Another thing that bothered me about our escape was that I hadn't seen Charlie or Marie, who should have been the first to meet us. They were both incredibly smart and would have had no problem deducing where we were, but they could be airheads, so it was possible that they were just screwing around somewhere. Whatever the reason, it didn't matter, as they would find us eventually.

As we came upon a steel double door that was easily twenty feet tall, a man and a dog were waiting by the door. I could tell right away that they were Charlie and Marie. Charlie was black and had always been the tallest of us all, standing at about six feet six inches, but like Connor, he was little more than a twig. He had black hair that puffed out from his head like a Q-tip. Charlie had always been the smartest of us too, but he was a bit of an airhead. Personally I thought he was just crazy. However, he was a capable fighter in any situation and was a prodigy at tactics.

"What took you so long?" Charlie asked, getting up from sitting.

"Can't ya tell, Charlie? They were helping all those people behind them," Marie said as she changed back into her human form and put on the clothes Charlie gave her.

I'd always known that she had the magic to change into any animal she knew, but seeing her change back always gave me the chills. It just didn't seem natural at all. Still, it didn't take away from the fact that Marie was a California dime, with mocha skin, curly black hair, and bright hazel eyes. I'd be lying if I said I wasn't a little jealous of Charlie.

"Doesn't matter now. We're behind schedule," Charlie said as he put his hand on the door, exploding it outward and sending the double doors out into the bright sky.

The first thing we saw was a courtyard filled with what seemed like desert sand, and lots of fighting. There were tall steel and stone towers all around the courtyard that had giant openings at their bases. Those openings must have been where others came out of. It took about a second for all this to sink in, and by that time, everyone behind us was surging forward. Connor, Annabeth, Charlie, Marie, and I had no choice but to get out of the way so as to not be trampled. Once the group we had just saved ran out, all five of us reconvened in the middle of the doorway.

"Lucy wants us to scale this wall and jump over. She's waiting with a car about a mile and a half straight out," Annabeth said.

"Why don't we just blast through?" Charlie asked once Annabeth was done talking.

"She said that there's over six hundred feet of straight steel behind the wall and would take too long to blast through it. It would just be easier to scale it and then run across."

If that was true, this would be a good time to test myself and the very little magic I could use without going crazy and killing everyone again.

"But I know that you're just gonna try it anyways," Annabeth said, turning her head and looking at me.

Smiling, I walked out into the courtyard and turned to face the giant steel wall in front of me. The others followed and stood behind me, waiting for me to do something. I sized up the wall, and it seemed that my calculations for the power seemed to be correct. I took a couple of steps forward and performed a straight kick to the wall, hitting it perfectly in time with my hips to create the most power. This action made a sound so loud that the four behind me clutched their ears and fell to the ground, as did everyone else within the encampment. The entire courtyard ceased fighting to find the source of the sound. For a second or two, nothing happened, and then a half circle going up half the wall formed. The wall had been kicked and blew back out into the open, creating a gigantic opening from which to escape the prison.

I turned around to face the others. They were still on the ground, clutching their ears. I extended my hand and walked toward them. They started to pick themselves up from the ground with my help while they recovered their senses. I realized that the sound created when I kicked the steel wall made me deaf. Everything the others were saying just floated over me, as I couldn't read lips and had no idea what was going on. Connor seemed to figure it out quickly when he said something to me and got no response other than a blank face. He then turned toward the group, yelled something at them, and pointed toward the opening. It was easy to grasp what he meant, and the group charged through the opening, staying as a group the entire way. As we ran my hearing started to come back.

We never slowed down; we kept the same pace even with our rucksacks. The first thing that struck me as we left the prison was that we were surrounded by nothing but sand. We were in the middle of the desert. Taking it in stride, we continued going forward, trusting that Lucy was exactly where she said she was. We ran for a good half an hour before stopping, far exceeding the mile-and-a-half distance Lucy had provided. By this time too, my hearing had come back completely, although there was still a ringing every now and again.

"Where's Lucy?" I asked Annabeth as we were resting.

"Coming," she said, pointing to a cloud of sand in the distance. "Since we didn't go directly up the wall like she wanted, we left at an angle and ended up three miles away from her."

We fell silent after that, waiting for the car to get here. We didn't have to wait long. Lucy pulled up next to us in a Jeep. Without saying anything to each other, we threw our rucksacks in the back and piled into the car. Annabeth rode shotgun with her sister, while Connor and I sat in the middle, and Charlie and Marie sat in the back together.

Connor and I said nothing to each other for the beginning of the drive, but we could hear Annabeth and Lucy updating each other on what they'd done the past six months, and we could hear Charlie and Marie doing the same. The mood continued like this until Annabeth got sick of seeing the two in the back go at it and froze everything around them, causing them to stop. Annabeth had gotten a lot stronger since our imprisonment. She didn't even need any hand movements anymore to create ice. Thankfully, this lightened up the mood between Connor and me. He was in a bad mood, but he'd been like that since we met in my cell earlier today. The only plus so far was that there were mountains and a forest coming up, so we would be getting out of the desert soon.

"Hey, you good?"

"Just thinking about some stuff, man," he responded.

I was sure I knew why he was being a bit mopey, but I asked regardless.

"Taylor?"

"Yep."

"How'd it go?"

"Well, she never exactly gave an answer to the question. She kind of just stood there looking shocked."

"That it?"

"No, we were attacked a couple of seconds after I asked. Turns out she's a magic user like us and pretty capable at that," he said.

"What type of magic does she use?" I asked.

"Destruction like Charlie and probably stronger."

Connor's statement piqued Charlie's interest, and he immediately leaned forward between us, listening to the conversation. He usually did this, so we just ignored him and continued with the conversation.

"Hey, have you guys seen anyone come in in the last few months? My friend and I got separated a while back. He told me he'd meet me at the forest up there, but he isn't there," Lucy said.

"How do you know that? The forest is at least four miles away," Annabeth said as she sat next to Lucy.

"Just because my power doesn't kill doesn't mean it can't get stronger."

"What does he look like?" Charlie asked.

"He's about your height, Charlie, and he's got wavy blond hair, built like Bryce. Also, he was probably placed with you guys at some point," Lucy said, looking in the rearview mirror while talking.

"He has a scar from one of his ears to his lip, right? And burn scars on the left side of his face and neck, right?" Charlie asked.

"Yes. Do you know where he is now?" she asked.

"No, he went a different way to escape. When we went right, he went left. I couldn't tell ya where he is," Charlie said to Lucy.

She looked like she was going to cry. Instead, she stopped the car, opened her door, and threw herself onto the sand. There she crisscrossed her legs and sat straight up with her eyes closed. She was probably trying to find the mind of the boy she had mentioned. Ten minutes passed before she moved again. She sprang up and sprinted toward me.

"I need you to go in this direction as fast as you can right now," she said with desperation, pointing in the direction of the prison. "I need you to save Shane. He should be just outside the prison."

I rushed out of the car and faced the direction in which she had pointed. We were at least one hundred miles away from where I needed to go. Using the same amount of power used on the door should be enough to get there in a couple of seconds. Ramping up my power just a bit, my body lowered into a sprinter's stance, and after a couple of seconds, I boomed off in the direction of the prison.

The prison was in front of me five seconds after booming off, and three people were fighting, but it was more like two people beating up on one. They were all Heaven's Justice users, the second-strongest magic and the only real counter to my magic. Heaven's Justice users were normally pure white, but these guys were pitch-black and emanated a humongous amount of power. The one being beaten up was powerful but nowhere near as powerful as the other two. Not a second after taking this all in, one of the black ones knocked the white one toward me. Catching him, I set him down.

He was knocked out on the ground, but he looked exactly as he had been described. Before I was able to check if he had any bad wounds, one of the black Heaven's Justice users attacked me from behind. I turned my body like lightning to face him. He was charging me with an eerily black sword and shield with the same-colored armor. He raised his sword as he closed the distance between us in preparation for a strike.

Once he was close enough, he brought the sword down at me at a lightning-like pace. The world seemed to stop, and his every movement was clear as day. Taking advantage of whatever this was, I immediately took a step to the right and swung at his shoulder joint. His shoulder moved after he was hit, it was easily dislocated, and the joint was probably shattered. The world then sped back up again, and his sword came at me at a sideways angle, but it was too easy to dodge, as the pain from his shoulder registered with him. This caused him to drop his sword before it even got halfway to me and fall to the ground. He was holding his shoulder, completely defenseless.

His defenselessness was too big of an opportunity to miss. I started to walk toward him, thinking about all the ways to finish him quickly.

My guard went down completely, and because of this, the other black Heaven's Justice user came out of nowhere and hit my left shoulder with a hammer. Luckily, however, my instincts kicked in at the last moment, and my body was covered in scales. He didn't let up either and kept swinging his hammer over and over again. After a couple of times, they became easy to dodge, as he telegraphed every one of his swings. After fifteen repetitive swings of the hammer and repetitive dodging, I shot directly at him as he finished a swing with a wide-open chest. My hand went completely through his chest, creating a hole in the middle of it, and for a moment, sparks of electricity electrocuted the air around me.

By the time the one who had been impaled by my arm fell back onto his back, the other black-colored Heaven's Justice user had already retreated to the prison. He floated over the wall to the other side and back to captivity just to get away from me. He must have been really scared. I looked back toward the unconscious kid behind me. He looked about fifteen, but you never know.

After I spent an ample amount of time checking his body for injuries of any kind, he seemed to be in good shape, considering he had just taken on two obviously psychotic Heaven's Justice users. He fit the description that Lucy had given me earlier for the person with a scar going from his left ear to his lip and minor burns around the scar on his face and severe ones on his neck. Wanting to save time, I picked him up and threw him over my shoulder and got into a sprinter's stance with one hand holding the kid over my shoulder. Then I boomed off in the direction of the car.

When I arrived at the car, there was a giant brick of ice behind it, and everyone was outside waiting for me to come back. Lucy, however, was on the ground with her back resting against the car. She was out cold and had a makeshift sling on her left arm made from one of Annabeth's pant legs. Everyone looked to be a little banged up but nothing as serious as Lucy. Still, Charlie was tending to all of them as I arrived. When he noticed me, he stopped talking to Marie and casually walked over to me before inhaling and exhaling a deep sigh.

"I know you just went through a lot, and I'll forever be thankful because of what you did, but next time please check your surroundings when you take off like you did."

"Why? What happened when I pushed off?" I asked.

"The shock wave you created when you took off flipped the car in the air toward Lucy," he said, gesturing with his head toward the unconscious girl. "She was just able to get out of the way so it wouldn't crush her. However, she couldn't fully avoid the car, and it clipped her arm. She's lucky to be alive, Bryce. Now, as for the car ..."

"Can it still drive?"

If the car was broken, that was a huge problem and a way for people to find us.

"The axle is definitely damaged, and one of the wheels is starting to lose pressure. Otherwise, the car is fine, but I don't know how much farther it will be able to take us," he said.

"Do you know of anything close by that we could safely get to with the car?" I asked him, surveying the horizon but finding only a couple of bumps that were too far away to tell what they were.

"Well, over there seems to have some type of mountain we could hide in for a while," he said, pointing to one of the larger bumps on the horizon.

"What about that mountain?" I asked, pointing to one north of us that looked gigantic and even had ice toward the top.

"I thought about that one too, but it's too close to the prison for me. I already did the math, and we would only be about 450 miles from the prison, and only about 700 miles from Slăve HQ. I want to be farther away than that," he said.

"We'll never make it farther than we already have without running the risk that they'll know exactly where we are at any given moment. As soon as we go back or through any type of city, we're screwed. They'll be on us like bears to honey. We need to stay away from that, so I think that the mountain over there is the best option," I said while pointing to the mountain I had mentioned earlier.

He seemed to contemplate this question, and I could see him weighing the pros and cons of both situations.

"What about water? It's not like we can use Annabeth's ice. It would kill us all," he said.

"Look at all the green around the mountain. Either there's a river, or it rains a lot. Water shouldn't be a problem, and we have the supplies to clean the water if need be. I grabbed them while we were going through that supply room."

"Ah," he said with an irritated tone, "let's do it."

"You think we can make it in the car?"

"The axle isn't damaged enough where it wouldn't survive that. What I'm worried about is that we'll run out of gas before we get there."

"Do you know how much gas is left?" I asked him.

"About thirty or forty miles' worth, and that was when we stopped, so we should have enough ... I hope."

"Well, let's get going," I said. "No time to lose. They probably already sent soldiers after us."

Charlie barked to the others to get their attention, and they came over to us. We then told them our plan. They didn't voice any complaints, and when we asked them if they had any better ideas, none of them answered. With that, we started to pack everyone into the car again. We had to make some adjustments with the rucksacks so that we could open up a third seat in the back, but that took almost no time. The kid whom I had saved was put in the far back, along with Lucy and Marie, who made sure nothing could worsen the injury while she was still unconscious. Charlie ended up in front with Connor, and Annabeth ended up with me in the middle. We didn't speak for the longest time, just like earlier with Connor, but when she finally did open her mouth about twenty minutes later, we began driving again.

"What was she like? Taylor, I mean. I want to know more about the chick who caught the pickiest man in the world's eye," she said in a hushed whisper.

"Really? That's the first thing you want to ask about after six months in prison?"

"I'm curious," I looked at her with a blank face for several seconds before sighing.

"Well, she could tell you everything about every plant and animal on the planet right now, like she was reading from a script. She loved botany and animals. She was a bit high-strung, but she was like the unofficial mother of our group when we hung out together," I responded after a few seconds of thinking.

"Okay, I got all that, but what did you mean when you said she was a genius like us?"

"Oh, I forgot to tell you. She's a magic user like us. She uses destruction, like Charlie," I said, and Annabeth's eyes widened in shock.

"Wow, I can't believe that she was a magic user. What did she look like then?"

"Imagine a really strict but hot teacher with panty hose and all. She even had her hair tied in a bun above her head, and she had a strict but beautiful face with glasses to go along with it. Well, that was what she almost always wore, at least," I said. It was a lot of detail, but I got used to memorizing stuff like that from going to a guys-only boarding school. You'll memorize the look of just about any girl.

"When do you think he started to like her?" she asked.

"What makes you think I would know the answer to that question?"

"I don't know. I just thought you would've noticed a change in his behavior," she said, still in a whisper.

I knew exactly what she meant, but that was something Connor should divulge, not me.

"No, sorry. I never noticed anything different about him. He hid his liking for her really well," I said to her, deterring her from asking any more questions until we got to the forest that stretched about five miles from the mountain. We had just barely made it too. Just as we were arriving, the axle gave out and disconnected from the car. Thus, the car flopped to the ground.

We all got out of the car, grabbed our gear, and began walking into the forest. Before we could enter the forest, Marie changed into a hawk and scouted ahead of us. I honestly expected more from the forest, but it was a very generic one, to say the least, and didn't really stand out very much. It was quite literally how you would expect a forest to look. The only thing that was different about it was that plant life was incredibly abundant and there seemed to be almost no animals except for bugs. This was disturbing to me, as it probably meant that these plants were poisonous. Two minutes after noticing this and plant life getting even more abundant as we continued to walk into the forest, I told everyone not to touch them, just in case.

Marie swooped down and landed on Charlie's shoulder and told him that we were going in the wrong direction, and we needed to turn left. He told me this as Marie flew back up into the sky. Following her instructions, we all turned left and went in that direction. Gradually, all the plants that had been there before began to disappear, and we ran into a deer. We completely froze when we saw it, and it did the same. We stared at each other for a couple of seconds before I realized that it was only a fawn no older than three months and posed no threat. We continued walking, but a giant buck the size of Charlie came out of nowhere and tried to hit me in the side with its antlers, probably thinking that we were going to hurt the fawn. My scales were protecting me in an instant, and the buck died on impact.

"What do we do with it?" Lucy asked. She was the first one to speak up in a while.

"I don't know, but we can't just waste it and leave it here," I said.

"I could probably get a decent amount of meat out of it if anyone has salt," Charlie said, stepping up to look at the deer.

"I didn't know you hunted," Connor replied.

"I did when I was younger, but that was before my magic presented itself and my dad bolted," he said, putting everyone in a somber mood. I was the only one in the group who didn't have at least one parent walk out on them because of it. "But seriously, did any one of you grab salt?" Charlie asked again, which snapped everyone out of their haze.

"I think I have some," Annabeth said, dropping her rucksack and rummaging through it.

It felt like this took ages until she finally pulled her hand out with a triumphant grin, displaying the salt to everyone present.

"Great, now we just need a decent tree to hang it from. We could probably get one by the lake we're going to," Charlie said, getting up and taking one of my rucksacks. He then proceeded to throw the deer over my back. It was a lot heavier than it looked on the ground, and it almost caused my knees to buckle out from under me, but I handled it.

We began to walk again in what we thought was the right direction, but after only a few minutes all the plants started to come back. We turned left just like we had done before and began walking. It wasn't long before we came to the mouth of a cave. We decided not to go into it and took a left around the cave, with me at the front and Annabeth at the back. Just as Lucy and her friend had gotten away from the entrance of the cave, we heard a slight rumble within it, and a gigantic black bear came out of the entrance. Annabeth, who was the only one left for the bear to see, jumped back away from it by creating ice at her feet to propel her away. She then pulled off the rucksack, set it down, and faced the bear. I would have intervened, but it was obvious she wanted this one.

The bear charged her, and after waiting for the very last second, she jumped out of the way and created a wall of ice, which the bear slammed into with its left shoulder. It got up from the impact, but its left shoulder was unusable, as its left arm hung limp as the bear favored its weight to its right side. It hobbled toward Annabeth, who stood less than fifteen feet away, knowing that the fight was already over, but it kept going. This bear wanted to die fighting for its territory. It didn't want to die after running away. It knew what was coming.

Annabeth granted its wish with a flick of her wrist. Ice protruded from the ground and went straight into the bear, ending its suffering. She then proceeded to retract the ice from the bear, leaving a hole by the neck of the beast. I knew right then that she had changed in more ways than just her power. She was merciful to the bear, something I'd never seen her be to anyone or anything before now. There was a short silence after that, but it was broken by Charlie.

"You see them too, don't you?"

"Yeah," she said, hanging her head.

I looked over to Charlie and was about to ask what that was about, but he had a sad look on his face. It was better not to prod.

"Charlie, can you call for Marie? I want to know how far away we are from the lake," I said to him, breaking his somber mood,

Without missing a beat, he whistled to Marie. She landed next to him and changed back into a human, completely naked. The first thing she did was ask for her clothes from Charlie, who gave them to her. As soon as she was dressed, she turned to me and said, "It's about one hundred feet this way." She nodded her head in the direction that we were going. "It's a bit smaller than I thought it would be, but the water is incredibly clear and clean."

We followed her to the lake. There was no fish or really anything in the lake either. It was completely untouched by everything around it. I couldn't believe how lucky we were to find this place. And to boot, there was a river coming down from the mountain with sheets of ice under it. It was literally a funnel from the melted snow to the lake, and all we had to do was follow the river to get around the mountain. I glanced around at the others, who all had the same look of disbelief on their faces. This was the best thing to happen to us in a long, long time.

CHAPTER

5

Since we found the lake just over two weeks ago, I had only slept three times. Each time came with horrible nightmares about what had happened in Omaha and the torture that they put me through. At this point it didn't matter if sleep came to me anymore, as the sleep wouldn't be good anyway. As a result, sleep deprivation and sleep with horrible dreams were my only two options, and neither was appealing.

At least my tent was nice, keeping me from the bugs of the night, but as always, around two in the morning I needed to get some fresh air. I stepped out of the tent and headed toward the now-fading fire in the middle of the camp and crouched by it, getting some of the remaining heat. I stoked the fire, and it started up a bit again but not too much. It was there that the waiting began, not only for morning but for someone who had been watching from the other side of the lake. This individual had come every night for the last four nights and just sat there on the other side of the lake.

Whoever it was probably thought they were hiding their power well enough not to be detected—and they were, to be honest, but not against Lucy. She knew they were there, and that it was a girl. At around three in the morning, the presence reappeared for the fifth time in a row. One hour later, like clockwork, the person left, and the sun came up, dawning on day sixteen of our time at the lake. The person who had been watching us was either a friend, making sure we were friendly, or an enemy, who was scouting us. However, that was only guesswork.

The day proceeded as it normally did. My friends didn't wake up until around ten, and they slowly moved around, doing their morning routine. This usually entailed brushing their teeth with toothbrushes and toothpaste from the storage area at the prison, bathing themselves with the water from the lake, and going somewhere in the forest to relieve themselves. At around noon, we grabbed some of the bear meat that had been salted and smoked from the makeshift refrigerator Annabeth had made on day two to keep our food good longer. After we were all done eating, Marie spoke up.

"We should follow the river up the mountain. I know this place is fantastic, but it's too close to the base and way too visible. For us to stay hidden, we need to go up the mountain following the river," she said in a matter-of-fact tone.

They didn't know exactly where we were, but they knew the general area in which we went, so it couldn't be that much longer until they happened upon us. We all knew it was true, so no one protested, but when it came to picking who would go to scout out the path, they never gave me a say.

"Only Bryce will stay behind. The rest of us will go," Connor said.

As my mouth opened to protest, everyone shot me with a knowing glare. They all could tell that I basically hadn't been sleeping since the first night, so they were giving me time to sleep while they scouted out the path up the mountain.

They left not long after that. All they did before they left was grab some food and water just in case they needed it. Once they had put these items into one of the rucksacks, they were off, leaving me all alone. Taking advantage of the situation they had given me, I went to my tent, laid my head down, and closed my eyes. Sleep enveloped me almost immediately, but not long after, so did the nightmares.

It was the same one as before, with the screaming and terrified faces of everyone who had been killed by my hand. Their faces became more and more distorted until they looked like demons coming to get me. This was when I ran in my dream, trying without hope of success to get away from the demons. The chase never lasted long, as they enveloped me, pinned me down, and started attacking me. And like always, my body shot up, drenched in sweat, my throat was sore from yelling, and I was fully aware of my surroundings.

It was now dark out, as there was no light coming into the tent. I went outside and looked around the camp to find no one was there, but the moon was out and high in the sky. It was probably the longest I'd slept in a while, but it was terrible, and right now something felt off. I looked around, and the cause of the feeling stood up from a bush, covered in black camo and raising a gun toward me. He had a different aura from that of the person from the last few nights, so he wasn't the same person, but there were about two hundred soldiers behind him, judging from my senses.

My eyes closed as my body got covered in scales so that I could concentrate fully on feeling for the soldiers who were about to attack me. It was too dark to try to fight them with my open eyes, as they would be able to avoid me easily with their black camo. It was much easier to rely on my other power-enhanced senses than to rely on my eyes. Just as my senses were ready, the people on the other side fired, but it wasn't loud. The bullets bounced harmlessly off my scales with a distinctive pinging sound. It didn't take a genius to figure out that they had just made a very dumb mistake.

The boom made by me charging them was louder than thunder, and a lot of the soldiers fell to the ground clutching their ears. This made it incredibly easy to finish all two hundred of them in a mere two minutes, leaving only two of the soldiers alive. The forest where the soldiers had been was once green and lush but was now crimson and degraded. I looked at my hands and seeing the blood on them I couldn't help but feel remorse, but it was either me or them. That was my world now.

I pulled my eyes away from my hands and looked at the two who were still alive. They looked terrified. One was a man and the other a woman, both roughly the same height. They were rather stoic in their positions, not saying or doing a thing. They were dressed in the same black camo as everyone else and held the same gear as everyone else. Maybe they could teach me how to clean the guns and use them. It would be useful for the others to know this.

"You," I said, pointing to the man, "show me how to clean a gun and how to shoot it properly."

"And what if I refuse?" he asked, looking at me.

"Then you die," I said.

"You wouldn't. You're the type of person who will only kill if you have to," he said, and as he finished the sentence, my arm covered in scales had gone clean through his chest. The woman was shocked into a stunned silence, evident by her face.

"Now will you do what I asked him to do?" I asked the woman, who nodded her head and proceeded to pick up her rifle. Over the next hour, she showed me how to properly clean the gun with a kit that she explained every soldier had. She explained how to shoot both the rifle and the pistol that the soldiers had on them. She even went the extra mile and told me what a lot of the soldiers carried on them, and most of things that she said they carried would be incredibly helpful to us.

After almost three hours of her teaching me these things, it was over. She had told me everything she could. I let her leave alive, holding up my end of the bargain. It was good for us to be known, as rumors always spread, creating fear, and fear was excellent to have on our side. Not long after she left, I hefted everything possible, carried it to the other side of the lake, and dropped it in the middle of the tents. It would take eight trips to get everything, and by that time, everyone was coming back, and they looked shocked to see what was waiting for them.

"Bryce, what the hell is all this?" Charlie asked almost immediately after seeing everything.

"Weapons," I stated, dropping the final gun onto the pile.

"From what?" Shane asked. It was obvious that he and Lucy were together, but they never announced it, so we never said anything. They probably thought that they were slick.

"Soldiers who wanted to kill us," I said, gesturing to the other side of the lake. They couldn't see much because of the dark night, but they could smell the blood.

"Oh," Connor said. He was the first one to catch the smell. "Well, what now?" he asked.

"Learning," I said and then proceeded to show them what the soldier had shown me.

The process took a little bit longer when teaching them, not only because it was my first time teaching it but because there were six of them instead of one. They were all fast learners, and within an hour and a half, they were all able to do it by themselves. In about the same time, they were able to shoot the guns fluently too. After this accomplishment, they went to bed. The only thing that bothered me was that the same presence as before was back but this time more in the direction from which everyone had come back. Was it stalking someone from the group? I called to Lucy before she headed to bed to talk about it.

"Did you feel it while you were going up the mountain?" I asked her.

"No."

"Can you point to where exactly they are?" I asked.

She lifted her left hand and pointed to the other side of the river that I thought was the right direction.

"Go this direction exactly without changing course, and you'll find her ... and Bryce," she said as I started in that direction, "she's powerful and wounded, so be careful approaching her. Make sure she knows you're friendly."

I nodded my head in thanks and headed off.

It had been almost an hour since the camp had disappeared behind me, but the aura Lucy had told me about was still nowhere to be found. The only thing to do was to keep walking until it came around, which didn't take long. It wasn't five minutes later, while I was stepping over a fallen tree that was rotting on the inside, that the power of the one who had been stalking us came to me. It was faint, and there was something wrong with it, as Lucy had told me. It was either wounded or sick, but it didn't matter; it was the nature of everything to be more aggressive against the unknown when sick or injured.

I followed the aura. It was the strongest right outside of a small cave that lay at the base of a forty-foot cliff. The person was inside the cave with nowhere to run. She was trapped, and I could tell by the slight increase in her aura that she could probably sense me outside the cave. Not waiting any longer, I walked into the cave slowly but surely, with my scales on and my body positioned to be ready for anything. Still, I was not prepared for something to happen above me.

The ceiling above shattered, and rocks came down toward me. I dove forward, so none of the falling debris hit me, but now my path back out was blocked. At least there was only one way to go now: forward. I took five steps down the path, and another part of the ceiling collapsed, but again none of the debris got to me. It didn't take long after the ceiling collapsed again to find whoever was there. I smelled blood as I walked farther down the tunnel and came upon someone with a familiar face

"Taylor?" I asked, looking at the girl barely illuminated by the small fire in front of her. She was wearing rags that at one point had been her clothes. Her glasses were still there too, but they were broken and held together by pieces of tape.

"Bryce? Why are you here?" she asked.

It then hit me that she had no idea that I was a Devil's Anger user, and my scales were now off.

"The same reason as you," I said, flashing my scales for a couple of seconds.

"Oh ... how'd you get here?" she asked.

It was an honest question on her part, but she was probably wondering something else, and so was I.

"A couple of friends and I escaped from a prison where we were all held. If I may ask, why have you been watching us for the past several nights?"

"I did no such thing," she said defensively, but after I gave her a look saying that I already knew, she continued. "Okay, well, I looked at your camp at night but could never tell who was there." When she was finished talking I saw the left side of her rib cage where her white shirt was caked red.

"You land on something?" I asked, bending down and lifting her shirt to see the wound. It wasn't deep or bad in general, but there was a decent amount of bruising—enough to make it hard to walk.

"Don't worry about the bruising. It's been there for about two days, so if it was internal bleeding, I would've already been dead," she said.

She was right, but I proceeded to poke around the bruising, focusing mostly on the ribs. After only a few pokes and prods, I could tell that most of the ribs on her left side were fractured and maybe one or two were broken.

"When did this happen?" I asked, still surveying her rib cage.

"Two nights ago, when I was coming back from surveying your camp, I tripped on some moss that was on a boulder and landed on it."

"Well, most of your ribs are fractured, and maybe one or two are broken on that side of your rib cage. Everything else seems to be fine and in working order."

"How can you tell?"

"You pick up a few things on diagnosing broken bones when you've practiced to the point of breaking them."

"Father?"

"Mother, actually. Dad was my main trainer, taught me over one hundred different martial arts, but my mom was the one who taught me how to take a punch. Which usually ended with me breaking something."

"Never would've guessed," she said as she stuck out her right hand to me. I grabbed it and pulled her up.

"Can you walk? I don't want to be lugging you around everywhere," I said to her as I turned around to face down the tunnel from which I had just come.

"Yeah, I'm good. You'll just have to help me a bit on the steep parts," she said, getting up and standing next to me as we walked down the tunnel all the way to where the ceiling collapsed the second time.

"Before I blow us a new hole, are you ready to see Connor?"

She seemed to contemplate it for a couple of seconds before nodding her head. So I destroyed everything that stood between us and freedom.

CHAPTER
6

When Taylor and I got back to the camp that night, everyone was outside around the fire. It got quiet really quickly when they saw her. Connor was the first one to react by standing up and walking over to Taylor with a face I had never seen him have before. It made sense once he got to Taylor because he just grabbed her and kissed her, hard. Taylor jumped a little in surprise at the action, but within seconds she was fully into it.

I was clapping and cheering Connor on and so was Annabeth. The rest of the group was too shocked to do anything about this and just watched it happen—until Connor pushed Taylor onto her back and got on top of her. Once that happened, Annabeth stopped clapping and stepped stepped in and blasted them both with snow. They were understandably angry for all of two seconds before they realized what exactly they had been doing. At that point Taylor's face got extremely red, and Connor had the biggest grin one could have. I fist-bumped him in congratulations as soon as I could.

After Connor and Taylor's little episode, we all went to bed on a high note. Unfortunately, it couldn't stay that way, as the demons visited again that night and they were fiercer than ever. Just looking at them in my dreams scared me even though I knew that they couldn't really hurt me. They kept on coming, giving me no time to rest, and they endlessly tormented me until my eyes snapped open from a sharp smack on my chin.

My eyes snapped open as Annabeth straddled my chest, with her right arm completely covered in her diamond-like ice. The fact that her ice had cracks in it was incredibly scary. I'd never seen it crack before, and I'd tested it myself. I looked around, and practically everyone was in my tent holding me down, and some of them even had light burns on them. I looked down at my body, and it was fully covered by my scales with sparks all around me.

All their eyes rose to look at me. Their faces showed just how scared they were, but when they saw me awake, their faces filled with relief. It freaked me out to see them scared of me. My demons were winning within me, and it was far too easy to tell.

Everyone, including myself, got out of the tent. The sky was just beginning to brighten. Dawn was just around the corner, and that meant that we would be leaving this sanctuary too. We had decided on the way back from the exploded cave that we would head up the river and up the mountain. They said that they made it about a quarter of the way up the mountain when they scouted it two days ago. So it should be only a two- or three-day journey, and with everyone now up because of my episode, we began to get ready to leave.

Last night we had packed everything into the rucksacks, so all that was left to do was to take down the camp. It took us just under an hour to collapse all the tents and put them into the rucksacks. That also included the bear and deer skins we had gotten over the past two weeks. However, the skins didn't fit into the rucksacks, so we just carried them over our shoulders. We began to leave, with only the dead soldiers and the charred remnants of a fire left behind.

About twelve hours later we had made incredibly good progress for the day, and we weren't even done yet. We had stopped only three times throughout the day, once to eat and the other two times for water. With that said, we did have two injuries, one of them Shane's and the other Annabeth's. Shane fell off the side of a small hill after he tripped on a branch and cracked a rib or two. He could keep going, but his rucksack needed to have some things taken out—most of which went to me. Annabeth, on the other hand, stepped on a hornet's nest about two hours after Shane fell. She had bite marks from the hornets all up and down both of her legs. Annabeth simply shrugged off the stings after a few minutes' rest, and we continued. She was a bit too stubborn for her own good sometimes.

It was about time we stopped. We were almost even with the cliff we had spotted on our first day. The cliff was still some distance away, but we were at about the same elevation as it was, so getting there shouldn't be that hard. I raised my hand in a fist, and everyone took the signal and plopped down where they were. There wasn't room for everyone to lie down, so some people doubled up in their sleeping bags. The people who did so were pegged as couples, and if we weren't 100 percent sure about them before, we were now. Connor doubled up with Taylor, Shane with Lucy, and Charlie with Marie. This left Annabeth and me to have our own sleeping bags, which we were happy about. It was a hassle to share sleeping bags with people.

About forty-five minutes after everyone had gone to sleep, I heard a distinct click and saw the flash of a camera behind me. I turned in my sleeping bag to see what it was. Annabeth was standing right behind me, taking a picture of the others doubling up in their sleeping bags.

"Where did you find that?" I asked her.

"When I picked up one of the rucksacks from the soldiers you killed, this was inside of it, along with a solar charger," she responded. She then put the camera back in said rucksack and went to bed.

Not long after she was asleep and snoring, my body gave up and succumbed to sleep. The dreams started the same way, with everyone dying in front of me, but this time, when the demons showed up, the entire dream changed. I was standing in some type of grand building, but everything was blurred out except for one thing. It was standing in front of me, taking agonizingly slow steps toward me. The sight of it made my body freeze and cower in fear. It was otherworldly. The left side of its body was completely white, and everything on that side seemed to be going upward, ripping the floor to shreds. The right side of its body was pitch-black, and everything seemed to be forced downward. That wasn't all. Its eyes were the opposite color. The left eye was black, and the right eye was white. However, two streaks of red started from below each eye and went down its face. It then opened its mouth and roared.

My body shot up in the sleeping bag, completely drenched in sweat, and there was no water to wash myself, so the stink would stay with me for the day. No one else was up, and the sun was just peeking above the mountain in front of me. It was probably around nine or ten; it was just about time to get everyone up so that we could make it to the cliff before the end of the day. If we really pushed ourselves, we could probably get there before two o'clock.

Before long we were traveling to the cliff. We didn't go at the speed to make it there by two, but we would got there by three. However, we eventually came across a drop-off inside the mountain that was about one hundred feet wide. We could have gone around it, but it would have added at least two hours to our travel, so Annabeth decided to create an ice bridge going across the gap. It was a normal bridge, but she added more ice on the sides that curled up, almost making it into a tube. I would have been able to power up and carry everything, but we needed to know the area in which we were going to be living. At least relatively so this was better.

After crossing the ice bridge, we continued our journey to the cliff. It didn't take long to arrive. We stopped at a clearing and could see the river, as there were no trees or anything blocking it. The clearing was huge too, easily big enough to put a mansion on it. Once we had fully taken in the clearing and its surroundings, which took about ten minutes, Marie flew up into the sky to see exactly where the cliff was. Not five minutes after that, she flew back down and told us that it was only about a ten-minute walk directly opposite the river to our right.

After she had given us directions to get to the cliff, Taylor, Charlie, and I took the route while everyone else set up camp. Charlie and Taylor paved the way to the cliff by exploding the ground and debris in front of us at a minimal rate to create a makeshift path. Once she got to the other side, Taylor went back to get the others and had one of them who didn't know the way try to follow the path. The path was even more of a success than I had expected, as everyone got there without a hitch.

Once we were all at the cliff and taking in the view, most of us let out a slight gasp in amazement at how beautiful it was. The forest below and in front of us was stunning, and the endless desert right behind it was just as breathtaking. Then to the right of the cliff, between the desert and the forest, was a small town. It was clearly abandoned and quite old, from what I could tell, but there still might be some salvageable things down there. It wasn't exactly the time to go exploring. It was time to settle down and rest for a bit.

Over the next hour, we went back to the camp as a group, and I decided to go hunting by myself to see what type of wildlife there was around the area. We weren't that high up the mountain, so there should still be deer and other forest-dwelling animals. It didn't take long to find a deer, as there was a small fawn in front of me, but it wasn't all that far away from a buck. It was worth the risk. Either we got a fawn whose meat was juicier than a buck's, or we got both. It was really a win-win situation. That was exactly how it turned out too, as the buck heard me kill the fawn with my claws, and it charged with its antlers first. And just like the last time, almost twenty days ago, it died.

By the time the two deer were brought back, everyone was set up in their own little areas, but there weren't eight tents; instead, there were only four. Apparently, the couples had decided to bunk up, and of course no one decided to help me out and make my tent. Charlie then noticed the two deer by my feet and immediately took them. I went over and made my tent between Annabeth's and Connor and Taylor's tents. Charlie had already finished gutting, skinning, and hanging the buck, and he had already gutted and skinned the fawn but hadn't hung it yet.

"Hey, Charlie, wait," I said, jogging over to him.

"What's up?" he said, turning to me, away from the small fawn in front of him.

"Let's cook the deer," I said, pointing at the small fawn.

"With what? We don't have any cooking supplies."

"No, but we can make a spit with one of the rifle barrels. The fawn is pretty small, so it should work."

"What about holding the spit in place? And how are we gonna rotate it?"

"Annabeth can make ice forks so that it will stay, and she can create a handle for us to turn it too. Besides, even if she can't, I'm sure we can find a way. We are in a forest after all. There's bound to be some sticks that we could use," I said, throwing a look over my shoulder to Annabeth, who was busy carefully rebuilding her ice fridge.

Nodding his head in agreement, he called Annabeth over and told her what they were going to do. While he was explaining what to do, I left and made my way to the cliff to try to get another glimpse of the fading light before it was all gone. What awaited me at the cliff was much more entertaining. Once the forest cleared into the edge of the cliff, I saw two people very close to each other. As I walked as quietly as possible, their faces came into view. It was Connor and Taylor, and they were kissing. One side of my brain was cheering for Connor, while the other side was giving a slow congratulatory clap for my best friend.

As the sun went down over the desert, the view faded from sight. I dangled my feet over the edge and saw something heading our way. It looked to be a company or two of soldiers heading our way with machine gun–mounted Humvees and transport trucks but no tanks or helicopters. Probably just scouting out the area.

"If you guys are done eating each other's faces, you can help me deal with our new problem," I said, breaking the silence. I could hear Taylor squeak in shock and Connor say some choice words under his breath. I couldn't help but smile at their reactions.

"Help you with what?" Taylor asked as she recovered from her surprise.

"With that," I said, pointing toward the mass of soldiers coming at us. "What's the plan?"

"Well, this is how we're gonna do it without any of the others knowing. Connor, you'll piggyback on me, and I'll jump down there so that you can get into the sand and change. You'll then create ditches in the sand for the vehicles to get stuck in, and I'll take care of it from there. The soldiers are mine, but if any get to the village over there," I said, pointing at the old abandoned town I had noticed before, "that's where you'll come in, Taylor. You'll have had enough time to run down there and set yourself up near the frontal buildings where the soldiers will undoubtedly go if they escape. If any of the soldiers do make it to you, I want you to explode every building there is. Got it?" I said to them.

They both nodded.

Getting up, I was covered in scales. I pushed off from the cliff, jumping with Connor on my back. We were in the air for a good twenty seconds before landing about four hundred feet in front of the town and at least half a mile from the cliff. After landing, Connor got off my back and immediately knelt to put his hand in the sand. He changed into sand and went off to do what we had planned. It took him about five minutes to get back, and by this time, the soldiers could see us, but their vehicles were damaged, so it didn't matter. They were all effectively dead now, and they knew it as soon as they saw me less than five hundred feet away.

Covering myself in scales, I stretched a little bit of my power, using more than I had before. It wasn't my smartest moment, to be honest. The sand and my feet instantly changed into glass tendrils of blue flames that floated off my body. I took a couple of steps just to gauge myself. I smiled, and my body boomed forward faster than ever. The soldiers hadn't even shifted their weight by the time I arrived. They looked terrified, and they should have been. The ones closest to me were ripped to shreds within a second. Then I conjured a ball of something—I didn't know what—but when I threw it at a group of soldiers, they were eviscerated by it, and I could feel my mind drift a little just by using whatever that was. I didn't even try to conjure the material again for fear of losing myself.

The fight went on for only a minute more before their force was completely decimated. Not only had they been ripped apart, but they were crushed by either me using one of their Humvees as a baseball bat, or by my feet or hands. That wasn't the end of it either. At one point I put both my fists together and slammed them on the ground. Everyone within two hundred feet of me was incinerated by the blast and pure heat that resulted from it. There were no survivors. It was frightening to see what my power was capable of, but even more frightening was that my power almost consumed me, as it had in Omaha.

I walked back to where Connor and Taylor stood, and Connor looked unamused, as he expected the display. Taylor looked horrified. She was still adjusting to my power, and that display wasn't even close to full tilt either. Nevertheless, she looked awestruck as she saw me approaching and passing her, heading back to the camp.

We picked up as much as we could and lugged it back to the camp. It got me thinking about just how lucky we were. In any other place our chances of winning were so much lower—not because we couldn't beat them but because we were on the perfect turf for us. It was a wide-open area, so we could complete a lot of our attacks in one long go. We couldn't really do that anywhere else. As powerful as magic users were, we were weak when it came to endurance with our powers. Few could properly control theirs for longer than ten minutes. It was probably why they caught so many of us at the beginning.

"Bryce?" I heard Connor say from behind me with Taylor at his side.

"You do realize I'll have to get you back for this right," he was referring to the moment I ruined between them.

"You can try."

"You've never won this type of fight Bryce and I've never lost. It's going to happen."

CHAPTER

7

Six months had passed since the two companies of soldiers were on their way to attack us. In that time, some things happened. For one, the three relationships that were obvious from the beginning were solidified; the last pair to come out with it was Lucy and Shane. This left me and Annabeth with nothing. Not to say she wasn't pretty, but she was more of a little sister to me, and her type had been painfully obvious to me since we met. She liked only girls. I heard the stories of how she seduced over ten women in her time at the prison, earning the nickname "She-wolf" from me, and it quickly caught on with the others. At first, she didn't like it, but she eventually warmed up to it, and she recently started to respond to it.

That wasn't all that happened. About three months ago, we found out that Taylor was pregnant. When we found out, Connor was seriously embarrassed, but Taylor, on the other hand, was ecstatic that she was pregnant. She viewed it as a completely new chapter in her life. As the unofficial mother of the group, she accepted it by saying she'd just be taking care of another baby.

None of us let Connor live it down for a solid month, until Taylor stood up for him and nearly killed Annabeth. This resulted in them fighting, and Taylor won by the skin of her teeth. If she hadn't injured Annabeth before the fight, she would have lost. After the fight, we had to separate the two so they wouldn't be at each other's throats. Annabeth, Shane, Charlie, and I went to the base of the cliff for a couple of days while they cooled down. Upon our return to the camp, Annabeth and Taylor made up, and they'd been getting along nicely ever since.

Presently, I was at the cliff with a pair of binoculars, scanning the horizon, looking for any movement. It was around six or seven in the morning now, as the short straw had been given to me that day, and that meant the early-morning shift (3:30–9:00 a.m.). Annabeth was with me, as we always did this in pairs, but she was fast asleep with the sniper rifle next to her and had been since we got there. It didn't really bother me that she was asleep and I wasn't, as the demons were still present in my dreams. More recently I had seen them everywhere. It probably had to do with the fact that I typically got about fifteen hours of sleep every two weeks, if that.

I pushed that out of my mind and continued to scan the horizon with the binoculars. Something appeared to the far left, close to the lake, where we had stayed early in our trip. There was a line of black slowly coming into focus. After I made a few adjustments on the binoculars, the view came into focus. The line of black was a group of soldiers, roughly four hundred, chasing one person. The soldiers didn't have any vehicles, which was weird, but the person in front of them probably had something to do with that. Said person was too far away to see what they looked like, but I was able to guess that it was a girl because of the length of hair. She was probably a rather capable fighter, but if she was running, then she needed help, and that was all I needed to convince me to wake up Annabeth.

"Hey, we gotta go help someone," I said to her as she groggily started to get up.

"Everyone at the camp can take care of themselves. They don't need our help," she said while sitting up and rubbing her eyes.

"Not them. There's someone by the forest near the lake that needs our help," I said to her, and she immediately stopped rubbing her eyes and stood up.

"Let's go help then," she said, turning around to face the direction of the lake.

Before I could say anything in response, she was already sliding down the cliff by creating an ice slide that ended parallel to the lake. This was about five hundred feet from the woman, and she arrived when the woman was only about a football field away. Not to be outdone by Annabeth, I covered myself in scales and exploded from the cliff, leaving the rifle behind. We got there at the same time, me landing and Annabeth jumping off her impromptu slide.

As soon as the woman saw us, she turned around and went at the soldiers. We just sat there and watched in amazement. Her magic had only been a rumor in our world; everything that came at her was instantly caught and sent back by an invisible shield. She was literally not even being touched by the soldiers as she decimated their ranks with ease. The only thing that I noticed about her was that her hair was red, tinted with a hint of ginger. Watching her fight the way she did had me falling for her before we even met. Say whatever you want about that—the way she fought was beautiful to me.

I could only watch as this beautiful woman ran through the soldiers like they were nothing. The efficiency and pure power display was enticing. She ended her fight by summoning orbs at her fingertips that destroyed everything in their path. It was impressive and beautiful.

When the battle ended, Annabeth started to walk over to the red-haired woman who, in response, sent one of the whitish-blue orbs at her. I reacted in an instant and hit her out of the way. The orb then hit me, and it stung, which was saying something, as it was the first type of pain I'd felt while having scales on. However, it wasn't effective at all, except for destroying my shirt, and the woman seemed scared as she realized this with me, being completely unharmed. She then began shouting at us.

"Why are you working for them! You're like me. They hunted and killed us! How can you be working for them!" She was getting visibly angry and glowing blue like before. It took me a second or two to process why she said that, but after looking at Annabeth, it hit me; we were wearing the soldiers' uniforms.

"We aren't with them!" I yelled. "We're just using these clothes because most of ours became rags long ago." There was no way she was going to believe me. My assumption turned out to be right, as she sent another orb at me.

"*Джец!*"

I didn't know what that meant, but it couldn't be nice.

Annabeth got up, and it was obvious that she wanted to fight, but when she looked at me for the go-ahead, I shook my head. A sad expression came across her face, but she backed down and let me go forward. The woman held her ground as she saw me advance. I let my scales cover my body, and flames came off my body.

CHAPTER
8

F ire was whipping out of his arms that were uncovered from the
black uniform the soldiers wore, and his entire body was colored in
bloodred scales. His face was emotionless in the current moment,
but his eyes burned with passion. The scariest part about him was that
he walked in a way that not only demanded respect but also told me he
wouldn't hesitate to end me if need be. The sense of power that came from
him would have been a turn-on if he wasn't about to fight me.

He slowly walked forward, and I sent ball after ball of my magic at
him, but it did nothing. When he got close enough to touch I reacted
on pure instinct and punched him across the face as hard as possible. It
sent him flying and he skidded across the desert. Getting up he looked
genuinely surprised but then he smiled, a smile that sent shivers down
my spine.

He moved so fast that he was completely disappearing at points as he
circled and bounced around me. There were no openings in this fight for
me to do anything offensively either, he was too fast and I knew that if he
got close enough to hit me it was game over. The best plan for me right
now was to focus solely on defense and just wait.

Doing exactly that I was able to drag the fight on for almost ten minutes before he finally seemed to be getting tired. His movements were slower and sloppy; idiot must be used to overpowering his opponents in seconds and never really had a fight before. I was using my orbs now to wear him down even farther. Around the time he was hit for the tenth time was when he finally stopped moving. Not wasting the opportunity, I ran up to him with an orb forming in my hand determined to kill him. It didn't exactly go that way.

As my orb came down to kill him he smiled and right there I knew that he had planned it all along once he figured he couldn't get past my defenses. In a movement faster than should've been possible, he grabbed my arm and bent it forcing me to go parallel to the ground. He kneed me in the stomach so hard the wind was knocked out of me. Following that up he hit me right on the shoulder blade, painful as all hell but no real damage. Then I went flying and as my eyes saw the sky and the sun they were blacked out by the man floating above me. Reaching out with his hand as we flew, he flicked me in the stomach and if my defenses hadn't been there, he probably would have split me in two. Still, it knocked all the energy out of me.

Lying on my back, my body refusing to move, I could hear his footsteps getting closer. My mind was screaming to run, but my body refused to move. I was too frightened to do anything. The footsteps got closer and closer until they stopped, and he leaned over my face, looking at me inquisitively. Closing my eyes, I prepared for death or worse.

"You okay?" a voice asked, and I opened my eyes.

"Uh" was my only response.

"My name is Bryce, and that over there is Annabeth," he said, nodding toward the girl I had tried to kill. "We're not with the soldiers. We're like you. The only reason we're wearing these clothes is everything else we have is either dirty or drying," he said, looking down at me with his hand outstretched.

After thinking it over for a couple of seconds, I finally decided that he had no reason to lie and grabbed his hand. Pulling me up, he looked at me up and down, obviously checking me out, and then turned around and walked away.

"Hey, where are we going?" I asked hurriedly, catching up to him.

"Back to our camp so you can meet everyone else," he said.

"Wait, there are others?" I asked, shocked.

"Yeah, just wait until we get to the camp, and you'll be able to meet them," he said, turning his head to face me. "Also, what's your name?"

"My name's Scarlet."

He smiled and turned his head back around and said, "Nice name." He continued forward, with me trailing about ten feet behind.

Most of the trip was dull and silent until we got to the forest. Once there, the woman he called Annabeth came up next to me and started walking with me. She had wavy blonde hair and sparkling gray eyes that just popped out at you. She was very pretty, to say the least, and she carried herself with a sense of purpose. Her face wasn't the only pretty part about her; she had very nice legs and a cute bubble butt. Her chest was a bit lacking but still okay. That wasn't all of it, however, as she was taller than Bryce by about an inch. Just by standing near them, I could feel the power difference. Bryce emitted power unlike anyone before him, and to keep it that well controlled was an amazing feat. Still, we walked in silence until we passed some trees that were taller than the rest, and then the blonde-haired woman began to talk.

"What's your name?" she asked, looking at me.

"Mine's Scarlet," I said, and she began to look me up and down, just as Bryce had done earlier. Was she checking me out?

"You're very beautiful, Scarlet," she said with a slight smile on her face.

My sister would probably love this, but it wasn't for me. Before I could respond to her to turn her down, Bryce spoke up.

"Annabeth, don't hit on the new girl. She's not like that."

"What makes you think that way, Joystick?" she retorted.

Joystick was definitely a nickname, as his back tensed up for a quick second or two, but it quickly relaxed.

"Just back off her, Annabeth," he snapped at her. Annabeth looked a bit taken aback for a second, but then she smiled. We walked in silence until we passed what looked to be an exploded cave. At that point, Annabeth started talking again.

"You're his type," she said out of nowhere, and my head instantly snapped to face her, and she was looking at me.

"I'm his what?" I asked, needing her to say it again.

"You're his type. You're the type of girl that he'll go after. I can already tell that both of you are interested. At least physically," she said, continuing to walk, saying all of this as if it was nothing.

"Word of advice too—he's a bit odd, to say the least. Although he's probably the best person I know, and I know for a fact that he'd do anything to help a friend. Also, under the rough macho-man exterior, he's a big teddy bear underneath. Last thing, he's a bit shy around new people, especially girls. You'll probably have to make the first move," she said, looking at me and I could only smile. I liked a challenge.

I looked up, making sure Bryce was out of earshot, and said. "Thanks." That was all the talking we did until we arrived at their camp about two hours later.

There was a taller woman with glasses, a slight bulge around her stomach, and jet-black hair. She was sitting next to a boy of about the same height as her with black hair like Bryce's. They were on a log that was in front of what looked like a fire pit. Next to one of the tents was another boy but with curly brown hair instead of black, and he was standing in front of a woman who was smaller than him in size and had dirty-blonde hair. The last two were lying on their backs on a blanket that looked like bearskin, holding hands and looking up to the sky. The boy had blond hair, and the girl had brown hair.

They all stood up, noticing us, and came over to greet me one by one. The first two were the curly-haired boy named Charlie and the one who had similar hair to Bryce's, Connor. Once they were done introducing themselves to me, they went over to Bryce and began to talk things over with him. They were quickly joined by Annabeth, who jumped into their conversation. She had obviously heard something interesting. The others quickly followed Connor and Charlie's example, and after only a minute or two, I knew everyone here. The woman with glasses was Connor's girlfriend, and her name was Taylor. The woman with dirty-blonde hair was Marie, and she was Charlie's girlfriend. The final two introduced themselves at the same time; the boy with blond hair was Shane, and the brown-haired woman's name was Lucy.

It was startling how big all of them were, as each one of them was at least six feet, and Bryce was only five feet ten inches tops. Even I was taller than him. I chuckled, as the strongest one here by far was Bryce, and he was the smallest by at least two inches. The only person under two inches taller than him was me.

By this time, everyone had gone back to what they were doing, which was generally nothing, until Bryce sent Connor and Charlie off to everyone else. They began directing everyone to do chores, from cleaning a spit and tidying up the place to washing the clothes at the river and cleaning the rifles. There were no rifles at the camp, as far as I could tell, but Marie and Lucy went off on a path that was close to the way Bryce had brought me. Connor and Charlie began to tidy up the campsite, while Shane began to clean what looked like a rifle barrel. Then I looked around. There was nothing to do, and Bryce had completely vanished. Before my heart sunk, Taylor waved me over to her. She had a rucksack of clothes as she walked down a clearing to a river easily visible from the camp.

"Thanks," I said to her as we walked down the short path.

"No problem. You seemed like you needed something to do, and I need some help. It worked out perfectly," she said with a motherly smile to me.

"So, what exactly are you guys doing here? Hiding?" I asked after a minute or so of silence.

"And training. The government probably knows the relative area where we are because of the satellites but not exactly where. When they do find us though, they'll attack with everything they have. So, in the meantime, we train so we're ready." Her voice changed from one of a relaxed and almost motherly tone to a hyper-serious one. That's how the conversation ended too.

CHAPTER

9

I t had been a couple of days since they took me into their group. Most were still hesitant around me, but I didn't particularly mind. Growing up with my family, you got used to being treated like that by others. Still, they were accepting of me for the most part, especially Bryce. Considering what happened yesterday with him, the others had been even more accepting of me.

I didn't know how it happened really, but Bryce fell asleep on my shoulder at the bonfire last night. Everyone reacted with absolute shock, even myself. As far as I could tell, Bryce had been running on maybe ten hours of sleep in the past week, and when he did sleep it wasn't pleasant for anyone, at least that's what everyone told me. The screaming, power surges, and general fear of being caught in the fire scared all of them, and I could only imagine how bad it had been. However, around me it didn't happen. He was calm and slept calmly; that fact made me happy.

Right now, however, Bryce was as focused as he could possibly be. This level of focus came out only when he fought and when he trained, which was what we were currently doing. He had taken us through several exercises, which included a ton of ab workouts, a six-mile run, and then some basic martial arts. Now, we were just sparring, but it was a bit different with Bryce's fight today. He had made a wager against Annabeth that if she could beat him in a fight, then she got her pick of rewards, but if he beat her, then she couldn't do anything for a month. This meant that if Bryce won, she wouldn't be able to do anything to the other girls of the group. Annabeth was a bit handsy with every girl there, uncomfortably so. In response, every girl was rooting for Bryce to win, but we had seen Annabeth beat Bryce in a fight before. The only other person to do so was Connor, and both won by the skin of their teeth. When they did win too it was heavily influenced by the number of people Bryce had fought before fighting them, sometimes the entire group before he got to them.

As we waited for the fight to begin, Charlie looked considerably happier than he had only a minute or two ago. So did Marie. Lucy also looked the same as Marie, and Shane had his arm around her, protectively smiling with obvious anticipation for the fight. Connor and Taylor, on the other hand, were rather quiet and reserved and showed no real emotions. This interested me, and I walked over to them to see why they were that way.

"Who do you guys think is going to win this?" I asked, walking up to them as Bryce and Annabeth were still setting their rules and making small talk with the occasional *She-wolf* and *Joystick* thrown in.

"My money would be on Bryce simply because of his clothes," Connor said without turning to me.

"Why do you say that?"

"Bryce is wearing shorts and a T-shirt, while Annabeth is wearing the soldier's clothing, which is much heavier than regular clothes. Bryce will have the definite upper hand for this fight, but Annabeth was trained by the same people, so she is no slouch by any means. If she takes off her clothes, which she might, it will be even in my mind. Either way, Bryce is still the better fighter, and I just don't see him making a mistake for Annabeth to capitalize on," he said, still looking at the pair before us who both then stripped to their underwear.

Bryce was wearing the same black boxers he had been wearing earlier, and his body was just as impressive and horrific as the night before, with scars covering his entire toned torso. However, his face was completely different from last night, when he had looked peaceful. He now looked completely serious. Annabeth, on the other hand, was wearing some bold choices of underwear. She wore a black lacy bra that didn't look like it was built to withstand fighting, and her panties matched. I looked around at the others. Their faces were steadfast, so either they were hiding their emotions, or they had seen it so much that it didn't affect them anymore. That was when their fight started.

Annabeth made the first move with a snap kick that sent sand flying toward Bryce's face, but he seemed to expect this and quickly rolled out of the way. As he recovered, Annabeth charged forward and jumped at him with her left knee leading the way, intending to hit him with it. Bryce deflected and countered this by pushing her knee to the left with both his hands and getting his body under hers at the same time as she twisted in the air. He jumped up with Annabeth on his shoulders and sent her flying into the air. I instantly thought it was over, as she would land and hurt herself. That turned out to be wrong, as she gracefully rolled out of the landing.

She instantly stood up almost twenty feet to the left, where they had started, and turned back around to find Bryce. He greeted her with a harsh kick that hit her right in the stomach, knocking the wind out of her. Bryce recognized this opportunity and immediately tried to sweep out her legs, but she jumped over them while still gasping for air. Knowing if she stayed there she would be easily overpowered, Annabeth jumped back a couple of feet, still facing Bryce, who let her catch her breath. It seemed that he wanted to win this fight on fair ground, although knocking the wind out of someone during a fight is fair ground to me.

Once she got her breath, she slowly got closer and closer to Bryce, while he remained in his stance. As she neared the five-foot mark, she repeated what she had done in the beginning and kicked sand at him, and again he was prepared for it, as he covered his face with his hands, staying stationary. However, he wasn't prepared for what she did next. She stepped to the side and sent a kick flying toward his back rib cage. It connected, and there was a resounding thump as she hit him, but she didn't put her foot back down. This confused me until I realized Bryce had trapped it with his left hand. He expected that and let her hit him. *Wow.*

Arching his back with her leg still trapped, he began to slowly adjust so that she faced him. He looked like he was about to do something to her ankle, but she jumped up and swung at him with her left leg. He dodged the kick, but in the process, he let go of her leg and she landed on her back.

Propelling herself back onto her feet with her arms, she landed gracefully like a basketball player would right after a dunk, but that ended the fight. As she was just about to land, Bryce took a step forward between her feet and threw a nasty right hook at her. It connected with her face, snapping it to her right just as she landed. She instantly fell back, body completely stiff, knocked out. Bryce won by KO.

Charlie, Shane, and Marie yelled out, "Oh!" while Bryce stood over Annabeth and then sat down next to her while she was lying there. It didn't look like Annabeth was going to get up anytime soon. This didn't delay Charlie, Marie, and Shane, who began to come at Bryce, but when he snapped his head toward them, they instantly backed off. His face was completely different, and his focus was replaced with a sense of protection and anger, as if to say, "Back off now." Charlie, Marie, and Shane then trudged back to the camp, where the others were already headed, having left without a word. Once they were far enough away, Bryce turned his head back to the river and remained silent. This left Bryce, me, and an unconscious Annabeth alone at the river.

I walked over to him and sat next to him in silence as he stared into the endlessly flowing river in front of us. It was my first focused look at the river, and it was relaxing, as it just flowed smoothly without interruption to an area unknown to me. Bryce seemed to think the same way. His entire body was relaxed as he shifted from a cross-legged sitting position to sitting on his butt with his arms behind him for support.

Something inside me pushed me to do something that I hadn't done in a while, at least not since this war started. Pursing my lips together, I began to whistle a tune of my own making. It was one that was spurred by the death of my family almost a year ago to remember them by. It wasn't long or complicated; it was short, sweet, and meant to move people. The tune lasted only a minute or two, and when it was done, Annabeth turned her face to me.

"That was beautiful," she said, waking up from her impromptu nap.

"Thanks" was the only word that would freely come out of my mouth.

Getting up, she went to get her clothes. As she finished putting on her clothes, she started walking back to the camp, leaving Bryce and me at the river.

CHAPTER

10

"So ... where are you from, Bryce?" I asked him, trying to start a conversation.

"Omaha," he responded, and my mind instantly drifted to the slaughter that happened there by a magic user, but the name eluded me.

"So you're a survivor of the slaughter," I said, knowing the answer to my question, as the answer about who Bryce was clicked in my head.

"Not exactly," he said with sadness in his eyes.

This confirmed my suspicion. He was the slaughterer.

"What did it feel like? Killing them?" I asked him, and his head snapped to face me instead of the river.

"I don't remember doing it. The only thing I remember is seeing my parents get killed and then just losing control. From the moment I could walk, my parents taught me how to control my power, and for good reason. What happened at Omaha could've been worse. At least I think it could've been," he said, still looking at me but now locking eyes.

"Do you think about what you did often?" I asked, wanting to know more about him, but at this point I felt like I was beginning to overstep my bounds.

"Every day for the last year, nightmares and demons of the people I killed have come to me in my sleep and sometimes while I'm awake. That is, until you showed up. There have been no demons or nightmares since you came around. I guess you're like my good luck charm or something," he said smiling and I couldn't help but to smile back.

After a couple of seconds of silence, he started to get up. He stretched out his body to get out all the soreness, and he was still in his boxers. For someone with enough scars for an entire continent, his body was grade A. He grabbed his clothes, and as he was putting them on, he walked over to me. Just as he poked his head out of the shirt, he bent over and kissed me. Without thinking, I swung my right arm to hit him for doing such a thing, but he easily caught it and held it while looking at me, smiling.

"The hell do you think you're doing," I snarled at him, only to receive an alluring smile back.

If he wasn't so damn good-looking, he'd have already lost an appendage.

We both became silent as we were deadlocked in a staring contest. Neither of us was willing to lose to the other as we looked into each other's eyes. My eyes were unbelievably dry, but neither of us gave up. About ninety seconds into our staring contest, Bryce leaned down toward my face with a cocky half smile plastered on his face. He was going for another kiss. Oh, did he have some balls! I was getting ready to send him through the forest, when Annabeth barged in.

"Oy! Stop that," she said with a rucksack in her right hand.

I broke eye contact with Bryce to look at her, and he took total advantage of the situation to kiss me again. Before I could retaliate, Annabeth threw the rucksack at us.

"You have to fold the laundry from yesterday," she said in a matter-of-fact tone. Her hand was on her hip as she leaned to one side, and then she left.

I stared daggers at him for what he had done, and he just shrugged it off. He was so damn cocky. *Oh my god.* This man was ridiculous, and Annabeth had said he was shy. She lied through her damn teeth.

"Were you ever captured?" he asked unexpectedly.

"What do you mean?" I asked him.

"Did you ever end up in a prison?" he asked bluntly.

"No, I never did," I said.

This was followed by a minute or two of silence.

"Did anyone else in your family use magic?" he asked.

"Yeah, my sister, Jessica. She would be about Annabeth's age now. I don't know what happened to her though. We got separated when we ran."

"How powerful was she?" he asked. I knew what he was asking, but for some reason nothing came out of my mouth. "Well, if you need something to compare her to, did you ever hear of the forest that froze over in Nebraska in the middle of a heat wave in only two hours?"

I nodded my head, remembering the incident, because my sister also had something to do with that forest.

"That was Annabeth. Did your sister ever do anything like that?" he continued.

She and Jessica seemed to be on equal footing.

"Yeah. You remember when the same forest burnt down about two days after it was frozen?" I asked him.

His eyes widened, realizing where I was going with that. "Your sister did that?" he asked with shock on his face.

"Yeah, she guessed that another magic user had frozen it and took it as a challenge," I said, and he still had the surprised look on his face.

"What did she look like?" he asked as he put one of the folded shirts into the rucksack.

"She looked similar to me but a bit taller. She also has a weird thing in her eyes. One eye was blue, and the other was brown. She also had cute little freckles that went across her nose, and her face was prettier than mine, in my opinion. She also had auburn hair like mine," I said to him, and he looked like he was thinking.

He then looked back to the camp and waved to Connor, who subsequently jogged over to us.

"What's up?" Connor asked.

"Tell him what she looked like. He'll be able to tell you if she was captured," he said to me.

He continued to fold the laundry as I repeated to Connor what I had just told Bryce. Connor seemed to contemplate my description for a minute or two, and then he jogged back to the camp, stopped in front of Marie and Charlie, and began talking to them. He then jogged back to me, stopping to walk the last ten or so feet.

"No, there was no one at the prison that looked like that when we were there," he said, nodding to Bryce and me.

Bryce responded by nodding his head back toward the camp, and Connor jogged back to it.

"So what does that mean?" I asked.

"It means that your sister could still be out there," he said.

"Oh" was my only response, but I was incredibly happy.

"Anyway, what brought you to the edge of the desert?" he asked, still folding the laundry.

"I heard that there was a powerful group here, and I thought, what could go wrong? So I grabbed what I could and came out here, only to be chased by the soldiers whom I subsequently killed in front of you guys," I said, telling him the truth. There was no point in lying.

"How'd you hear about us?" he asked.

"Rumor mill, you could say. Backstreet bars, shady places, mob centers, just about any place where information flows unregulated," I said.

"You worked for the mob?" he asked, sounding surprised.

"For about two months before I found out about this place. An old friend of my dad's runs this district for the Russian Mob. He let me lay low with them if I did the occasional job," I said, hoping he wouldn't ask what I did. The fewer the questions, the better.

"So what did you do?" he asked.

"I was a courier," I told him, hiding the fact that I had also done assassinations. I didn't want him to know that, and he didn't need to. We ended up falling into a comfortable silence after that.

It took me another five minutes to finish the laundry. After that we left to go back to the camp. The fire was going, and it seemed that everyone was doing the same chores they had done yesterday, only a different person was doing each job. All the guys were gone, and the rest of the girls were at the camp.

Taylor was spinning the rifle barrel on the spit, while Lucy, Marie, and Annabeth were just lounging around on skins that they had brought out. Lucy and Marie were out cold sleeping, while Annabeth was just looking up into the sky that was nearing darkness, with the stars starting to come out. The sky was beautiful, as it still had the faintest hints of dusk, creating every color imaginable. It completely distracted me for a full five minutes before Bryce tapped me on the shoulder. I turned to him and thought his reason for pulling me away from the beautiful sky better be good.

"You're lucky. This only happens once every three months here. It's a phenomenon unique to this area. It's beautiful, isn't it?"

"Yes, it is," I said, turning my head to look at him, but he was looking up into the sky with a look of happiness.

Turning my face back to the sky, I caught Bryce turning his head to look at me. It brought a smile to my face. It wasn't every day that the strongest man in the world was infatuated with you, even if he was a bit of an ass. He was still a good person at heart. That much was easy to see.

We stayed like this, looking up at the stars, until they fully disappeared, and at that time, someone was cooking a deer that looked like the one from last night. The guys were also back, and they were with their girlfriends, except for Annabeth, to whom everyone gave a wide berth. She looked like she was about to freeze everything around her, but more importantly, she looked as if she needed someone to talk to. I hadn't really interacted with anyone but Taylor and Bryce, so it might be good to talk to her at least for a bit.

"Get up. Let's go," I said right in front of her after I had walked around the cooking deer.

"Why?" she asked without moving and with a lot of attitude.

"Because you're obviously pissed and need someone to talk to," I replied and began to walk toward the path that would take me to the cliff.

I continued on the path until it reached the opening. Annabeth followed me all the way there, and as I sat down in the middle of the clearing, so did she. She sat next to me as we both looked out over the cliff and into the seemingly endless desert. She was the first to speak.

"I've never seen Bryce as happy as he is with you. The fact that your presence here stopped his nightmares means so much not only to him but also to the rest of us. So when I say this, take it to heart. If you do anything to hurt him besides when we're training, we'll end you," she said with a stony complexion. By the tone of her voice, I could tell that she was 100 percent serious.

Her words shocked me to the core, to the point where talking was impossible. Sensing this, Annabeth got up and headed back to the camp, leaving me to ponder this. I didn't think she needed to worry about that. He was most certainly an ass, but there was something about him that just made me smile. I wanted that feeling to be permanent.

CHAPTER
11

L ying at the cliff with the sniper rifle, overlooking the entire landscape before me at the hottest point in the day, was not fun. The only thing that kept my mind occupied was that it had been one month since Bryce blocked me from flirting or doing anything with the girls in the camp. My mind had been taking heavy hits because of this, especially because of Marie, who liked to tease me for not being able to do anything. Even when Bryce wasn't around, he was still able to creep into my mind and stop me from doing anything, which was possibly the most frustrating part of it all. Having him inside my head restrained me from doing anything remotely sexual with anyone, including myself. It was going to be the death of me. The insane heat didn't really help my frustration at the moment either; my face was covered in sweat, and both of my sleeves were soaked in sweat by now.

The only plus out of this whole situation was that the full moon had been two nights ago, and that was the last time to see if I would win the bet on Scarlet and Bryce or not. The bet had been to see how long it would take them to get together, and just from the way they acted it was surprising, at least to me, that anyone expected them to get together within two weeks. They had been hell-bent on just annoying the crap out of each other and doing outrageous things in front of the other, and that's me saying that! However, they ended up getting together, and I ended up winning the bet, because I expected it to take longer than two weeks. Connor was the only other one to bet the same way as me. Because we won the bet, everyone had to individually give us either a blanket or an animal fur from their collection.

My victory was short-lived though, as Bryce seemed to shove in my face the fact that he was with Scarlet—who, in my opinion, was probably the hottest girl I'd ever seen. She had the perfect body with a perfect bubble butt and a bust that wasn't too big or too small. Her face was unbelievably beautiful, and her hair seemed to be blessed by the gods. The only downside was that she didn't swing my way.

Still, we had talked a lot in the past month and became pretty good friends—so much so that she'd even gone into detail about her family. For the most part I was only an ear for her to talk to, but then she started describing her sister. I immediately absorbed every detail she told me about her sister; the only reason I was so attentive about that was that Scarlet said she swung both ways. There was some hope for me then. Scarlet had told me that there were rumors about us in the outside world, and she hadn't been caught. All there was now was hope that she would make her way here.

Those were my last thoughts before something on the horizon caught my eye. To the far right of me on the complete opposite side from which Scarlet had come, someone was running toward the city. A horde of soldiers were following said person, easily equaling the number of soldiers that were chasing Scarlet a month earlier. The person was way beyond my visual range, but I could tell it was a girl from the whipping hair behind her. They were going at a breakneck pace, and they weren't going to be able to keep up for much longer. As they neared closer, they headed straight into the town, hoping for cover. It was a good idea, but they did not know the layout of the town. She was going to need some help.

After creating the ice slide as I did a month ago, I slid down to the front of the town to see where the soldiers were going. Most were following the girl straight into the town, but some were going around to try to cut her off. They were mine.

None of the one hundred or so that were on the outside closest to the desert survived me, as they were either impaled by my ice, frozen in it, or slashed by it, or they died of hypothermia. It made it easy to kill when I could make ice as cold as dry ice and as tough as diamonds. They were quick work, taking me only about two minutes to deal with, but that was too long. Most of the soldiers were in the town. It was time for close quarters.

Creating an ice pillar below me that touched one hundred feet, I surveyed the entire village in front of me and pinpointed the soldiers' locations. Some of them shot at me, but I expected this and had covered myself in my ice, which essentially worked like Bryce's protective scales. It took only seconds for me to spot the girl. It was clear as day that she had exhausted her magic earlier. Now was the time to act, as they slowly closed on her.

I drew on my power, and it didn't take long for the soldiers to look down at the scanners on their belts and go crazy. Every single one of them looked at me, but it was much too late for them now. I exploded off the ice pillar, my speed easily exceeding five hundred miles per hour, and the person who looked to be the commander of the group now stood in front of me a mere blink of the eye later. His face was filled with fear and remorse, but it was far too late for him, as he got impaled and lifted by makeshift ice swords. Unceremoniously, dropping the commander I exploded toward the rest of the soldiers, slashing, kicking, punching, and freezing anyone who got in my way. This was all in an attempt to protect the person in the middle who was now facedown on the ground and had a fair amount of blood around her.

The fight with the soldiers didn't last all that long, maybe five minutes, and that was because it was in the town and not in a wide-open area. Letting the last one make it out alive didn't sit well with me, but it was what we usually did whenever soldiers came to our area—to spread rumors to increase our fear factor was the way Charlie and Bryce put it. As they were running away, I headed back to the girl and picked her and her pack up before booming toward the bottom of the cliff, still using a lot of my magic. I created an ice pillar like before, but instead of one hundred feet, it got up to about five hundred feet. Standing on top of the pillar of ice, I took a minute or so to figure something out. It wasn't a good idea, and its success rate was probably low, but the girl in my arms was losing blood and was unconscious, so time wasn't really in my favor.

Taking one last look at the girl in my arms whose face was covered with her auburn hair, I hoped that she'd be okay and took the jump toward the cliff. I was able to propel myself toward the side of the cliff, courtesy of an ice pillar made at my feet at the exact moment of the jump. Just as my feet were about to hit the cliffside, another ice pillar exploded out and sent me upward at an incredible speed, getting me just under forty feet from the top of the cliff and directly over my previously made slide. The plan ended when my feet contacted what had been my slide going to the town. Just as my feet hit, spikes formed at the bottom of my feet to create a grip on the slide.

I slowly brought myself up, taking longer than I planned to do so, but it was worth it, as we were now safe on solid ground. Being far too tired to do anything else, I yelled out for Bryce, who was there almost immediately with a blast of wind from his speed. He needed no explanation as he grabbed the unconscious girl and took her back to the camp to see Charlie, Taylor, and Marie, who were our medics. After all that, my body shut down and flopped backward. It had been a long time since my power was used to that extent, and if we hadn't been doing as much endurance work as we were, this probably would have made me pass out. I'd have to talk to Bryce about incorporating some magic-only days into our workouts.

After a couple of minutes on my back, I got up and walked to the path back to the camp. My mind began to wander to that girl. She seemed to have a slender body, and her skin felt nice, to say the least, when she was in my arms. It felt good to be the one saving people, but the fact that I didn't get to see her face was gnawing at me, as if it was important. I brushed it off and tried to focus on the path in front of me as I made my way to the camp.

The path ended and cleared into the camp, and silence ensued. No one seemed to be moving from their places around the campfire pit, except for Scarlet, who was shaking and saying something in another language. I took a closer inspection of Scarlet, and she seemed to be crying into Bryce's arms as she was shaking violently. Judging from the faces of those around the campfire, the outlook on the girl didn't look good, but if anyone here could save her, it was those three. They were all smart and crazy enough to try anything with the small knives, pincers, gauze, and painkillers we had.

Not wanting to disturb the mood or make it any worse, I made my way next to Scarlet on the log she shared with Bryce. She was still shaking, and there was nothing for me to do except put a reassuring hand on her, with Bryce already doing the same. With both of our hands on her for reassurance, she started to calm down a little, which made me wonder how she had been before Bryce had gotten to her. After a couple of minutes, she started to calm down even further, to the point where she looked like she was asleep. Her peace didn't last long, as one of the three working on the girl swore incredibly loudly, and this made Scarlet go right back to her tears. With the way she was reacting, she must have known the girl.

The sun was starting to set now, and the girl had been with Taylor, Charlie, and Marie for a minimum of six hours. It was disconcerting waiting there, as none of us did anything for that entire time. The only thing that happened that made any of us move was when Marie called for Scarlet to come into the tent. She was typically in there for about fifteen minutes, and then she'd come out pale and immediately down as much water as possible. This could only be caused by a blood transfusion, and Scarlet couldn't do it much more; she had already been in there three times. Any more could be fatal.

When the sun had all but disappeared from the sky, there was a shout of joy from the tent, followed by one of the three yelling that the girl was stable. There was an audible sigh of relief from everyone around the now-lit campfire pit—especially Scarlet, who looked to be crying but with a smile on her face while she hugged Bryce. We were so elated to know that another person would be joining our group and that she was okay that we literally started to yell and cheer as loudly as we could. That was until Taylor, Charlie, and Marie came out of the tent and shut everyone up. They said that we all needed to go to sleep and that the girl would remain in Taylor's tent, so she and Connor would have to share with me. Although I was displeased at this, there wasn't anything for me to do, as she had just saved a life.

The exact time eluded me, but sleep absolutely refused to come to me. This was probably caused by Connor and Taylor being in my tent with me, making it more cramped than usual. Still, sleep should have come easy to me, as it had been an exhausting day, but nothing worked in my attempts to go to sleep. It finally became too much for me to deal with, so I walked out of the tent and took a stroll around the camp and the surrounding forest.

There was nothing particularly interesting to me about the forest, as it had been imprinted in my mind for the past seven months. It was still beautiful though. The bugs in this region lit themselves up at night, giving the forest an incredible glow. They didn't light it up like the sun did, but it was enough so that you knew where you were going, and the forest became almost mystic because of the bugs' glow. Besides the bugs, there wasn't much inside the forest, as the animals knew that they should stay away if they wanted to live. For that reason, we started freezing and reusing the kills we made so that our supply lasted longer. Even so, we didn't do that all that often because of the amount of MREs we had scavenged off the soldiers. We were very well off on food for the foreseeable future, but it never hurt to be conservative just in case.

After spending a half hour in the forest, it was time to go back to the camp. It was easy to find the way back. The dimmer the bugs got, the closer the camp was. Finding the camp still took me about five minutes, and I went into the closest tent upon entering the clearing. The tent seemed familiar, but after a couple of seconds it dawned on me that it was Taylor and Connor's tent and currently the med bay for the girl. Even with this realization, it was far too late to do anything, as my eyes were already heavy. The last thing I remember before falling asleep was flopping down behind the girl, with her back facing me.

My eyes opened the next morning, and I had a warm sensation all throughout my body, and hair was in my face. My right arm was over the side of the girl, and my legs were on her legs that curved in a bit. After a couple of seconds, I realized that we were cuddling. It was awkward to be doing this with someone whose actual identity was unknown to me, but she was so warm. A couple of seconds later, my eyes closed again and sleep took me over.

I woke up again in the same position as before, and the sun was shining through the tent and directly onto my face. The glare practically forced me to get up. Groaning as my body moved and slowly stretched within the tent, I was careful to avoid touching the girl. I tried to leave the tent, but there was an ever-so-silent "No" that had to have come from the girl. I turned around to look at her, and she had turned her head to face me and was pleading with her face for me not to leave.

"What's your name?" I asked almost out of impulse.

"I'll tell you if you lie next to me," she said with a devilish smile on her face. She had the face of an angel. Cute freckles went across her nose and face, greatly complementing her auburn hair. She also had differently colored eyes, one being a sparkling blue and the other being chocolate brown. The smile she gave me at that moment warmed my heart. She looked familiar to me, but it was too early in the morning, and my mind wasn't working.

"So what exactly is your name?" I asked, lying next to her as she got on her back.

"Jessica. You?" It then clicked that this was Scarlet's sister, but I made no mention of it to her.

"Annabeth."

"That's a nice name. Where ya from?" she asked pleasantly.

"Can't remember. Parents abandoned me and my sister before we were ten."

"That sucks. My parents were always supportive of my sister and me," she said, turning her head to look at me.

"So, what can you do? You were out of magic before I could see what you could do," I said, changing the subject to one easier for me to handle.

"Fire. You?" she asked in an almost monotone voice.

"Ice," I replied. There was no real talking for about a minute after that.

"Say, were you in Omaha about three years ago?" she asked.

"Yeah, why?"

"Were you the one that froze the forest during the heat wave?" she asked, and it dawned on me that she could be the one that burned down the forest two days later.

"Don't tell me you were the one to burn it down."

She smiled, knowing that I had caught on.

"Yep, it was fun doing that," she said with the same smile that warmed me up, but it did tick me off a bit.

"Well, it wasn't fun for anyone else. That was the only place in the entire city that wasn't blazing hot," I said, a little pissed, but it's been three years.

"Sorry ... about ... th—" was all she got out before she went unconscious.

At first, I thought something was seriously wrong, but after I took her pulse, checked her breathing, and checked her stitches, everything seemed to be as it should be. She was just tired.

As she slept next to me, it was hard not to notice that Scarlet had left out some of the more specific details about her sister. For example, when she slept, she was incredibly cute, with just a slight snore that sounded like a wheeze. Not only that, but she had several scars along her arms. I became curious after seeing them, so I turned her hand over to make her wrist face up. Very distinct scars lingered on her right wrist. She self-harmed, and the scars matched the ones on my left wrist.

This was something that a lot of magic users did, as a lot of them weren't able to handle the discrimination. It was even harder for people like me, as there was still discrimination against gay people, even among the magic users. That was mainly why Bryce and Connor were so dear to me. They were the only people who treated me equally. They certainly weren't the best people in the world, but they were a couple of the few who judged people only by their actions. The number of people who supported me the way I was gradually increased over time. Charlie, Marie, Taylor, Shane, and Scarlet didn't care what someone was and only cared about how they acted toward others. With this lingering in my mind, sleep enveloped me again. But I woke up as quickly as I had fallen asleep, as Bryce was shaking my shoulder.

"How'd you get in here?" he asked, looking at me and then at Jessica.

"I went in through the door," I said to him, straight-faced.

He took a very long sigh before responding. "Have you been in here since last night?"

"Yeah, why?"

"Well, it's almost three in the afternoon. The others are beginning to worry. Should I tell them that you went down to the lake to recover?" He gestured toward Jessica, who was still sleeping next to me.

"Yes, please," I replied with a genuine smile on my face.

He responded to my smile with one of his own and left. Jessica began to stir as soon as he zipped up the entrance of the tent.

"I never thought that I would meet him here," she said in a monotone voice.

"Are you talking about Bryce?" I asked, surprised that she might know him.

"Yeah. Every magic user in the world knows about him," she said in a way that made it hard to judge if that was a good thing.

"Is that a good thing or a bad thing?" I asked her to find out which one it was.

"Both. The media and government are using him as a poster boy to tell people that magic users are bad, but most people aren't buying it. Also, a lot of magic users believe if he stands up to the government, we'll have our freedom, but they're a bit radical. The remaining people and magic users alike, like me, believe that he could be used as a deterrent to create some type of peace within this screwed-up country." She was exhausted.

I had never thought about any of that. Bryce was just my friend.

"What do you think he'll do?" Jessica asked.

"I don't know, but I believe that we will be forced to make a stand within the next year, and if we win, magic users will have freedom again. But if we don't, I fear that our lives may be forfeited. That is what I believe will happen," I said, and she seemed satisfied with that answer but a bit curious.

"Why do you say within a year?"

"Because increasingly more soldiers have come to this area. Most of them are just scouts that we let pass most of the time, but if they get too close, we end them. The rest of the time, battalions like the one chasing you come around just on a training mission, but we know they're scouting the area. We generally tend to leave them alone, but again if they get too close, we take care of them. But there was that one time Bryce was in a bad mood about two weeks ago when a battalion parked themselves by the lake we originally stayed at," I said.

Jessica's next question was obvious from the face she made when she heard that Bryce was in a bad mood. "What did he do?"

"He killed all of them but one, which has become a type of pattern whenever we kill the soldiers. We tend to leave someone alive, and typically that person is high-ranking," I said, dispelling nothing. She was going to find out sooner or later either way.

"Why do you do that?" she asked.

"Bryce says to create fear and spread the rumors that we are stronger than people believe."

"Well … I'm tired again. Good night," she said before passing into sleep again.

I followed her lead only minutes later, and sleep enveloped me for the umpteenth time in the past day.

CHAPTER
12

It was another day in a fantastic hell where the only things available for me to do were to sit around, train, and do paperwork. Doing nothing behind a desk while my secretary did basically all my actual work was beyond annoying. I'm not saying that I wasn't thankful for that and the extra money the job brought, but there was no one for me to share it with, and it had been months since the higher-ups had allowed me into the field. They said that it was too much of a risk to send me anywhere, because the last time didn't end well. Bryce had escaped when he was my responsibility. I was lucky they hadn't given me my DD-214 and thrown me in prison. Instead they had grounded me, giving me a "promotion" and throwing me behind a desk. It wasn't all that bad. The plaque they had given me for my name was pretty. "LTC Reiner," it said in big bold letters.

It had now been a little over eight months since most of the magic users had escaped, but most had been recaptured. This was overshadowed by the fact that Bryce and probably the strongest magic users on this side of the world were still at large, sort of. We knew their relative location, in the mountains right out of the Sierra desert, mainly from readings we got off sensors. No one could conceal the amount of power they had, even if they were masters of their powers. However, their exact location was still a mystery. Their powers were so extreme that there was a three-hundred-mile radius within the mountains, desert, and forest that lit up like Christmas trees on the sensors.

The thing about all this, though, was that we weren't sure that Bryce was even there. All the power readings we had gotten weren't coming from a Devil's Anger user and instead from all the powers Bryce's friends had. The only reason we believed that he was there was that every once in a while, that entire side of the country would light up, and it was because of a Devil's Anger user. That was our only reason for believing that he was there, and that wasn't even a guarantee. The scariest part was the amount of power that he was using, if he was there. Compared to the amount that he used when he fought me and the two Heaven's Justice users—one was dead, and the other was doing something unknown to me—it was utterly miniscule. The power he used to fight them and me was caught on the satellite sensors, and it lit up over half the continent.

Out of nowhere, I heard a pounding on my door, and a voice came through it. "LTC, the higher-ups want you," my secretary said as he came through the door.

"What do they want?"

"How the hell should I know?"

I gave him my hard look, and he backed down a little. We were great friends, but at work we needed to be at least somewhat professional.

"Maybe because they told you to get me."

"Do you really think that they would tell me anything about what they want to talk to you about? Now go and talk to them before I get yelled at for no reason," he said with his arms crossed, leaving the room.

It looked like another boring meeting with the same boring colonels would take place. They'd do the usual: ask me how training was going, wait for me to give them a response, and then they'd hear a varied version of what they'd been told once a month for the past eight months. They didn't even ask me to fight anymore or personally train the newbies along with the sergeants. That was the best part about being a LTC—I got to help with the newbie training. Usually the sergeants did all the work, but it was fun to get involved every once in a while.

I clicked the *up* button at the elevator door, and it opened almost immediately. A handsome man was in the elevator, but my stomach turned over at the sight of him. It was the head of the Slave. We had once been proud to wear our uniforms, but because of him, we were essentially bounty hunters of magic users. There was no pride or honor in anything we did now. It didn't help that anyone who said anything derogatory to him would usually find themselves discharged within two weeks. He was the damn dictator of the military and had no reason to be here; thus, everyone despised him.

"Morning," I said to him, not bothering to look at him. I pressed the button for the desired floor, hoping he wouldn't say anything, but it didn't work that way.

"Fine evening we're having, LTC, but not as fine as you," he said, making me scoff at him. He'd done this every time he'd seen me.

"First, no matter how many times you hit on me, it won't work, so please stop for both our sakes. Second, only people who've earned my trust while I fought with them can call me LTC," I said with attitude, but he just brushed it off.

"Ah, well, one day you'll accept. How is Major Smith by the way? He is your current secretary, isn't he?" he asked, giving me a knowing look, which I answered with a nod. "I did a little bit of research on him, and as it turns out, his entire family were war heroes at some time or another, and he doesn't seem to be much different. He even has a silver star, and after I read the report on how he got it, it seemed he should've gotten the Medal of Honor instead. But his actions were overshadowed by a certain someone," he added, giving me the same look as before.

"You're right. He should've gotten it," I said, stepping out of the elevator and letting it close behind me.

But before the doors closed, he said, "Call me."

I looked down at my side, and he had somehow been able to put a sticky note on my uniform. God, that man was insufferable.

Taking it off and throwing it into the nearest trash bin, I proceeded down the hallway to the conference room where the meeting would take place. Usually, there was only some random private at the door by the time my butt got there, but not today. Today there were special ops sergeants whom I knew standing with their guns locked and loaded. They had their usual straight faces, but their presence set off alarm bells in my mind. This was more than just a normal meeting. This was probably big.

I pushed open the door and walked in. There was only an empty room. Either I was the first and only one here so far or the meeting had been canceled and they were just screwing with the sergeants outside. Most likely, they were late. Who in the military would be late for a meeting unless they didn't care if they were late? That would mean that they were ridiculously high ranked. The only thing to do now was wait. It didn't take them long to arrive and I wasn't disappointed, the people that were holding the meeting were the three highest ranking generals in the military. One of them being Bryce's grandfather.

The meeting with the generals was eye-opening—mostly because of the weird questions they asked me. They ranged from what Bryce could be motivated by to subtler things like if he could be bought. I answered their questions as honestly as possible. There was no reason to lie. At least I was home now, and that was all behind me ... for the moment.

I turned on the TV, and a news show came on. I immediately changed the channel. There was no need for depression about the world when I was part of the group that was trying to fix it. The next channel was some local sports network. I usually would have enjoyed this, but today wasn't the day, so the search for a good channel continued. After almost an hour of this and the destruction of five out of six beers, the history channel surfaced. This channel would stay. It kept my eyes glued to the screen for the next hour. I took my eyes off it only to go get the hard liquor and another three beers after I finished the six-pack. Today was a heavy-drinking day—that was for sure.

By the time the show ended, an entire six-pack plus the three beers and a half a bottle of Jack Daniel's had been downed. It went without saying, but I was wicked drunk now and in no real control of my actions. A blackout quickly followed. Later, my secretary told me of my actions. This resulted in my calling my sister twice. Thankfully, she didn't answer. I then called my secretary, who answered.

"Hoowelk d ya syy baoom?" were the words out of my mouth.

"You're drunk," he said.

"Frrrt nahme," I said.

"You are drunk," he said again.

"Frrrt nahme!" I said again, apparently yelling that time.

"You're drunk, Julie. I'm coming over before you do anything really bad," he said.

Later he told me that he actually did come over. When he arrived, he took me to bed and made sure I did nothing idiotic until I was fast asleep.

When I woke up, the headache caused by last night's drinking was insane and made me want to get drunk again just so that it would go away, but I knew better. It didn't stop my secretary from worrying though, as he had taken all of my booze, leaving only his signature hangover cure (Gatorade with lemon) and a sticky note behind saying that he was taking all the alcohol and that he would be monitoring my credit card for the next month. He couldn't do that legally, but he would do it anyway, and if he explained the situation well enough to whoever caught him, they'd agree with him. I had a bit of a problem with alcohol.

CHAPTER
13

Since Jessica had arrived about a week ago and got with Annabeth, something had been calling me to the town. I didn't know why, but today I was going to find out what exactly was calling me. Not wanting me to go alone, the guys in the group had decided to come with me. We made a beeline for the shortcut. It was one that we had discovered not all that long ago near the edge of the cliff, about five hundred feet from where we posted as lookouts. Calling it a shortcut was a bit of a stretch, as it was more of a fall. The end of the path was a drop-off about five hundred feet down, but it was at a big enough angle so that we could slide down it without having to worry about hurting ourselves. Still, we kept it a secret from the girls so that they didn't have to worry.

Thinking about it now, I wondered why we never actually explored the town. I guess it came down to the fact that we just didn't want to—that or we were just too scared of any soldiers coming after us. It didn't bother me now, because we were exploring it.

Meanwhile, getting on the path and down the side of the cliff took us a little more than ten minutes, instead of the half hour it usually took. It gave us a decent amount of extra time to explore the city from which we were now only a mere half mile. The only problem was that we had no idea who would be exploring each area, as doing it all together would take way too much time. It seemed as if I wasn't the only one who picked up on this.

"How are we going to split the city up? It's not like we can all search it together," Charlie said as we walked toward the town.

"I'm taking the top-right part, the part that will be farthest from us when we get there," I said immediately.

That was where my instincts were practically yelling at me to go. After deciding on who would have what section we went to go to our respective areas, resolving to meet in the middle of the town.

When we got to the edge of the city, the first one to break off from the group was Charlie, as the part of the city he was exploring was right in front of us. Shane left not much later to explore his part of the city, leaving only Connor and me together for the remainder of the walk. It didn't take long for us to split ways, with him going to the left and me to the right.

The first thing that I noticed about my area was the sheer size of the buildings. They weren't all that big, being only two or three stories at the max, which wasn't much bigger than the rest of the city, but the shape that these houses were in was a lot better than the rest of them. The change in quality was sudden too, going from basically rubble and mismatched stones to perfectly shaped houses. Whoever had lived here before had a very conspicuous gap in society. It just went to show how some things in life were inescapable, though a bit exaggerated in this case.

Not letting it freeze me, I started my journey to find whatever had been calling out to me for the past week. The moment I passed the first house, my head began to pound uncontrollably. It was agonizing and most definitely the worst headache ever, but as soon as it started it stopped. It left me baffled as to why it happened, but not a second after it stopped, my mind was given an image of a house that had several white roses around it. The house looked just like the ones around me. Maybe whatever had been calling out to me just gave me some directions. This begged the question: what exactly was calling out to me? The question had been poking at the back of my mind for a couple of days now, and I was going to find the answer.

As I was walking past the buildings, I noticed that some of them had gardens overrun with weeds, some were just plain dead, while others didn't even have a garden. This usually wouldn't have registered with me, but the image in my head clearly showed a house with white roses around it.

When I turned left after passing another house, the headache came back. This time it lasted longer and was unbearable. It went on for what felt like minutes, and at the end of it, another picture popped into my head: a view of me clutching my head on the ground between two houses. Upon seeing this, I whipped around in every direction, looking for something that could fit the bill.

Bingo, there it was! Right in between the two houses to my right was a house surrounded by white roses. It was a bit bigger than the one in my image, but it looked the same. As I approached the house, what jumped out at me was the fact that on the front door there was a picture of a white dragon curled up into a ball with one black six on its head, one on its back, and one on its tail. It was an exact copy of the birthmark that I had on my back. *What the hell?*

Slowly, I pushed the door open and walked into the house. It was completely barren on the inside, and the outside was just a shell. As I walked around inside the house, I noticed some stairs. Maybe the top floor would be more fruitful.

Walking up the stairs came with a lot of uncertainty, as every step was greeted with the creaking of the stairs, but they held firm and let me get upstairs. Much like the bottom floor, the top floor was completely barren. I looked for anything that might have been calling to me. *Nothing. This must be the wrong house.* There was nothing there.

Going back to the stairs to leave, I noticed a door. It wasn't open, but there was definitely something on the other side. I could feel it. In response, my body instantly went into a fighting stance. There was an unknown on the other side of the door, which called for me to be ready for anything. As I edged closer and closer to the door, my hand began to outstretch. Upon making contact with the door, it slid open effortlessly.

I entered the room, and there was nothing in it that presented any type of danger, so I dropped my stance and began to look around the room. It was small, with no closet or bed or anything except for a table and what lay on it. On said table was a sheathed sword with a note attached to it. The sheath was colored black but was elaborately painted with pictures of white roses attached to stems that had thorns on them.

Beautiful was the only thought that came to my mind as I observed the sheath, eventually picking it up. It was surprisingly light and felt good in my hands, but why had it been left there? Maybe the note had a message in it. It was encased in an envelope that was tied to the hilt of the sword with a thin white string. I untied the string at the hilt, pulled the envelope free, and subsequently pulled a folded sheet of paper out of it. It read,

Dear Bryce,

I am truly sorry for you to be receiving this like this, for it means that I have passed on, and for that, I couldn't be any sorrier. Although I do hope that this finds you in good times, and you are happy with everything around you, there is no chance this is the case, as people will always fight what they are ignorant of, and our magic is included. We will be hunted until our dying day unless we can do something. However, no matter what we do, we will always be disliked, and for that, I couldn't be any sorrier. But in this one case, you will need to continue to stand up against everyone in the world who hates us. You must never give up or give in at any time ever. If you do, our hope will be gone for eternity, gone with you. You are our beacon of hope for everyone, myself included, and you must fight for the future of everyone no matter the cost to yourself. Please remember that.

I can't help but be disappointed in myself, as I feel like I am throwing everything onto your shoulders without regard for what you want, but it is too late now. If maybe I had been a better father to you, things might have turned out differently.

Still, I am sorry, and I will always love you, Bryce. Even after my death, I will continue to love and guard you.

Sincerely,
Your father, Xavier Ceribri

This sword was a last memento from my father, and as I held it in my hands, my eyes began to tear up. With all my effort, the tears stayed in my eyes. It was not easy, but it was accomplished, and as my eyes cleared, I picked up the sword again, looking it up and down just like before, but this time I unsheathed it. A blast went through my mind. It felt the same as when Lucy touched my mind.

So I finally get to talk to you. It's nice to meet you officially, Bryce, a voice said in my mind.

Um, who are you? I said into my mind.

I'm someone you will be able to rely on even if you aren't my future host, the voice said before it felt like it disappeared.

This was starting to get weird. Who or what had just been talking to me, and how did my dad's sword have anything to do with this? I didn't seem to have much control, so I would have to take what came at me and fight it. There was really no other option at this point, as all the possible ways to research it were far away from where we were. I hated everything about this situation and how in the dark I felt. Did everyone know what was going on in this world except for my friends and me? How could this sword literally talk to me? *What the hell is that? Magic and powers are a stretch for any world in and of themselves, but sentient swords, really!* This was probably only the beginning too, because my whole story seemed to be in its adolescence. Hopefully my questions would be answered one day, sooner rather than later.

I sheathed the sword, made my way out of the house, and walked toward the city center, where we had decided to meet up. I walked past all the bigger buildings, and it felt different to see the smaller buildings again. It was a lot easier to travel around the smaller buildings, as they were all ten feet max, and there was plenty of rubble to step on to look over them. It wasn't long before Connor and the others saw me sticking my head over a house and waved to me. Noticing them, I made my way over.

As soon as I arrived, my head began to throb again, but instead of a picture of a location, it was a picture of a being, the one in my dream from a couple of months ago—the only thing that actually scared me. The left half of the being was pure white, and everything around it seemed to be violently rocketing upward. The right side of its body was pitch-black, and everything around it was crashing downward. One of the two abnormalities was its eyes; the one on the white side was pitch-black, and the one on the dark side was pure white. There were two red lines that started right under its eyes and went down its face, ending at its jawline. Its pure presence made me shake in fear, and just like the last time, I didn't last five seconds before passing out.

"Hey, Bryce, are you okay?" Connor asked, sticking his hand out to me as I began to pick myself up from the ground.

"Yeah, I'm good. Just a bit of a headache," I replied, taking his hand.

Once up, I got to take a good look at what everyone had been able to get while they were exploring the village. Shane's finding was the only one that looked remotely interesting. He had some stone tablets that were covered in an ancient language.

"Where'd you find that, Bryce?" he asked, pointing at my weapon.

"Found it in one of the houses I searched. It's still sharp too," I said, drawing the katana and then lightly touching the tip of the sword to my left index finger, causing blood to draw immediately. None of the three noticed this, as they were still staring at the blade. Then they looked at me. That was when I got what they were trying to ask silently.

"Yeah, I didn't find anything else in my district worth grabbing. Sorry, guys."

There was a collective "It's okay" from the three present.

In all honesty, I wouldn't doubt if there was something of good value out there, as I hadn't been paying as much attention to my surroundings as I should have. The only thing that had been on my mind was to find the house and subsequently the sword.

"Hey, guys, we may have a problem," Lucy said in our minds, popping into them suddenly.

"A magic user popped up on my radar. He's not all that far away from you guys, only about a three-minute walk north toward the mountain. Thing is though there are two more magic signatures who are doing a good job of hiding, or they're just traces of the person I'm picking up."

"What do you mean 'traces'?" Shane asked both out loud and in his mind.

"It's exactly how it sounds. The person left a trace of their power somewhere. This only really happens if either the person is incredibly powerful, or their magic has something to do with attacking from a range.

Annabeth creating her ice and throwing it at people is a good example of that."

This got an "Ah" out of all of us except for Charlie, who stayed silent, probably already understanding what it was.

"So you're saying that we're dealing with either someone reasonably powerful or three people?" Shane asked, summarizing what Lucy had just told us.

"Yep."

"Thanks, Lucy. We'll get back to you soon. Check up with us through Connor in about an hour," I told her, and she wordlessly obeyed, cutting the connection that we had.

All four of us looked at each other at the same time, and we instantly knew what everyone was going to do. With our plan all but actually discussed among ourselves, we started toward the position she had described to us. As soon as we got within a few hundred feet of where she had said the signature was, we split up so that we could surround the person or persons.

It would be another couple of minutes before I was in position and another two minutes for both Shane and Charlie to get into position. Connor had already been in position and waiting when I got there. What we saw was kind of surprising. In the middle of a clearing there was one lone kid, maybe a year or two younger than me, sitting down with his back up against a boulder. He was petting a rather large silver-haired wolf that was lying across his lap. His hand was slowing as he nodded off, and as the minutes progressed, he fell asleep, and so did the silver-haired wolf on his lap.

All four of us quietly entered the clearing, looking around for any form of danger, and in a matter of seconds, it came. A browned-haired wolf came straight out of the bushes to Shane's left and Connor's right. It bolted straight for Shane at an impressive speed for such an animal. Shane was barely able to get up the white armor he used as his magic to stop the animal from ripping out his throat. As the wolf clashed against Shane's armor, it bounced off and bolted over toward the sleeping human and wolf, quickly barking at them.

They were instantly up and prepared to fight us. That kid was huge, probably reaching six foot eight. I didn't want to fight them, as they probably had no idea who we were, and we were just defending ourselves.

However, my friends didn't really make us look friendly, as they were instantly on high alert. Shane was fully bathed in the white armor, with a shield and sword accompanying him this time. Charlie had little explosions going off all around his body—I had never seen that before—and he looked ready to kill. Connor had already pulled out a knife and was fully prepared to absorb the dirt at his feet and charge. This wasn't exactly the best way to make new friends.

"Stand down!" I barked at my three friends, trying to lessen the tension in an already terrible situation. Thankfully they listened, albeit reluctantly.

"It's okay. We aren't here to fight," I said, taking a step forward with each word.

My plea fell on deaf ears as they tried to blow me up—or at least the boy did. He reached out with his magic and was intent on exploding and killing me. That being said, it made him interesting to me, as most Destruction users had to touch what they wanted to be destroyed. It seemed that this kid was an exception to the rule. The explosions worried me slightly, as my scales always negated any damage from Taylor or Charlie, but as he was the exception, he could have been the exception for me too. However, it turned out that I had worried for nothing. There was not even a blemish on me.

The boy freaked out when he saw me casually walking out of the smoke toward him, with a shirt now in strips and soot-covered pants, all the while with my scales on. The two wolves at his side were adamant about protecting him. They growled the closer I came, but the boy was a different story. He was too scared to even move. Once only a mere two feet separated from the boy and me, the silver-haired wolf jumped at me with its claws and teeth ready to rip me apart. The rush of the wolf attacking sent a shiver down my back, but it also gave me life. Fighting was what drove me, and that was what I did too, reaching out with my hand and grabbing the wolf by the throat.

This action broke the boy out of his petrified state. When he saw me holding the wolf by the neck, dangling to his side, he showed the first signs of fear since the fight started. It looked as if he cared for the wolf in some way, and it wasn't that hard to understand. The wolves had probably been his companions for a while. When I looked into the eyes of the wolf, there was something in there other than an animal. There must have been someone in that wolf. It was probably a Morpher, like Marie, and the eyes of Morphers never lied. There must have been someone in there, and whether the kid knew it or not, he cared deeply for them. This was a good first step to get this kid to calm down so we could talk.

After deciding my course of action, I gently placed the wolf down, never once taking my eyes off the hulking figure of the boy. Once the wolf was set free, it nipped at my hand, growled at me, and slowly backed away. I sat down, crossing my legs in front of the boy, and gestured for him to do the same. He did, and an awkward silence ensued. He was the first one to break the silence.

"I know who you are."

It was a simple statement but not one of significance. It wasn't like I was the most wanted man on the planet now or something for killing over three million people. Nope, not at all.

"A lot of people know who I am. What of it?" I asked him.

"A lot of people still think you're dead, and a lot of people believe that it was a gas explosion that helped people escape the prison. Not you who quite literally kicked out close to one thousand tons of steel over a thousand feet. That is what I'm saying."

"You were there?"

"No, but a friend of mine was."

"Is he dead?"

"Yes." That was something not to bring up again. He looked like a kicked puppy now.

"Have you been traveling around all that time?"

"No, I've been with the Teller for most of the time since they started imprisoning us."

That statement got a rise out of Charlie, who firmly believed that the Teller was just a bunch of baloney. A person who could accurately predict the future down to the tiniest detail was just too far-fetched for him—even after he'd seen some of the stuff I'd been able to do.

"The Teller is only a child's tale. What makes you think that we would believe that garbage?"

The boy whose name I had yet to know only chuckled at this.

"Why are you here?" I asked the boy, taking the conversation out of Charlie's hands.

"I want to change the world for the better, and what better way to do that than to be with the group that will undoubtedly go down in the history books."

I turned to Charlie and Connor and silently asked them whether or not they were okay with the kid joining. They both gave slight nods of approval.

"What's your name, kid?" I asked him, standing up, and he followed suit.

"My name's Albert," the hulking boy said, and for the first time, I decided to get a good look at him. His skin was mocha colored, and he had blue eyes. His hair was military short with a fade to the top. He was no pushover. He was built. He probably played a sport. Football or basketball was my guess.

"Well, Albert, welcome aboard," I said, outstretching my hand to him as he stood almost a foot taller than me. He took it and flashed a quick smile at me.

"So what now?" he asked, and he was answered with three rucksacks being thrown at him.

"You carry our stuff back to camp. It won't take that long," Connor said.

We headed back to the camp in silence while the wolves followed obediently behind Albert.

CHAPTER
14

This was the sixth—or was it the seventh?—meeting I'd had with the generals. It wasn't like it mattered anyway. I still had all the notes about what we were going to do with Bryce's group. We were still trying to pinpoint their location. Whenever the satellites tried to find them, the images were always blurred out by the power surges in the area, no doubt caused by Bryce. He did this to practically the entire mountain range near the prison, leaving us with only manpower to find out exactly where they were. However, in this whole situation it felt like, at least to me, that the generals were delaying.

We still had no idea what we should do about them. To attack or not to attack—that question had already been answered, because if we let them gather more people, then the fight would be that much harder. What we were really discussing were what tactics we should use to attack them, and right now the tactic of attrition was winning out. It made sense, as there couldn't be more than ten, maybe twelve, people in his group. They would eventually tire out.

Still, it wasn't finalized, and we were currently going over exactly what units we were going to use—something for which I did not need to be here, but the generals wouldn't let me leave. They wanted me to stay the entire time, taking away my time to do my own work, and I was thanking my lucky stars that Smith was my secretary. If it wasn't for him, there was no way that any of my work would be even close to being done.

One thing that kept me interested in these meetings was the possibility of finding out more about the Reapers. They were myths to the rest of the military; they were given patches of a black scythe, but no one had ever seen one until I saw it on the inside of the general's jacket when he took it off five meetings ago. Being in the same room as a former one was a privilege of untold proportions. At least to me it was. Unfortunately, every time I asked him if he would tell me more, he always shot me down, but today would be different ... maybe.

"That concludes our meeting for now. We'll meet tomorrow at the same time," General Ceribri said as he sat in his chair.

These words snapped me out of my trance, and as usual, I waited until the other generals and their assistants left, as General Ceribri was always the last one to leave. As his assistant left, the last one in the room besides us, neither one of us made a sound or moved. When the general finally decided to talk, he leaned forward in his chair.

"I think it's about time I told you about the Reapers. Maybe that will get you to pay attention during the meeting next time, eh?"

I could only nod in agreement with the general.

"So what is it that you would like to know, Lieutenant Colonel?"

"I have several questions if you don't mind," I started, already picking out a couple of questions that had been circling inside my head lately.

His response was to only nod in silence, exactly as I had done before.

"Why the name *Reapers*? How'd you guys get that name?"

"Now that's a good one," he said, shaking his finger at me, smiling. "We got that name because of Bradly, Lieutenant Bradly. Best hand-to-hand guy I've ever seen. He was actually Bryce's teacher for a while, if you can believe it. He got us the name Reapers, because whenever he had to fight in close quarters, he used a sickle instead of a knife. So one day, they just started calling us Reapers because of it, and it stuck. Too bad he's dead now ... heart attack," he said with an expression of sadness, but he quickly recovered. "Any others?"

"How long were you a Reaper?"

"Oh, about fifteen years, I'd say, maybe a year or two more. It was hard to tell in all honesty. The years just blurred by."

"That must've been hard on your wife."

"I didn't have a wife back then. I was a Reaper almost as soon as I joined. The youngest ever in their books, I was only seventeen when I was accepted into their ranks, and I don't think anyone will ever get close to that record. I didn't meet my wife until I was thirty-three and didn't marry her until I was thirty-five. Xavier came along not too long after that."

"So what was it like being a Reaper?" I asked, as what he said about the years passing by like they were nothing really intrigued me.

"Well, if you want a family, it's not something I'd recommend. There is no tour. There are no breaks. You're either training, or you're in the field. My fifteen or so years with the Reapers were one continuous long tour. You only got one full day off a year, and if there was an emergency during your day off, your free day became null and void."

"Sounds terrible," I said.

"It wasn't too bad. That was only if you didn't have a family back home."

"Okay. Was your son a Reaper?" I asked with a bit of apprehension, as I assumed that it was a sore subject for him.

"Yeah. He was the second-youngest at twenty-one, but he only lasted about three years, which is the shortest for any Reaper ever."

He sounded kind of proud about his son being the second-youngest ever, and he seemed to be even more proud when he said that his son got out after only three years.

"Why'd he leave?" I couldn't help asking.

"He met a girl. Broke a lot of Reaper rules to do it too. Nearly got himself court-martialed for it, and it probably would've happened if I hadn't interfered. He didn't get off scot-free, of course, and as punishment he had to serve another year around the clock with no breaks."

"How'd that go over with the girl?" I asked.

"She accepted it and actually began to hang around my wife and me a lot. Before I knew it, about two months into Xavier's last year as a Reaper, she was basically living with us and did everything we asked of her. She was a good person and the only person outside of my family and the Reapers who gained my full respect. That woman was willing to do anything for family," he said with a smile on his face the entire time. But right before he started talking, I heard him whisper, "I just wish she had done it in a different way."

That made me curious about this woman, but I decided not to ask about that. If I got her name, that would be enough.

"So what was her name?" I asked.

"Her name was Madelyn Argentum."

The name resonated with me, and I felt like I had heard it before, but I pushed it aside for now. It wouldn't be that hard for me to find out about her through our records or on the internet.

"Now if you don't mind, that's all I have time for. It was nice talking with you about this, but be advised it will not happen again. Got it, soldier?" he asked in an authoritative tone that instantly made me bolt to attention and salute him.

"Yes, sir," I said back, saluting him, and he saluted back before walking out of the room, leaving me alone in there.

Now the only thing left for me to do was work. *Better not avoid it any longer.*

Several hours later I was finally done. We had extra paperwork today, as some of my subordinates got into a brawl during training, and it fell to me to read through all the reports and then make a final decision. One may ask where their superior officer was during this time, and the answer would be that he was doing paperwork for me because of the meeting earlier. It really annoyed me that the meeting that really didn't involve me made this happen, but it wasn't like the past could be changed.

All the paperwork wasn't what was really bothering me. It was the name of Bryce's mother that the general had told me earlier. I'd never heard it before, but it resonated with me—more specifically my magic, and it made me afraid. Just thinking of the name of the general's daughter-in-law sent shivers down my spine. The only person to ever do that to me was MO. Maybe they were connected. It was doubtful, but it didn't hurt to check into it, and Smith owed me a favor. He'd get MO's file and look up the woman for me.

"Smith, get in here," I said into the phone that worked as an intercom system between our two offices. It took him all of a couple of seconds to come into the room.

"Yes, LTC?" he said, going to attention in front of my desk.

I simply waved him off, silently telling him to relax and to take a seat.

"I need you to do a bit of research for me."

"On who?"

"MO and Madelyn Argentum." Just saying those two names in the same sentence unnerved me.

"Why, if I may ask?"

"Just a hunch, and get the files to me by tonight at my place. You still owe me a favor, so you'll be cooking," I said, smiling at him. He returned the smile with one of his own, nodded his head in affirmation, and then proceeded out the door.

Now that that was taken care of, the only work left to do was to decide what I was going to do with the people who got into a fight earlier. The two who started it were good people. From what Smith and others told me, they'd both had issues at home recently. Considering everything they did, mostly to each other (in addition to one broken window and the accidental detonation of a concussion grenade in a crowd of my soldiers), I made up my mind. They would both go on forced leave—not a suspension per se, as it wouldn't go in their records as suspensions, but they needed time at home. They both did. Everyone knew that a healthy family meant a healthy soldier, so the faster they fixed the problem at home, the better they'd perform, and the easier my life would be. It was a win-win for everyone.

I sent the recommendation for the soldiers' punishment to the colonel and then began to clean up my office. It took only a couple of minutes, and by then, the colonel had responded, telling me to go ahead with my plan. With his approval, I sent an email to the two captains so that they could tell them their "punishment."

One would have expected my proposal for the soldiers to be denied, because I was a magic user, and with the world in its current state, it was not hard to expect discrimination, but that was not what happened. The majority of the military actually supported magic users, as there was a decent number in the military, but they were spread out all over the units. Only the Slāve absolutely hated them. The rest of us really treated them like normal people. It had gotten to the point where there were rumors that a military coup could happen any day now in support of the magic users, but I doubted it. No one was that desperate … yet.

It was not my place to worry about that. It was time to go home and wait for Smith to come over with the file on MO and anything he found on the general's daughter-in-law. He likely had everything and was just waiting for me in the parking lot so that he could follow me. When he wanted to, he could quite literally get things done in minutes that normally took hours. He seemed good at manipulating people.

As I closed the door to my office and walked out of the building to the parking lot, my suspicions were proven to be correct. He was lounging on the hood of his Jeep, reading a book. As soon as he saw me, he shut his book, got into his Jeep, turned on the engine, and waited for me. I started up my sedan and pulled out of the parking lot. Smith was right behind me, and the drive home took a bit longer, as I had to make sure we didn't get separated. He still didn't know the route to my house by heart, which was a bit annoying. Once we got inside the house, he gave me the file on MO and a notebook with all the info he could find on the general's daughter-in-law. Then he went into the kitchen and made us something to eat.

For the next twenty minutes, I skimmed over the two files. To say that what was in there was pleasing would be a complete and utter lie. Half of the MO file was blacked out and subsequently useless, and there was a compartment for pictures in there, but they were gone. And the notebook for Bryce's mom didn't tell me much either. It included only her birthdate, social security number, and credit score. It also included a list of jobs. The first one was a waitress, when she was sixteen, to pay for her dance team's tournaments. At eighteen, she was a bartender while in college. She was a stripper from twenty-two to twenty-six, which was around the time that she got pregnant with Bryce. And at thirty-one, she became a successful investment banker for a couple of years before retiring.

At all her jobs she was given above-average ratings from everyone, and all the reports that Smith gathered showed her to be well liked and respected, especially while she was a stripper. Apparently, she was the main act for practically her entire time there, and to be honest, I could see it. From the pictures Smith had gotten, this woman was gorgeous. She had exotic sparkling white hair, dazzling blue eyes, a slender body, and pearly skin, with above-average assets. This woman was the epitome of beautiful. I couldn't imagine the tips she got when she was working as a waitress.

"Hey, Julie. Do you want yours spicy or not?" Smith suddenly asked from the kitchen, breaking me out of my little trance.

"What are you making?"

"Curry."

"Spicy, please!" I shouted back at him before closing the notebook and turning on the news. Both leads ended up being dead ends, except the fact that the pictures were missing from the file. I'd be paying the archives guy a visit soon. That man was always a pain to deal with.

The rest of the night went smoothly. We ate the curry that Smith made, drank beer, and watched the news. It was quiet and peaceful the rest of the night, until just before Smith was going to leave. A news story came on about the magic user who had been attacking practically every military establishment from one side of the country to the other, with the last attack occurring about three months ago. This wasn't the part that had Smith pissed. It was when they stated that the military still had no idea what the person looked like. They had minimal information: the person was female, she had red hair, and her magic made her damn near impossible to kill. Because of this, the media came up with a nickname— the Untouchable Queen—and it stuck. This pissed Smith off, because he ran the information side of special ops, and for him not to know something made him mad. It also didn't help that the woman was practically a ghost, appearing and then disappearing, as if she had been told to hit the places. Needless to say, Smith was not very pleasant afterward.

While he was at my house, he knew to be tame, but it took a bit of coaxing and a beer or two before he really calmed down. He took a seat on the couch, beer in hand, and passed out. He looked so peaceful sleeping on the couch that I couldn't help but smile, though I did have to take the beer out of his hand. I grabbed a blanket and swept it over him to help him sleep a bit more comfortably.

"Good night, Smith," I whispered as I draped the blanket over him.

His response was to grunt and then smile. I smiled in return before heading off to my own bed to read over the files again. Maybe I missed something.

Not changing into my sleepwear, I went straight onto my bed and opened the file on MO. As before, it was basically immaterial, showing only the least important facts, but if I really analyzed the information, I could get a relatively decent idea of what was being hidden. Coincidently, it helped that I used to be the person who did the blacking out.

The file explained in detail what happened to the areas that were attacked, and at the end of each description, the final paragraph was blacked out. I looked at the news reports about what had happened at the end of each attack. At least I got some pictures of what happened. The news reports didn't help much, which was expected, but what did help were the pictures.

The bases were not destroyed, but they were certainly broken. One part was always torn up the most, and this usually warranted suspicion, but they all had a common denominator. Each place that was destroyed the most at the bases was where they housed the prisoners.

This wasn't common knowledge, as the military didn't like the public to know everything, but I'd seen the inner workings of practically every base, and it was safe to say that every base held the prisoners below ground, even back then. Practically no one besides me and a handful of others knew that, and this completely changed how I viewed MO. They were looking for someone, but whom? My only thought was the back of the file, where it discussed MO's motives behind the attacks. A single line was blacked out, and there was no doubt that it contained the name.

Going over the files again definitely helped. Now the only thing left to do was to get the files for the prisoners—that is, if they hadn't been destroyed yet.

CHAPTER
15

It had been just two weeks since Albert had joined our little group. He had adjusted nicely, all things considered, as he didn't butt heads with anyone and seemed to get along with most. However, when we got into our training, he got his butt handed to him on a silver platter several times by not only myself but everyone else. Even Lucy was able to take him down. Still, he was improving, and it was mainly because he had never been trained to fight. For someone who had never been trained to fight to last as long as he did in some of the fights was an accomplishment in and of itself. All in all, he was a good kid, but he had a ways to go if he wanted to be even a halfway-decent fighter.

Our runs were usually between five and sixteen miles. We would run in the shallows of the river right on the edge to make it harder on ourselves—these we did every day, barring that nothing stopped us from doing so. Albert did well on these for the first mile and a half, and then he just couldn't do it. The first time he ran with us, I had to quite literally carry him over my shoulders for the last three miles, as he had collapsed. After that, he started to pace himself more instead of running like he usually did, and I came to find out that my earlier assumption about him being a prodigy in sports had been correct. Football was his forte—more specifically wide receiver, for obvious reasons. Still, it didn't help him one bit with us.

One thing that really caught my eye since he'd been with us was that the wolves basically never left his side. Even when we went on our runs and trained, the wolves were always near him. That made me even more suspicious of them. They always seemed to keep their distance from me but not anyone else. I couldn't get a grasp on whether my original assumption had been right or not. It was starting to get infuriating.

Smack!

"Ha! I finally hit you!" yelled Albert as he proceeded to do a little dance he called a celebration. "Oh yeah!"

We were in training, and I had just spaced out. *Wow, I'm actually ashamed of myself right now.* What added to my embarrassment was that when Albert started his so-called celebration, the silver wolf barked, as if it was congratulating him. Also, Annabeth looked like she was about to say something.

"Don't you say it," I said, with my right hand on the bridge of my nose and my left one pointing at Annabeth.

"Okay ... party pooper." She said the last part under her breath, but I paid no heed.

"Hey, Albert," I said to get his attention, and he turned around mid-celebration. "Match is still going."

He merely nodded and immediately got back into the stance I had taught him—low to the ground with his feet out wide and hands separated with one in front of him and the other at his head. This stance was usually reserved for someone with a different body type, but he had quick enough reactions and fast enough hands to get the job done. It also made him harder to hit, and it was easier for him to defend himself. Although he had the stance down, he couldn't attack for crap. If he kept working with his stance and attacking, he'd become a force to be reckoned with.

"Now how about a little wager before we begin?" I asked him, and he relaxed a bit but was still ready to move if I attacked suddenly.

"What's the bet?" he asked simply.

"If you can last thirty seconds against me, you won't have to do any type of cleaning duties for the next two weeks."

"And if I can't last thirty seconds?"

"You and only you are going to make a new latrine the next time a new one needs to be made."

We put the latrines well away from actual camp in case the smell got too bad. We dug a hole about ten feet deep and four feet wide. From there, we propped up some wood from a felled tree and put a hole in it. After it was all set up, we used it for about a month, give or take a couple of days, until we, as a group, built another latrine only about five feet from the previous one. The dirt we dug up was used to cover the old one. The process was long and usually took a whole day, as a group, and we never used our magic. We took the time we spent together as a gift, even though we were making a hole to crap in. If Albert used his magic, he could probably get it done in the same amount of time.

"I'll take that deal," he said, brimming with confidence as he got back into his stance.

"Anyone going to place their bets?" I asked the others watching.

"No," they all said in unison. I guess they knew what was going to happen.

"You ready, Albert?"

He only nodded in agreement.

"Then, Charlie, start the clock."

I exploded forward, and the distance between us shrunk from twenty feet to nothing in less than a second. Albert reacted on pure instinct from seeing me close the distance that fast and threw a punch, one that was child's play to dodge. Grabbing onto his now-extended arm, I started to spin him around me for maybe two rotations before letting go. He stumbled forward a couple of feet but quickly recovered, only to see me in front of him, and by that time, it was over. My first punch landed right in his sternum, knocking the wind out of him. As he doubled over, I got behind him and kicked the back of his knees, causing him to go to his knees. From there, finishing him off was nothing. An open-hand strike to the left side of his face knocked him out completely, and he landed face-first onto the dirt.

My immediate concern was flipping him over just in case he got his face in something—better safe than sorry. I also needed to make sure he was still breathing, which he was. What further confirmed my suspicions of the wolves was that the silver-haired wolf was now even with my face and glaring at me all the while growling, as if it was planning to kill me.

From this position I could see its eyes again, and the same light that had been there two weeks ago was still there. That confirmed it for me. That wolf was definitely a Morpher like Marie.

After a couple of seconds, the wolf stopped glaring and growling at me to go to Albert's side, where it did the same thing I had just done. It checked for breathing by putting its head over his mouth, and it checked his pulse by putting its ears to his heart. When the wolf was satisfied with the results, it snuggled up against him as he lay prone on the ground. We probably weren't going to be able to have any more matches today with them in the middle, so now was as good a time as any to call it. Besides, we had spent an extra hour practicing strikes for Albert.

"We're done for the day, guys. Go get some rest since you'll have to wait until Albert's back up to wash yourselves."

I got up and proceeded to make my way back toward the camp, until I got a tap on the shoulder.

"We need to talk," said the voice.

I turned around to see who it was, and the voice belonged to Marie. I nodded to her, and she gestured with her head toward the forest, where we stocked our extra ammo and weapons. We walked there for about a minute until she was satisfied we were out of earshot.

"There's no way those wolves are just wolves," she said, turning around to face me with her arms crossed.

"You'll get no arguments from me. I was actually planning on talking to you about that. When do you think we can actually confirm it or not? They're almost always with Albert, and I've rarely seen them leave his side."

"Well, that's the problem, isn't it? They're very good at covering up their own tracks. I've never been able to find out where they go even when they do leave. It's like they vanish into thin air," she said with a bit of annoyance.

"I think I can help with that," a new voice said, slightly startling us.

We were concentrating too much on how to track the wolves. It didn't fully alarm me, as I recognized the voice immediately. It was Lucy.

"And how will you do that?" Marie asked, looking past me and directly at Lucy.

"Well, they do have a magic signature. So I could track them and you at the same time and direct you on where to go if you lose them. That sound good?" she asked the both of us, but only getting a nod from Marie.

"The plan's good with me, but are you sure you can do it?" I asked.

"Don't underestimate me, Bryce. I've got some surprises up my sleeve," she said with a smirk plastered across her face.

She wasn't wrong. I had started to underestimate her, and as someone who could literally go into your mind, that was a bad person to underestimate.

"All right then. We'll do it tomorrow. Today, however, rest. You both did well today," I said, nodding to them and walking back to our camp with them right behind me.

As it always was after training, the camp was dead silent with the exception of light snoring coming from Connor's and Annabeth's tents. Taylor was the one snoring in Connor's tent, and both girls snored in Annabeth's tent. It was just the way they were. As soon as we arrived, Lucy and Marie both went to their respective tents to be with their boyfriends, and that left me in the middle of our semicircle of tents alone, staring at the burned-out fire.

The silence that accompanied me there was rather soothing—no fighting, no death, no people talking; it was beyond peaceful. It almost lasted too. From the campfire, a figure with black mist as a body and glowing red eyes rose out of the ash and looked me straight in the eyes. I forgot how scary they were.

This hadn't happened since before Scarlet came around. He—or she possibly—was what I liked to refer to as a demon. They were all inside my mind. That was obvious to me, but that didn't make them any less scary when they did nothing but torment me. Just out of reflex, as soon as it appeared, my scales flared up and covered my body. When it took one step toward me, I took one step back, but that just seemed to make it even more menacing, as it started to grow larger. Then it took another, and my feet refused to move, so it took another and another until it loomed directly over me.

By this point, my body was completely drenched in sweat, and my heart was pounding at one hundred miles an hour. For months the demons were always looming over me and my friends, looking as if they were about to slaughter us all. It had been incredibly difficult, but, eventually, it became just another everyday thing, and the fact that it became an everyday thing was what made it so terrible. However, after not seeing one of these guys for so long, my defenses were completely down. It must have realized this, as it slowly reached out its misty hand and grabbed my throat. When my scales started to flare up even more, I could feel my fire start to go out of control. Just when it was about to strengthen its hold, it snarled at something behind me and then disappeared in a wisp of smoke.

I collapsed to the ground, unconsciousness quickly taking me.

Waking up with a headache, I looked around and recognized my tent, which stopped me from freaking out. Still, it felt weird to wake up without Scarlet next to me. Pushing the demons out of my mind, I got dressed and walked out of the tent, only to be immediately confronted by Scarlet.

"What happened yesterday? I've been worried sick."

I was surprised at how gentle she was being about it. I thought that she was going to have a little mini freak-out session about what happened yesterday. Everyone else was going about their business, as if nothing happened, so maybe she was just going with the flow of the others for now, but it was hard to tell.

"Just a hallucination. They happened all the time before you came. That was the first one I've had since you came, so almost three months now. I wasn't prepared at all for it."

"The hell does that mean, Bryce!" she hissed at me with both concern and anger. "You could've burned the camp to the ground! Possibly killing all of us! What was really going on?"

We were standing now and shouting at each other.

"I saw a demon, Scarlet! What else is there to be said? I got scared and freaked out!"

"That's not a damn answer, *Bryce*! Demons don't *exist*! They never have, and they never will!"

"Well, they exist to me! Every day, every godforsaken day since I murdered the whole damn city that I lived in my entire life, they've been there. Now, they were bad while I was being tortured for six freaking months, but it didn't compare to how they were when we escaped! I saw them every day killing everyone! Each day was different too on how everyone would die! Sometimes it would be drowning. Then the next day it would be explosions, stabs in the back, shooting, you name it. And don't even get me started on the nightmares! Those were the worst, when the worst of the worst came out. I almost killed Annabeth twice and

Connor thrice, because I would freak out in my sleep and send my power everywhere.

"But that's not the worst part. The worst part of all this was that after a while I got used to it. I got used to seeing my friends die in front of me every day. Do you know how it feels to actually get used to seeing your friends die—people that you've spent practically your whole life with— and knowing that you could do absolutely nothing to stop it? I would do almost anything to keep them alive! There wasn't a day that went by where I didn't think about killing myself to stop that and to protect everyone from myself. So, yeah, I freaked out a bit when I saw one of the monsters responsible for that!"

Everyone was staring at us wide-eyed. It took me a couple of seconds to register that we had just had that fight in front of everyone, and it took me a few more seconds to realize that I had never told any of them that. It was time to get out of here and now.

CHAPTER
16

B ryce and Scarlet started arguing while Connor was rubbing my stomach, something he liked to do with the baby. Not even five seconds into their argument they were both glowing—actually glowing. Bryce had his scales in full, completely covering him while he glowed a dull red at the beginning of their fight, and by the end, it was like a flashlight was right in my face. Both his arms and legs were billowing out flames while they argued. Not to mention Scarlet. By the end of the argument, her hair was whipping around, as if she was in the middle of a tornado, and she was glowing the brightest blue I'd ever seen. Aside from her glow, she had literal floating balls of energy all around her. They both put the fear of God into us in those moments, because we knew that if they went at it, we'd get caught in the cross fire, and no one here was even close to their level.

Thankfully, once Bryce finished his rant, he took off toward the mountain, jumping almost halfway up the mountain, leaving us to ponder what he had said. To be honest, we never thought it was that bad. We always thought that they were just really bad night terrors, and the few times he did lose control of his power during the day, we assumed he was just stretching his power after not using it for so long. We never knew, and that made it so much worse. His closest friends, us, had no idea that he was suffering. What good friends we were.

As soon as he leaped to the mountain, Scarlet collapsed into a crying mess, balling on the ground and incessantly saying that this was her fault. She was about as inconsolable as they come, and it took me and Marie almost five minutes to just get her to stand up and get back to the camp, where she continued to cry in the safety of her own tent. I went into her tent and started to calm her down by incessantly stroking her hair and shushing her cries. She just felt really bad about all this. I couldn't blame her. She was just trying to find out what happened so she could help. We were all going to do the same after training anyway, so this result was probably going to happen either way.

It was almost a half hour before she was fully calmed down, and that was because she had no more tears to cry. At that point, I left her alone to sort out her thoughts and went outside to see the others waiting around the fire pit, where they were roasting a couple of squirrels. Everyone was dead silent, all obviously going over what Bryce had said earlier and how the hell we had missed it all. Albert and Jessica, who never knew Bryce during that time, were looking around aimlessly, not knowing what was going on. Jessica had Annabeth to fill her in a bit, so she knew a little, but Albert had no one and, hence, knew nothing at all about the situation. Everyone else just looked like kicked puppies, and someone needed to do something.

"Well, we screwed up big-time," I said to the group, making my presence known to them.

"You're not wrong there," Annabeth said, looking up at me from the fire.

"What are we supposed to do? What if he doesn't come back?" Albert asked from his part of the logs that worked as our seats.

"He'll come back. We're his family, and if he doesn't come back for us, he'll certainly come back for Scarlet. He loves her," Connor said as he was turning the spit where the squirrels were.

"So what should we do in the meantime then?" Shane asked.

"We'll train until we're sore to the bone. What else is there to do? And besides, it won't be all that much longer before the world comes knocking on our doorstep," Connor said as he took the squirrels and the spit away from the fire and had the squirrels hanging to cool down.

"What makes you say that?" Jessica asked, looking at Connor curiously.

"It's just a process of elimination. I saw what Bryce looks like from a satellite, and he looks like a flashlight being shown wherever he is on a map. His power even when he didn't use it at all reached to this mountain range when we were still in the prison. It sounds as if it would be impossible to find us in the smoke screen, but what do all of you think those soldiers we saw were doing? They're finding out where we are if they haven't already. They'll be here soon enough, and we better be ready for them, because if we aren't, we'll die, and the hope of others like us will die with us. And, personally, I'd like to see my child grow up in a world where we're accepted."

Everyone shut up, contemplating what he had just said. They all knew that he was right. The training that they had been doing was just to warm everyone up. The real thing began now.

"Great," Albert said, heaving a sigh, much to the amusement of everyone there, who all began to laugh, including myself.

CHAPTER
17

It was the dead of night, probably around one or two o'clock in the morning. Both of us were uncertain as to what to do now. Our instructions were to wait to reveal ourselves when one of the groups confronted us or Albert about it, but Bryce might have been the only one onto us. This could be a serious problem if what we were told was to come true. I looked to Regius as we walked to the clearing, where we always met to talk, and he portrayed no emotion in his wolf form. He was always stoic when he changed, but once he was in human form again, he'd tell me what the plan was.

We changed back into our human forms, and he said nothing for what felt like the longest time. "You can come out now, Marie. Bring Lucy too, please," he said in the calmest voice possible for the situation. He must have smelled them now, and he took a whiff at the air. The wind was coming at us from the camp. It would have been easy for him to spot them. I, on the other hand, was never really good at the finer aspects of changing, like the sense of smell and sight, but their instincts always worked well with me.

An owl dropped down from one of the branches and changed into

Marie. She stood there, looking us up and down for several seconds before Regius began speaking again.

"Where's Lucy?"

"She'll come when I believe that you mean her no harm."

"Fair enough. I assure you that I only mean to talk and to reveal our identities to you and, by extension, the group."

"Then why wait until now?" she asked, shifting her feet a bit. She was getting ready to fight. I couldn't really blame her. I probably would have been fighting by now.

"We were told to wait until someone discovered us," he said, staring her down, which made me feel a bit awkward, as we couldn't wear clothes when transformed, meaning all three of us were currently naked.

"I'm guessing you were told to do so?" she asked, which he answered with only a nod.

Marie motioned with her arm, and Lucy came out of the forest and stood next to her. She proceeded to whisper something into Marie's ear, to which she smiled.

"Well, it seems it's your lucky day. Lucy here says to have no ill will toward any of us, so I guess you guys are in the clear for now. That being said, what are your names?" Marie asked, looking at us with a smile on her face.

"I'm Regius, and that there is Argentum," Regius said, gesturing toward me.

I smiled and gave a slight bow toward the two women in front of me. My foster parents had taught me to always bow toward people you just met or people in authority. It was a sign of respect. To my pleasant surprise, they both bowed back. It had been a long time since anyone had bowed back, and that was when I was meeting my foster grandparents.

"As a stand-in for Bryce and Connor at the current moment, we would like to welcome you both to our little group." They both smiled at us before Marie continued. "We do have an extra tent at the moment, but it isn't near the camp and is where the guns and bullets are, if you're okay with that."

"That'll be fine with me. Argentum here already has another place in mind," he said with a smirk, making me blush. He knew how I felt about Albert, and he hadn't stopped teasing me about it whenever the situation arose since he found out.

"Albert's tent, right?" asked Lucy with a gigantic smirk on her face, and it made me blush furiously.

Regius laughed, probably excited that he now had a partner in crime to tease me. He hadn't stopped teasing me since he found out I liked Albert.

"That is correct. Isn't it, Argentum?" he said, stretching out my name and smirking.

I just put my head down and began to walk back toward the camp. After a couple of sets of clothes were thrown to me—courtesy of Lucy, who also gave clothes to Marie and Regius—it took me over two minutes to try to get the clothes on before giving up, changing back into my wolf form, and walking with the rest. When I put clothes on from now on it'd be when it's absolutely necessary, meaning when others were around me.

All of us walked together back to the camp, but when we were about a minute away, Marie and Lucy stopped us and proceeded to tell us that we would break the news as to whom we really were tomorrow before our training. After that, we split up. Marie and Lucy went to their respective tents, while Regius went to find a quiet place to sleep in the woods. I, on the other hand, went to talk to Albert. It was about time he found out the truth.

I stopped right outside of his tent. My mind began spinning about how he would react. Part of me hoped that he would take it all in stride and be fine with it, but my rational side, after knowing him for almost a year, told me his reaction wouldn't be too good for me. He hated being lied to or tricked, and this certainly fell under that category. This could be bad.

Finalizing my plan and going inside the tent still as a wolf, I nudged him with my nose and sat down in front of him, looking as expectantly as possible. It was my signal to him that a walk was needed. He rolled over to face me, and when he saw me, he let out a long sigh, knowing what was expected. He was still wearing the jeans he had worn on our first day at the camp and a white T-shirt. After slowly getting on his tennis shoes, he followed me out of the tent, and we made our way toward the forest to the left of the river. That part of the forest was always more beautiful at night.

We didn't even make it ten steps into the forest before we found our first firefly. These things always roamed around the area, and they made it beautiful. Older trees with hanging branches everywhere barely illuminated by fireflies screamed romantic, along with the serene nature of the forest, made me fall in love with this area the first time I saw it. Albert didn't really mind any of this, and that was probably because he was hardwired for sports and adrenaline, not for romance. Still, it was nice to think that he at least enjoyed the walk. This walk would probably be in his mind for a long time, hopefully.

We stopped when we reached what must have been the oldest tree in the forest. He plopped down at the trunk of the tree, while I walked around and picked up a stick in my mouth. Bringing it to him, he looked at me with an amused expression before he spoke.

"You woke me up in the dead of night to take you on a walk, and now you want to play fetch?" he asked with a smile on his face, which I could only return with a half-hearted whimper, but it was enough.

"Fine." Sighing, he took the stick out of my mouth and whipped it into the forest. Thankfully it was far enough away so he couldn't see me change.

Playing the part of the happy animal, I sprinted after the stick and into the darkness for a couple of seconds before stopping. There was no turning back now for me, even though part of me was screaming not to do it. I knew that if he discovered this from anyone but me, he probably wouldn't ever talk to me again. Psyching myself up and changing into my naked body, I prepped myself to go out and face him.

"You should at least wear some clothes."

I was beyond startled and whipped around to see Connor there behind me. He was holding out some nice-looking clothes, like those you would buy from a store, not the military ones everyone had scavenged. To boot, he was looking away from me as he held out the clothes. It was nice to see a gentleman.

"Thank you. But how did you know?" I asked before taking the clothes and throwing them on. The underwear was a bit tight but comfortable. The tight jean shorts went down to my midthigh, and those must have seen better days, as they were faded to the bone, but they fit well enough. The top was a loose brown V-neck that would have been big on me if I was a boy, but it fit snugly on me because of my chest. It made me feel embarrassed, but it looked damn good.

"I make it my business to know everything about everyone in the camp. I am Bryce's right hand after all. What would I be worth as his right hand if I couldn't find out basic information?"

"That doesn't answer my question, Connor."

"An educated guess really, followed by a bunch of stalking."

"Great, just another thing to worry about. A stalker and the military."

He chuckled a little bit. It wasn't dark or intimidating; it was a genuine laugh.

"You'll get used to it, Argentum. Bryce needs to know how everyone is doing in order to lead effectively, and he lets me get the information. Plus, it helps that I can go anywhere at any time, and you'll never know I was there. Besides, it doesn't matter. I arranged this for you two, and even though I'm a stalker, in your words, I make sure that everyone is happy or at least has closure."

"He must have so much faith in you to let you do that. Bryce, I mean."

"You have no idea."

I was about to ask another question, but as I blinked he disappeared. He needed to teach me that.

I stood there in the dark, now fully clothed, thanks to Connor, and my mind was running a mile a minute as I thought of every possible outcome, ranging from the good to the bad. The best scenario was that he would take it all in stride and just continue on like this wasn't a change at all. The worst and probably more likely scenario was that he would get mad enough to attack me. But there was no more waiting. This was the time to move.

Taking a couple of steps toward him to stay out of sight, I saw that he was awake and still sitting up against the tree. "A-Albert ... please don't freak out."

He was instantly up and looking at my silhouette. I took another three steps to get out of the darkness so that he could see me. When his eyes met mine, he froze, looking at me, trying desperately to comprehend what was going on.

"Albert. It's me," I said, trying to break him out of his shock. To help, I put my hand on his shoulder as gently as possible, trying to convey as much trust and comfort as my body could. That was a mistake.

"Get the hell away from me," he snarled at me, smacking my hand from his shoulder.

"B-But, Albert, i-it's me, Argentum, your wolf," I said with a shaking voice, praying to whatever gods there were that he would forgive me, and I put my hand back on his shoulder.

"I said get the *hell* away from me! Do you realize the things I've done in front of you and the *infinite* amount of trust I had in you? Just when the *hell* were you planning on telling me that you are human, huh!" he shouted at me and shoved me to the ground. It didn't hurt physically, but emotionally, I might as well have taken a rocket to the chest.

I can't deal with this. I knew it would be bad, but I never thought it would get this bad. I've got to get out of here. And so I did, with tears pouring out of my eyes. The only sound I could hear was my own sobbing as I ran into the forest.

CHAPTER

18

"Wait, Argentum, I'm sorry," I tried to call out to her, but it was far too late. She was already gone into the forest. "Way to go, Albert," I said to myself, releasing a heavy sigh. "You just had to make your best friend of the past year and a half cry and run away in shame. Real man you are, idiot."

"Can't really argue with you on the last part there. You're an idiot," a voice spoke from behind me.

I whipped around to see who it was, but no one was there. Instantly, I prepared to fight. I frantically scanned my surroundings until my eyes spotted a figure crouching on a tree branch.

"Who are you?" I asked him, not letting my guard down in the slightest.

"You know who I am," the figure said, dropping down from the branch and walking close enough that when he was illuminated by the fireflies, I could see his face.

"Connor? What are you doing out here?"

"I take a vested interest in everything that happens here, including someone overreacting to something very trivial. And to actually hurt the person who made them overreact with a blatant disregard for their feelings and how they felt ... well, that is something I will always take an interest in."

"So what? You can use it as gossip?" I asked angrily.

The way he was saying he took an interest in these types of things infuriated me to no end. He was just a gossip whore.

"No," he stated in a tone that suggested if I interrupted it would be my head. "I take an interest in these matters, because the sooner you make up, the better it is for the group. Besides, do you really think that she just wouldn't tell you without a significant reason?" he asked.

He wasn't wrong. I thought about it for a little bit, and he wasn't wrong. Why would she hide it, knowing the entire time that I would probably react like this? That was the million-dollar question. *Why?* She would have gained everything and lost nothing if she had told me right away, but instead she didn't and waited until now. There must have been a reason.

"So ... what do you think I should do?" I asked, looking up at him, and he laughed at me.

"What makes you think I would know? She's your girl and a woman. I'm not quite sure they even understand themselves."

His statement shocked me into silence, and for the mere millisecond my eyes wandered off, Connor disappeared. Sighing, I looked around, trying to find any sign of my wolf so that maybe my mistake could be forgiven. It wasn't all that hard to find the signs either, for she had just run off without trying to cover her tracks. That was my fault also.

I followed the tracks, and she came into my sight only three minutes later, and it wasn't a very pleasant sight. She was crying incessantly, sitting with her back resting against a tree. If she hadn't been crying so much, she would have been stunning. She had long, slender, and toned legs with a healthy tan to them. In fact, her entire body was toned, from her legs to her stomach to her arms. Not to mention her assets. *My god.* Her hair and eyes too were unlike anything I'd ever seen. She had snow-white hair and sparkling ice-blue eyes. Her crying made me feel awful.

"Hey, Silver," I called out to her, making my presence known.

She hiccuped a couple of times and tried but failed to stop herself from crying.

"H-H-Hey, Albert," she barely choked out.

I sat down next to her at the tree, and she shied away instantly. Before she could get too far away, I put my hand on her shoulder—not as a means to keep her near me but for me to know that she was still there.

"I'm sorry. I overreacted. I never should've harmed you or yelled at you."

I could feel myself getting choked up toward the end, and I bent my head down so that she wouldn't see. Luck didn't favor me that time, though, time, as she backed over to me and nudged my shoulder with her head like she usually did but only in her wolf form.

"It's okay, Albert. Mistakes will happen. Just don't do it again," she said, no longer crying and with a surprisingly even voice for someone who just stopped crying.

I lifted my head, and she snaked her head under my right arm and rested it on my chest, nuzzling into my chest just like she did in her wolf form. Just as she got comfortable, there was an audible click and flash. We were both up instantly and ready to fight, but all we saw was Connor standing there with a camera—from where he got it, only God knew—adding insult to injury, ruining the moment before my wolf, who, I now realized, never told me her real name and looked like a bright red lollipop. She was flushed.

"Don't worry about the picture too much. You're not the only ones to get caught by me," he said, checking the picture on the camera.

"Who else?" we both asked in unison.

"Everyone."

CHAPTER
19

S leep wasn't particularly kind to me at the current moment. Even with it being well past midnight, I didn't even feel the slightest bit tired, and that was probably because Bryce hadn't come back yet. It had been only about half a day since our fight, and although that was a short amount of time, living it felt like weeks—especially considering most of my time was spent crying. Waiting here was too much for me.

So instead of waiting, I got up and left the tent, still dressed in my earlier clothes, and walked toward the mountains in the direction of Bryce. Walking there without powers would take too long, so I began to do something that my body hadn't done in a while.

I focused on the deepest level of myself, and a golden light began to envelope me. When it had enveloped my entire body, I opened my eyes. Everything became enhanced; all of my five senses increased in sensitivity at the same time, allowing me superhuman senses and strength. I looked for any signs of Bryce in the mountains, and it wasn't that hard to find him this way. He was in possession of essentially the world's magic power several times over, so he wasn't all that hard to find. He looked like a miniature sun, and it really did hurt to look at him.

I tapped into my actual magic, not this separate part of me, and made my way toward him by running at speeds far exceeding Formula One drivers and by jumping distances that would have made track coaches faint. Getting to him didn't take all that long, but before we actually met, I stopped a few hundred feet from where he was and began to slowly make my way to him. It took way too long in my opinion, as my entire body and mind just wanted to be near him, but going too close too quickly would make him attack, and right now that wasn't what either of us wanted.

I finally got there and noticed the faint glow of a dying fire that was invigorated by a scaled hand reaching into its ashes and stoking the embers of the fire. There was no doubt it was Bryce. Slowing down even more so as to not put him on edge, I made my way to him. When he saw me entering the light of the fire, he looked happy and even smiled.

Smiling back, I made my way over to him and sat down next to him. I pulled him down to rest his head on my lap. He gave no resistance, and soon he was looking up at me smiling, but in his eyes were sadness and shame.

"None of that now, okay? We both made mistakes and overreacted today," I said, leaning over and kissing him on the head.

He simply looked at me with gratitude, and that's all I needed for an answer. But he got up and turned to face me with a look I hadn't seen on him before. It was feral and primal, but it was sexy and intriguing at the same time.

"Bryce. Wh—" I didn't even get to finish my question, as his lips came crashing down on mine. God, this man was a snake, but I'd be lying if I said I didn't like it.

I awoke to Bryce running his hand through my hair. Normally, this would have prompted me to hit him, but after last night, it didn't matter. He could do whatever he wanted to my hair if he didn't cut it off.

"Finally awake, sleepyhead," he said cheerfully as he looked at me.

My head was on his chest, and my body was practically a blanket for him. I didn't dignify him with a response and instead chose to stretch out my body, pushing on his chest and chin, making him fall over beside the tree he had been propped up against.

"Thanks for tha—ugh!" He stopped being sarcastic as soon as I planted my foot on his stomach and pushed myself up.

"You were saying?" I asked, standing above him with a confident smirk on my face.

"Thanks for the view" was his only response as he looked me up and down.

Following his eyes, I was greeted with the sight of my own naked body. I let out a small squeal and tried to kick him, but he ducked out of the way.

"Where are my clothes?" I timidly asked, trying desperately to cover myself. I still had at least a little bit of dignity.

"In a pile by the fire. I took the liberty of picking them up after you fell asleep," he said, pointing to a pile of clothes by the now burned-out fire. I bent down to pick up my clothes, and Bryce spoke up again.

"Again, thanks for the view."

Without even thinking about it this time, I summoned my magic and threw a blue ball of energy. The ball was about ten feet in diameter, and it eviscerated everything in its path, leaving nothing but smoking edges of trees and mountain. However, Bryce was still just sitting there with his scales, smoking a little. It was hard to tell whether it was because of my magic or his.

I stared him down for a couple of seconds and summoned more balls of magic that spun by themselves in my hands. He raised his hands in defeat and turned around. It took me about a minute to fully change into the clothes I had been wearing yesterday—a pair of rather plain underwear, a white shirt that was too big around the chest, and the jeans and shoes that I had worn on my first day at the camp. Turning around, Bryce was completely ready to go, as he had also gotten dressed and was now waiting on me.

"So about last night," Bryce said out of nowhere.

"What about last night?" I asked, looking over at him.

"We never really talked about the argument that caused everything, and I don't want to just avoid it. I don't think it would be good for us to just ignore it."

Oh, that's what he's talking about. Now I kind of feel like an idiot.

"Oh, I just really want you to let me know. If you have a problem, then it's also my problem, so please just let me know," I said with a caring smile.

"I can do that," he said with a smile. "Just as a warning, if my demons have really come back, expect a couple of nightmares. I should be okay though."

"Okay." And that was the end of our conversation ... at least for now.

"You all ready to go, Scarlet?" he asked simply. In his voice was sincerity. He wasn't asking the question out of impatience but to make sure that I was actually ready to go.

"Yeah. Let's go," I said, going for his hand, which he had offered.

We began to make our way back home hand in hand. It was mostly in silence that we walked back, but every few hundred feet we'd pass by some type of animal, be it a deer or a squirrel. There was never any real silence to enjoy, although the sounds of nature were quite relaxing. I would have been even more relaxed if I wasn't sore.

About two hours into our walk, we came across a mother bear walking around with its cubs. When we spotted each other, we both stopped dead in our tracks. The cubs of said bear immediately went behind their mother when they saw us. Normally we would have killed them and taken both their meat and skins, but we hadn't done that in months. Seeing the mother with its cubs behind her, it just felt wrong. At least that's how I thought about it; Bryce didn't look so sure.

He wasn't even looking at the bear. He was looking all around us, as if he was looking for anything that might jump at us. This left me and the bears in an uncomfortable silence, and the bears even looked frightened to be near us. After another minute or so of silence, Bryce began walking toward the bear, tugging me along. He stopped right in front of the bear, and the bear responded by getting on its hind legs, preparing to attack, but in the instant it did, Bryce disappeared from sight, leaving the bear to swipe at air. When the bear landed back onto all fours, it looked at me and growled. But before it could do anything, Bryce appeared right next to me with a dead doe in his hands.

There was no sound as he laid the dead doe in front of the mama bear and then grabbed my hand and brought me past the bear and its cubs. We walked for another ten minutes in total silence, and this left me to contemplate what had just happened.

"Hey! You okay? You're spacing out a bit," Bryce said, breaking my train of thought.

"Y-Yeah, still thinking about what just happened," I said, looking at him.

"Are you talking about how you almost just walked into that tree, or are you talking about the bear?" he asked with a smile, prompting me to look forward, and there was indeed a tree barely a foot from my face. This caused me to slightly blush with embarrassment, but that quickly faded.

"The bear."

"Oh, I just felt like it was the right thing to do. We have more than enough skins to last us at least another year comfortably, and we have more than enough food stored in Annabeth's fridge to last us a couple of months if we care for the meat, not to mention the MREs that will last us even longer."

"Well, that's good," I said before walking again, leading him this time on our way back home.

We walked for another two hours before we finally got to the river, where we could see our home on the other side of it. Before I could prepare myself to jump over the river, Bryce picked me up, bridal style, and jumped with me in his arms over the hundred-something-foot gap. Landing on the other side, we saw no one, but they came splashing through the shallow part of the river toward us and the road leading up to our home.

When they saw us, they all stopped, and Connor slowly strode from the front of the group to us. He looked like his normal slightly impassive self, with an air of confidence that demanded respect just like Bryce. He seemed apprehensive and slightly nervous. About what, I could only guess.

"What is it, Connor?" Bryce asked in a calm tone.

"You were right about them."

Okay ... what are they talking about? I hate being out of the loop.

"Well, are they against us?"

"No. I have a schedule for Lucy to screen them every morning and night just to make sure. We still don't know much about them other than that they were told by the Teller to keep quiet until discovered. But if you're asking if they've earned my trust yet, then it's a no. However, I do believe that they at least deserve a chance."

"That's enough for me—for now, at least," Bryce said, nodding toward the others, and they nodded back in affirmation.

They all passed by him, with the addition of two individuals. One was a tall man, probably around six feet four inches, with military-style hair and the look of someone who'd seen too much. He looked to be in his late twenties, maybe early thirties. The other one was a stunningly beautiful girl, definitely a year or two younger than us. She had long exotic white hair with diamond-blue eyes, and she held herself in the exact same way Bryce did, demanding respect with a lot of confidence. But she may have had too much confidence, with just a hint of silliness. For some reason, Bryce stopped her by holding his hand out in front of her. Albert was at her side in the next instant.

"You're her," Bryce simply said, lifting a finger to her face but stopping in front of it. "You're the girl I lost to, aren't you?"

Marie, Albert, Regius, Shane, and Jessica's full attention was on them, while the rest turned to look at Argentum, and then all had a collective look of realization.

"She's the chick you lost that award to," Connor said, pointing toward the white-haired girl whose name I still didn't know.

"Yeah. You were that fencer who won Best Junior Athlete of the Year award two years ago. I still can't believe I lost to you," he said with a smile on his face.

"Well, I was just a better athlete than you," she said teasingly with a smile on her face. That actually got a little chuckle out of Bryce.

"I guess so. Anyways, it's good to have you here. Maybe you can teach some of us how to use a knife the right way," Bryce said, gesturing to everyone.

I was confused about how we even got here, but at this point I trusted Bryce with everything and hoped that he knew what was going on.

"I'm sure I could," she said, stretching out her hand to both of us. "My name's Argentum, by the way."

"Bryce."

"Scarlet." I made sure to interject myself in there. This girl was too pretty to be left alone with any one of the guys.

"It's nice to officially meet you two, the Untouchable Queen and the Devil Dragon."

I hadn't heard someone say that name since I had been roaming. I guess I got a little more famous than I originally thought. I looked at Bryce, and it hurt me to see his face when she mentioned the nickname he had been given after Omaha. It was something he obviously didn't want to remember, but in an instant his grief and pain were gone and replaced by curiosity.

"Untouchable Queen?" Bryce asked incredulously, looking from me to Argentum and back. "Care to explain, Scarlet, as you are the only one she could possibly be talking to?"

"It was the nickname—really code name—the Slăve gave me while I was making my way here. I'm pretty sure I officially got it after I destroyed one of their manufacturing plants and came out completely unscathed."

I avoided eye contact with him and everyone else that entire time, a little ashamed of what I had done. No one should ever be proud of killing, even if it was necessary to survive.

"Oh ... I like it. It fits you," he said with a rare genuine smile that warmed my heart. He didn't smile all that often, but when he did, he truly meant it.

"Now let's get to practice. Scarlet and I will stretch while everyone else does the usual routine. Charlie, show Argentum here the ropes," Bryce said, getting his voice loud enough to address the entire group at once. As they went about to follow his command both Annabeth and Jessica gave me a knowing smirk. I didn't acknowledge them at all.

They all followed his command. Argentum looked a bit miffed, but she still followed the order. Albert didn't look particularly happy when he heard that it wasn't going to be him helping Argentum, but he'd been there barely three weeks. He hadn't earned the right to show anyone the ropes yet. The other one who came with her just stood there at full attention, surveying everyone around him. Bryce seemed to notice this but made no attempt to go over to him while we stretched together.

Everyone was running through the various drills we had been doing for about a month or so now. They were just slow run-throughs of the new moves we were learning. Bryce always had something new for us to learn, but every time he gave us something new, he also forced us to practice an old move with it so that we didn't forget a particular move. It made for a rather well-balanced fighting strategy for all of us. On occasion, Bryce would put all his attention on one individual, like he did with Albert at the current moment.

Bryce and I finished stretching a solid ten minutes after we started. He let me go to Marie, who was my partner this week, while he went off to Albert to work with him. Regius, who was the other new addition, didn't participate and instead decided to watch from the sidelines. It set me on edge a little, but I pushed it out of my mind. He was here for the same reason we were: to survive.

CHAPTER
20

When I arrived home, Smith wasn't inside waiting for me, as I had asked him to. He was sitting on his car in the driveway, and in his hands was a black folder with bold red letters that said *Top Secret*, so he must have gotten the file, which was nice. The day was already good, but it seemed to be getting better by the minute. He also had a bag of groceries with him. *Even better than the folder.*

"Hey, Smith, you got it," I said, gesturing toward the folder with a slight smile on my lips.

"Yeah, but I'm not so sure about this anymore, Julie."

"And why would that be?"

"He just gave it to me. I didn't even have to ask. No exchanging of favors, no smart talk, no talk at all. When he saw me come down to him, he immediately went into the back, grabbed the folder, and brought it back for me. This whole situation just doesn't feel right at all. I don't think this is a good idea," he said, looking highly apprehensive and with genuine fear in his voice.

"Did you take a look at the file?" I asked, reaching for it, but he didn't give it to me.

"Yes. And I don't know how you'll react, but let's go inside before you look at it. Okay?" he asked, and I nodded my head and went inside my house.

Smith followed me inside, put the file on the island in the middle of the kitchen, went to my fridge, and got some food to prepare. I looked at the file with a lot of apprehension. The file seemed to be mocking me, telling me that whatever was in there shouldn't be known. But Smith had looked in the file, and he found what was important, so it couldn't be absolutely terrible.

I opened it up to find a couple of papers detailing prisoner transport to each of the nine bases that MO had attacked. At first I looked over the papers, and nothing really stood out, as most of the names were blotted out in random patterns. It wasn't until the second time I went over the papers that something really jumped out at me. Every list was in alphabetical order, and a name was blotted out in the same place in all nine of the bases. Was it possible that MO had attacked all those bases just to get someone back?

I began looking through the pictures in the file, and it didn't take long to notice what was going on in them. Most of them just showed the damage that MO did to the bases, specifically to the prisoner parts of the bases. However, the last few were the surprising ones. In the middle of the ninth base was a giant pillar of bright blue fire. In another picture, the fire was dying down and two figures appeared. The final picture shocked me the most. It showed Bryce's mother clutching a man who must have been Bryce's father, crying her eyes out as fire billowed out from her arms and legs. The man looked like he had been through hell, and he was hugging her back just as hard as she must have been hugging him.

"You have got to be kidding me."

"So you found it," Smith said, looking over at me from the stove. All I could do was nod.

"Flip over the photo. We need to talk," he said with a sense of foreboding.

I immediately got a bad feeling, and flipping it over didn't help at all. On the back of the picture were a few elegantly written letters that spelled out *We know.*

"Great, now I feel like I'm in a video game."

"You and me both, Julie."

"Do you know who 'they' could be anyways?"

"No idea whatsoever."

"Great," I said with a sigh, hanging my head. "What now?"

"Well, I'm going to go about my business as usual. If these guys are actually able to know about this, then it's a pretty safe bet that they can get us at any time. So I'm going to do the two things that actually calm me down in this world: hanging out with you and working."

"I agree with hanging out with you, but I'd rather drink until they kill me instead of working."

"Okay, have fun getting hammered. You mind if I stay here tonight, just in case?"

"Safety in numbers?"

"Yes."

"You know where the guest room is?"

I went to the fridge and grabbed the hardest liquor I had. I poured myself a drink, and the glass got halfway to my lips, when it was taken away from my grasp by Smith.

"The hell, Smith!" I angrily snarled at him.

"After you eat," he replied with a monotone voice as he handed me a plate of the most delicious-looking stir-fry I'd ever seen.

"How do you make this stuff? This looks amazing."

"I brought my own ingredients. I can't very well make stuff like that with just alcohol and junk food."

"Don't insult my choice of food, but thank you for the meal," I said, smiling as I dug into my plate of food, which didn't disappoint. It was amazing.

"Julie, that isn't food. That's liquid and garbage. How you stay in shape I'll never know," he said as he dug into his meal, completely ignoring the dirty look that I gave him.

We ate in relative silence, with only the sounds of our forks against our plates filling our ears. Neither of us uttered a word while we ate our meal in silence. It didn't take that long to finish either; within ten minutes of the food being placed in front of me, it was gone. Smith was even quicker, finishing before me. We put our plates away, and Smith went to the couch while I grabbed the hardest liquor available. We shared the liquor as we watched the news.

As we watched the news, a thought came to my slightly intoxicated mind. *Why is it taking so long for the generals to attack Bryce and his friends?* All it would take would be most of the soldiers that we had. It would take a bit to mobilize them, but this was the only good way to get it done, and we'd been talking about this for almost two months. It didn't take long to create a strategy that was essentially only to attack until they were dead. *Do they want Bryce to win? No. There is absolutely no way they would. Would they?* At least those were my last thoughts before falling asleep.

Waking up the next morning was a lot more pleasant than expected considering the amount of alcohol that I consumed. I wasn't complaining, especially since the first thing to hit my nose was bacon. I looked around and saw the bacon resting on the island where the black folder with the pictures and prisoner records was. I ignored that and went straight for the plate with bacon and dug in until my heart was content, and that was when the bacon was gone.

I put the plate away and went to get dressed, taking only a couple of minutes to do so, and I was driving to work within the next five minutes. The drive was pleasant, as always, and no one was playing at the park today, but that was to be expected. It was a school day. Arriving at work and parking my car went as they usually did, with no interruptions, but going to my office was when it became worrisome. No one was in, and no one was around my office, but when I went into my office, everything seemed okay. Even the usual email from the generals to meet them in the usual place was there.

When I got to the conference room several floors up, it really began to go wrong. Opening the door, I was greeted with Smith sitting off to the side. The room filled with an air of utmost seriousness, and to say it didn't frighten me would have been a lie. I took my seat in silence, and the generals stopped whispering to each other and looked at me collectively. One thing that popped out at me was that their assistants weren't here. *Why?*

"We know that you know who MO really is," said the air force general, General Grahm.

"Yes," I responded, trying desperately to keep my bearing and look unfazed.

"Well, if we understand each other, then let's continue on with the meeting," General Piken, the Navy general, announced.

Smith and I exchanged confused glances. We were expecting death, in all honesty.

"Wait, that's it?" I asked.

"Yes, unless you have any questions as to why we're letting you live and not just outright killing you for finding out something that was never supposed be anywhere near you," General Ceribri calmly stated.

"I do actually." The words were out of my mouth before I could stop them, but it was already too late, and the generals were motioning for me to continue. I might as well get at least a couple of my questions answered. "If you know who MO is, then why haven't you apprehended her? This entire situation could've been avoided."

"No, we couldn't. The damage that she had done to the image of magic users of the world was beyond repair. What you're seeing now in the world would've happened eventually either way. Besides, she needed to be out to teach Bryce how to control his powers when he was born nine years later."

"Wait, you had no idea Bryce would be born. Why take that precaution on something you couldn't have had any idea about?"

"Have you ever heard of the Teller, Colonel?" General Piken asked this time.

"I have, but I thought that it was only a myth."

"*She* is far from a myth. She is also the reason that we have done what we have done lately."

"Does that include the imprisonment of almost all the magic users?" I asked with a little edge sneaking into my voice.

"Yes, it does. Do you wish to know why?" General Ceribri asked with calmness comparable to a monk.

"Yes."

They then proceeded to tell me a story and explain why they had done everything they had done. It was the most incredible and yet insane story I had heard, yet there was nothing that could prove it wrong. After they told me everything, I couldn't help but feel that they were leading me down a rabbit hole that would never end.

CHAPTER

21

O ur usual morning routine of training went as it normally did. However, when we got to the eight-mile mark on our run, a shot rang out diagonally across from us within the forest. All of us immediately stopped and crouched down. Having been training and running at a good pace, we weren't really in a condition to take on more than ten soldiers by ourselves—with maybe the exception of Bryce, and even he didn't look all that good.

Turning around to face us, Bryce pointed to Lucy and then to his head, and in the next second, we were all hooked up telepathically. Regius, Argentum, and Albert, who had yet to do this, were a bit unnerved to start, but they got the hang of it after about a minute. Once they were all set and ready to go, Bryce started doling out orders to all of us.

"Marie and Regius, I need you two to scout ahead of us and see where exactly that shot came from. When you've found its source, don't engage. Just come back to us, and tell me what you found. The rest of us will begin to slowly move in the direction we heard the shot, at a crawling pace. Finally, Argentum, I want you to scout ahead just a little so that if someone comes while we're moving, you can give us an early warning. Everyone ready?"

We all nodded and began to do what we were told, moving into the forest at a pace comparable to that of a sloth; at least we weren't crawling. Marie and Regius changed into some type of bird and sped off into the forest. Argentum did the same but stayed in visible range.

For about ten minutes, we moved at the same pace toward the location of the shot. Along the way, the shots became so frequent that they sounded like a full-blown firefight. This could get ugly. It wouldn't be all that bad for us, especially if we were able to get the drop on them. Eventually, Regius and Marie came back and told us what they had found. Apparently, a company or two of Slăve soldiers were being held back by one man with a machine gun. This immediately piqued our interest, because this man was definitely an ally and well versed in fighting. It came to no surprise to us that said man had his back up against the bottom of a drop-off, leaving him vulnerable to attacks from all sides, not giving us much time. Thankfully, they were fighting only a few hundred feet away, but before any of us could move, Bryce stopped us.

"I know you want to rush in there, and so do I, but if we do that, someone will get hurt," he said with concern, and only because we knew that he would be on the front lines with us did we stop moving and listen. "Jessica and Annabeth, go on the sides of the drop-off, and hit the soldiers with everything you've got. Marie, Regius, and Argentum, get behind them, and get them by surprise. It'll also be your job to get anyone trying to escape. Scarlet, I want you to get in front of the man and protect him for as many bullets as the Slăve fires and then send them all back. When she does this, the rest of us—Charlie, Shane, Connor, and I—will all jump from the drop-off and charge forward. And, Albert, give us cover with your explosions, and then get the person out of the kill zone. Now move."

We didn't need to be told twice. We were off like lightning.

The first one of us to be in position and ready to go was, of course, Scarlet, who, in her haste, didn't stop to check where everyone else was. It didn't matter, as she wasn't offensive right now, getting in front of the man we were saving. There was an instant where there was no firing of bullets from the Slăve, but a second later, they were firing at full force at her. The rest of us got there and saw that she was holding thousands of bullets. We used the attention all the soldiers were giving to her as an advantage, and everyone else was able to get in position.

Bryce gave us the signal through the link, thanks to Lucy, who had just told us that we were up against two Släve companies. Jessica and Annabeth were the first to act, unloading on the soldiers from both sides, distracting them just long enough for Scarlet to send all the bullets right back at them. Since most of the soldiers were firing from cover, they weren't affected by the returned bullets, but the soldiers caught out of cover were very much dead. That was our signal too.

We ran and jumped over Scarlet and the man. When we landed on the ground, Charlie slammed his fist into the ground, and a ripple of explosions erupted, killing a couple of the closest soldiers but making almost all of them lose their footing. The firing almost completely stopped, and we charged the soldiers. Shane was covered in a white glowing knight's armor courtesy of his magic. He literally looked like a white knight. Charlie had mini explosions going on all around his body, which I'd seen only a couple of times before. I still had to ask him about it. Bryce was his usual self when he was fighting, covered in red dragon scales with flames licking at his fingertips. I was now composed entirely of dirt. They couldn't harm me even if a tank ran me over.

All four of us charged at the soldiers as they were picking themselves up and desperately trying to protect themselves from the ice and fire coming at them. As desperately as they were trying, they didn't stand a chance. They were being attacked from so many angles. Marie and the other two had made it behind the soldiers and were now starting to pick all of them off one by one. It also helped that they were now trapped in their own kill zone. Needless to say, we tore through their ranks like a knife through butter, destroying everything in our path and letting Jessica and Annabeth pick up on any of the people we missed in the charge.

It didn't take long for their once-one-hundred-strong soldiers to be reduced to two—both of whom were on their knees in front of us.

"Now the only thing left is, who are you?" I asked, looking at the man we had saved.

The man had brown hair and brown eyes that looked a bit off, but I couldn't place why. His chest was strapped with so many kinds of explosives and extra magazines that I couldn't tell how big his chest even was. He also had a giant machine gun strung over his shoulder, and he handled it like it was a pistol. His pants were generic army ones with basic camo, but his boots were nicer than most, even if they were extremely dirty. He looked to be in his late forties, maybe early fifties, and had the eyes of a man who had probably forgotten more about war and sacrifice than we'd ever know. He was someone from whom Bryce and I could learn.

"His name's Erik, and he's my friend."

All of us were surprised, mostly because Regius rarely spoke, but for this guy to be a friend of Regius was an even bigger surprise. We honestly didn't think he had many, if any, friends.

"Man, I thought you were dead. You went dark after they started to round us up, and you weren't at the safe houses. Where were you?" Erik asked as he walked over to Regius and shook his hand, smiling.

"I had the promise to keep, brother. Couldn't leave messages or do anything. There wasn't enough time." When he spoke of a promise, he said "the," which was rather specific.

"Oh, well then, I understand. Where is she, if I may ask?"

"She sent me and her granddaughter off about eight months ago. She's probably alive, but I don't know for sure."

"Um, excuse me, but if I may interrupt your reunion, I'm going to ask the million-dollar question. Why are you out here?" Annabeth spoke up, interrupting their reunion.

"I'm looking for the group of magic users rumored to be out here. I want to join." We all gave him curious looks, but then he continued. "Don't tell me this is all you guys have. The rumors are that you guys are a good hundred strong of the strongest in the world."

"No, this is all we have," I said, switching more to an interrogation mode after that. "What did you and Regius work as?"

Bryce usually left this stuff to me. He liked to watch silently to see if someone was lying or not.

"We were in the military together before we began to work as mercenaries," Erik said, and then he began to scan everyone. His eyes widened when he looked at several of us, including myself. When he was done scanning us, he spoke again. "Well, the rumors might be lying about the numbers, but they certainly weren't lying about your strength."

"What do you mean by that?" asked Jessica as she made her way over to Annabeth.

"I mean, out there in the world, everyone here except for Regius, the kid who got shot, and his overprotective girlfriend are ranked as the deadliest people in the world. Every one of you has a comfy price on your head."

"Oh, cool," Annabeth said, a little more excited than she should have been. "How much am I worth?"

Before Erik could answer that, Charlie interrupted him. "Okay, as much as I would love for this to continue, we should really take care of the mess we made." He had just stepped back into view with a red-eyed Marie clutching his arm and shying behind his back. *What the hell happened?*

"Can you just kill us or let us go already?" one of the two soldiers asked as he fidgeted around on his knees, interrupting our talk.

"No. You're going to give us a little bit of information first, and then we will probably let you go," said Bryce right next to me.

"And why would we do that?" asked the other soldier, who was slightly taller than the first. From the patch on his chest, which he had forgotten to remove, he was apparently a captain and probably one of the commanders of the companies.

When he spoke up, a rustling sounded behind me. Checking it out, I saw both Marie and Charlie looking like they had seen a ghost. They were both clutching each other desperately and had pale faces.

What is going on? Could this be the guy they told me about?

"Well, you don't have to, but think about it. We control if you live or die, and after all the rumors out there about us, are you really willing to take that chance?" Bryce asked with a malicious smile, looking at the two soldiers.

The two soldiers then leaned closer to each other, talking over something. I didn't like this at all, and after maybe a second of their whispering, I began to walk forward to get them apart. But they snapped away from each other, with the smaller of the two with a pistol. As he raised it and fired, I dove out of the way, rolling and getting back up right away.

I looked around to assess the situation, and everyone seemed okay until I heard someone groaning over by the ledge. Bryce and Charlie were staring intently at the two soldiers, one of whom still had the gun up. Leaving those two to keep an eye on the soldiers, I went over to the ledge and climbed up to see who got hit. My eyes quickly fell upon the shirtless giant that was Albert. Thankfully, the bullet had gone straight through his trap, the muscle between the shoulder and neck. He was lucky.

"Who got hit?" came Bryce's voice.

"Albert," I responded, looking back at him.

As soon as he heard the name, both he and Charlie took several steps back from the soldiers, both of whom were now smiling, thinking they were home free. Little did they know …

"Good choice," said the taller of the two, who didn't have a gun.

Again when he spoke, both Charlie and Marie visibly flinched and paled. This had to be the guy. My blood began to boil stronger than ever before.

Before anyone could react, including us and the soldiers, Argentum exploded out from behind the soldiers as a gigantic black bear, swiping the gun out of the man's hand and chomping down on his neck. His screams of pain were chilling, but they didn't last long. Only a minute later, Argentum came running out of the bushes fully dressed while she wiped blood away from her mouth.

She came right for Albert, panicking like anyone would when the person they liked got hurt. Her hands were glowing a bright green as she applied pressure to Albert's wound, hurting him more than helping. I tried to tell her, but she was having none of it. Just as Scarlet was about to help me pull Argentum away, I saw a flash of green from her hands. Scarlet and I used this opportunity to take Argentum off Albert, only to see that the wound was completely healed. There was only one explanation: Argentum had two kinds of magic. That shouldn't be possible.

"Everything okay back there?" came Bryce's voice.

I looked back, and it seemed that he was still having the standoff with the soldier.

"Yeah. Everything's all good," I said, jumping back down into the divot and walking up to Charlie and Bryce.

The first thing I noticed was that Charlie was staring the man down with the pistol pointed straight at the man's head. Looking around for Marie, I noticed that she wasn't here. Walking over to Charlie, I grabbed the gun while it was in his hands and eased it away from him. He looked at me with steely eyes and only nodded before sprinting off to find Marie.

"What's his problem?" asked the soldier.

"You remember San Antonio on the Day of Shattered Dreams?" I asked.

A bit of realization dawned on the soldier's face. Bryce looked at me for answers, and I leaned over to whisper what he and some of his soldiers had done to Marie and Charlie on that day.

Bryce was instantly scale bound with blue flames licking at his arms. He then walked up to the soldier, grabbed him by the neck, and raised him high above. Most of our group watching didn't know what the soldier had done to Charlie and Marie, but they didn't care. For Bryce to be this mad at anyone meant that they did something unforgivable. That was all they needed to damn the man.

Now with the man above him, Bryce's grip became tighter and tighter, and the desperation of the soldier became even more apparent as he pulled out a triple-bladed knife and began stabbing at Bryce. However, Bryce just grabbed the blade and yanked it out of his grip. With the man disarmed, he gave up, going limp in Bryce's grip, with only his eyes pleading for mercy. He wasn't about to get it though.

"This will be brutal," Bryce said to us as a final warning if any of us didn't want to see what was going to happen. None of us moved even a centimeter.

Bryce dropped the man to the ground, and he lay there gasping for air, only to get a scaled foot from Bryce straight into the stomach, knocking what little wind there was out of him. The soldier curled up in a ball, desperately gasping for air as he pathetically tried to crawl away. He didn't make it five feet before he was punched upside the head, sending him facedown into the dirt. The man tried to push himself up to escape, only to be stepped on by Bryce. With the soldier under his foot, Bryce reached down to the man, sinking his scaled fingers into the man's back and around his spine. This was the brutal part. Bryce then ripped out the man's spine, with his skull connected to it. He spun the spine and head once before shattering the skull over his knee.

Several others gasped, but I knew exactly why he had done that. Bryce had always been a bit of a religious man surprisingly and a fan of ancient cultures. Many of which believed the soul to be in the skull, and if it was destroyed, that person couldn't pass to the afterlife. So, in Bryce's eyes, he had just damned this man to eternity, wandering the world without hope of ever having peace. It was the ultimate sign of disrespect for Bryce, and it was exactly what the man deserved.

CHAPTER

22

No one made a move for almost a minute after I had ripped the man's spine and skull out of him. The first ones to move were Scarlet and Jessica, both of whom came over to the body and said some choice words to the corpse. However, I understood none of what they said. It was in a different language, but they spit the words at the corpse. One could only assume they were condemning him. When they were done speaking, it was again silent, but this time only briefly, as everyone made to leave except for Jessica, Erik, Annabeth, and myself. It didn't take long for us to clean up, and Jessica and Annabeth left.

"We'll be right behind you," Scarlet said as she turned back to me and Erik. "So, Erik, what's your magic?"

"I can see people's souls."

"No, no, seriously … Oh, you're actually being serious. I didn't even know that was possible."

"How does it work?" I asked, giving Scarlet's brain a chance to reboot.

"Think of it as glasses, and when I put them on—that is, activate my power—I'm able to see exactly what someone's soul looks like."

"That's ... actually pretty cool," I said, voicing my opinion on his power, and I wasn't lying. That was cool.

"If you don't mind me asking, what do you see our souls as?" Scarlet asked, gesturing to both of us.

"Well, you, Scarlet, look like a sleeping tiger. Bryce ... well, Bryce is unlike anything I've ever seen before."

"Like how?" I asked.

"You sure you want to hear what your soul looks like?"

I gave him only a nod as an answer, but it was enough for him.

"All I really see is a blackened glass bottle chained up, and it looks like it's been through hell and came back. It just doesn't look right at all, but when I look at it, I also see hope. Don't ask me how, but it just emanates hope like the sun gives out heat. It's really weird."

"Cool ... well, uh ... let's get going" was my only response.

Neither of them had anything else to say, so we left what had just been our killing ground.

It didn't take all that long to find the river, as all we had to do was take a right as soon as we climbed out of the pit and follow the tracks that everyone else had left behind. When we got to the river, I could see the others in front of us. The closest were Jessica and Annabeth, who were maybe a thousand feet in front of us. The next closest were Argentum and Albert, who were only a few hundred feet in front of Jessica and Annabeth. Even at a distance, I could still distinguish Albert, as he towered over Argentum. *It must be nice to be that tall.*

Other than those four, there was no one in sight, as the river curved to the left and the trees blocked everything off. It was nice to walk without anyone to bother us. Erik, having seen that Scarlet was holding my hand tightly and pulling me along, jogged ahead with his gear still on and a machine gun over his shoulder. He was far stronger than he let on. He kept on jogging ahead of us until he was out of sight, but it didn't bother us at all. We got to be alone for the first time in a while.

We weren't planning on doing anything, but as we walked, she turned to me and gave me a quick kiss before turning her head away. I tried to kiss her again, but she pulled away. What came out of my mouth sounded like a whimper, and she began laughing as soon as she heard it. She turned back to me, pulled me toward her, and gave me an actual kiss this time.

"C'mon, Bryce. We have to catch up with the rest," she said, giving me a smile that melted my heart.

She turned back around and started to pull me along again.

Damn this woman and what she could do to me.

"What in God's name did I do to deserve you?" I asked.

"If you keep wondering how you got what you have, then you'll never be able to make it better."

"God, I love you."

She instantly turned around, and for a brief moment she said nothing, scrutinizing my face before smiling and pecking at my lips again. "I love you too."

She turned around again and continued pulling me along. *What just happened?*

My question went unasked and, thus, unanswered. Honestly, it was all fine with me, because I'd probably say something wrong, causing her to be mad at me. So I stayed silent.

We spent the next hour in silence, enjoying each other's company. The only sounds around us were those of nature and the river flowing downstream. It kind of sucked that there were no fish in the river. It would have been nice to have a different source of food for once. We'd barely had even the slightest variety of food in our diet for a long while.

Deer meat, usually smoked and salted for days, with the occasional MRE was starting to get seriously bland, even with the diversity of the MREs. It had gotten to the point where if you got peanut butter in your MRE, you had to hide it, because if you opened it near the group, everyone began to fight for it. Albert opened up a packet of peanut butter as we were sitting around the fire a couple of weeks ago, and Argentum punched him in the stomach, causing him to double over and drop the packet. She picked up said packet, but before she could even take a bit of it, it was snatched from her hands by a bird that perched on a tree branch at the edge of our camp and changed into Marie. She too was about to get a taste of the peanut butter, but the branch snapped, and the packet fell. We all watched the packet go into the fire. We let out a collective sigh and just went back to eating our meals.

CHAPTER
23

As we walked back to the camp, only one thought went through my mind: I had two powers, something that was thought to be impossible. Scientists said that it wasn't possible for the human body to contain two powers. My luck was astronomical, or I was the outlier of the century. It was a bit crazy, but if I didn't have the powers, Albert might have been seriously hurt. He was all right, albeit a bit wobbly. It was just the shock the bullet gave to his system. By the looks of how he moved his shoulder and where he was shot, it was easy to tell that he was having phantom pains.

"Al, it's phantom pain. It'll go away eventually. Just try to focus on other things until then," I said as I was still supporting him so that he wouldn't fall over. He was still stumbling every so often.

"It still hurts," he complained.

"Oh, will you just grow a pair, you little girl! You got shot. Just deal with it. You've been shot before, and those times were worse," I said, stepping away from him so that he had to support himself.

He looked like he was going to collapse, until he saw that I was going to let him fall. When he noticed that, he stopped and righted himself.

"See, it's a miracle. You're all better now."

He looked at me with squinted eyes before turning his head forward and walking off without saying a single word to me.

Before I could walk after him, my head felt like it had just been shattered. This headache was unlike any before. Pure white shone in my eyes, and I felt only pain. Then I saw a flash of an image. It was a katana with a beautifully sculptured sheath painted black with white roses. Surrounding the sword were what looked like furs and military blankets, which could only mean it was in one of our tents. The vision lasted just long enough for me to make out the sword, sheath, and immediate surroundings but not long enough for me to see anything else.

When the white faded from my eyes and the pain subsided from the headache, I saw Albert holding me up with my arm draped over his shoulder. His face showed an incredible amount of concern and fear. My legs were shaking, and they felt like they were giving out on me, but before they could, Albert picked me up off my feet and put me on his back like a piggyback ride. I wanted to protest, but he silenced me before my protests could be heard.

"I don't know what that was, but you obviously can't walk right now. Just be silent, and fall asleep if you can. I'll wake you when we get back to the camp."

I probably would have been able to fall asleep immediately if it wasn't for the fact that he smelled like sweat and blood—not to mention that he didn't have a shirt on. Again, I was about to say something, but I was interrupted.

"What happened?" came a completely new voice to me. I opened my eyes to find where the voice came from, and I saw the new guy whom we had saved today.

"She fainted," said Al, breaking me out of my trance.

"She okay?" came the stranger's voice again.

What's his name again? Eren, I think. My head was still a bit fuzzy at the moment.

"She's okay, I think. Just a bit dehydrated probably. I'll be getting her water when we get back and making sure she gets some rest," Al responded, continuing to walk with the newcomer.

They started talking about sports, and this caused me to immediately zone out. My eyes got heavier and heavier as I rested on Al's bare back. It didn't take much longer for my eyes to completely close. I was sleeping.

A dream awaited me when my eyes closed. There was nothing but darkness around me, and nothing seemed to be moving except for myself; my body just aimlessly floated in the darkness. Floating in the endless darkness became increasingly worrying the longer it went on, but it wouldn't last forever. When it seemed like an eternity had gone by, a single voice rang out through the darkness. It was deep and somber, sounding like someone who had seen death too many times.

"What is your name?" the voice asked me.

Not knowing whom or what I was talking to, I was obviously very hesitant, but my curiosity won out in the end, and the voice got an answer.

"Argentum. What's yours?" I asked the dark void, hoping that the voice would respond.

"Deathwalker. That is my name."

Okay, if that wasn't ominous, I didn't know what was. Who or what the hell was named Deathwalker? But I knew instantly who—or rather what—this voice belonged to.

"Are you the voice of the sword that I saw?" I asked the endless abyss.

"Yes," the voice drawled out. "Now you must answer a question for me."

"Ask away," I said, simply extending my arms outward to make myself look open and vulnerable. I didn't know if the voice could see me or not, but this would at least show it that I had no qualms about it asking me a question. What was the worst that could happen?

"What is the one thing that the sharpest sword will never be able to cut?"

Now that came straight out of nowhere. It resonated with me, though, as I was one of the best swordsmen alive, but still, *what the hell?* It was a very perplexing question, as everything could be cut. The only things that couldn't be cut were ideas and ideals, things that really didn't exist in our tangible world. The real question now was what idea or ideal was the one that he was talking about. Unfortunately, there was no way to zero in on the answer, so it was just a guessing game. It was time for me to give it my best shot.

"I have my answer," I declared to the abyss, and all I got in return was a slight hum. That was the best answer it was going to give me. I opened my mouth to give my answer, but I stopped at the last second as clarity washed over me. What if it was talking about not ideas or ideals but something completely different?

"The answer is the human soul."

There was complete silence for a couple of seconds before the voice came back.

"Impressive."

Instantly my left forearm felt like someone was taking a blowtorch to it. The pain was unbearable, and my screams of pain were so loud that they must have escaped the dark void. The next thing I knew was that Al's face was in front of mine. The pain was still there and still unbearable, soliciting another bout of screaming. My world was consumed by pain, until it finally disappeared and my world grew black.

CHAPTER

24

P ain, pain, and more pain. The world was white around me, but at the corners of my eyes, it was beginning to come into view. The pain was beginning to fade, but my arm still felt like it was in an oven. It took several minutes after the pain began to fade for me to be able to open my eyes, and even then, it hurt.

The first thing that came into view was someone leaning over me with two of her fingers at my neck. This person was going to choke me! I acted without thought and cracked whoever it was across the face with my fist and sprinted out of the tent only to clothesline after a couple of steps.

I was on my feet before the person who clotheslined me could move and run away. My entire being was screaming to run, and nothing was going to stop me from doing so. Even plowing over another person who tried to get in my way didn't faze me. Taking only two more steps before changing into a bird, I took off, but not before someone grabbed one of my talons and took me back down, changing me back into a human.

I got up from being thrown down, and everyone was in front of me. There were eleven people in front of me, but I heard footsteps behind me. It was too late to react though, as they tackled me to the ground from behind. Next thing I knew, they were straddling me, and my instincts kicked in. Thrashing out with everything available to me, I swung wildly with my hands, trying to hit anything and connecting almost every time. That was until my arms were pinned down and my body was completely immobilized.

"Argentum, calm down. You are okay," I heard a voice saying to me.

But the pain still hadn't left, and my instincts were still screaming at me to run and hide, to get to a safe, secluded place. That mind-set resulted in a series of events that should have never happened.

Suddenly, there was a shot of pain and a new weight in my right hand, and everyone who had been on me jumped off. Opening my eyes to see why that happened, I saw Scarlet clutching her side as blood was seeping between her fingers. Everyone was looking astonished at what had just happened, myself included. But I recovered first and started to sprint away with what I now recognized as the stunningly beautiful katana in my hands.

Seconds later someone blurred in front of me and slammed their fist straight into my face, making me do a complete flip and land facedown into a rotting log. I got up immediately and saw a furious-looking Bryce. He was covered in blood red scales with flames billowing out from his arms and legs. That wasn't all that was coming out of him. A black mist seemingly ebbed out of his body and swirled calmly around him. To top it all off, it looked as if he was ready to kill.

I should kill her. She hurt Scarlet, so she deserves it. Make her suffer. Show her true pain. Maybe even keep her alive just to make her suffer more. No ... no, she doesn't deserve that. She was morphed for months. Her animalistic instincts probably took over her common sense once she started to get the headaches Albert talked about. Wait, she deserves death. No one touches my Scarlet. No one, only me. She is mine! All those who hurt my family are enemies and must die!

"Bryce!" a voice snapped, stopping me mere inches from killing the traitor. Turning around, I saw Connor looking at me with shock and apprehension. "You okay?"

"Of course I am. What would make you think otherwise?" I sneered at him. He had interfered in my protecting our family. This girl was a threat. I should just kill her, end her existence.

"Because it looks like you're about to kill Scarlet."

What! This isn't Scarlet, is it? Turning to look back down at the person below me, I realized that he had tricked me. This became alarmingly true when he punched me across the face.

"Wrong move, Connor."

"Yeah, I know. But you aren't in control." And with those words out of his mouth, I backhanded him across the face and sent him flying through the forest, stopping only when his body hit a tree. He wasn't down for more than a couple of seconds before he was standing up and facing me again. *The insubordinate little brat. He'll pay for trying to protect the one who harmed my Scarlet!*

With that, we clashed fist against fist. We moved faster than most normal humans could ever even fathom. Even in his stone form he was keeping up with me—barely but he was. Our traded blows blew back shrubbery and any other debris, creating a rather nice circular battleground for the two of us to fight. This was the true extent of the difference between Connor and me. He truly had to try to keep up with me. I could do this in my sleep. He was nothing, but he was a friend and one of the best at that, and that was the only reason he was still alive.

As we traded blows again, I grabbed his arm and bent it backward, subsequently forcing him to do the same. When his head was at the perfect place, I raised my fist to finish our fight, but before I could do it, a gigantic piece of ice slammed into my back, forcing me to release him. I looked at the culprit, and Annabeth stood proudly and without fear, prepared to fight. She was always the one to fight no matter the odds.

"Forgot about me, jackass?" came a voice behind me, and when I whipped around, no one was there until a fist came up from under me and exploded on contact, sending me flying into the air. While in the air, someone tried to axe kick me, but it didn't matter. I grabbed their foot, spun in the air, and whipped them at a tree, which they went straight through. Once they landed, I saw Connor, Charlie, Annabeth, and Jessica all prepared and ready to fight me—all with their magic activated and radiating toward me, but it was nothing compared to mine. Showing them what real power was, I released some of mine at them, and it visibly shook them.

"You don't stand a chan—"

What the hell is going on! I can't see anything! What is going on?

Then a voice shot out through the darkness—one that sounded purely demonic in every way.

"I will intervene just this once, boy! Do not let yourself lose control again."

And as soon as the voice disappeared, my vision returned, but I was dizzy and woozy, and before I knew it, I was stumbling over some debris before passing out.

"Thank God that's over," said Charlie, who just sat on his butt in relief.

"Can someone tell me what the hell that black mist was around Bryce? And why the hell did he just collapse in the middle of the fight?" asked Jessica who was brushing off wood splinters from the tree she had been thrown through.

"That wasn't Bryce, Jessica. That was what is commonly known as a Prime. As for the black mist, I can only say it shows up when the Prime does. And for him collapsing, I got nothing for you there. That was weird even for me," Annabeth said, plopping down like Charlie had.

"Aren't Primes only a hypothesis?" Jessica asked.

"Technically they are, because it's never been officially proven. However, there have been enough unconfirmed cases and eyewitness reports so that one assumption could be made for them. Everyone who activated their Prime tried to kill and destroy everything in their path until they fell unconscious," I explained.

"All right, Connor, that makes sense, but there's no way Bryce would just collapse like that in a fight. He barely looked like he was warming up," Jessica said.

"At this point, don't question it. Just be glad that it did happen, because the way that fight was headed, we would all be dead."

CHAPTER
25

W*here am I?* I opened my eyes, and that same question kept pricking at my mind, as the time around me seemed to continue aimlessly. The only thing that stayed constant was the ceiling, and that was because I couldn't see anything else and my neck was immobilized. Every second seemed like an eternity, and every minute was pure torture. It was hell, especially with my animal instincts being on high alert and with my not knowing what was going on.

Finally, after what seemed like days, my constant view changed. Instead of the boring ceiling of my entrapment, it was a face—a recognizable face. Albert was looking down at me, but he wasn't looking my face. He was looking at my stomach, and he looked concerned. *Why would he be? What would make him concerned? We had the fight with the soldiers and saved that one guy, Eren—I think that was his name. Then we walked back and … my arm!*

My head couldn't move, and my arm wasn't responding either. Why wasn't anything responding to me? I wanted to scream, but my mouth wouldn't even open to allow me to. Insanity slowly began to creep toward me, but it was halted as Albert looked at my face and saw my open eyes.

He looked shocked and then instantly relieved. He gave me the brightest smile and let out a loud and heavy breath that he must have been holding.

"Hey," he said as he pushed back a few strands of my hair behind my ear. "If you're wondering why you aren't moving at all, well, that was Connor's idea. Since you freaked out last time when you woke up, he, as well as the rest of the camp, decided it might be better to paralyze you with hemlock."

My eyes widened like dinner plates. *Isn't hemlock lethal?*

"You don't need to worry. Erik apparently majored in botany in college. You only got enough to last one, maybe two, hours, and it won't kill you. You may throw up though, so I've been with you since they gave it to you. They just needed to be sure you didn't go crazy like you did last time. Oh, and before I forget, do you remember anything? Blink once for yes and twice for no."

Needless to say, I was very pissed that they had intentionally poisoned me. No matter the reason, that was a bit uncalled for. As for what had happened, the details were still a bit fuzzy, but I remembered an angry Bryce with black mist around him. That was it, and if the others were saying nothing, then that should be my course of action too. With the decision made up on that matter, I looked at Albert and blinked twice.

"You fought Bryce and got your butt kicked—not going to lie—but then he went haywire and started attacking the others. Then all of a sudden he just collapsed. It was so weird, but you don't have to worry about that now. Get some rest, Argentum," he said before leaving the tent.

I took his advice about getting some rest not five minutes after he left.

Waking up felt really weird. My entire body felt like it had been through a ten-hour kendo match, and it had only just ended. I slowly tested my hands and feet to see their movement, and everything seemed in order. Moving around was one thing, but actually trying to do anything was a whole other story. It took me three minutes to sit up, and even that was tiring. Not discouraged, I was able to stand up a minute later and walk out of the tent the next.

My walking was by no means graceful, but it did the trick, and getting out of the tent gave me a view of a burning fire. I looked at the illuminated bodies, and it seemed that everyone was there and enjoying the warmth of the fire. Walking over to them was not quiet by any means, so they all saw me coming. No one said anything, and only Al helped me to my usual spot next to him. I got to look at everyone, and I saw some of my handiwork.

Taylor had a good-size bruise on her face and a black eye, and Connor was giving me the stink eye, but it was not nearly as bad as I had imagined. It was a lot worse after he caught me stealing his peanut butter. There even seemed to be forgiveness in his face this time. Scarlet, on the other hand, had some bandages around her side, and they looked freshly changed. She didn't look the greatest, but she didn't look terrible, and she too had forgiveness in her eyes, as if it wasn't my fault. *She's hurt because of me, damn it.* What was new was that Jessica had a nasty bruise on her leg, but that was it. Maybe it was me too? Either way, apologies were in order.

"Sorry for hurting you guys. It was my fault," I said with apprehension and shyness. God, I sounded helpless, and I hated it.

"It's okay, Argentum," Bryce said.

Everyone went silent again, as if that was supposed to be it. *That can't be it.* I was expecting him to beat me or something or give me some type of punishment at least.

"Is that it? How can that be it? I hurt you guys. I hurt our family!" I practically yelled at them. It just didn't feel right for nothing to happen to me at all. Something must have been wrong with them.

"Yes. Yes, you did," Bryce said, lifting his head from looking at Scarlet. "However, you weren't really in control of your actions. You were obviously in a great deal of pain, and given your particular circumstances, this was inevitable."

"How, in God's name, was that inevitable for me? I stabbed Scarlet and punched Taylor. How can you just shrug it off like that!" This time, I yelled.

Surprisingly, it was Charlie who responded to me. "Oh, believe me when I say that we're still furious about what happened, but we also understand that there wasn't much you could've done about it." I was about to interject, but he held up his hand, silencing me before continuing. "You were changed for six-plus months with very little time to change back. Now that doesn't sound like much to you, but when you're changed for that long, there will be side effects. Even Marie will sometimes bounce her leg like a dog if you scratch behind her ear, and she doesn't change for more than ten minutes. Your side effects aren't that dull, but they're dangerous because the side effects you got affected your instincts. You'll have better reactions, better hunting style, senses, and anything like that. However, you'll react irrationally in some situations, and you'll obviously have to control certain urges."

"What do you mean 'urges'?" I asked, now understanding why they could react the way they did, but the urges they were talking about worried me.

"Well, if what happened earlier today was any inclination of your instincts, then it isn't out of the question that you will have to control your instinct to hunt and kill. Also, you'll probably go into heat like normal female animals would."

"Please tell me you're joking," I said, looking at him with hope.

"No, but it's only a theory. I could be wrong. However, if it's true that you were a wolf for that time, then you'll inherit most wolf tendencies and instincts, so it would be in your best interest to start to prepare yourself. We're closing in on fall, and the urges will start to show themselves. And if I were you when fall ends and winter hits, I would invest in a chastity belt. Just saying."

A chorus of laughter broke out from everyone except for Al and me. I didn't know what Al looked like at the moment, but I was freaking out internally and had become singularly interested in the ground at my feet.

"Not funny," I said, crossing my arms and gaining just enough courage to raise my head and look at them with hopefully enough determination to persuade them to not make it into a joke.

"It kind of is, and besides, you punched Taylor in the face and stabbed Scarlet. Intentional or not, it doesn't matter. You should expect this for at least a little while," Charlie said, recovering from his laughing fit.

That really hit me, as I hadn't even asked Scarlet or Taylor if they were okay. I looked to said individuals, and they had both stopped laughing too, but it didn't look like they didn't find my situation funny. It looked more like they couldn't laugh due to pain. Maybe that could change. Hell, apparently, I had a second magic, and it was healing—an extraordinarily rare magic with no documented cases. And it was my second one, which shouldn't be possible. It was like being a main character in manga. When this was all over, I was going to the closest anime store and buying everything.

Shaking my head to get those thoughts out of there and focusing back on the injured girls, I dug deep into myself. Reaching the deepest part of me didn't take all that much effort for me. My kendo and karate instructor had forced me to meditate, saying inner peace was a good way to think clearly about any situation. It didn't take me long at all to find the new power that had previously been hidden and bring it to the surface. I didn't know how to control the newfound power fully, so it exploded out from me without any control. It washed over everyone there, and the effects were immediate.

I, for one, felt great. My body was no longer aching, and everything around me became a lot clearer. Most of the group tried to dodge the unknown power but didn't succeed, as they had been too focused on laughing at my duress earlier. The wave of magic didn't seem to do anything to most of them and just washed over them, as if it was nothing. Bryce had been instantly enveloped in his scales and had gotten in front of Scarlet before the wave had even gotten a foot from me, and he seemed unaffected. Scarlet seemed to be unaffected, as a result, but Taylor wasn't.

The giant bruise and black eye that had previously occupied Taylor's face had completely vanished. She noticed right away, touching her face and trying to feel for the pain that had been there previously. She tapped Connor on the shoulder and asked him if the bruise was gone. He looked at her, and his face automatically contorted into one of pure shock. He could only slowly nod. By then everyone else had noticed and obviously connected the dots—Bryce included, as he whipped around to look at Scarlet, who had already begun to undo her bandages. She did it slowly though, just in case hers didn't heal, and as she pulled back the final strip, there was nothing on her side but a thin scar.

Scarlet looked amazed and happy that the wound was now healed, and she was only able to mouth the words *thank you* to me. Bryce turned to look at me and merely nodded in thanks before looking back at Scarlet with a happy expression on his face. The mood was then a lot more stable and less hostile—toward me, at least. It got better too as I got peanut butter in my MRE. Of course, this wasn't shared with anyone as it made its way to my pocket and away from prying eyes, even Al's.

"I don't feel too good anymore," I said, gradually becoming green, and my stomach started to feel like a war zone was going on in there. Al—bless him—was on his feet in a second, and in the next second, he was helping me into the woods so that I could empty my stomach out there instead of around the fire.

Clutching my stomach in pain and preparation of what was to come, I let Al guide me to the woods while everything that I had in my stomach was coming out—and not peacefully. I just barely managed to make it to the forest; the contents of my stomach came out in a fit of retching that would best be forgotten as soon as this experience was over for me. It never seemed to end either. But eventually I was able to breathe freely.

"Are you okay now, A?" Al asked as he was still holding my hair behind my head.

"No, I just puked my guts out. What do you think?" I said, irritated, but I regretted saying it as soon as the words were out of my mouth. Looking at his face, I wasn't surprised to see hurt, and it broke me. "I'm sorry, Al. I shouldn't have been that harsh."

"It's all right, A. I understand," he said in his usual understanding and forgiving tone. "Let's just go to bed. It's been a long day."

I could only nod my head in agreement.

CHAPTER
26

Waking up with Scarlet at my side was weird after yesterday. I had a lot of questions, most of which revolved around why I went off the deep end. However, those questions could wait, as we had more pressing matters. Apparently, on his way here Erik had spotted a soldier base. We needed to act and destroy it before anything else could happen, so we got ready, grabbing any guns and ammo we might need before we started to move through the forest with Erik taking the lead.

He, of course, had his gun out and at the ready, waiting for any sign of attack, but we had walked only about a mile by now. He was really on guard for the distance we'd gone, but I couldn't blame him. He was a soldier, and that mind-set was imbued into him. It was certainly that way with my dad. He never told me what branch he worked for or what he did in the military, but I could tell that whatever it was had changed him for good. Erik was no different except for the fact that his eyes screamed of someone who had seen too much.

These thoughts bugged me for the remaining three hours we trekked to our destination. The other major thought that crossed my mind was

Taylor's pregnancy. She had to be close to giving birth or at least going into labor. It would become difficult to fight with one down the entire time, but we'd been doing it for months now. It shouldn't be a problem. Just because she was pregnant didn't mean that she couldn't kick some ass, at least using her magic. She was still one of the strongest in our group, and it wouldn't surprise me if her hormones made her slightly more powerful than she had ever been.

I was left with nothing but the upcoming fight to think about. It would mostly involve improvisation, but a lot of it would depend on Lucy, as she kept us all connected through her mental link: telepathy. This would have been something to worry about two years ago, but now not so much, if at all. She'd made incredible progress, and so had everyone else in the little time we'd all been together, which had been over a year for most of us. If anyone got hurt, we had both Marie and Charlie to take care of them, and it was almost guaranteed they'd have doctors there too.

Erik held up his hand in a fist, signaling us to stop, and motioned for us to get down. When we went down, I turned around to look at Lucy and nodded my head toward her. Not five seconds later we were all connected in our minds. For Erik this was completely new, but it didn't take him that long to adjust to it. When he was in the loop about how this worked, Erik began to tell us that there was an enemy patrol coming up on our left. He said that there were about twelve people, and we were more than likely within two miles of the lake now—something I agreed with after looking at the surrounding forest and recognizing bits of it, mostly the tree that had my claw marks on it.

"Bryce, what do you want to do?" Charlie asked through the link.

I took almost a minute to think it over.

"Ambush and interrogate. Let's not kill them if we don't have to, but we don't have enough information on the base that we can just let them go. Connor, Argentum, Marie, and Regius, I want you four to get on behind them and on their right. The rest of us will take the left and front. Move out."

We moved silently and slowly through the forest, surrounding the soldiers with the help of Erik giving us their location. We followed them for a little over ten minutes as we made to surround them fully, listening to their radio chatter and conversations. Most of what they talked about was mundane—mostly about women—but they did mention something about a new vehicle that they just got. We had already taken too long to initiate the ambush, so Erik gave the signal through the link, and we ambushed them.

"Hands up, guns on the ground now, or you all die" came the no-business voice of Connor as he emerged behind them and with others on their side. They all had their guns aimed at the soldiers. The soldiers didn't lower their weapons but raised them toward Connor and his little group. That turned out to be a mistake. A single, silenced shot resonated in the forest around us, and one of the soldiers dropped. The rest of us then emerged, and Charlie's pistol was smoking out of the silencer.

"I'd suggest you all listen to him," Charlie said as smoke was still coming out of his gun.

They didn't comply right away, but when their eyes found me staring at them, completely covered in scales and looking ready to kill, they began to comply. There were positives to everyone in the world thinking you were a mass-murdering lunatic. Slowly, they lowered their weapons, as a group, and placed them on the ground. Not taking any chances, Erik searched the group and took the radio from the radio man and any other communication devices they had on them, including some phones. After he had taken away everything of use to them, Erik nodded to Connor, who began to interrogate the soldiers.

"How many soldiers do you have at your base by the lake?" was his first question, and it was met with a stern silence from the leader of the group, who was a staff sergeant. He then looked expectantly to the other soldiers, who again gave him silence as their answer.

"Okay ... how about, how long has the base been there?"

This thankfully did get somewhat of an answer. One of the soldiers just recited his name, number, and position. After he did, every one of the other soldiers did the same. By this time too, I was out of my scales and looking normal again, but it didn't matter. They would have given that answer no matter the situation. They were Släve and highly trained.

"Lucy, you're up," Connor called to her.

This surprised me a little. She had always been able to communicate with people mentally, but if Connor was asking for her now, then he must have believed that she could go in and extract information from someone's mind. It sounded dangerous, as the last time she tried this, she almost got trapped inside the person's mind, and that person was me.

I approached Connor and whispered to him. "You sure she should do this? She could get trapped in their mind."

"I know it's a possibility, but they aren't you, and I believe in her."

With that, I believed in her too. Connor had never led me astray, so I trusted him with almost everything, and if he believed in Lucy, then so did I. Backing away to where I was before, Connor began to speak again, only this time with Lucy next to him.

"All right, last chance before I let Lucy here have her way with you. If any of you want to answer the last two questions, you won't need to go through this, but if you don't, I can't promise anything."

Again there was no response, and the soldiers stayed eerily quiet, watching Lucy the entire time Connor was speaking. After a full minute of silence, he motioned for Lucy to do her job. She walked toward the soldiers, stopped in front of their commander, and knelt in front of him, looking into his eyes. Nothing happened for the longest time, but suddenly Lucy's hand shot out from her side and gripped his forehead. The soldier began convulsing, and he began to foam at the mouth. His eyes rolled back into their sockets. Lucy looked completely unfazed, eventually dropping the soldier to the ground, where he continued to convulse and foam at the mouth. His squad mates looked completely terrified, but Lucy looked like this was an everyday thing. Even people in our group were surprised and mildly scared at what had just happened.

"I have everything," Lucy stated calmly as she dusted off her pants.

"Everything?" all of us asked in unison, beyond surprised.

"They've been there for two months, and they have roughly a thousand soldiers, give or take. I'd like to interrogate the radio man, though, to see if he has any more information," she said, starting to walk over to said man, who was completely frozen in fear.

"No. You've already interrogated the sergeant. You won't get anything new out of the radio man," I said sternly, stepping forward and grabbing her shoulder to take her back.

"What about the new vehicle they were talking about?" Charlie asked, throwing in his two cents, as it was something we should know.

"He didn't know much. Only that it was a prototype and a couple of minor details. It was based on the LAVs of old. It's supposed to have the speed of an LAV but the power and armor of a tank. It's also supposed to have something that's antimagic," she said in a monotone voice.

That last part was a bit concerning, but it shouldn't be a problem, as long as we didn't all get hit by it at the same time. It was only a prototype, so it shouldn't be able to do much to us. We had the most dangerous magic users in the world right now in the group.

"Did you see where it was located in the camp?" I asked.

"Yeah, it's right next to the lake. In a black tent" was her very monotone response.

I'd never seen her talk like this, but it had to be because of whatever she had done.

"Then let's get a move on. What do you think we should do to these soldiers?" Annabeth asked, making her voice heard.

"Will your ice kill them if you freeze them?" Regius asked.

"Oh yeah, they'll die. My ice can do many things real ice can't, but letting a human live while frozen is not one of them" was her quick response.

"Well, we can't just leave them here ... alive, at least."

That was surprising coming from Albert. I had never really pegged him as the type of guy to kill without reason, but he wasn't wrong. If we left them, there was no doubt they would get free (although it would already be too late by then).

"We'll leave them be. Tie them up and just leave. That way we won't have to worry about leaving survivors like usual," I said.

Everyone seemed to agree, so we proceeded with that. Erik ended up tying them all up together. Just as we were leaving, with me in the rear, one of the soldiers called out and got my attention. I told the others that I would catch up and to just go.

"What is it, soldier?" I asked, crouching in front of the tied-up man.

"Why didn't you just kill us?"

His squad mates got instantly mad at the man and were about to berate him, but I raised my hand to stop them.

"I don't see a need to. I'll kill only when I have to, and none of you are currently a threat to any of us."

With that, I left the soldiers, jogging a bit to get back to the group. It took about five minutes to find them again, as the farther I went into the forest, the denser it got, making visibility even worse. Actually, finding the group was a job in and of itself, even with Lucy's telepathic link telling me where to go. When I did actually find them, they were at a standstill, with Erik's hand in the air signaling to stop.

Lucy's voice came through the link. "Bryce. Plan."

It took me less than a minute to explain the improvised plan to them, upon which they immediately acted.

As they began their assault, Charlie and Annabeth turned their backs to me and crouched down, preparing for the attack. I readied myself for a second more, concentrating my power away from my hands and into my legs and back. Then I bounded forward, grabbed both of them, and leaped into the air so high that I was at eye level with an incoming helicopter by the camp. Reaching the apex of my flight, I threw Annabeth into the middle of the camp, reaching it in mere seconds and creating a giant ball of spiked ice. Not a moment after the ice was formed, Charlie was thrown at it. When he hit the ice, it exploded outward, ripping through almost the entirety of the base. It must have killed at least half the soldiers there and injured even more. It was absolutely devastating.

Surveying the base while falling was an odd experience. However, it dawned on me about halfway down that there was a helicopter coming in. Even though it was only a transport helicopter, it still had guns on it, which would be a serious problem if it got to the base. So doing something I never thought would be possible for me, I put more of my power into my legs and pushed toward the helicopter in the air, only to go way farther than needed. I completely missed the helicopter. Spinning in midair to get back on track and adjusting the power in my legs, I kicked again, sending myself right into the helicopter and through the closed door.

Looking around inside, I didn't see anyone, which led me to the conclusion that the helicopter was just called to come over. It didn't matter though, as the only ones in the helicopter now besides me were the pilots, who were staring at me with wide eyes. It wasn't really my place to kill them yet, so instead, I ripped off both of their mounted machine guns and opened the door that had a massive hole to leave, but not before turning back to them.

"Leave … if you want to live."

I jumped out and exploded my way toward the base, which was now in the middle of a battle.

The soldiers had already been pushed into a corner on each side. The group on the right didn't see me coming from the helicopter and landing in the middle of the few hundred soldiers backed into a corner. They all turned to face me, but it was already too late for them. They were all dead within the next two minutes, and I only had to kill about two hundred. After those first few hundred were gone, the rest of the group swept in and obliterated the rest with a little bit of help. I focused my attention on Regius, since he wasn't bulletproof like the rest of the ones in that group. Once they had control of the situation, I left them to go to the other group.

I got there and repeated almost exactly the same thing, but instead of landing in the middle of them, I just went right through them, which was easier. They stood literally no chance, and as I carved a path through them, the rest of that group followed, picking up the pieces everywhere they went, slaughtering the soldiers. The fight would have been different a year and a half ago when numbers meant something for them, but after continuous training for over a year for most of us, they stood literally no chance, especially with only a few hundred soldiers.

In the middle of the fight, the sound of gunfire and screams of pain deafened my other senses, but it didn't matter. The fight was already over. Taken by surprise in their own base in the middle of the day, they had no idea we were coming. Instead of joining the fray, I decided to just observe all that was around me and maybe take out those trying to escape. That plan of leisure ended as soon as an unknown shot echoed throughout the base. It was unlike anything I had ever heard.

Another shot rang out, and this time it was followed by a scream of pain. Shane landed in front of me alive but unconscious, and he smelled like electricity. I looked around for whatever could have caused this, and it made its presence known to me. Exploding out from behind a tent directly in front of me was an old-looking LAV. What was mounted on it was something completely foreign to me. It looked like an average cannon, but electrical wires were all along the cannon, and it looked deadly. I didn't run, instead choosing to examine the machine. It didn't share my same curiosity and fired its gun maybe ten feet from me.

When the gun fired, my body reacted on pure instinct and dodged the shot. Not wasting any time after dodging the shot, I grabbed Shane by his collar and threw him to the side. In that split second, it fired another shell. This time dodging wasn't an option. By the time I saw it, the shell was barely a foot from me, so instead of dodging it, I caught the shell. It pushed me back a couple of feet, digging up the ground and going through a tree in doing so. What I didn't bank on was that the LAV would fire another shell. I didn't notice it until it hit me, and my world absolutely erupted into pain and sent me cascading backward.

The shot hadn't pierced my scales, and wouldn't no matter what, but I could already feel my entire chest and side bruising. The others started to run over to me, but they stopped once the black LAV whirred to life and started to move around, firing shots at them intermittently. In the fray, Connor had made his way over to me to see if I was okay. Before he could get close enough to ask, I waved him off.

"I'm good! Just, whatever you do, don't get hit by it!"

He nodded and went to help distract the LAV.

Standing up hurt like you wouldn't believe. While the others were distracting the LAV, I was charging myself up to hit the LAV. It was going to hurt more, but I hated being on the sidelines. If I could help, it was going to happen. It didn't really work out that way, unfortunately, because the LAV noticed me and trained the cannon on me as I was charging up. In this state, not only could the LAV kill me by crushing my organs, but my body wouldn't be able to move at all.

The cannon then fired at me, and as the shell approached, I felt the air around me charge with electricity and pressure. My life was over, and with it hope was gone. I failed as a leader. However, the pain of death never came. Instead of death, a hurricane howled past my ears. Opening my eyes, I saw Argentum standing in front of me with the sword in her hands. Had she just cut the shell in half? *Damn, that's impressive.*

My happiness at being saved lasted all of about two seconds, as the cannon fired again and again in rapid succession. Argentum was just barely keeping up after the third shot, and it was obvious that she was fatigued. She was breathing heavily, sweat was spraying everywhere, and her movements were getting slower and slower. She wouldn't last much longer. As the LAV fired the sixth shot, Argentum fell over. She didn't even cut the shot in half, instead deflecting it. As she fell, I acted upon instinct and covered her with my body, intent on protecting her.

As the air was charged with electricity again and the howl of the shot continuing through the air, a shell was closing in on us. Luck shined on us there, because the shell was at an angle where it was deflected by my scales and not a direct hit; a direct hit probably would've killed us. Before another shot was fired by the LAV, the cannon on top was encased in ice before exploding into tiny frozen pieces. Not bothering to think on it, I took the opportunity to destroy the LAV. Digging my clawed hands into the front of the LAV, I ripped it open. Argentum took it from there, finishing it off by cutting the LAV in half with one swipe of the sword, killing the soldiers inside in the process. With that done, we both just sighed in relief and sat down on our butts.

"Are you okay?" Scarlet asked, running up to us and dropping down in front of me with a first aid kit.

"Relatively, but I'm alive," I said, visibly flinching at my breathing and retracting my scales to reveal a nasty bruise all over my chest and side.

Scarlet grabbed the first aid kit and was about to help out but was stopped by Argentum, who waved her off and began to glow, healing my bruise. When the bruise disappeared, I felt so much better, but Argentum passed out. Albert immediately ran over and began to check her out with Scarlet's help.

"What is that?" Annabeth asked as she arrived with Charlie and Marie.

"It's a rail gun," Marie said, taking only one look at the cannon before knowing.

"Modified for LAV and tank use. It's very dangerous for us, but it seems to be a prototype. We may get lucky, and this'll be the only one we see. Don't bank on it though," Charlie said.

Lucy came up to us with two soldiers right behind her. Seeing that everyone else was okay, they went to explore. She stopped right in front of me and forced the soldiers onto their knees in front of us.

"I'm going to tell you something. You can either give us good answers to our questions, or you cannot, and she'll just take them from you," I said, turning to the soldiers and gesturing toward Lucy. "Just so you know, the last person she had to extract information from d—"

"Bryce, we have a problem," Lucy interrupted from behind me.

I looked at her for an explanation, but she was pointing at the sky. I followed the direction of her gesture, and my stomach dropped immediately. Flying maybe two thousand feet up in the sky was an AC-130.

"Everyone, get to Scarlet *now*! Annabeth, shield *now*! Brace for explosions!" I screamed both through the link and vocally. It took everyone only a matter of two seconds to form up and be protected by both Annabeth and Scarlet. All that was left was for me to destroy it.

At the exact moment everyone was protected, the AC-130 fired a shell. It cascaded directly toward us, and for whatever reason, I shot out at the shell. The shell struck me about a thousand feet off the ground, and it threw me back down to the ground like a rag doll. It was far more powerful than I expected, but it didn't even leave a scratch on my scales; it left only a ringing in my ears and a giant smoke screen in the air. That was good.

Using the improvised smoke screen that I had created, I focused on slowly charging myself up to make the jump, making sure not to use too much so as to lose control, and not too little so as to fall short. This took a little too long, as the smoke screen cleared, and the AC-130 began to fire its mini guns at Scarlet and the others. She was able to protect them, keeping up her shield and catching most of the bullets, but there were thousands and thousands of rounds that she had caught in her shield, and it was beginning to be too much for her.

It was just in time too. Exploding off the ground, heading straight for the plane, I didn't account for the machine guns. Just short of the plane I kicked with my feet in the air and shot above the plane. Once I was above the plane, landing on it was easy.

Punching a hole through the roof and dropping down, I came face-to-face with four guns being pointed at me. This wasn't a time to stall or go soft on any of them, so in that instant, I flared my power just a bit, and the flames that exploded from my body incinerated all four soldiers who had pointed guns at me. I ran up to the cockpit, kicked open the door, and crushed one of the pilots' heads into the radio on the dashboard of the plane. The other pilot looked at his partner in horror before he looked at me and immediately raised his hands in surrender before he could be killed.

Then a shot went off, and as I looked out the cockpit window, a howitzer shell was flying down toward my family. I looked back at the pilot with anger in my eyes, and he had his hands down on the stick of the plane and was turning it. This plane was too big and too slow to do that. Thus, he got himself killed with a quick slice to his carotid artery. I left him and exploded out of the cockpit to try to catch the shell, but it had too much of a head start. It reached them before I did, but it didn't hit the ground. Instead it hit Annabeth's shield of ice … and her shield held. Even as I landed on the shield a moment after the shell did, the shield held.

As I slid down the slanted wall, my scales retracted by shredded clothes that barely covered me. That didn't matter to me, and I ran around the wall to check on everyone. Expecting the worst rounding the corner, I found that no such result awaited me. They were all okay. Scarlet looked out of breath, but other than that, everyone seemed to be okay. The first one of them to notice me was Annabeth.

"What took you so long?"

CHAPTER

27

S o, *yeah, that just happened.* My ice stopped a howitzer shell coming from an AC-130 and completely negated the shock wave. I guess that showed how much stronger I'd become in the year we'd been out here—all thanks to practicing and experimentation, and Bryce was to thank for that. If it wasn't for him, we'd all still probably be in prison, or we would have been recaptured after escaping. Still, it would have been nice if he had taken care of the AC-130 faster, because even though my body didn't show it, I was winded; it took a twenty-foot-thick and thirty-foot-long wall of ice to stop the howitzer shell from killing us all, and that was no easy task.

"What took you so long?" I asked as I saw him coming around the corner of the wall.

"Had to take care of something" was his response.

A loud explosion went off in the distance.

"That the 130 crashing?" Charlie asked as he went around to everyone, checking to see if they were okay.

"Probably," Bryce answered. "Who can still walk?" he continued.

Everyone raised their hands, producing a pleased expression that disappeared as soon as it appeared.

"Anyone hurt then?" he continued.

This time Regius, Connor, and Jessica raised their hands.

"How bad?" he asked as he walked up to those three, who were near the exhausted Argentum, who could barely stand up because of magic exhaustion from healing the injured, and Marie, who was tending to Connor.

"I got some shrapnel from a grenade in my side, but I was far enough away that all the shrapnel is still poking out of my skin," Connor said as Marie slowly plucked shrapnel out of his side.

"Clean through my shoulder, and it hit nothing. I got lucky," Regius said as he was stitching himself up.

"Shrapnel to the leg, same condition as Connor's, and a bullet to the stomach," Jessica said, just waving off the fact that she could be dying like it was nothing.

I looked at Argentum, silently asking if she was okay.

"She'll be fine. Just a ricochet, so it didn't go deep at all and no organ damage. Plus, I already got it out, and that rules out infection. Now, it's just stitching the hole up," Argentum said as she proceeded to stitch up Jessica.

"All right then, let's get going. We still need to check the camp. There might be some salvageable material just yet."

He turned on his heel and left us there. Scarlet scurried after him, which amused me to no end. They were both whipped, and it was honestly disgusting at times. Once they had left, the rest of us got up on our own time and went looking too, with Connor, Charlie, and me being the last ones to leave.

Everyone went their separate ways in searching, but they eventually got into pairs—girlfriends, boyfriends, or just friends, in Erik and Regius's case. This included me and Jessica. We walked around the camp, which was now more of an assortment of craters than a camp. I was sure we'd be a great demolition crew if we ever needed the money. Nothing seemed to be different between the time we dealt with the soldiers and the crashing of the AC-130—just maybe a few more craters. The problem was that the two soldiers who had been the commanders were now dead. Jessica and I found them. They both had a severe amount of shrapnel all over their bodies.

The sight was disgusting, but we searched them just in case they had anything on them. Neither of them had anything of much importance, but one of them had a map with locations marked. We didn't know why, so we took it just in case. After we were done looting, Jessica incinerated their bodies. This was always a sobering experience for us, as we knew that if we had just been a little less alert or a little unluckier, it could have been us on the ground dead or dying. I was reminded of that as Jessica's hand gripped mine in desperation to know she wasn't alone here. Still, we stopped thinking about it eventually and continued searching the base for anything interesting or of use.

The only problem with finding anything of use was that most of the area was destroyed or already searched by everyone else. However, in the area that we were searching, one tent seemed undamaged. Looking at each other, we nodded and then went into the tent. At first, we were disappointed, as there didn't seem to be much in there except for bunks and a few personal things that would never be touched again. A curtain hung on the other side of the tent, and after a quick look around the bunks, we found a couple of needless things, including an explicit men's magazine, which I tucked into my pants. Swinging for the other team did have its perks sometimes.

We walked over to the curtain and pulled it away. What we saw behind the curtain was a bit surprising. It looked like a command center. There were some radios around and some information on the table. On the table in the middle of the room there was only a map. I compared it to the map I had looted from the commander and found that they were a match, but the one on the table was far more detailed, going so far as to show troop numbers. We now knew exactly how they were going to attack us. Finding this was the equivalent of finding gold in war.

"Get Bryce. He needs to see this."

Jessica silently nodded and ran out of the tent to go find Bryce. It wasn't quietly, because as soon as she left, she was yelling to Bryce that we found gold.

This, of course, caused everyone to pack into the tent. It wasn't crowded, as we were only thirteen, and this tent was meant for at least twenty. Over the next couple of minutes, everyone explored the tent, including the control room, reacting differently to it. Regius and Scarlet sat down with both shock and excitement overloading them. Charlie,

Marie, Albert, Argentum, Shane, Lucy, and Jessica were so giddy with excitement that they went outside to cheer. Bryce, Connor, and Erik were all stoic in the moment, thinking about what to do with the information. I was currently putting down as much information as possible onto the map, adding locations, troop movements, and such that weren't on the smaller map. Everyone still in the tent was interrupted in their thoughts as the radio blared to life.

"Base S, this is Motherbase. How copy? Over," came an official-sounding voice from the radio. All of us looked at each other for a second in complete silence before Connor spoke.

"Intimidation. There's no way they won't figure out their plans aren't compromised."

"We hold the upper hand. Don't be cocky," Erik added as Bryce grabbed the radio and began to talk into it.

"Good, copy, Mothership. This is the Devil Dragon speaking. How copy? Over."

At the mention of the name Devil Dragon, all of us looked at him in silent unison, wondering how he came up with that name.

"They'll know it's me if I use that name."

It made sense. That name would inspire fear in them, knowing that enemy number one on their board was now in possession of their plan to fight him. It seemed to do its job too, as the other person didn't speak for the next several minutes, during which time everyone made it back into the tent. They had been initially boisterous, but as they saw Bryce at the radio, they shut up and sat down. Jessica came over to me at the table and held my hand tightly. A lot rested on this conversation, and it was getting to us all. Eventually, the silence became unnerving, and Bryce spoke again.

"If you are waiting for your AC-130 to destroy the base, then it's already too late. He flew far too low to survive," he said through the radio.

Again there was silence. This time a shiver went down my spine, and I went outside the tent to just cool down. I looked to the horizon, because the feeling just wouldn't go away. Sure enough, two black dots appeared.

"Are those what I think they are?" Jessica asked from beside me, scaring me a little.

"I think so."

"I'll get Scarlet and Bryce."

And so she did. In the next instant, they were both outside. They looked at the dots as they increased in size, coming at us at high speeds.

"Scarlet, you know what to do. Protect everyone. Your spheres are too slow to do anything to them."

Bryce prepared to attack the planes in the air. He was already covered in his scales and had blazing fire around him so hot that both Scarlet and I had to back away. As we did, Jessica walked up to him and put a hand on his shoulder, and her entire body was also covered in blue flames. They seemed to be on the same page, as Bryce nodded, and Jessica held her hands to her side and separated, as if she was holding a basketball. A red flame erupted between her hands. It quickly turned blue and then pure white, which I couldn't see but sure as hell felt. The heat coming from the flames was so insane that I had to put up a wall of ice to protect Scarlet and myself even though her shield was up for us.

The planes were now so close that we could tell that they were A-10 Warthogs. Then an amazing thing happened. Jessica's ball of pure white flame disappeared for a split second before coming back in full force as lightning. She looked like she was straining too, as it was evident on her face, but it was relieved immediately as she released the lightning toward the planes in a bright flash followed by an explosion that cracked the ice between us.

It caused me to blink, and as I opened my eyes, I saw both planes explode and fall to the ground. Those planes must have been miles and miles away. Damn, my girlfriend was powerful.

"My God."

"My sentiments exactly," said Bryce, who casually appeared out of nowhere, before a resounding crack almost deafened me.

Disregarding Bryce, I immediately ran over to Jessica, who was starting to stumble around like a drunken fiend. I grabbed her before she could fall on her face. Once she held onto me, she could walk normally, breathing a bit more heavily than normal and sweating buckets. Bryce, on the other hand, looked more mentally strained than anything else. It didn't take that much to figure it out. Getting the right amount of power to use without losing yourself to it was difficult, and anyone would be exhausted mentally.

Still, he recovered in about the same time as Jessica did. He was starting to look angry—brows furrowed, jaw clenched, and a scary look in his eyes. I got only a brief glimpse of his face before he went into the tent and right up to the radio. He ripped it from where it rested on the table, somehow not tearing the cord in two, and began to shout into the radio.

"Put your commanding officer on the phone right now! Unless you want to keep wasting money, then by all means keep sending your Warthogs and AC-130s! We'll gladly rip them out of the sky again! Over!"

With that last *over*, he restrained himself just enough to gently put down the radio, knowing that if he didn't, he would destroy it. He then proceeded to storm out of the tent. Scarlet tried to follow him, only to be stopped by Connor, who appeared out of nowhere, merely shaking his head and raising his hands in front of him, causing Scarlet to stop. Connor wasn't always the talkative one, but when he said something or even when he didn't, people listened, even Bryce. So, of course, she did listen, and she sat down on the same cot on which Jessica and I were sitting.

Not a second later we heard Bryce shouting obscenities, some of which I had never even heard before. Next came the sound of things exploding, followed by the crackle of fire. It took him about two minutes to fully calm down and come back into the tent, which had been completely silent, as no one here besides Lucy, Connor, Charlie, and me had ever seen him in one of these fits. It was a good "destressing" technique for him, but he usually never needed to use it, as either it was too late—the other day was a case in point—or he just wasn't angry enough. This was the first time he'd ever sworn during it, so that was new.

When he came back into the tent, he looked serene. Venting the way he did was very effective, but it was really only for certain situations, and today was obviously one of them. As soon as he stepped into the tent, Scarlet was on him like a fly to honey. The extent to which they loved each other was disgusting. Even the others, mostly Charlie and Marie, agreed with me.

"Why don't you two put your affection for each other away for once? We get it, you *love* each other," Charlie said.

Bryce looked like he was about to respond, but the radio crackled to life, and a very familiar and chilling voice sounded.

"Hello, lost children. I hear you've been destroying things that aren't yours. Now you asked for me. What do you want?" the voice sneered at the end.

I instantly recognized the voice, and so did everyone in the room. It was the commander of the Slăve, Edward Mors. He was responsible for most of our imprisonments, the taking of our freedom before this, and the stripping of our basic human rights. He made us appear to the public as no more than savages.

Everyone in the room felt a cold shiver run down their backs as he spoke, and Scarlet looked especially affected. However, Bryce quickly calmed her down, and she sat down next to Jessica and me. Bryce then walked over to the radio and spoke possibly the boldest thing that ever came out of his mouth.

"I wasn't talking about you, ingrate. You know who I want to talk to, so put him on the radio, and don't even try to attack us with anything. It'll only make you look even more pathetic."

The looks of absolute shock swept through the tent like wildfire. Then came the incredulous mumbling, usually consisting of profanities. Some of us were completely speechless, including myself, Charlie, and Connor. Charlie proceeded to laugh so hard that he fell to the ground, and Connor simply covered his mouth in pure shock. The radio was completely silent too for another two minutes before it came back to life.

"Hello, Bryce. Over," came another similar voice.

I couldn't place this one exactly, but from the looks of Charlie and Connor, they could. They didn't really look all that surprised.

"Hello, sir. How have you been? Over," Bryce said, seriously confusing us all as to the level of familiarity he was showing with the voice on the other end.

"Bryce, this is no time for pleasantries. You know that we're about to bring the whole world down around you. Over," said the voice.

This time I recognized it as Bryce's grandpa, known to most as the general of the army. I knew little about him, but I did know that he was a good man.

"I wouldn't expect anything else from the military. Will there be media personnel there, if I may ask? Over."

"There will be. No one expects you and your group to put up a good fight. In fact, most soldiers think they'll be done in a day. Over."

"And what do you think, sir? Over."

"I think … you might just win."

After that surprising statement from the general, the radio shut off, and all we heard was static.

We all stared at each other, not knowing what to do. None of us had expected that to happen. We expected soul-crushing reassurance that we would lose, but what we got was nowhere near that. We got the oldest- and highest-ranking officer in the military right now saying that he believed in us. If that wasn't the biggest morale booster in the world, then I didn't know what was. Even the others, who didn't know who was on the other end of the radio, knew that the speaker was incredibly high on the totem pole to outrank the head of the Slăve. None of us spoke for a solid minute after the radio shut off. Charlie was the one to break the silence.

"Well," he exclaimed, jumping up from the cot, "there's only one thing left to do. Win."

For the longest time, no one said anything, but Charlie kept standing there, looking as proud as he could be to have said what he did, and it didn't take long for Bryce to walk over to him.

"You're right. There is no other option. We will fight them outnumbered almost one thousand plus to one, and we will win."

Those last few words were said with such conviction that my body instantly jumped up and joined them. Jessica and Scarlet followed me right away, and so did almost everyone else. Only Connor stayed away. We all gave him curious glances before he finally made his way over to us and began to speak.

"You've all read the history books, and you've all heard the stories of how a group of people rose up and fought for their future. So why not show the world that they aren't just stories or pages in history? That it is real, that it can happen? This is our time to show the world what we are truly made of and to carve our names into the annals of history so that we will never be forgotten. This is our time!"

None of us could resist our roars of agreement, which were so loud they must have scared off any type of wildlife in the area. We all gave each other smiles of encouragement, but we knew that even if we did win, there was no way all of us were getting out alive. So we took the time to memorize each other's faces. It didn't take long, even though it felt like an eternity. Eventually everyone made their way out of the tent and toward the trail leading back to the camp.

The walk back was consumed with happiness. We chatted our worries away and smiled to conceal our fear of the coming battle, and it was enough for us. For the briefest moment, we were truly happy, but more importantly, for the first time since the Day of Shattered Dreams, we had hope for a better future—a future we wanted for our children and their children, a future I would happily die for if that meant that others could have it. This might be our only real chance to make that possible too—the most dangerous people on the planet all piled into one little group, ready and willing to die for the idea of freedom and hope.

But all of that died down when we heard a cry of pain up ahead of us. We recognized the voice as Taylor's, and we instantly moved as fast as we could toward the noise. What was in front of us shook me to the core. Taylor was being used as a meat shield with a gun to her head, and twelve soldiers all around her were pointing their guns at us. They were the soldiers we had spared too. That imbued far more hatred than imaginable, as we had given them a chance to live, and they had thrown it back at us. It was too bad that they were all going to die now—and probably not peacefully. The only problem was the guy holding the gun to Taylor's head.

It was still hard to grasp that not only were they holding a pregnant woman hostage, but said woman was also a stand-in mother to most of us. She took care of us whenever we needed it, and she had always been there for us in the past year and a half. I could feel the rage boiling inside me, and it was palpable from the others. However, Connor looked serene, and that was what scared me. That face was recognizable from anywhere. It was the face he had when he was going to kill viciously and without mercy.

"If you want your precious pregnant friend to get out of here alive, I suggest you let us go," said the man with the gun pointing at Taylor's head, breaking the silence that could have been cut with a knife. None of us said anything. Connor simply looked at Bryce and held out his hand. Bryce also said nothing and put the knife that was hanging at his waist into Connor's open hand. Connor then unsheathed it and looked it up and down before nodding his head and throwing the sheath back toward Bryce, who caught it. Then Connor disappeared, only to reappear above the man holding Taylor hostage, with the knife already in the man's head.

When that happened, Bryce exploded forward, grabbed Taylor, and exploded right back to the group. As soon as he made it back, I threw up an ice wall in front of us. The remaining soldiers just stared in absolute confusion at their fallen leader. Connor was nowhere in sight, and then another one fell—this time with Connor crouched in front of him and the knife straight in his neck. When Connor disappeared again, blood spurted out of the soldier's neck as he fell to the ground backward. The remaining ten soldiers started to blindly fire everywhere, trying desperately to hit Connor. Even I was confused as to how he was moving around. There was absolutely no trace of him anywhere; he was just appearing and disappearing at will.

"Still trying to figure out what he is, huh?" Bryce said, poking my shoulder from the side.

I was surprised to see that he had left Taylor's side, but Charlie and Marie were attending to her. There was nothing to worry about now.

"Yeah. I just … I just don't know what he could be."

"He can become anything that—"

"Yeah, I get it. He can become anything he touches. I *know*. But he's not actively touching anything. What the hell could it be?"

"You didn't let me finish, Annabeth. He can become anything he touches but also anything that's touching him."

"That still doesn't explain anything, Bryce," I snapped at him.

I turned back to the scene and watched Connor appear again with the knife in the spinal cord of one of the soldiers, instantly killing him. He disappeared again before the other soldiers could react, and looking at them now, I saw there were only four left.

"Okay, then here's a hint. What is every single one of us actively touching at this very moment?" I was about to shout at him to just tell me, but then it dawned on me. But it didn't seem possible. However, it would explain how he could be so sneaky all the time. I looked back to Bryce again to confirm my suspicions.

"He's the air, isn't he?"

"He's actually the oxygen in the air, but, yes, you are right in a sense."

"Ho-"

"He told me."

"That makes more sense."

I saw Connor standing above the last remaining soldier, looking down at him with his shoe on the man's neck. The man was positively pleading for mercy, but it was far too late for that. Connor put the tip of the knife right between the man's eyebrows and slowly pushed down into the man's skull. His screams were horrible, and they probably would have lasted much longer, but Taylor yelled for him to stop. I don't know how he heard her, but he did, and he ended the man's suffering by plunging the knife the rest of the way in and killing him.

With the last of the soldiers dead and lying in their own blood, Connor ran over to Taylor, who proceeded to run around the ice wall to him. They met right in front of the wall, and it was heartwarming. At the very least it was nice to see that they were both happy and together. That, of course, didn't last all that long.

"Guys, my water just broke," said the frightened Taylor as she held Connor out at arm's length.

CHAPTER
28

"**Y**ou get the hell away from me right now! *You* did this to me. *God, I hate you!*" came the screams of my wife as she was in labor and yelling her heart out me.

It was only the pain that was making her say those things, but that didn't mean that the words didn't sting, especially since she currently had the power to back up those words. She hit me with her power for the third time now, sending me violently cascading away from her. I got up again, as nothing would stop me from seeing the birth of my child. It was mine as much as it was hers, so we were going to share in the moment the baby came into the world. I walked up to her for the fourth time. She looked at me for a couple of seconds with only rage covering her face, but it quickly dissipated.

"*Fine*. You can stay, but I still hate you for doing this to me," she said.

Even though she was letting me stay with her, she was not happy about it. She would periodically hit me with a small explosion, and she was gripping my hand as hard as she possibly could. I was certain that she had broken at least one of the bones in my hand.

The real concern was time, as we had been in the process of labor for almost five hours now. I didn't think my body would hold out much longer. At least Scarlet was here. She calmed Taylor down whenever she could, and she saved me from Taylor's wrath at least twice now. Charlie and Marie were also helping, but they were helping to get the kid out of Taylor and not calming her down or keeping her from killing me. Thankfully, after many hours, Marie gave me relief that the end was in sight.

"The baby's crowning, Taylor. Just a long push now," said Marie, and those words were like sweet honey to my ears, bringing relief to my soul.

"Get this thing out of me *right now*!" came the angry screams of my wife right next to me.

Her shouting right in my ear did not help my hearing one bit. I was pretty sure she hit me with another explosion too, but at the moment, the pain was dulled out by everything else.

"Just one last push. You can do it," said Marie.

With an agonizing scream, Taylor pushed as hard as she could, and when her scream died out, we heard the crying of a baby.

Charlie held the baby in his hands as Marie cut the umbilical cord and cleaned the baby off with the wet and dry towels Scarlet had gotten earlier. She wrapped the baby in a blanket and then gave her to Taylor, who was now crying tears of joy as she held our kid in her hands. I was also crying with joy as the baby opened her eyes and looked at us. She had sparkling eyes full of joy and curiosity, just like her mother. Just seeing those eyes made me smile as wide as possible.

Seeing the brightness in Taylor's eyes as she looked at our baby filled me with joy, as well. This little thing was ours and only ours. We had brought her into the world, and she would be ours forever.

"She's beautiful, isn't she?" Taylor said. It wasn't really a question but more of a statement, to which I couldn't agree more.

"Yes, she is," I said, stroking my baby's little head with my pinky.

"So what are you going to name her?" Scarlet asked.

"I don't know yet, but what's the date? I want to know when my baby's birthday is," Taylor said.

"It's the twelfth of June," Charlie said, looking at his digital watch he had swiped off a soldier a while ago.

Scarlet seemed a little surprised.

"What is it, Scarlet?" I asked.

"It's my birthday. I'm twenty now."

That made a little bit of sense. Taylor just smiled at that, and I knew that smile. She had just thought of something.

"I think I know the baby's name," she said, and she glanced at Scarlet before she continued. "I'll name her Carmine."

Shock spread across Scarlet's face, as well as Charlie's and Marie's. I had no idea what naming our kid Carmine meant to Scarlet, but it seemed like it was an extremely high compliment. Judging from Scarlet's face, it was a compliment to her. It didn't surprise me, as those two were good friends. Still, if it was a compliment, it flew right over my head. I looked to Charlie with a curious gaze, and he came through.

He whispered, "Carmine is a synonym for Scarlet."

Oh, now it makes sense.

"Charlie, would you please go get the others and tell them to come and greet Carmine?" Taylor asked in a cheerful voice as she tickled the chin of Carmine, who giggled slightly in response.

Charlie did as he was asked and went to get the others. Before they came back, Taylor looked over at me.

"Thanks for staying. I don't think I could've done it without you," she said with probably the happiest smile I'd ever seen on her.

"It's okay, and you're welcome," I said in response, smiling, and leaning over to kiss her.

It just so happened that everyone came to us at that moment, and all of them let out an "aw" upon seeing us. I saw that everyone was there except for Bryce, which wasn't like him. He'd usually be here in a heartbeat, so where was he? I got up, and Taylor looked at me, but when she too noticed that Bryce wasn't there, she nodded to me to go look for him.

I left the group that had gathered around Taylor, and the first place that I looked was downstream from us, where it was always quiet, with just the flowing of the river as noise. He usually meditated there, but he wasn't there today. That didn't leave many other places. After checking the cliff, I knew there was only one other place that he could possibly be, and that was up the mountain a couple of miles away from the camp. A cave was there that he would go to when he wanted to sleep without hurting everyone, before Scarlet came along. However, walking that far was not part of the plan, so I went back to Taylor and the others. I grabbed Lucy and asked her to see where Bryce was. She told me that he was on the other side of the town about an hour's walk from here with the shortcut.

"Why the hell would he be there?" I asked. It didn't make any sense for him to be there.

"I don't know, but his power's been fluctuating sporadically a lot in the past six or seven hours. I think he's trying to do something."

I thought I knew what he was trying to do. If he'd been able to do it, he'd have been the third in history, according to the rumors. The first two were MO and some woman in the military named Julie.

It was smart of him to get away from the others to try it, but he should be meeting his niece now. I walked over to where he was and decided to wait until he was done with his current meditation. If he was interrupted and surprised, he could lose control and attack me without realizing it was me. So sitting back and watching was the better idea. Plus, it was way too hot to even get close to him now. The ash of the forest around him was evidence enough of that.

What I got to see though for Bryce was not failure but success. Ever so slowly, his body began to change. Instead of being covered in scales, his skin and scales shattered, and he was only a skeleton. In that moment, his entire bone structure changed to that of a dragon, with four legs and two wings. It must have been at the towering height of over two hundred feet. The muscle, fat, and organs all went into the dragon and solidified it. Finally, the scales reformed and covered up the body. Bryce opened his eyes and smiled. At least that's what I thought a dragon's smile looked like. Then he roared in triumph, shaking my skeleton to its very last bone. If any enemies heard it, they knew they would die.

In the next instant, he spread his wings so incredibly wide that they must have been close to one thousand feet in length from tip to tip. And then he took off from the ground, propelling himself upward almost five hundred feet. Not wanting to lose sight of him, I changed into oxygen and got myself up to the tallest branch of the tallest tree in the area to see where he was going. However, when I got up there, I was greeted with the sight of what must have been thousands of vehicles coming from the horizon and several helicopters ahead of the group. Bryce seemed to be going in for the attack against the helicopter pilots right away.

CHAPTER
29

When I was finally able to successfully change myself, the joy was insurmountable, but it was quickly dashed when I noticed what was coming toward us—thousands of vehicles with possibly the whole military with them. Then four helicopters were in the air far ahead of the vehicles coming toward us. It seemed that this would be the perfect time to test out my dragon form.

I stretched out my wings as far as they would go, and it seemed like they would be able to touch the mountain. Even with the soldiers so far away, there was no way they weren't seeing this right now. I thrust down with them, propelling myself at least five hundred feet into the air. This made me look gigantic, even with the mountain behind me. I felt powerful, and that power wanted to come out. Now it was time to show the soldiers just what they were truly up against.

Propelling myself toward the soldiers with the power of my wings, I was into the desert within a minute. They were still a couple of miles away at this point, but they had definitely seen me by now, and the fear they emanated produced a delicious smell. Once they were within one mile of me, the four helicopters that were ahead of the main group made their way toward me. If they wanted to survive, they should have sent more.

We were only about four hundred feet apart when they attacked. They sent two rockets each at me, but it was rather easy to dodge them by propelling myself upward. However, when I did that, the rockets still followed me. They were heat seekers. I should have seen that coming, but it wasn't the time to dwell on that right now. I wanted to breathe fire on the rockets to destroy them, but I hadn't figured out how to do that just yet.

Flying around for about a minute with them still following me was a lot harder than I anticipated. It took another minute before I came up with a good plan to get rid of them. After flying almost one mile up, the plan began once I reached the peak of my flight.

I fell straight down past the rockets toward the ground, but they still followed me. When the ground was only fifty feet away, it was time to make my move. I suddenly jerked myself from falling straight down to flying horizontally, parallel to the ground. Four of the rockets weren't able to change their direction fast enough and blew up in the desert, and two more blew up on my sides. It most certainly hurt like hell, but there was no damage to my body, so it was okay. With only two rockets left, it was time to finish the plan. I flew toward the four helicopters, and they fired even more rockets, but they weren't heat seekers, so it was easy to dodge them. Once they were within one hundred feet of me, I reached out with my two front legs and grabbed two of the helicopters, instantly crushing the two pilots in each. I spun them around to face the two remaining rockets, which were about three hundred feet away. I had to wait two seconds until they were within one hundred feet. Once they reached that mark, I dropped the helicopters that were crushed in my claws into the rockets, taking care of that.

I turned to face the two remaining helicopters, and rockets were already coming at me. There was no time to dodge. They had backed me into a very tight corner, and I wasn't sure if breathing fire would work. There was something else that I could try. I went inverted, with my body straight up, and thrust my wings together as hard as possible. This created a gust so strong that it threw the remaining rockets together, creating a huge smoke cloud.

The cloud was so dense that the pilots of the remaining helicopters couldn't see through it, and that meant they couldn't see me. Taking advantage of this, I dove down under the cloud of smoke and went straight up into the helicopters, destroying the closer one by biting it in half, and once the other one had turned to see what was happening, it was too late. My tail came raging up and wrapped around the cockpit, crushing the pilots in it.

As the helicopter that was bitten in half fell toward the ground, one of the pilots was able to get out and deploy his parachute before hitting the ground. This was the perfect situation to have them hear our message. I flew toward him, and he was probably scared shitless. Once I landed, I changed into my human form so that he wouldn't be intimidated. Walking toward someone after changing from a dragon to a human—and while completely naked—was weird for not only him but also me. Additionally, he had just seen most of his comrades die, which was probably traumatic.

He struggled to get off his parachute that was flapping in the wind, and he was barely able to keep his feet planted. When he was finally able to get free of it, I was only about twenty feet away. He immediately pulled his sidearm and began shooting at me. It was futile, as my scales were already covering me completely, and the bullets bounced off harmlessly. Once he ran out of his clip, I exploded toward him, grabbed the gun out of his hands, and knocked him to the ground. It was at that moment that he began begging.

"Please don't kill. I ... I ... I have a family, please," he said.

"Don't worry. I'm not going to kill you since you're the only one who survived. I just wanted to give you a fair warning about what you guys are really getting yourselves into," I said.

"Okay," he said as he tried to stab me in the neck with a knife. His moves were so obvious to me, so stopping him from doing anything was easy.

"No, no," I said, shaking my finger. "Now who said you could do that?"

I took the knife out of his hand and plunged it into his leg, away from the arteries so he would feel it all. He didn't scream, though, and instead looked at me with eyes full of hatred.

"You're scum. You don't deserve to live if you're okay with doing this to someone," he said, thinking that the knife was bad.

"I understand how you feel about me now, but imagine that feeling times fifty. That's how I feel about the people who killed my family and all the people who tortured my friends and me. We did nothing to you, and you attacked us because we're different! All we wanted was normal lives. We don't like to kill, but we will do anything to protect our families, and if that means we kill, then we kill," I said with the most conviction possible while looking straight into his eyes.

"I don't care what you say to me. You killed my brother when you escaped last year, and I will never forgive you for that," he said, starting to tear up from rage.

"I get that, but I came to talk to you for one reason and one reason only: to tell you what will happen if you attack us. You will kill some of us, but there is no way in hell that more than five of you will survive this fight. So either tell the soldiers coming to turn around, or die," I said.

"Screw off, scum. You don't deserve mercy," he replied, standing up, heavily favoring his non-stabbed leg.

"Neither do you."

And with that, our conversation was over. I walked away, turned back into the dragon, and flew back to the hole. I continued with my plan of changing and then rushing back over to the group to get ready for the night op.

I sprinted there, so it didn't take long. However, informing them of the change of plans took a bit longer, mostly because I had to explain my actions to them and then tell them the new plan, which was really a revision of the old one.

Scarlet, Erik, and Shane would go into town and set up the traps there. Argentum and Marie would go into the enemy camp and basically scout it out. Connor's job was to be the overwatch for Argentum and Marie and inform them if anything went haywire, while my job was to monitor Scarlet's protection of the group and taking out soldiers or providing overwatch for Argentum and Marie. The rest of the group, except for Lucy, could sleep. Lucy and I needed to keep our minds connected for communication.

This was the beginning of our fight for survival and the end of our journey. Whoever won this would change the world, and we all knew it.

CHAPTER

30

I looked at my watch, and our drop zone was coming up in about two minutes. As the engine of the plane roared around us, the group of soldiers under my command looked calm and ready to fight. We were the best of the best, handpicked from the various branches for this. This was just a regular mission for us, even if we were going up against the strongest group of magic users ever. With ammunition dipped in magic-neutralizing material, we felt more than confident that we could kill Bryce and his people.

"Thirty seconds to drop. Get ready," the pilot said over the speaker.

Getting my men up and checking their equipment took all of ten seconds, as they were already standing and I was the only one sitting. Getting to the front of the line and preparing to shuttle them out was nerve-racking for some reason, probably because of my brother, but this wasn't the time to think about that now.

"Drop," the pilot said over the speaker.

"Go! Go! Go!" I screamed to my soldiers.

All ten of us jumped out of a perfectly good airplane to go fight people who had nothing to lose. We landed about five miles to the west of where the dragon had been spotted coming to life. The intel people had assumed that was where their camp would be, but after they were briefed on this s0000, the idea that he would do something so dumb seemed improbable. But you never knew with human stupidity.

After regrouping with everyone about four miles east of the point, we started to slowly make our way to the area. It was only 2400 hours at the time. We arrived at a point a few hundred feet from the location at about 0130. I sent one of my troops to scout it out, and it turned out that there was no one there after all. This s0000 lived up to my expectations. It was time for a new plan.

"Bird, I want you to find a sniping position around here that will give you a clear line of sight all around the town. I want you to cover us while we go through it to the other side," I said to my sniper of the team.

"Roger, wilco," he said, pulling from the group and running off to find his position.

"If you were paying attention, then you know the plan, but just in case you weren't, the plan is to go through the town and up onto that cliff on the other side. Everyone got it?" I asked, looking at them.

They all gave me a nod that the message got through, and we continued on with our mission: eradicate the magic users.

CHAPTER
31

"How's the progress with planting the explosives coming, Scarlet?" I asked her through the link.

"We're a bit ahead of schedule, but we still won't be done for another hour or two" was her response.

"Well, at least we're ahead of schedule. For now keep up the good work, and don't rush setting them up. No use in setting them up if they aren't going to work."

"Wilco," replied the curt and militaristic Erik, which ended the link.

Erik was developing into quite the person since being integrated into the group. Everyone liked him, to an extent, but he didn't really talk to any of the group except for Regius. Even then he always maintained a high-standard military manner, much the same as Regius. His presence made Regius interact with everyone, and that subsequently made Erik do the same. If he had arrived earlier, I had no doubt in my mind that he would be at least decent friends with everyone here. The only thing that really outshined his introvert manner was his ability with weapons, explosives, and the like. That included information on basically every vehicle they could throw at us.

That information would be invaluable. It was time to check up on Argentum and Marie, who were currently scouting the enemy encampment. Last time we checked in with them was almost an hour ago, and they were just getting into the camp as snakes. By now, they had probably switched to something like mosquitoes or the small lizards that lived out in the desert.

"How's it going down there?" I asked them through our telepathic link.

"It's going pretty well for now. We've had a couple of close calls, nearly being swatted by some people, but it's been smooth sailing otherwise," Marie responded.

"How many tents have you checked?" I asked.

"We've gone through eight hundred tents in total with about eight people in each. We probably have a few thousand more tents to go through, not including the leadership tents, and then we have to go and check on the helicopters and tanks," Marie said.

"Just from looking, it seems like Charlie's estimate for the tanks and helicopters will be pretty accurate at three hundred each," Argentum said, butting in without giving me time to respond to Marie.

"How about soldiers? Can you give me at least a rough estimate now?"

"I can, but it will be the very definition of rough."

"That's better than nothing now."

"I'd say at least half a million infantry and another three hundred thousand in fighting forces. That's including tank and helicopter personnel. There's probably another one hundred thousand in maintenance and other jobs here, but that's about it."

"Okay, thanks. Report back in an hour or so. Otherwise, do what you can, and if possible, find the command or tech tent, and do a bit of sabotage."

"Got it."

With that, she went silent. Lucy tapped me on the shoulder.

"They're here. Coming from the other side of the town."

Connor and I looked at each other and nodded in silent understanding. We had expected this, and they were coming. We figured we might as well show them what walking into a trap felt like.

Moving back to where the sniper rifle was, on the edge of the cliff, we set up as we normally did—me on the spotting scope and Connor with the sniper rifle. We set out immediately to check our scopes and get them zeroed in on the other side of the town. The only thing left to do was to instruct Scarlet to get ready.

"Hey, Scarlet. They're coming. Get ready, and be as silent as possible. We'll be overwatch for you from here, so no need to worry about where they are. You'll know."

"Got it."

We could see her make commands from here, as she motioned to both Shane and Erik to get into cover and get ready. All of them got their weapons ready too: Scarlet with her submachine gun, Erik with his SCAR assault rifle, and Shane with his white armor. He cocked his Beretta pistol and armed himself with a white sword. Scarlet set up on the right wall that was closer to the cliff, but there was a space between the two houses behind it, leaving an opening. Erik set up on the right side, farther from me, while Shane was the farthest, two whole houses in front of the others.

Now it was time to find that other sniper. They must have had one. He definitely had the upper hand here too, so it would be difficult to find him. He was on lower ground than I was, so he'd be able to hide more easily. With the trees and no real moon tonight, he'd be able to hide quite well. My position had its advantages though. I was able to see a lot more around the area, and because of how we were set up, there were only eight places in the area where he'd be able to get a shot at either of us. Finding him and eliminating him should take no longer than twenty minutes, especially since Connor would be helping me look.

About five minutes in, there was slight movement in the second spot that we were checking. A few twigs were moving, and the ground was moving too. We waited three minutes before the object that we were looking at came into an area that we could properly see it. Unfortunately, it was only a snake and not the sniper that we were hoping for.

"I thought we had him for a second there," Connor said with a little bit of anger. He always hated to be the one looking instead of hiding.

"You're not the only one that thought that, man. It would've been nice to find him right away, and then we'd be able to support Scarlet and the others."

"You can say that again, but I guess lady luck decided not to give us that."

"When was the last time we were ever lucky?"

"When we found the girls of our dreams and managed not to kill them."

His statement took me by surprise, as I hadn't thought about that. He wasn't wrong though. The happiest we'd been this past year was when we found the girls we were with now. Connor with Taylor, and me with Scarlet—our journeys together were just beginning.

Thinking it over after Connor made that statement, I realized that happiness had always avoided me in my life. Even when my parents were still alive, my mom always scolded me for the littlest things, and my dad made me train until my body literally couldn't do anything. What they did, as parents, was probably the only reason that I was still alive. If it hadn't been for them, I wouldn't have been as disciplined as I was. Thus, people would have died because of my mistakes.

I mulled this over while still looking for the other sniper, and suddenly I realized that Scarlet was literally the only person who could make me happy and pull me out of my robot-like existence besides Connor, Annabeth, and Charlie. My friends held me in check too. They made sure that my head was always held high no matter what, especially Connor. He was the reason that we'd made it this far. He kept me from breaking during the nightmares after the escape and my torture sessions, and he took care of me after we escaped by cleaning my cuts that regularly opened due to our travel and my workouts. He was the one who fixed me, and he was the only one here, besides maybe Scarlet, who knew just how truly broken I still was.

Just then Connor spotted some movement in his last section.

"Bryce, I got something. The last one I'm supposed to check under the bushes next to the tree with a broken branch hanging down."

"I see it. I think we might have him. Just a few more seco ..."

I noticed a faint glint on the other side of the tree, and there he was, the other sniper. Just as I was about to tell Connor that he was on the other side of the tree, Connor fired, but so did the sniper. Both guns were silenced, as neither could see the flash of the other or hear the other. However, it didn't matter. I saw the sniper's bullet coming right at Connor, and in a split-second decision, I extended my hand in front of his face, enveloping my hand in scales, and caught the bullet with the palm of my hand. We made eye contact at that moment, and he let out a very big sigh.

I looked back through the scope and saw the sniper was propped up against a tree, lifeless. Connor had seen him and made the adjustments himself.

Connor returned to the scope of the rifle, looked through it, and called out positions of the soldiers to Scarlet through the link. I separated myself from him and went into the bushes. I put my hands together and proceeded to pray. I wasn't asking for strength or forgiveness; rather, I wanted to warn God.

"Dear God, I don't know if you're out there or not, but I want you to hear this. The only thing you have ever given me in this world is Scarlet and my friends, and if you take them away from me, not only will I become a god myself to protect them, but I will utterly destroy you for letting them die."

I was strangely calm for someone who had just threatened God. I crawled back to Connor, who was still looking through the scope and calling out the soldiers' positions to Scarlet's group. My mind was occupied with two questions: *How many more will die? And how many will be lost in this war?* This war would bring more bloodshed, and peace for magic users would no longer be possible. But maybe peace for our group *was* possible. Maybe we could rise above all of this with thousands of bodies below us and show the world just how powerful we really were. We would show them that we were not to be trifled with, that we were not prey. We were the hunters of this world. They would witness the power that we possessed when we were fighting for our families' future. Just maybe, like Connor had said, they would realize that leaving us alone was their best option.

"Scarlet, I'm going to be forcing the soldiers toward you guys. They'll be focusing on protecting themselves from me, so they probably won't even consider you guys, but be careful nonetheless," I heard Connor say through the link.

"Okay" was her only response.

Connor made some adjustments with his scope based on the information I was giving him. His finger flexed on the trigger and fired the sniper rifle. The bullet ended the life of the third guy to the right in their nine-man formation. It went straight through his head and into the ankle of the guy behind him. This made him a sitting duck and an easy target, but instead of finishing him, I convinced Connor to wait and see if they would try to get him to cover. Instead, the remaining uninjured people reacted like cats and jumped to the wall closest to us. They couldn't save their comrade who had the bullet in his ankle. With no way to get to cover without endangering his comrades, he was essentially dead, and he accepted it as he closed his eyes and said something to his friends. During that short period, Connor made a slight adjustment on the scope and repeated the process. The bullet went straight through his forehead, ending his life instantly. Seven were left.

For the next couple of minutes, the soldiers stayed away from the open air, clinging to the walls. However, this made it easy to push them toward Scarlet and the others, who were all holding back on their magic at the moment, not because they couldn't but because we needed to conserve our energy. Needlessly using magic would just make us more vulnerable to the soldiers tomorrow. Most of the buildings they were in were already collapsing and blocking ways, and they would have been in the open air to go over them, so they had to follow the path, which led right to where Scarlet and the others were set up and waiting. There was a little space between the buildings behind Scarlet, so that was an area that needed to be watched once they got there.

CHAPTER

32

I looked across the opening between the houses, and Erik and Shane looked really tense but ready nonetheless. Erik had his SCAR out, and Shane was in full battle armor with his Beretta pistol and sword at the ready. We were at a huge disadvantage here. Erik and I had brought only one magazine each. Because of all the traps and explosives we carried down here, we couldn't carry any more. It was a truly stupid move by us, especially since we knew this might happen, but we couldn't change it now. We'd have to make all our bullets count. *This is now war, and they won't look to capture us. They'll be looking to kill us.*

"Be prepared down there, guys. They'll be coming around the corner two hundred feet from you guys in about fifteen seconds. I count three buildings that they could slip into, so at least take a few out before they get into one," Bryce said to all three of us through Lucy's telepathic link.

"Thanks. We'll do it," Erik and Shane said simultaneously, which was surprising.

"Also, Connor and I can't see much from up here, as they're hugging the walls, so you guys will mostly be on your own. Be careful."

At that moment, the soldiers came around the corner, hugging the wall to avoid Bryce. By the look on their uniforms, they were the GROM unit, which was the same unit that killed most of my family. They were highly trained and very good at their job, which was killing people like us. However, right now they were the prey—very wide-open prey.

I signaled over to Erik and Shane to fire and attack when they passed the first house door. Five seconds later, I gave the signal, and Erik and Shane poked out from where they were and fired at the soldiers. Erik fired, hitting the lead man in the head. He was dead instantly. Then Shane threw a spear, which had been his sword, toward the group. It was cool to see him make his weapons change, but it had its drawbacks, as now he had to retrieve it to use it. Nonetheless, the spear impaled the man right behind the one Erik had taken out, and he fell like a ton of bricks.

Shane then got on one knee and hid behind his shield slowly inching forward, while Erik and I fired at the remaining five soldiers but weren't able to seriously injure any of them. They, in turn, returned fire, forcing us to take cover. It allowed them to retreat back into the first house. We didn't leave Shane out to dry though. We kept our weapons trained on the house, but not everything went according to plan. An object flew out and blew up, blinding me for a second. I could hear Shane scream in pain during that second, and as soon as my vision was back, I fired a couple of shots at the house. Shane was nowhere in sight.

"Shane, where are you?" I yelled through the link, trying to keep my voice in check, but relief soon entered me as he responded.

"I'm in the house next to the soldiers. I took one to the side, shoulder, and one grazed my neck. Otherwise, I'm fine, but I don't think I'll be able to summon my armor," he said.

Even though the words implied confidence, he was straining to say them. He wasn't in the best of shape.

Now it was time to make up a strategy to take care of them inside the house and fast. We could get one of the Destruction users down there, but that would take too much time. We could call down Bryce too, but whatever they had thrown had obviously interrupted Shane's concentration on his armor, and there was no way that was their only one. Bryce was an asset we couldn't afford to lose. There were several other options, but they all would either take too much time or just not work. Our only real option was to go into the house and clear it. But that would be a problem, as both Erik and I had only about a half magazine left each.

Deciding that it was our only option to attack them through the house, we started to move into the road between the houses. Before we could, Bryce told me that there was passage between the houses behind me. I turned around and saw a little passage, and he was right. I started to move to it, and Bryce shouted in my mind to stop when I was about five feet away from the path.

I looked at him from my position, and he looked focused. Assuming that someone was around the corner, I got onto one knee and crouched so as to become a smaller target. Connor proceeded to tell me the plan that he came up with for the guy.

"There's someone in the alleyway, but he's not far enough out of the path for me to kill him. I'm going to shoot the wall next to him so that he'll hug the other wall. That's when I want you to peek around the corner and finish him off. You ready?"

"Of course."

Surprisingly, my body was really calm even though I was about to kill someone. It used to be hard for me to kill a fly, but now, since this living nightmare started, it had become different. Maybe it was because my mind and body were realizing that killing to survive wasn't a bad thing. It was obvious that I was no longer nervous when the trigger was pulled and the target ended up dead. The people who died because of me would come to me in my dreams. I couldn't imagine what it was like for Bryce. His body count had to be past the three-million mark after destroying half a city, a government torture/prison facility, and more soldiers since then. The others had told me about the nightmares he had, but I was never there for one, so I never knew.

"Ready, Scarlet?"

"Ready. Go when you want," I said back.

"Okay … one … two … three."

Connor fired, and the bullet hit the wall. The thud of the soldier going to the other wall made it to my ears, and he appeared in front of me. Without hesitating, I pulled the trigger, and three bullets went into the man—one in the head, one in the neck, and one in the collarbone. He was sufficiently dead. Four soldiers remained, and only twelve bullets were left.

Giving the all-good sign to Bryce, I turned the corner to go down the alleyway. Erik, who had been on the other side of the wall just watching, now began to walk down the street. We arrived at our positions at the windows of the house at the same time. Using Connor as a middle ground, we coordinated an attack at the same time for maximum effect. However, what we didn't expect was for them to jump through the windows and into the house next to them and the one Shane had been in.

We wheeled around and fired three bullets each before I put up my shield and caught a couple of bullets before they stopped. Not knowing if we had gotten any of the soldiers, we slowly backed away from the building and made it to the other side of the street before I fired the bullets back at them. Releasing the bullets was the cue for us to get cover in the building behind us, and we did.

Well, it looked like I was the last one standing. By some luck the two outside were able to hit both my radio man and the sergeant in the head as we jumped into the building with their friend. Their friend subsequently killed my second-in-command before I could do anything about it. He didn't make it unscathed, as he wound up with both a knife and a bullet in his chest. There was no point in checking if he was dead. No one was coming back from that.

I had to give it to them though. We had completely underestimated them. They weren't only powerful with magic, but they were devils with weapons. I wondered how many soldiers they'd killed and how many weapons they had in storage—probably hundreds, if not thousands. My death was coming soon too, so I might as well see if I could bait them into coming at me and at least maim them in the fray.

"If you haven't fired back already, you must be out of ammo. What a pity for your friend. Now do you have any last words?" I said loud enough for them to hear me and know that their friend was about to die.

"You should never get this close to a dying animal," said a voice to my side.

What I saw shocked me. The kid had pulled out the knife that was embedded in his chest and threw it at me. It went right through my chest cavity and into my heart. The life left me as he burst my heart, and the blood flowed endlessly inside me. I could feel everything—even the malice emanating off the kid—as I fell to the ground.

My breathing was getting more and more labored, but I refused to die here. I tried to crawl away from the kids, but that didn't work. I felt pressure on the small of my back before I heard the click of a gun. I closed my eyes, and an inevitable end came fast.

CHAPTER
33

N ow that was unexpected. I didn't think Shane had enough energy left to do that, but he was right—never back an animal into a corner it can't get out from. It will only get stronger. Even so, he was dying, and there was nothing we could do. He had maybe five minutes left.

Sending a message to Bryce to go get Lucy now, he knew immediately what had happened and understood that this would be her last moments with Shane.

Losing someone on the first night was completely unacceptable to me, especially since I believed that we could have saved Shane. *If I had just been willing to ask Bryce to come and help.* My arrogance and my feelings for Bryce caused Shane to die. He didn't deserve to die like this.

Shane then looked over at me and beckoned for me to come to him.

"I'm going to die, and I know it. Could you tell Lucy something for me?" he asked with strained breaths, but I simply shook my head.

"Tell her yourself. You will survive long enough to say it to her yourself. Okay?"

He nodded and then looked up at the ceiling, as if it was the eighth wonder of the world.

Not a moment later, there was a crash outside. It was Bryce covered in scales with Lucy in his arms. She jumped out of Bryce's arms and ran into the house to be with Shane in his final moments.

I walked over to Bryce, whose facial expression I had never seen on him before. It was sadness, but as soon as he noticed me, it was gone. He was hiding his emotions, but I was beyond happy that he was still alive.

We hugged each other, and neither of us said a thing. We were both immensely happy that the other was alive. This was only the beginning of the fighting, but there was a feeling in my gut that Bryce wouldn't let me die. There were some things he couldn't protect us against, and I would just have to rise to the occasion when that time came.

The moment of silence we were sharing was shattered when Lucy started to hysterically cry. That was our cue to get Lucy before she went crazy. We also knew that Shane had passed. However, as Erik went over to get Lucy, it was already too late. A beam of light red shot up from the building, and Lucy came out bathed in the same color. None of us had any idea what was going on, but we felt it as she raised her hand toward the soldiers' encampment.

Terrible pain shot through our minds, but we could tell that this was just a fraction of what the soldiers were feeling, as it wasn't directed at us. Next we heard thousands and thousands of shots of all kinds fired at the same time. Lucy passed out and collapsed onto the ground. The bloodred color that had been there only moments before was gone.

CHAPTER

34

After Erik left with Lucy knocked out on his back, Scarlet and I carried Shane's body out of the house and then scavenged the soldiers in the street and in the house. Scarlet had the ones in the street, and I had the ones in the house. Connor was taking care of the other soldiers who were killed earlier.

What we found on every one of the soldiers in the house was unexpected. They had at least seven pounds of explosives on them. I went outside to ask Scarlet if she had found the same explosives on the soldiers she was looting, and she looked at me with the explosives in her hands. She had the same expression written on her face that I had on mine. However, we didn't say anything and continued scavenging all the soldiers. We knew what the explosives would have been used for: to kill us and to erase any evidence of our existence.

After we finished scavenging in the house, all their weapons and ammo were in the street, along with the explosives but those were in a different pile. Connor met me outside with his own separate pile of gear that he had scavenged off the soldiers he killed, including the one Scarlet had killed in the alleyway behind the houses. All of his people also had the seven pounds of explosives. This was a peculiar situation, but their reasons for having the explosives were depressing. They were going to leave no evidence that we ever existed, which meant that they were going to quite literally eviscerate us with the explosives.

"You do realize why they have all these explosives, right?" Connor asked both Scarlet and me as we were starting to put the scavenged material together.

"Yes. I'd rather not think about it right now" was Scarlet's curt reply.

We stayed quiet for the rest of the night as we took the materials back to the camp. It took us three trips to get everything back to the camp. With all the salvageable weapons back at camp, we proceeded to put them in a tent away from our camp that acted as our storage area.

Marie and Argentum reported in after getting through half the camp. The total number now was exactly half of what they had predicted earlier, with 500,000 soldiers, 120 tanks, and 95 helicopters, and that was only half the camp. However, when they made the report, they were still in the camp, and this was an excellent opportunity to talk to their commander. I told Marie what to do. She was hesitant at first but accepted and did it.

I ripped off all the soldiers' dog tags and put them in one of the bags they were carrying. Then I grabbed Shane's body and took him to the edge of the town. I buried his body and made a crude cross over the grave from some building parts. It wasn't much, I knew, but it was better than just throwing his body into a mass grave like we did to the soldiers. He deserved better than what we could give him. Hopefully he understood.

I propped myself up against a nearby building and rested my head on the handle of the shovel. I watched the bustling of the soldiers in the fort across from me and knew that tomorrow would bring so much death. It felt good when Scarlet came silently and rested against me, falling asleep almost instantly. Just having her there made me feel better, at least for the moment.

This was the first sleepless night I'd had since Scarlet came into my life. It was probably the sorrow of Shane dying and the nervousness of the fight to come. This was only the beginning of it all, and there was no way that he would be the only casualty. As much as it pained me to say that, it was true. When it reached the breaking point for our group, either we became legends, or we fell—never to be seen by anyone ever again. That was the reality, and it would happen in only one of those two ways.

The sun was beginning to dawn on the edge of the horizon, and the chirpings of the early birds could be heard from every direction. This was the perfect time to start walking out into the desert to meet the commander. Scarlet was still sleeping, and she'd be asleep for a bit. Waking her up was out of the question. She did not function well if someone woke her up; she was at her best when she woke up naturally, which was usually early.

It was closing in on eight o'clock, and Scarlet had just begun to stir. Since she was already in my arms, I picked her up princess style and started to walk toward the Släve camp. The commander would come to meet me halfway at about nine o'clock.

By the time we reached the designated area, Scarlet was awake but faked snoring in my arms. It was kind of cute to see her think that she got away with it. Instead of gently putting her on the ground, I dropped her to the ground. She wasn't happy with that at all.

"Bryce, what the hell?" she yelled at me while punching me in the shoulder.

"Maybe you should wake up next time," I said, moving my body in a way that seemed to be mocking to her.

"Shut up, you jerk. You knew I was awake, didn't you?" she said, obviously angry.

"Maybe," I said in the most mocking tone possible. It made her angrier.

The commander and a major who had been awake late last night arrived via their own feet. I noticed them, but Scarlet didn't, as they arrived behind her.

"Admit that you knew that I was awake right now, or I'll never have sex with you again," she said.

It was hard to tell if she was serious, but it wouldn't be surprising if she was serious and if she followed through with it. She was very stubborn at times. Now it was my time to counter.

"Okay, I admit that I knew that you were awake. However, can you admit that you've faked being asleep before to get out of chores and so you wouldn't have to walk back to the camp after training?"

Just then the commander cleared his throat behind Scarlet, and she turned to face him.

"How long have you been there?" Scarlet asked, hoping they hadn't heard the previous conversation, but they already had.

"Not long. We just arrived, but I decided to stop you before you got into a lovers' quarrel," the commander said with a sly smile.

The first movement I made was to grab the bag of dog tags from my pocket that we had collected from the soldiers last night. Taking them out and throwing them to the commander with supreme nonchalance took him by surprise, but he didn't open the bag right away, which was a good thing for us.

"So the reason I called you here is that I know there will be a lot of dead lying around during our fight, and I thought that if you were okay with it, we could cease fighting every day at six thirty so that you could pick up your dead," I said to him.

"That's very considerate of you but also a very bold statement. What makes you think you'll even last the first day?" he asked.

"It's not bold if I know it's going to happen," I said.

"Huh. Quite the confidence you have there, Mr. Ceribri."

"Thank you, sir. You can look through the bag if you want to. I swear on my honor that no harm will come to you if you do."

He gave me a curious and apprehensive look, but he eventually cracked and began looking through the bag I had tossed him. When he saw that they were dog tags, he began sifting through them quickly, as if he was looking for one. His face changed from anger to sadness as he picked one specific one that still had a little blood left on it; that was the special ops commander's dog tags. He completely lost his composure too. It looked as if he was about to cry, and my observation of this was solidified when he asked his question.

"Where are the bodies?"

"In town," I replied with a sharp, almost angry, tone, realizing this would be a good time to see if I could turn him into another McClellan.

"Can we have them so that they can be returned to their families?" He asked with an even shakier voice. He had to be related to one of them.

By the look of his major next to him, he had never acted this way before.

"In two days. They killed someone who was a part of my family and who was the boyfriend of someone whom I think of as a younger sister. I hope you understand."

He looked distraught and sad, but at the same time it seemed as if he understood the circumstances. He then turned around to leave, but before he could, he looked back at me and asked, "Do you really think that you can win this?"

"Yes, I do," I responded.

"Why?" he said.

"Because we know just how much the future depends on these next couple of days, and we will do everything to make sure the future of our family and all others like us is safe and secure."

"I don't agree to your terms."

And with that, he left, choosing not to even acknowledge what I had just said.

This was the beginning of our legend.

CHAPTER
35

It was time, and I ran to the edge of the cliff, passing Lucy, and jumped off. About halfway down, the power surged through me, and my entire body changed in an instant, a lot faster than it had changed before. The pain was exponentially magnified, as it felt like the skin and muscle on my body were instantly ripped off, allowing for only my bones, and then my bones were stretched out and forced to become bigger. After that, everything that had been ripped off my skeleton was forced back on, and when the dragon scales came onto my body, they felt like burning coals that were hot glued onto my body. The wings sprouted out of my back from what had been my shoulder blades. The transformation was complete, and there I stood on the ground in front of the cliff, over three hundred feet tall and over three hundred feet long, not including the tail, with the sun shining off the scales, making it look as if my body was fire.

Instead of flying back up the cliff—which would have been easier to do but would have made it a lot harder for Albert to get on—I began to climb up the cliff using my claws. Surprisingly, it took very little time to get to the top and stick my head out for Albert to get on. However, it turned out that he was really inept at getting onto my head. After about three minutes of him repeatedly failing to get up, Lucy became annoyed, picked him up, and tossed him onto my head. He didn't seem to be prepared for it at all. He was very nervous, as his heart was beating into my head.

"You ready, Albert?" I asked in my dragon voice. Its deepness seemed to surprise him.

"As ready as I'll ever be, but give me a sec to get to the base of your neck," he said.

I reached up with my right front arm, grabbed him gently with the claws, and tossed him down to the base of my neck. He did not like that and displayed a unique vocabulary of swear words. It was rather entertaining to see him use words that were probably made up but used as swears. I surveyed the battlefield, and it became painstakingly evident that the group in the forest would need our help, as most of the tanks were on that side.

"You ready, Albert?" I asked again.

"Just go," he said.

Taking off after that, we sped toward the Slăve in the forest. Just as the first tank fired the first shell, I was in front of the forest and took the hit from the tank. It didn't feel like much, but there would definitely be a bruise come tomorrow morning. Then the second one hit my side, and then a third, fourth, and fifth. Now it was my turn to retaliate. Before they had a chance to react, my legs had already propelled my body toward them. Just from my landing, two of them were crushed under my legs and claws. Then the closest one of the remaining three got grabbed by my front left claw and was thrown close to six hundred feet away.

The next closest tank tried to go up behind my right hind leg. He was able to fire before I noticed him, but what happened next was beyond comparison to anything. I smashed my hind leg into the sand right next to the tank, and it went flying up into the air. As it hung up there, my whole body twisted around, and my tail hit slightly under the tank and sent it flying. There was no fighting as the tank flew. It just continued to fly, completely denying the world, and landed on the mountain, which was no less than three and a half miles away.

Over the next couple of minutes, there was absolutely no sound of any kind produced by fighting. Everyone just stared at the tank and the smoke that was rising from it. That was probably the coolest thing that I had ever done, and it probably wouldn't happen again.

Although the feat of sending it that far was awesome, there was still a fight going on. With everyone staring at the tank and the smoke it made, it was easy to finish off the last tank in the area by crushing it with my front left arm. After that, there was a line of infantrymen who were just starting to realize the situation that they were in, but it was too late for the ones close to me. Spinning around again with my tail on the sand, I swept that area, taking out at least one entire company, sending their bodies flying.

The others in the forest didn't waste any time when they saw me attacking. They took the opportunity to start pushing forward through a cloud of smoke created by Charlie's Destruction magic. All the soldiers in the smoke were subsequently torn apart by Marie and Regius within seconds. There went another company. If things continued like this, then the forest would be easily protected, but it wasn't going to happen. Not all good things could last. But for right now, we made the most of their blunder by allowing them to be distracted. They should be reduced to about half their force in the next two hours or so. The time for me to leave came sooner than expected, as there was an explosion behind me.

"Bryce, the helicopters are here," Albert shouted as loud as he could from the base of my neck. It was time to move.

"Got it," I said as I took off from the ground, leaving the soldiers to Charlie's strong group.

I turned around to see how many I was fighting, and there were forty. Nope, thirty-nine. Albert had just blown up the closest one. *This is going to be hard.* I yelled for Albert to hold on for dear life.

Every single one of them fired several rockets at us. Even with the enormous propulsion of my wings on the ground, I wasn't fast enough to dodge all of them. At least half of them hit my side. It definitely hurt, but it wasn't even close to the power required to crack the scales, which was good. As my wings continued to flap, the remaining rockets continued to follow us. They were heat seekers. There were at least twenty of them coming at us. This was going to be really annoying.

Flying straight up was the only option at that time, and so that's what happened—I flew straight up. To my amazement, it had already been over two hours since I jumped off the cliff, which became a problem, as I was starting to get tired. There wasn't that much time left to fight today; it was almost four already.

That wasn't the thing to worry about, as there were twenty heat-seeking rockets coming at us. Now was the time to see if becoming a dragon really meant being one.

CHAPTER
36

This whole situation was both exhilarating and extraordinarily frightening, especially after losing Shane. Last night we were reminded that we weren't invincible.

Sitting down behind one of the buildings at the beginning of the town, I reloaded my gun. It had been an UMP at the beginning of the fight, but there were no more bullets for it, so one of the extra SCARs we brought became mine. This was actually starting to be interesting. We would probably have to retreat into the town soon if we didn't want to be overrun, as there were still two tanks left. They were really annoying too, as they continued to destroy our cover.

Having Bryce deal with them right now would be really nice, but as I looked over at the forest, it seemed as if he had his hands full. He probably wasn't going to be available for the rest of the time, since there looked to be around twenty-five helicopters right on him. Refocusing on our fight, I turned the corner of the house, put up a shield with my right hand, and fired my SCAR with my left while making my way to the other side of the road. One of the remaining two tanks fired at me but stopped five feet ahead because of the shield. If it hadn't been for that, it would have ripped me in half. However, since it had fired at me and it had been caught, it was over for that tank.

I sent everything in my shield right back at them, destroying the tank and killing about twenty soldiers at the same time. Now the fight was a lot easier, as we didn't have to deal with two of them, but the last tank was more advanced than the previous twelve and was located toward the middle of the soldiers. This meant that four hundred soldiers stood between us and the tank. Only Bryce would be able to deal with that.

I looked over again toward Bryce and the others, and the fight with the helicopters had just started. The smoke from the first exploded helicopter was still in the air, and Bryce was flying straight up with about twenty rockets coming after him. As they were about to hit him, he did the most amazing thing.

He breathed pure red fire at them, hot enough to make all but the farthest two from him explode from the heat. He then spun sideways, just barely dodging them, and headed straight toward us with the two rockets close behind. He must have noticed that there was only one tank left on our side, as he changed his course to head straight for it. If he didn't pull up soon, he was going to slam directly into the ground, but that looked like it was part of the plan.

Just as he was about to hit the ground, he pulled up parallel to the ground at almost twenty feet above. I saw Albert on his back, holding on for dear life and looking as though he was about to crap himself from the stress of holding on. Also, when he pulled up, the two remaining rockets slammed into the tank, ending the crew inside and the couple of soldiers near it—not to mention that Bryce's flyby caused a huge gust of wind to push practically all of the soldiers down into the desert sand. Now we went on the offensive against these guys.

Looking up at Jessica and Annabeth, who were both on top of a small building, I signaled for them to push forward with everything they had. Argentum came running over to me, prepared to push forward with me by her side. It struck me as odd that the entire Slăve force wasn't there attacking us. We were only fourteen people, and if they attacked with full force, they could probably win. It wasn't as if it was bad for us, but the commander might have not been in the right thinking right now. It might have had something to do with how Bryce rattled him earlier today. Maybe he was trying to keep as many people alive as possible, but more of them would die because of his foolishness. There were so many possibilities, but the general in charge could have just been a coward.

Jessica, Annabeth, and Argentum had already begun to move forward, leaving me behind. Jessica started moving forward by sending a horizontal line of blue flame toward the soldiers, making them duck and killing some. Then she shot another line of flame that hit the sand and created a smoke screen. Before moving forward, Annabeth gave all of us, except for Argentum, a giant shield of pure ice to move forward. Argentum was already ahead of us, dealing with all the soldiers in the smoke as either a tiger or a gorilla. She made quick work of them and was back to us rather quickly, leaving behind what looked like mangled bodies.

As we traveled out of the smoke, about a thousand soldiers were still in front of us, but most were already retreating, much to my chagrin. That didn't stop the zealots though. They immediately fired at us, but Annabeth was able to get her ice shield up, protecting her and Jessica, while I was able to get my shield up before the bullets got there, protecting Argentum, who was right behind me. After sending all the bullets back, Jessica sent another line of blue flame, making the soldiers drop, which bought Annabeth enough time to create a giant shield of two-foot-thick ice.

The barrier that she put up turned out to survive the entire day, even in the heat of the desert. Not once did a bullet go through the ice, and we ended up making our own shooting holes later so that we wouldn't have to lean around the corners to shoot. It wasn't the greatest spot, as the others couldn't effectively use their powers from it, and that caused the fight to last a lot longer than we had wanted it to. But it did the job, and there was no complaining on my part. The only plus was that my orbs could go right through the ice without damaging it.

CHAPTER
37

They were magnificent—the way they worked together as a group and didn't back down even when they were so ridiculously outnumbered. If these kids were in a different situation and they had a normal life, every one of them would become successful—Charlie's hidden intelligence, Marie's caring, Argentum's tenacity, Scarlet's looks and brains, and not to mention Bryce's leadership, and that was only the tip of the iceberg. They would have all had something to offer the world, and they probably would have changed it for the better without violence, but that was not the situation we were in. I truly believed that if we survived this, they would change the world for the better for magic users like themselves.

Their fight was worthy of praise. They were so far beyond me or anyone on the battlefield right now, especially with Jessica's fire and Annabeth's ice. Bryce deserved more of a mention than those two because of the pure size, strength, and power he had as a dragon, but he was on such a higher level than anyone else there that it was not even fair. Despite his power, he could still be overwhelmed with sheer numbers. Evidence of this was in the sky with him fighting what looked like nineteen or twenty helicopters. Although he had destroyed half of them by now, it was obvious that he was starting to get tired, and he might not be able to keep it up much longer.

For some reason, I felt that Bryce would find a way to win and protect everyone. He may have thought that he was hiding it well from the others, but I'd seen enough people like him to know that even though he was unemotional and kept most people at a distance, he viewed all of us as his family, and he loved every one of us unconditionally. When the time came, when enough of us died or a certain someone died, he would break, and seeing his true power would be exciting.

"Hey, Erik, stop freaking daydreaming and fire back. Jeez!" Charlie shouted at me from a nearby tree.

He was right. This wasn't the time or the place to be daydreaming, especially when I had bullets firing in my direction. *Even without offensive powers, I am not powerless.* Putting it to the test for the umpteenth time, I peered around the tree, located three soldiers right away, and fired three quick shots. *Boom! Boom! Boom!* All three of the shots hit their targets square through the head, and they were dead instantly.

After a few more minutes of fighting from the forest, Charlie again blew up the sand to make a cloud, which allowed Marie and Regius to again devastate at least fifty soldiers in the smoke cloud. This also allowed me to take care of four soldiers in the smoke with the manacle and my gun. This was the fourth time we'd done this, and the results weren't as good. Previously we'd gotten at least eighty soldiers in total. But it didn't really matter, as we were still advancing and slowly trimming down their numbers. They had only about four or five hundred soldiers left in this area, and the number seemed to be about the same in the town. Today's fighting was almost over. The soldiers were getting increasingly more passive in their attacks, and some were even starting to pull back. They were going to be in full retreat soon!

CHAPTER
38

This was really starting to piss me off. The helicopters had been circling and firing at me for the past half hour without making a single mistake, and I hadn't been able to get close to any of them. Albert was about to pass out too from using his magic so much, but he was doing an excellent job at protecting me as best he could. He'd even been able to blow up most of the rockets that had been shot at me.

Even with him lessening the damage, it was still a big problem, as they were hitting their marks once every ten minutes after the heat seekers. This amounted to twenty hits on me in various spots all over my body. If there weren't bruises on my body after this fight, then I'd take it as a blessing from God.

Albert then blew up another rocket that was heading straight at my head. Using the smoke from the exploded rocket, I went straight through it and chomped down, hoping to get something. It looked like luck was on my side. The entire front end of a helicopter was in my mouth. I spit the destroyed helicopter out of my mouth, and it was apparent that the two pilots weren't in there. Either I had swallowed them, or they had already fallen to their deaths. Either way, it wasn't important; while I was in the dragon form, people were tasteless to me. It was weird to think about that.

With their formation finally broken after getting that helicopter, it was time to wreak havoc on the remaining seventeen helicopters for the last fifty minutes of the day. First up were the two closest ones who made the mistake of being too close to my wingspan and being too close together. Without giving them a millisecond to react, I inverted myself upward and slammed my wings together. The resulting force of wind caused the two helicopters to slam together and spiral down toward the ground. They crashed and burned in the desert not thirty seconds later. I could hear Albert screaming as he held on, but I trusted him to not let go.

The remaining sixteen helicopters knew better than to get too close, and they immediately backed off and made a giant circle around me. It was annoying since I couldn't get close to them to do anything, and my fire couldn't reach that far quite yet, although it was increasing in distance with every use.

Then three of the helicopter pilots who were right in front of me fired rockets dead at me, and there was no way for Albert to blow all of them up in his tired state. Taking that into account, I told him to hold onto me with all of his might. When the rockets were less than one hundred feet away, I lifted the right side of my body, tilting to the left, and then propelled myself as hard as possible in the opposite direction, making me spin in midair.

The three rockets that were fired at me missed by about ten feet to the left, five feet above Albert's head, and eight feet to the right of my right wing. All in all, it was pretty damn cool that it even worked. However, while regaining my balance in the air, Albert threw up on me. I couldn't really blame him. It was surprising that he even stayed on me through all this so far, to be honest.

One of the helicopters behind me started creeping up. It was right over my tail, and Albert yelled to me about its location. I turned to face the helicopter, and it immediately froze as the pilots made eye contact with me. In that split second that they were motionless, I whipped my tail up, wrapped it around the helicopter, and crushed it. After that the helicopters and soldiers began to pull back. They should have kept up the attack, but they didn't. This was a gift.

None of us got much sleep that night, all of us being too on edge. However, some sleep was better than none at all.

CHAPTER
39

The next morning everyone was back in their assigned spots; they never actually left them from the day before. Some of them had gone to the other side to see loved ones or check up on others. We were just waiting for the soldiers to make a move. We could take the fight to them, but we weren't nearly powerful enough to do that and get most of us out alive. Instead we made them come to us, and that was better for us anyway.

It was a suspiciously calm morning, but as soon as the thought crossed my mind, reality came crashing down. Out of nowhere, what looked like two missiles came into sight, one going for the town and the other for the forest. As the first one to spot them, I shouted at Lucy to link me up to everyone. "Scarlet! I'm coming to get you. You're going to have to send back the missiles coming at us. Everyone else, take cover just in case we fail."

I jumped off the cliff without Albert, changed instantly into my gigantic red-scaled dragon, and headed for Scarlet in town. Again the transformation hurt beyond belief, but it wasn't anything compared to the torture from them, and they never made me scream out in pain.

It took me thirty seconds to arrive in town, and by then the missiles were only about ninety seconds away from impacting. It took another thirty seconds for Scarlet to get on and get secured. They were only a minute away now. Our only chance to avoid them exploding was for Scarlet to send them back at the same time, but they had to be right next to each other, and they weren't. One of them was going to explode unless we did something amazing or really stupid.

"Scarlet! Trust me." That was all I said before heading for the missiles.

Although it was likely to work, I thought the pain that would be inflicted on me would probably be worse than anything I'd ever felt, but now was the time to see how hard dragon scales really were.

There were fifteen seconds until they got within reach. I spun horizontally and stretched my body as far as it could go to cover the maximum distance. Five seconds. Four ... three ... two ... one ... zero. The missiles were within a couple of feet of us. Scarlet was just barely able to get into position on my head, catch the missile with her shield, and send it right back from where it came. It had gotten so close to impacting my head that I could read what the soldiers had painted on the side of it: *Go die in hell, Devil Dragon.*

As if to add insult to injury, the missile that was supposed to hit my tail missed and started flying toward the town. We recovered as fast as we could, and we were after the speeding missile with only about ten seconds to catch up to it. There was no way we were going to catch up, so we proceeded to do something stupid. Scarlet, who had been on my head after sending the first missile back, jumped in front of my mouth and landed on one of my teeth. She patted my nose, and this told me what to do. I spun my head to the right and jerked it forward, sending her right in front of the missile. There she did the incredible by catching the rocket with her shield. She had one hand outstretched and the other hand on her arm, holding it steady with a look of complete concentration on her face and nothing but her pure will to succeed in her eyes. Then she sent the missile right back to its senders.

As she was falling the last thirty feet to the desert ground, I reached out with all my power and caught her with my left front leg. She didn't hit the ground and instead went into my arm as my body hit the ground. A couple of the houses closer to the desert were destroyed because of the crash. Luckily, both Scarlet and I were okay.

As if things couldn't get worse, my assumption that the Slăve had other magic users was proven correct. Over seventy thousand soldiers appeared a little over half a mile from us with at least ninety tanks, and it looked to be the same by the forest. Dropping Scarlet off by the others, I sped off up to the cliff and threw Albert onto my back. We both turned to face the horde of helicopters that were now in front of us—at least one hundred—and a dragon that rivaled me in size. This was now very interesting.

CHAPTER
40

"What the hell? Where did they come from?" I heard Regius ask as the soldiers seemed to appear out of nowhere less than a quarter mile from us.

"Doesn't matter," I shouted back. "Just be ready to move. I'm throwing up a smoke screen."

Nodding to him as if to tell him to get ready to move, I leaned around the trunk of the tree and touched the sand there. One of the soldier's shots grazed my left shoulder. It hurt but wasn't terrible—definitely not enough to make me yell and not even close to enough pain to stop me from giving us cover. All my focus was on making the sand explode.

Nothing was going to stop the sand from exploding as my hand connected with it. Not even a second later, a gigantic cloud of sand was in front of us. With this new cover, we took the opportunity to move back in the woods and run over to our attacker's right. It was easy for us to move as a group, and for the most part we never really had to talk to each other, because we always knew what each other was doing. I was usually the only one to talk, and it was never out loud. Lucy had linked me up with her and Scarlet, as we were the leaders of our two teams.

"Lucy! Can you tell me how many of them are near us or at least a rough estimate with the tanks also, please?" I said through the telepathic link.

"Don't expect me to count them, but if I had to guess, I'd say around seventy thousand soldiers with at least eighty tanks. Don't give in," she said.

All that was available for me to do was to forget the numbers and focus on winning against them and not dying in the process. As we reached an area close to 150 feet from where we were previously, we looked out of the forest and fired at them with both our guns and our magic. We dropped a few hundred of them before they realized where we were.

"Go wreak havoc with the soldiers, Connor. Do whatever you can, but don't be dumb," I shouted at him, and he simply nodded before disappearing.

We began to move after Connor left. The tanks knew where we were, and we couldn't do anything against them, so we had to either continue what we were doing or retreat into the forest. Neither choice was the clear favorite in my mind, but now it was up to the others to decide.

"Do you guys want to keep moving around, or do you want to lure them into the forest?" I shouted to everyone.

In complete unison, they shouted back at me, "Lure them into the forest!"

Their unanimous response was unexpected, but they had remembered something that I had not—we had both Connor and Bryce out there, and if we could buy a couple of hours in the forest to let them deal with the tanks, we could definitely win this. We couldn't just go right into the forest, so we moved around a few more times to make them think that we were planning on staying. We weren't able to do all that much damage to them, as the tanks were on high alert, with several of them exploding and one even firing on another one. *Thank God for Connor.* Still, there were too many tanks out there, and each time we moved they found our location after we began shooting.

The tactic was over, and we ever so slowly trickled back into the forest, giving the false impression of retreat. Connor had already taken care of seven tanks, and Bryce had taken out four tanks and one thousand soldiers. This left around sixty-three thousand soldiers and at the most sixty-nine tanks left to deal with.

They took their sweet time coming after us, but they eventually did, and that was a mistake on their part. They were at a complete disadvantage, as we knew everything about this area and what animals not to piss off and where they were. It also helped that both Marie and Regius were here. They could help direct the animals. We'd still have to fight, of course, but it would be a lot easier for us. But holding our ground didn't mean anything if Scarlet's group couldn't hold theirs.

CHAPTER

41

It was one o'clock in the afternoon, and my group was already exhausted. Everyone had thrown up at least once, myself included. We really needed something to stop the fighting; otherwise, we weren't going to make it to the end of the day. It also didn't help that the tanks were destroying the ice that was protecting us. Although Annabeth's ice was as hard as diamonds, it could still be destroyed eventually. We were in way over our heads. The only thing that was keeping us alive was that Annabeth, Jessica, Argentum, and I were all doing our specific jobs. Most importantly we kept the soldiers at a relative distance from us so that those grenades that had disrupted Shane's magic couldn't be used on us.

Considering how many times I had to run from side to side and how long we had been there, we didn't receive that many injuries. However, my luck did eventually run out. As I was running to Argentum's side between the houses, a bullet went through my butt at a weird angle, grazing the other butt cheek, as well. I screamed like a little girl, and Argentum came running. She patched me up the best she could in only a minute or two. She didn't use her magic so as to conserve her energy.

We got pushed into the town shortly after that, and we all fought side by side. I heard Annabeth scream out in pain, and she grabbed her arm. Her gun had been shot, and the shrapnel from the gun had gone into her arm. As she screamed and writhed on the ground, I pulled her behind cover and put my shields up so that Argentum could help her. My shields got so many bullets that it was a miracle they hadn't killed us already. Jessica and Argentum went around the other side of our cover and hit the soldiers as fast and as hard as they could before sprinting back. As soon as they were out of my range, I fired all the bullets caught in my shield back at the soldiers. This took out so many, but it didn't get us out of the woods.

The distinctive sound of rail gun shell whistled behind Jessica and Argentum, into the building next to them. The building subsequently exploded outward and got the girls in their backs. Both of them were wounded but somehow got their way into cover. I poked my head back out and fired several haywire bullets into the crowd of soldiers before Annabeth erected a giant slab of ice and kicked it at the soldiers falling on them and the tank destroying them all. Immediately after that she erected another giant slab of ice in front of us to protect us. Both Jessica and Argentum were able to go on and fight, but they needed attention fast. Argentum had a rather big piece of wood in her shoulder, and Jessica had one in her hamstring, along with a couple of small ones in her back. All the pieces were subsequently removed. Argentum couldn't heal without being out of the fight, so instead we used Annabeth to freeze the wounds closed.

It didn't look as if Bryce was doing much better than we were. He looked dead tired, and he was moving slowly, even for a dragon as big as he was. He looked to be only around five hundred feet above the ground instead of his usual two thousand feet. The helicopters needed to refuel soon, so he'd probably get a reprieve at that time. If I was the commander, it would be an easy decision to just send another sixty helicopters up there and then have the remaining forty helicopters come back. Then that happened. Another thirty helicopters appeared to be coming toward Bryce. He was going to be tired, and Albert was probably having just as hard of a time. At least he got up the balls to give us a strafing run against the soldiers in front of us.

CHAPTER

42

All that Albert and I had been doing for the last four hours was fighting the helicopters and the dragon. They wouldn't stop. They kept coming after us with no restraint, and now that the original group would be out of fuel, another group of thirty helicopters showed up to replace them. However, the dragon that was in the air with them didn't need a break, so it kept coming after me, giving me no chance to rest. As we connected in midair, we could see the shock waves coming from us and the blood that each of us caused the other to leak. The situation didn't improve at all now that the dragon had support from the helicopters while I had nothing.

To protect Albert from the fire, I had to do a lot more spinning than usual. My chest had to face them for most of the time. My underbelly scales were stronger than any metal on earth, but they were still weaker than the scales on every other part of my body and could probably break if hit enough. It was unlikely that they knew about this, but they took advantage of my exposed underbelly and opened fire with rockets and machine guns. They didn't break through, and most of them missed anyway because of the dodging, but the ones that made contact hurt a lot more than usual. The dragon took full advantage of that, biting me, breathing fire on me, or hitting me—the latter happening the most. Any damage they did to me though was reciprocated ten-fold.

As the fighting for the day continued, it got increasingly more difficult to deal with the dragon and the helicopters. The dragon was smart. It didn't attack me all out all the time, but it let the helicopters run interference against me and only struck when an opening appeared. It made them incredibly hard to deal with, but when they attacked I always counterattacked at least once or twice.

More concerning than my well-being was the condition of everyone else, especially since I hadn't been able to help as much today. They were probably in the same condition as Albert, which meant that they were also probably throwing up. The only two who wouldn't be throwing up would be Lucy and Taylor, who were just sniping without moving. They'd helped by spotting soldiers or killing them if they couldn't point them out well enough. They were probably good on ammo, seeing that Lucy was a great shooter, and Taylor was an even better spotter. Nonetheless, they were a very deadly and helpful team up there.

CHAPTER

43

Boom! Lucy managed to take another one down. That had to be around fifty today alone from over a half mile away. She was a prodigy, and she stopped asking for help around the fifteenth or sixteenth kill. She started doing it without any wind or distance calculations. She missed only twice. If it wasn't for this war, she would probably have been an Olympic shooter.

Lucy had completely changed since Shane died. Her demeanor had always been bright, happy, and energetic, and she kept us all upbeat. But since he died, she had lost her brightness and happiness. At least she had kept her energy. She had become what Bryce was like when I first met him. He never talked to anyone but Connor and kept a straight face, never showing any emotion. Lucy used to hate killing or hurting anything, but when Shane was killed, she completely changed. The sniping she'd done had been magnificent, but she hadn't changed her expression since we began yesterday, and when we ate, she went into her tent and ate by herself.

Spotting for her had become just sightseeing and taking pictures with the camera that Annabeth had scavenged almost a year ago. It had solar rechargeable batteries, so power had never been an issue. However, the camera didn't have enough zoom to get any action besides Bryce, but when the lens was through the spotter scope, it got pretty good pictures somehow. This had led to eight pictures each of Scarlet's and Charlie's groups fighting. There were still over twenty available pictures left too. We used this once before to take a group photo before the fighting with the GROM unit on the first day. It was the only thing that helped us to remember everyone, and it would be made into a photo one day no matter what happened to me.

I looked around the battlefield, from Scarlet's group in the town to Charlie's group in the forest. It looked like half the soldiers on Charlie's side were fighting in the forest. This was a good thing for Charlie and his group. They were by far the best at making regular traps and using the forest as an effective battlefield. The remaining tanks on that side couldn't do anything from outside the forest to help the soldiers inside of it, so the soldiers were at an even bigger disadvantage. It also looked like some of the tanks were blowing up on their own too, or they were randomly firing at their counterparts and then blowing up. Connor was the only explanation.

At least twelve thousand soldiers came sprinting out of the forest, passing the tanks going back. The soldiers who were outside of the tanks, numbering around forty thousand, followed their lead and retreated along with the tanks. Charlie's group was at the head of the forest, routing the soldiers who had attacked them.

I looked toward the Slăve camp. Right above them was a rocket that was coming right for Charlie's group. Bryce was almost two miles away at the mountain and wouldn't be able to reach them, so my only option was to tell Lucy to tell them. It looked like two of them had gone about one hundred feet in front of the forest and were uncovered. Grabbing and flipping Lucy over to face me, I told her the situation as fast as humanly possible, and she got on it immediately.

It was just in time. When the rocket was only a thousand feet away from them, the two still in the forest ran forward. Now it was only five hundred feet away, and the two who ran forward grabbed the other two. One was thrown back to the forest, while the other one was covered up by the other. The rocket exploded too close in front of them, producing a huge cloud of sand. Two streams of light then burst into the air from the sand cloud. One was yellow, and the other was red. There was then a huge rush of power from the area.

CHAPTER

44

No, no, no. Why the hell is Marie running forward? Erik's too close to the tree line too; they need to get back now!

Lucy called out to me. "Charlie, there's a rocket coming for you guys. Get back to the forest, and take cover!"

It was too late for them to run for cover, and they couldn't hear my or Regius's calls for them to come back. There was only one option. I looked over at Regius, and we silently agreed to do it. Even if it meant our lives, we had to at least try to save them.

We rushed forward toward Erik and Marie. By the time we got to them, the rocket was only two seconds from hitting the ground. In those two seconds, Regius grabbed Erik and threw him almost three hundred feet back to the forest. It must have been the animal inside of him that caused that strength, but he was glowing red. *What is going on with him?* That kind of power wasn't in my possession, so all I could do was jump on top of Marie and hope that the woman I loved survived, even if it meant my death.

The next thing I knew there was a giant explosion and then nothing but yellow. I stood up after a couple of seconds, and the desert was still there. Marie was on the ground at my feet, unconscious but alive. There was a huge dust cloud from the explosion, and something red formed in front of me.

It was Regius. He was covered in black wolf's fur, he had fangs for teeth, and his hands were claws. Also, he was surrounded by a red aura that was shooting up into the sky. I saw a yellow light shooting up into the sky. It was mine. That was where the power was coming from, and we both had maximized our magic's potential, or EFFs.

Anger unlike any before rushed inside of me. *They tried to take my precious from me. They tried to kill Marie, and for what reason? There is none!* They were trying to kill her for being different and for fighting against people who wanted to kill us for being different. We were nothing but failures and outcasts in their eyes. *They will all die!*

As the dust cloud cleared, Regius and I saw the entire group of soldiers who had attacked us today. They were just waiting to be slaughtered. Regius boomed forward. He moved as fast as Bryce did when he was in his speed mode. Without even thinking about it, I thrust my hand into the sand and willed the entire front line of soldiers to explode.

They all exploded upward in pieces—over ten thousand targets that were over one thousand feet away; this was the power of an EFF. Regius was about one hundred feet away from them, and he kept moving to the next line of soldiers, knowing that the path was clear for him. Next for me were the tanks.

Before I could repeat what happened with the soldiers and destroy the tanks, a tank shot at me. It exploded next to me, and the shock wave was huge. There was no real damage to myself, but it then proceeded to reload. It had no time, and it knew it. My hand plunged into the ground, and by sheer force of will, all the tanks except for one exploded, and it was the one that had just fired at me. Before I could make my move, Connor appeared next to me and yelled that he was going to see if Erik and Marie were okay. I merely nodded before turning my head back to the tank.

It fired at me and did not miss. It hit me directly in the chest and sent me flying backward, but it didn't kill me. It caused a giant black mark that was starting to bruise, but no blood or cuts appeared. I was impenetrable. This was a game changer.

"Prepare to die!"

CHAPTER

45

After exploding toward the soldiers, there was only one thing on my mind: kill all the soldiers in front of me. There would be no peace for us if we didn't kill all of them. I hoped they were prepared to die, because there was no way that I was going to let any of them live.

The looks of terror in the soldiers' eyes were amazing. It was great to see how they looked when confronted by something they knew would kill them if they crossed the line. That was how it was when I was with Bryce. Seeing that expression on his face was exhilarating.

They all started firing at me, but it was too late, as I had already moved around them. In the next couple of seconds they were all dead— via my legs, my teeth, or my claws. It was a bloody mess—one hundred down and more than thirty thousand to go. This was really going to be something, and it was time to test my limits with this new power.

The speed was incredible. It was as if nothing could stop me, and all my previous limits were shattered. This must have been how Bryce felt when he fought. It was me though, and every one of the soldiers seemed so much slower than normal. This power was so much more than anything I had ever experienced, and it felt so good.

Booming forward to the next group of ten took less than a second. I stopped right in front of the lead runner, looked him dead in the eyes, and told him to die. They all raised their guns and began to fire at me. It was futile though, as all their bullets missed me. Either they were bad shots, or I could see the bullets coming at me, and that made them easy to dodge.

I moved around, and the bullets were no problem. It was time to show them why it was a bad idea to ever screw with us. I then attacked the closest one. My claws went clean across his chest, and they severed at least two major arteries. He was dead before the others realized what had just happened. My next victim was the next closest. To finish him, I spun on the toes of my left foot and roundhouse kicked him in the neck, crushing his windpipe and flinging him backward five feet. He flew into one of his teammates, and they knocked heads. The guy was out cold and might be dead, but it was too hard to tell, and there wasn't enough time to check. Next up were the two right next to the guy who was just hit by his flying friend. They were distracted by the flying body, and by the time they looked up, it was too late for them. My claws had already done enough damage for them to be dead twice over. It was now time for the other five, who were behind me.

They didn't stand a chance. I exploded backward with my elbows up. This instantly took out two of them. It was pure luck that they were both right where my elbows would hit their necks. The next one got taken out by my kick to the side of his head. His head snapped at a weird angle, and he collapsed to the ground. The one next to him dodged my punch aimed for his head and survived, but following through with the punch put me right next to the other guy. The only thing that came to mind was to head-butt him. He fell back onto his butt, dazed and spinning around. The guy who had somehow dodged my punch was too slow this time around. My claws again swiped across his chest and severed at least two arteries.

I turned around to face the final guy. He fired his gun, producing at least thirty giant booms. They all struck home in my chest and sent me staggering backward, but there was no blood, only a pounding on my chest. The bullets were halfway in my skin and halfway out. I wasn't bulletproof—more like bullet resistant. This made me laugh—a good and hearty laugh that had the last soldier looking at me with pure terror in his eyes. I then picked him up by his neck and threw him as hard as possible back toward the forest. He landed about ten feet from Erik, who then proceeded to finish him off with his gun before he could realize what had just happened.

I turned back toward the ever-closing mass of the thirty thousand soldiers. It was now time to really test my new powers. I heard a giant rumble, and then at least half the soldiers in front of me were consumed by explosions. It must have been Charlie. I turned around to see him with his arm in the sand right next to a tank with the hatch open. After pulling his hand out of the sand, he resembled a ghost. He looked so tired and worn out. He then went behind the tank in a hurry and probably retched, but he was back in front of the tank within a couple of seconds, using the tank to support himself.

He would recover. Now it was my turn with the big group. I boomed forward toward the mass of soldiers. There was a bit of terror in my stomach, but it quickly faded as my fight with them began. Kicking, slashing, jumping, grabbing, throwing, and overwhelming pain were the only things I knew for the next fifteen minutes. There was so much blood everywhere, and at least two-thirds of the once-massive group of soldiers in front of me were dead. Their forces went from fifty thousand to under nine thousand in less than twenty minutes. This was the power of an EFF.

It couldn't last, and I could feel the power fading. The red aura surrounding me that was once bright was not much more than a dim fading light. My body felt like it weighed ten times what it usually did, and it was moving incredibly slow, although my speed was probably back to normal. I tried to finish off the remaining two soldiers, but one of them popped a grenade, and it exploded in my face. All the magic in me vanished.

This sucked, but at least I took a lot of them with me. One of the soldiers about thirty feet away raised his gun at me. It wasn't the end for me, not quite yet. I was going to fight to the very end.

Boom!

"What in God's name was that?" I said with reanimated strength.

I turned around to see a tank charging right at me. Was it going to run me over? It stopped a mere two feet away from me. The hatch opened, and out popped Charlie.

"Look what I found," he said with a grin that stretched from ear to ear.

"Yeah, I see that. What now?" I asked with actual curiosity. *What possible use could we have with a tank now?*

"We use it to blow up the tent with their communication systems. Then we take it back to the forest and park it for later use." He said this as if he was taking the tank out for an afternoon spin.

But when will I ever get to ride in a tank? "Sure, why not? Let's get it done," I said while climbing into the tank.

Charlie sat in the driver's seat, so it was only natural for me to sit in the seat that controlled the cannon fire. It looked really complicated to me, but Charlie explained how to aim and then fire. He made it look like it was a child's toy, but it made perfect sense to me, so why not go with it? To test it out, I aimed it at one of the closer tents that were still at least a quarter mile away.

The cannon fired just as easily as he said it would, but my aim was off, as I had forgotten to compensate for the drop. The shot missed the tent by at least one hundred feet, maybe more. It was hard to tell from the distance. With the next shot, nothing needed to be redone, as we had covered the distance it had previously missed. So when I fired the next shot, it was a direct hit on the tent. There wasn't much of an explosion, which was disappointing, but at least it hit its target.

Now we had to find out what tent had their communication system in it so that we could blow it up. Apparently, when I asked Charlie how we were going to find this out, he said that he already knew where it was. Taylor had asked Argentum through Lucy where that might be, and then they told him where it was. It was located at the back of the camp, exactly three rows in and in the dead middle of the row. It was going to be hard to find a spot with a clear line of sight, and we didn't exactly have the time, so we had to hurry.

Not five minutes later, we found the perfect spot from which to fire at the tent. Charlie stopped right there, and the cannon was already turned toward the target, so we just had to compensate for the drop of the shot. We did this in ten seconds, but in those ten seconds, a soldier was able to run up and put charges on the rails of the tank. I was able to fire the cannon before it exploded, shaking the tank left and right.

The explosion caused a huge cloud of smoke in the tent. It had been a direct hit, but now we were stranded, and we were being surrounded. The soldiers then started running away or getting behind something thick.

"Wonder why they're running away" escaped my lips when I already knew the answer.

"Because helicopters are coming for us," Charlie said, peeking his head outside the hatch.

"Hell of a way to go out."

CHAPTER

46

After Charlie and Regius died, the fight died down as we pushed the soldiers back. They had ordered a retreat after that for everyone. Even the dragon and helicopters pulled back. We pulled back and gave Charlie and Regius a proper grave, even though we couldn't recover their bodies.

He didn't sleep again. I could see it in his eyes and the way he carried himself. It was as if he had been thinking for a thousand years, and his eyes looked tired. His body seemed to be preparing for something. *For what? And why would it keep him up all night?* This war we were involved in was bringing out weirder things every day. It was like everything went to hell, and the multiverse was determined to screw with us.

It felt even more real and devastating to think about when we were around the graves of Shane, Charlie, and Regius. Each one of us was silent and in mourning as we stood in front of the graves of our friends in the early hours of the morning. The only one who was not there was Lucy, as she was at the cliff conducting overwatch for us as we mourned. I didn't think she wanted to be here anyway. She was still in denial about Shane's death. We were there for a half hour before Bryce said anything.

"We should keep the groups as they are, but someone from Scarlet's group will have to go over to Marie's group now," Bryce said, looking at me.

"I agree. My proposition is that you let me ride you today."

"Okay, where will everyone go then?"

"Albert will go to Marie's group, and I will ride on your back today. Also, Jessica goes to Marie's group, and Erik comes to mine."

"That's fine with me. Marie, are you okay with that?"

All she did was nod her head in agreement. She didn't seem to be in the mood to speak to anyone, and no one could blame her. The heart knows no limits for sorrow, so we were just thankful that all she was doing was ignoring us. I hoped she didn't try to do something crazy now.

The groups set out, one to the forest and the other to the city. A couple of minutes after they left, Taylor and Lucy went to the cliff, and we accompanied them. We would wait there until there was any movement from the other camp.

We sat there in silence, just watching and waiting, until finally, around eleven o'clock, a single military truck came from their camp. It had a white flag on the side of it. A Slăve symbol was on the side of it too, so it wasn't a fake, as far as we could tell.

"Lucy, can you tell if there's anyone in it?" I asked.

"Two people, both women, but I can't tell if they're armed or not."

"They do have a white flag raised on the side of the car, so don't kill them," she stated without looking away from her scope.

"Hey, they stopped a few hundred feet from the town. What do you think they're doing?" Lucy asked aloud.

"They're waiting for me or at least someone to talk to," Bryce said.

He was bent over right behind us. He scared both Taylor and me, as the last time we saw him he was leaning up against a tree, spacing out into his own world.

Straightening up his back, he looked at me and said, "Best not to keep them waiting. Let's go." He smiled innocently.

"Let's go then."

Bryce grabbed me and jumped off the cliff toward the truck.

We landed in front of the truck, and the driver's side door opened. Then the door behind it opened, as well. Two women proceeded to get out of the truck. They were both unarmed, but I got the feeling that they were prepared for the worst if it went that way for them. They seemed to be cautious as they got out of the car and looked at Bryce in his gigantic dragon form. Both groups just sat there and waited for me to get up, and Bryce lowered his head to the ground to make it easy for me to get off. He then changed back into his human form. This wouldn't have been a problem if we hadn't forgotten his extra clothes, so he was entirely naked.

We noticed this way too late, as he was standing beside me—naked—and right in front of the two soldiers. He acted as if this was completely normal for him and that there was nothing to worry about. He was standing there with a straight face, arms crossed, and feet spread, so absolutely nothing was hidden. What made it worse were the faces of the two soldiers in front of us. They were initially disgusted by the scars, but then their eyes lowered, and their disgust transformed into curiosity and that pissed me off.

"He's mine. Back off." The words escaped my mouth before I realized what was happening, and Bryce laughed.

"I never thought I would see the day where you got jealous." He chuckled. "I just didn't expect you to be the type," he continued, making me blush and look away.

"I'm not jealous. I'm just establishing my position on the matter," I said, trying to level my voice.

He laughed even harder before saying, "So you're really jealous. Never thought I would see the day," he chuckled a little after that but stopped as soon as he saw me giving him the stink eye. Noticing that he held up his hands in defeat but gave me a smirk that was just begging to be punched off.

"Well, if you guys are done being all lovey and annoying, we actually have business to discuss, and it would be much appreciated if you would comply," the taller of the two women said.

She was about my height, but she had shorter legs. Her hair was a pretty blonde color, and she had pale blue eyes. The other woman was a lot shorter, maybe five feet three inches, and her hair was jet black mixed with some gray, and her eyes were a dark brown. She looked to be around forty, while the other one was twenty-five max.

"So what was it you were planning on talking to us about?" Bryce asked.

"Our commanding officer would like to suspend the fighting for today in order to get all the dead home to their families," the taller one said.

"So what exactly are you asking us for? You could've just done that without telling us," Bryce said.

"He knows, but he wanted us to tell you so that you don't attack us while we're sending dead soldiers back to their families," she said.

"Okay, your message is received. Now leave," Bryce said rather candidly.

Neither said anything as they left.

I got the feeling that there was a lot more to their transporting the dead back to their base and then to their families. They had to be planning something more, but for now we couldn't worry about it, as we needed to rest. Bryce didn't look happy about this at all. As a matter of fact, it looked as if he was even more serious than before.

"You think something's up, don't you?" I asked him.

"Yeah, I do, but I think that they're sincere about not fighting today. They're probably planning on bringing more soldiers back when their transport helicopters come back. Or at least that's what I would do," he said, looking at their camp with his arms crossed and his weight shifted to one side—still naked.

"There isn't much we can do, is there?" I asked.

"No, there isn't. We can't just up and destroy their helicopters that are transporting the dead, even when they're coming back. That would piss too many people off and as much as I hate to say it we'll need people out there, political and otherwise, to support us if we want to live peacefully. We're in a no-win situation really," he said.

"So, what now?" I asked.

"Well, you and I can go back to the cliff, and the others should stay in their positions for now, at least," he said and began to walk back toward the cliff.

"Bryce, you're still naked. Couldn't you change and we just fly back?"

"I could, but I want the sun. It's good for the skin."

That was it. That was the conversation. *God, sometimes this man …* It wasn't like I could stop him though, so I sighed and walked with him.

CHAPTER

47

As we made our way back to the cliff, the uneasy feeling I had gotten earlier only grew stronger, and my gut was telling me that my earlier assumption would prove to be right. They would bring more soldiers and supplies back today when the helicopters came back from dropping off their wounded and dead back at their base or hospitals. We needed to finish the fight soon, because if they did bring back soldiers and supplies, we wouldn't be able to hold out much longer. But we would fight to the end no matter what.

Of the people who were originally captured, only Annabeth, Marie, Lucy, Connor, and I remained, and all of us knew exactly what was at stake if we were captured. We didn't ever want to go back to that hell, and I doubted we would ever be able to recover if we did, especially with the damage we'd done—not to mention that a lot of people would be looking for revenge. The girls would, unfortunately, fit the bill for them. I would personally never allow that to happen to any of them, even if it meant killing them.

We arrived at the cliff ninety minutes after talking to the soldiers. It usually took less time, but my knee was still sore from the rocket yesterday.

Lucy was in the same position that we had left her in, lying on the ground with the sniper rifle. Taylor was nowhere to be seen, but that was expected, as she still had to take care of the baby. In all honesty it surprised me that she even went out here.

As we walked up to the edge, Lucy turned her head from the scope, tossed me some clothes and asked, "What took you so long?"

"We walked," Scarlet answered as I got dressed.

"I've been waiting on you to tell me what the meeting was about so that I could tell everyone else what was up!"

I just stood there looking at her, not saying a word. Scarlet was right next to me, also not saying a word. We then looked at each other, back at Lucy, and back at each other again. Scarlet then nodded to me, and she headed back toward the camp. Once she disappeared into the forest, Lucy spoke up.

"You going to answer my question or not?" Her tone was surprising, something that I never thought would come from her mouth, but having someone who would literally die for you did things to people.

"They want the day off to take their dead back home. And before you say anything, yes, they'll more than likely be bringing soldiers back. We can't do anything though. It'll only make us look worse."

She looked like she was going to say something but stopped herself. With her not talking, I decided it was time to leave. Before I did, I stopped right at the edge of the forest on the cliff.

"Lucy, if you ever speak like that to me again, I'll remind you of the difference between us."

I didn't mean that at all, but if she was taking it out on me, it wouldn't be long before she started doing it to the others. That could not happen now.

Leaving her there in silence, I went back to the camp to be with Scarlet. It was obvious to me what was going to happen, but I wasn't going to stop it. If they had brought reinforcements in during the fight, then they wouldn't have even gotten close to landing. If I did it now, I would be beyond a terrible person, which was okay with me, in all honesty. However, attacking those who couldn't defend themselves was not something that would ever be on my résumé.

It wasn't long after arriving back at camp that Scarlet jumped me from behind. I knew that she was there the whole time, but sometimes it was better to let her have her way. That was exactly how it ended up playing out too. She took the initiative and the control out of my hands.

Once she got on top of me, however, I saw that she was crying. I sat up with Scarlet on my lap, and she was crying her eyes out. All I could do was hold her as tightly as possible and tell her that everything was going to be okay. But it was no use. She just wouldn't stop crying. She continued to convulse nonstop, the weight of everything coming down on her. After five minutes with no end in sight, there was only one thing left for me to do, and that was to sing as softly as possible to her. However, the number of songs available in my memory was next to none, so I ended up singing the song my dad sang to my mom whenever she had a nightmare.

You are my sunshine, my only sunshine.
You make me happy when skies are gray.
You never know, dear, how much I love you.
Please don't take my sunshine away.

The other night, dear, as I lay sleeping,
I dreamt I held you in my arms.
When I awoke, dear, I was mistaken,
So I hung my head, and I cried.

You are my sunshine, my only sunshine.
You make me happy when skies are gray.
You never know, dear, how much I love you.
Please don't take my sunshine away.

I'll always love you and make you happy—
If you will only say the same.
But if you leave me to love another,
You'll regret it all one day.

You are my sunshine, my only sunshine.
You make me happy when skies are gray.
You never know, dear, how much I love you.
Please don't take my sunshine away.

When I finished the song, Scarlet was fast asleep, and I went back to the cliff to help oversee the area with Lucy. After a couple of minutes of just standing there, an idea formed in my head about my power. It was about how, whenever I changed, I increased not only my strength and speed but also my eyesight and reaction time. What if I could control just my increased eyesight but nothing else? There was no record of that being done, but there was always a first time for everything. Hell, MO was the only person to be able to change into a dragon in Devil's Anger history before that military officer and then me, so what was to say I couldn't make one of my eyes change?

"Hey, Lucy, could you hand me the scope, please? I want to try something out," I said.

"Go ahead," she said, grabbing the scope and handing it to me.

I put the scope up to my eye and looked through it at the Slăve camp. It was smaller than I expected. Considering the camp was at least two miles away, it was a miracle that it was even seeable from here. I focused as hard as possible for my eyes to change, and they both did. The skin around my eyes evaporated to the bone and was replaced with my red scales. Even though it was only near the eyes that this happened, it hurt just as much as a regular transformation. After my skin changed to scales, my eyes changed. My pupils went from a circular shape to the shape of a cat's pupils, and that hurt a lot more than I remembered. However, my theory was proven true. I could change one part without changing my whole body. That wasn't the best part. My eyesight increased incredibly, and the Slăve camp now looked like it was less than one hundred feet away.

At their camp, there seemed to be increased activity. A lot more people were moving around than usual, but that was to be expected if they were really sending their wounded and dead home. That number must have been astronomical, but it still wasn't enough to win. Looking around the camp now, I felt an eerie silence of movement from everywhere else. The soldiers were probably in their tents, but there still should have been at least a couple moving about. The silence concerned me, but after viewing the entire area, I didn't see a real problem. I was just about to give the scope back to Lucy when something caught my eye.

Two people were walking toward us from one of the tents. What concerned me was that they weren't wearing any gear, and it didn't look like they were escaping in any way. The probability of their being magic users and working with the government usually wouldn't be high, but they had just walked out of one of those tents and were now walking toward us, as if it was nothing. More concerning was that everyone was asleep and now needed to be woken up. Changing my eyes back to normal, I handed the scope back to Lucy.

"Lucy, can you wake up Jessica, please?"

"Why?" she asked.

"Because there are two people coming from the enemy camp, and they're probably magic users for the government," I said, pointing to their location in the desert so she knew where to look.

After looking through the scope and finding the two people, she said, "I'll wake her," without even turning to face me. A couple of seconds later, she turned toward me and said, "She's up. A bit grumpy but up."

"That's fine."

"You want me to tell her about the two people, or do you want me to hook you in the message so you can tell them?" she asked.

"No, it's okay. Tell her yourself, but also tell her that Scarlet and I will be meeting her once they get to within one thousand feet of them."

My suspicion of them grew stronger. I believed they were trying to show off just how strong they were. They weren't concealing their magic powers; they were just letting them run wild, as if to say, "Prepare for battle." The showing off of their powers made me a little envious of them, as they didn't have to worry about the sensors detecting them and then soldiers coming to get them and/or kill them. They could do whatever they wanted with no worries of their families being hurt.

Their amount of power was starting to intrigue me. They weren't anywhere near my level, but it looked as if they would be a very good fight for Jessica versus the taller one on the left, who seemed to be a relatively high-class Devil's Anger user. The other one seemed to be a high Heaven's Justice user. If the government filled the spots of everyone who had escaped, these two would probably be the s0 and the s00. I would probably end up fighting them both, but knowing Jessica, if she came out to meet them with us, she'd want to fight one of them. She could win a one-on-one fight, but she would die if she tried to take them both on at the same time. Besides Jessica and me, only Annabeth, Scarlet, and Connor could win in a fight versus either of them.

After a minute of watching the two walking toward us, it was now time to move toward them. I walked over to Scarlet and gently shook her awake. She got up and grabbed my extra clothes that we had left here earlier. I walked over to Lucy to tell her to tell Jessica to come out if she wanted but to stay back and watch otherwise. Then I jumped off the cliff and changed into the dragon on the way down like before. The transformation was a lot less painful for me now, as my body had gotten used to the pain, like it had during the torture sessions while I was imprisoned.

I landed in the dragon form, climbed the side of the cliff like before, and put my head right next to the edge so that Scarlet could get on. She proceeded to get onto my head and then down to the base of my neck. We took off toward the two people in the desert. We noticed that Jessica was already in front of them, standing completely still with her magic in complete control, without letting out so much as a peep of energy in front of the two. Both had stopped in front of her, and the Devil's Anger user was looking her up and down, while the Heaven's Justice user was looking straight at Scarlet and me as we flew toward them. As we landed, both the government magic users had their eyes fixed on us. Jessica had her eyes toward them.

Scarlet made her way toward my tail and got off me that way. As soon as she was off, I changed back into a human, with no clothes on, in front of the government magic users. Judging by their expressions, they had never seen something like that—the dragon–human transformation—but it also probably had something to do with my having no clothes on. Scarlet gave me the clothes she had brought, which ended up being the shorts and T-shirt that Connor and I had stolen from the store after we escaped from the prison camp.

All five of us then stood in silence, facing each other. None of us indicated any need to move. Someone needed to speak up before we became statues. Scarlet heard my thoughts and decided to speak up at that moment.

"What do you want?" she asked.

"For you to die," the Devil's Anger user said.

He was quickly smacked on the back of the head by his shorter companion, who said, "We are here to fight you and your group, Devil Dragon."

"Why? You know you'll lose if we fight," I replied.

The taller one looked like he was about to speak up again, but he was cut off by the smaller one, who said, "You shouldn't be so candid when you say those types of things. It'll end up killing you one day."

"Fair enough," I responded. "But what—"

"Enough already! Let's start this," the taller one yelled as he boomed toward me.

His move would have been obvious to anyone, and he wasn't all that fast, maybe Mach 1. He would have died right there, but when he attacked me, Jessica had come out of nowhere and clobbered him on the right side of his face, sending him flying seventy or eighty feet to my right. Jessica chased after him. The Heaven's Justice user put his head in his hands, changed into his armor, and took out his sword and shield. He then boomed toward me, and he died then and there—but not by my hand, by Scarlet's.

Scarlet jumped in front of me as soon as he was moving. Once he was within a couple of feet, he swung his sword. As his sword came down toward her, she drew her M1911 pistol from her back and at the same time reached out with her hand to stop the sword with her magic. His sword got caught in her shield somehow, and it bounced back, causing him to lose his balance, and his helmet slid up a bit, revealing his upper neck. Scarlet pointed her pistol at the exposed spot and fired two shots. Both ended up hitting their marks, and he fell dead in front of us.

"Why in God's name would you do that!" I said to her, spinning her around.

I had no idea that she could block swords with her shield. I thought she could only stop projectiles.

"Because I knew I could, and if you were so worried, why didn't you push me out of the way?" she asked, looking at me with a somewhat irritated expression.

"I didn't move you out of the way, because I know that if you're going to do something incredibly dumb, you knew you could do it. Also, the reason I'm pissed off isn't because of that but because you were risking yourself for me. Trust me more," I said while flicking her ear.

"Ow! How about you trust me more then?" she said right back at me with severe attitude.

"Fine. But we will discuss this at length later. For now, let's watch Jessica fight this small fry, and then we can go back to the camp," I said, a bit irritated.

CHAPTER
48

The Devil's Anger user burst toward Scarlet and Bryce. Without realizing it, I had already shot forward to intercept him. I stopped him in his tracks and sent him flying almost eighty feet away from me with a flying kick. He got up immediately and boomed right back at me. His legs were in front, as if to kick me. It didn't work, as it was too easy to counter. I easily dodged the attack and countered, my fist going straight into his kneecap with all my force backed up by a propulsion of blue flames. As my fist made contact, I could feel his kneecap breaking, but my right wrist broke too.

We were now separated by only ten feet. He stood on one leg, and my broken wrist lay limp at my side. Rocketing forward again and stopping right in front of me, he hit the dead center of my chest and not only sent me flying back a couple of feet but also knocked the wind out of me, causing me to fall to the ground. I picked myself back up, and he was there again, this time kicking me in the ribs. He broke at least three of them. Again I picked myself up after that kick, and he tried to do the exact same thing, but my unbroken hand was able to grab his foot. Holding onto it, I rolled under his other leg, making him fall onto his stomach. Before he could do anything about it, his foot had already been twisted more than 180 degrees. This broke the ankle on his last good leg and made him completely immobile and helpless on the ground.

He knew he was done for too as he saw me over him. Although he knew he was going to die, he fought until the end. I made my way onto his chest by smacking away his legs and arms repeatedly until a hole opened up. This slightly knocked the wind out of him, and it was at this moment that my left hand wrapped around his neck. He began to fight, but it was no use, as his injuries were just too severe, and his energy was too low to produce scales around his neck. He didn't last all that much longer before his final breath escaped his lips.

CHAPTER
49

As Jessica finished off the Devil's Anger user, she stood up. The fight had taken a significant toll on her, and it looked like she had broken her right wrist and maybe a couple of ribs on her left side, judging by the way she was holding her arm. Before my body could move toward her, she fell to her right, completely exhausted. Bryce was there to catch her before she landed on the ground. He felt her right wrist and then felt his way up the left side of her chest. If it wasn't obvious that he was just checking for injuries, I would have slapped him silly. It still made me a little angry that he was feeling up my sister, even though he was just looking for injuries.

"She doesn't seem to be in too bad of a condition. Her wrist is broken, and she may or may not have a couple of broken ribs," Bryce said, looking up at me while removing his hand from my sister's side before continuing. "We should get her to Argentum so that she can do something about these broken bones," he said while looking down at Jessica.

"Yeah, you're right. Should we fly or walk?" I asked.

"Let's walk. I don't really feel like changing now that we're all the way out here, and I have some clothes on too that I don't feel like ruining," he said while he picked up Jessica, princess style.

We started to walk back toward the city, where Argentum was. However, before we made it even two minutes, Annabeth was already running toward us. It looked as if she had been crying. She probably thought Jessica was dead by the way Bryce was holding her. Bryce then told me to run and tell Annabeth that Jessica was okay but unconscious.

"Annabeth! Calm down. She's okay. She's just unconscious," I shouted to her when we were about one hundred feet away, but she didn't seem to hear me. I repeated what I had said when we were within ten feet, and again she seemed to not hear me at all. She seemed focused on only one thing, and that was getting to Jessica as fast as possible. Once she was within a few feet of Bryce, she fired some of her ice at Bryce's head. I had never seen her lose her cool like that.

"You were supposed to protect her! How could you let her fight and die like that?" she shouted at him.

He simply put Jessica down behind him. "Calm down, Annabeth," he said, looking up at her.

"I will not calm down! This is your fault!" she screamed, releasing all her magic.

The ground erupted at her feet, and she was surrounded by a cloud of wind so powerful that it blew me back a couple of feet. Sparks were flying around her. Everything within twenty feet of her was frozen, and she was surrounded by a blue haze of power. She looked like the devil incarnate, as her hair was golden and whipping around, and her clothes were blowing around like no other. An aqua-colored light shot into the sky. She had just gone into her EFF. At this moment, her power increased even more. Her power at that moment far exceeded anything I had ever experienced. She turned to look at me, and her eyes were ice blue. Her entire body looked as if she was made entirely of ice.

She then raised her hand, pointed at me, and said, "This is your fault too."

In those few seconds, Bryce grabbed Jessica and put her at least four hundred feet away from him back toward the way we had come. Annabeth turned back to Bryce, but before she could take a step toward him, he shouted, "I said calm down!"

He then absolutely exploded with power. The ground around us actually shook like an earthquake was happening, and the ground within five feet of him cracked. The power that he was emanating was light-years stronger than Annabeth's, practically dwarfing her display of power by comparison. Everything within one hundred feet of him was set ablaze with blue flames. Annabeth was almost caught in the flames, but she was able to leap back just in time. I was over 150 feet away, and his power blew me back at least another fifty feet.

Bryce put on this show for only a couple of seconds. He then looked at Annabeth and shouted, "Do you want to continue? Jessica is alive, you know."

She didn't hear him and shot toward him with no regard for the fact that he was our leader and that he had just dwarfed her EFF with ease. Before my body could react to her movement, there was a gigantic boom followed by an even larger boom. Then a giant rush of air lifted me off the ground and sent me back almost ten feet. The blast of wind was closely followed by a cloud of sand that passed me rather passively, as I had regained my senses and put my shield up. Even so, there was still a big cloud of sand 150 feet away from me, but there was no more aqua-colored light.

As the sand cleared, Bryce stood above Annabeth. Running over toward them, I paid no heed to Bryce, who looked fine. That wasn't the case for Annabeth, who was out cold. Thankfully, that was the only thing wrong. I looked up at Bryce after looking at Annabeth, and he seemed completely unfazed by all of this.

Unable to stifle my curiosity about this whole situation, I asked him, "If you have that much power, why haven't you used it yet? And why isn't the dragon that powerful?"

He then looked down at me and said, "Power was never an issue with the dragon. It was the transformation. As for my power, that was nothing."

"Then why don't you use it? You could've saved so many lives!" I said angrily.

"Because I would lose control of myself. I could barely control that amount of power for that little amount of time as it is," he said.

I could see his eyes starting to tear up. He probably blamed himself for everyone's death. He then boomed toward Jessica, who still lay unconscious. He picked her up and then boomed back and grabbed Annabeth and held her too. We both walked back toward the city, where Argentum was, so that she could treat the two. The walk was filled with silence. At least nothing happened for the rest of the day.

CHAPTER
50

Bryce had probably realized my absence by now, but it was far too late. I was already within one hundred feet of the Slăve camp with the bag of explosives and the detonator. It was a good thing I had found out about the birds around here. Thankfully, one was big enough to carry this bag, so it would be easy to get into the camp as a bird. I flew over the camp, and there were many targets to get, but the explosives needed to be rationed. It looked like they brought reinforcements on the helicopters that came back along with more helicopters. *Why not take those helicopters away?*

Swooping down to the end of the row of helicopters, I changed back to a human and planted two explosives on each one of the ten helicopters. This left me with about twenty-nine explosives left. Thankfully, all the explosives could be detonated remotely, so they could be planted everywhere and all blown up at the same time. Changing back into the bird, I flew back up into the sky to look for more areas to destroy. The communications area would have been my next target, but Regius and Charlie took care of it before they died.

I was thinking about them. Charlie had pissed me off so much that half my body had changed back into a human, and I was falling. Changing back and regaining my concentration stopped me from dying. I was flying again over the camp in search of the next place to destroy. My next target ended up being the tanks. There were about one hundred or so left now, and after planting two charges on ten of them, their numbers would be reduced. That left only nine charges and plenty of areas to destroy. It looked like the most important areas were the ones I had to prioritize.

Their war room seemed like the next reasonable area. It was one of the biggest tents in the camp and had a flag of the world above it. Four charges around it should destroy it. As I was planting the charges around the war room, I could hear people talking inside.

"So all the reinforcements are here today, right?" person A asked.

"Yes. We got everything we lost back and more," person B said.

"What about the Delta MKS? When are they coming?" person A asked.

"They'll be here tomorrow around midday," person B replied.

"How many of them are there?" person A asked.

"One hundred of the clones of s00 who supposedly can go EFF and Lieutenant Colonel Julie, the s000," person B said.

"So we just need to hold out till then," person A said.

"Yep," person B replied.

This was bad, but right now I needed to finish what I had come here to do, and then I'd tell the others. Next was one of the mechanics' tents that was less than one hundred feet away. Just to be safe, I flew toward it. It was all for naught, as someone saw me and started shooting. I had no idea where the guy came from, but he wasn't that good of a shot and only grazed my body while taking off. However, that wasn't the problem, as now the entire camp was on high alert.

Now I had to rush, as almost everyone was out and about looking for me. I landed next to the mechanic tent and made a lot of noise. I planted the four charges as quickly as possible. With only one charge left, there was only one place to go: their fuel tankard. Unfortunately, they had several of these massive tanks of gas, but taking out just one would do a significant amount of damage.

I landed right in front of one of the tankards and planted the charges, but as I turned around, there was a shot, and my leg went on fire. There were then another few shots—one in the other leg, one in my spine that should have crippled me, and one through my left shoulder. My right hand then went into my bag, and I turned around to face them. They shot me three more times—once in the stomach, once in my right arm, and once in my chest that punctured my left lung.

"How are you still standing, girl? You should just fall and die now like the rest of your friends will soon," one of the soldiers said.

"We will not lose to you, scum," I said before they shot me three more times—once more in my neck, once in my right shoulder, and once more in the stomach. That wasn't the end of it, as one of the soldiers came behind me and stabbed me directly in the spine, severing my nerves. But my body refused to fall.

"How can you even stand!" the soldier behind me said as he ran in front of me to the group that had shot me.

"Because we aren't fighting for ourselves. We're fighting for an idea, and it isn't freedom. *We fight so that we can have hope again,*" I said before hitting the detonator with my last ounce of strength, blowing up all the charges around their camp. The tankard behind me blew up, enveloping me, and all the other charges that went off did so much more damage. My life ended there, and the only thing that crossed my mind was that I was going to be seeing Charlie soon.

CHAPTER
51

Boom!

Standing on the edge of the cliff where we used to snipe, I could see everything that was happening at the Slăve camp. All their tents, which were neatly aligned in rows so far back that they were hard to see, were burning as if there was no tomorrow. Some of the tanks were burning on the far left of the camp, and about ten helicopters were destroyed and burning a few hundred feet from the tanks. Fortunately, the screams of the burning didn't reach me. They would have triggered some bad memories.

It was not long after the explosion that the rest of the group joined me at the cliff. Most didn't know what had happened, but after they realized who wasn't there, it dawned on them. Crying came from both Lucy and Annabeth; they had been good friends with Marie. If Charlie had still been alive, he would have blown up the entire cliff, all seven-hundred-plus feet of it gone. For how much of an energetic weirdo he was, he was just as smart and strong.

"Why … why does everyone keep dying?" Scarlet whispered in my ear as she hugged me from behind.

"I don't know. We will survive this and create a new world for us. Okay?" I whispered.

"Okay," she responded.

I turned to the rest of the group and waited until all their eyes were on me. "Tomorrow. Tomorrow this will end. Tomorrow, we'll crush them so badly they'll never want to screw with us again."

There was an overwhelming sense of determination from everyone. They looked stone-faced and pissed beyond belief. A minute of stone silence followed, and then Albert, the quietest of us all, raised his hand and said, "They die tomorrow. For our friends who have passed, for our families who have passed, and for everyone else who is still suffering in captivity because of them. Tomorrow we finish this war once and for all by any means necessary."

I couldn't have said it any better myself. Hearing that from Albert was a shock. Everyone recovered quickly and nodded their heads in agreement. They then left to go back to their tents to get what could be their last few hours of sleep. Eventually, everyone left except for Albert and me. We both stared at each other for a bit before Albert spoke up.

"Don't hold back tomorrow. Don't let fear control your power. Control it and everything about it."

I looked at him curiously and with apprehension, but he continued to speak.

"I can see the fear in your eyes, a fear no one else could see, because they had never experienced it. The fear of oneself will prevent even the strongest from surviving," he said before nodding his head toward me and walking away.

After that conversation with Albert, I began to wake up the others. They'd come full force after us now. Walking around to every tent and shaking or kicking everyone awake was how the morning started. Scarlet, of course, was the first to be woken up, followed by Taylor, Lucy, Jessica, Annabeth, Argentum, Albert, and finally Erik. They made their way to the center of our camp, the fire pit. There the plan for the day was laid out.

Everyone went to their usual spot, and instead of waiting like we usually did, Scarlet and I went directly to the cliff with Lucy and Taylor, and for the first time in this fight, my group was the first one to our area. We were viewing the entire desert in front of us, including the soldiers marching toward us with what looked like everything they had. Judging by what I knew from military structure, there were at least four hundred thousand soldiers and over two hundred tanks. Making matters worse was that they were already into the forest and the town. However, the good news was that the helicopters were just starting to move. It was time for me to change.

CHAPTER
52

Jumping off the cliff, my body went through the usual transformation to create a giant red dragon over three hundred feet tall. I climbed back up the cliff, and Scarlet got onto my head and then slid down to the nape of my neck, where she always sat. Next, we took off from the cliff and saw everyone—excluding Taylor, Lucy, and Jessica, who were only a five-minute sprint away. As I flew over the forest and town, I breathed one line of fire on both areas that slowed them down but barely. This was an utter disaster already and if something didn't change they would be overrun and killed. They needed to escape.

Going for another run to help the group, I was blindsided by the other dragon. It slammed me into the ground, no doubt breaking a rib or two. It was on top of me and went to bite the back of my neck. Scarlet got in the way, catching the dragon on the side of the face and snapping to the right. Not throwing away the opening, I kicked out the dragon's legs before getting out of the its hold and slapped the dragon away with my tail. I looked toward where the dragon had come, and there must have been at least two hundred helicopters flying toward me. Forty branched off and went to my left toward the two groups. As I looked back at them quickly, it looked as if the two groups had been pushed back enough to merge into one group. They were fighting side by side and looked as if they were only a three-minute sprint from Lucy and Taylor, who were now useful as only spotters for the group; they couldn't really support them without exposing themselves. All that could be seen from that area were blue flames, ice spikes, and explosions of ice, regular explosions, and a silver-scaled gorilla jumping around.

Because I was not paying attention to my surroundings, almost every one of the 160 remaining helicopters got a successful hit on me. They didn't really hurt anymore, but the fact that I had been that careless was the problem. There were so many of them, and they were all in tight groups, which made it easier for me, so I pushed all 160 of them back into the desert air within five minutes. Unfortunately, only fourteen helicopters had been downed in my group by then.

They surrounded me in the middle of the desert air with almost nowhere to go. Rockets were constantly coming at us, and either I dodged them, or Scarlet sent them back. The helicopter pilots caught on when Scarlet sent them back and would dodge them easily. The past couple of days must have been just information gathering for them, as they now knew almost every move I made before I even made it.

Deciding to change it up a little, I sent a gigantic stream of flames into a group of ten closely spaced helicopters instead of attacking them head-on. It took down four, while the other six managed to dodge it. As the smoke drifted up from the falling helicopters, a smoke screen appeared in front of the pilots. As I stormed through it to get the other helicopters, two were already done, and the final one was just too slow. It ended up crushed between my teeth. This had only begun.

CHAPTER
53

We were surrounded, and we were in absolute overdrive to stay alive. We were releasing and attacking with our magic—impaling, freezing, burning, shooting, smashing, or exploding everything around us, to a point where everything around us was split into three sections. The biggest area was mine, and it was completely frozen over and stained with blood from spiked soldiers. The next area was basically just ash with embers and fire everywhere. It created a perfect smoke screen above us, but the price was that we could smell everything—and I do mean everything. The last area was just what you would expect from forest warfare: crushed wood, splinters everywhere, and bullet holes with the ground covered in puddles of blood. We were in the center of this hell surrounded by fallen trees that we were able to move, creating an enclosed triangle wall of wood. It was high enough to protect us efficiently but small enough for us to be able to look over and attack.

All in all, we were doing well for the situation we were in. A large part of that was due to the spotting of Taylor and Lucy, which let us know about everything that was going on around us. This allowed us to be effective and safe without risking our lives to find out where they were. We were really pinned down, with nowhere to go. We were surrounded, and they just wouldn't stop coming. We'd killed three thousand, but that was but a little dent in the four hundred thousand plus we had started with. Something needed to happen and soon, or we were all going to die here.

"Uh … guys, I'm completely out of ammo," Albert said to us, looking like a lost puppy.

"Well, what do you want us to do about it?" Jessica yelled as some soldiers shot our little holding, sending splinters everywhere.

One of the bigger ones impaled my leg. Argentum, who was right next to me, pulled out the piece of wood, and then I closed the wound by freezing it. This was what we had been doing for the past half hour so that Argentum wouldn't get worn out. The only one who didn't have ice on them was Jessica, because it would just melt right away. Everyone else had at least one piece of ice, and this was how it went: Albert had some on his left forearm and right calf, Erik had some on the side of his neck, and Argentum had some on both her calves and on her back. Fortunately, all the injuries except for Erik's were from splinters.

"It's not like we can do anything right now, Albert," Argentum said, and she stood up and fired a couple of shots at the woods before dropping right back down.

"She's right. So unless you've got a plan, you're just going to have to only use your magic," I said to him as I sent spikes of ice at soldiers that were charging.

Needless to say, the ice wasn't blue for long. We had done so much killing by this point that we were more protected by mountains of bodies and the slippery blood everywhere than we were by the trees that we had set up.

Albert looked like he was about to say something again, but two explosions occurred on either side of us. These came from two of the forty helicopters above us. As a response to this, Jessica and I sent our fire and ice up into the air. I sent over twenty spikes in three seconds, and Jessica sent just as many balls of blue flame up into the air in all different directions. A couple of seconds later, we heard at least eight crashes. Another crash landed within five feet of the logs of wood that surrounded us.

Albert got up and rummaged inside the cockpit. He must have been looking for something, and soon it looked like he found what he wanted. He then pulled out what looked like an UMP-45 out of the cockpit. After getting the gun, he continued to rummage within the cockpit, and he pulled out at least seven magazines, all of which he tossed over the logs to us. He then cocked his newfound gun, leaned around the nose of the helicopter, fired a couple of rounds, exploded some of the ground around the edge of the forest, sending dirt and debris up into the air, and then sprinted the five feet to the logs and hurdled them, landing right back where he had been. Everything he did took about two minutes, and during that time, the soldiers' gunfire didn't stop, and neither did we, firing back with either our magic or our guns.

One soldier with a medic helmet and a white cloth on his arm came running out of the burnt region of the forest toward the flailing soldier. He was carrying a blanket. The medic didn't make it there, as Erik fired through a crack between our protective logs, hitting him dead in the head. Even though Erik didn't have any offensive powers, he was one hell of a crack shot. The only one doing more significant damage than he was was Connor, as he appeared and disappeared all over the place, killing soldiers left and right.

"Albert!" I said after throwing a ball of ice into the middle of the burnt forest.

He blew it up, sending shrapnel everywhere. I couldn't tell if it killed anyone, but one piece of it hit a soldier in the leg, and he collapsed. He was then dispatched right away by a shot to the head from Jessica. Add another body to the ever-building piles.

"We need to move now!" Erik said as he fired several shots through another gap in the logs.

It looked as if he got another soldier running between the destroyed and burnt areas of the forest, but he was starting to get back up. I got ready to send a spike of ice at him, but Jessica already burned him in every sense of the word.

"Where? We're completely surrounded with nowhere to go," I said as I looked over the logs.

I was answered with gunfire at the logs that sent splinters everywhere. This time, no one got hit by the splinters.

"I don't know, but we have to move somewhere other than here. The helicopters are getting closer with their shots."

Four explosions occurred around us from rockets. None of us got injured by them somehow though, so that was good. We didn't need to discuss it after the rockets exploded around us. Everyone poked their guns over the logs and emptied their magazines. Next, Albert blew the ground and trees around us to create a smoke screen. I formed ice in a circle all around us on the tree line, and Jessica sent flaming blue balls of heat at it, exploding it and creating steam as a more effective smoke screen. With the soldiers effectively blinded, we jumped over the logs and ran past the helicopter and through the frozen part of the forest.

We ran past soldiers and past an incredible amount of gunfire—all while somehow not getting hit. At one point we ran directly through a whole brigade of soldiers, firing our guns, sending spikes of ice everywhere and balls of fire left and right, and exploding the ground around us. Even with that, none of us got a splinter. We found a tightly packed group of trees and immediately downed them. We formed them into the triangle pattern and jumped into all of them, as we had done before.

Not ten seconds after we all jumped into the little encampment, the soldiers were already shooting at us. Practically the same thing happened to the forest surrounding us as it had at the previous area. One-third of the forest exploded and was smashed by Albert and Argentum, another third was basically burned to a crisp, and the final third was frozen. I looked up and recognized exactly where we were. We were right at the fork in the path of where we went, either to the town or to the forest. That meant that we were less than a minute away from Taylor and Lucy if we sprinted.

CHAPTER
54

"Don't, Lucy. It's not worth it at all. We have to tell them what's going on. We can't afford to take any risks here unless you want to die," I said.

Lucy had been arguing with me on whether or not to shoot at the helicopters around Argentum's group, which was only a few hundred feet away. She didn't seem to hear me, and she stood up. I reached toward her to grab her and pull her back down, but it was too late. The shot took out one of the pilots in one of the helicopters, and it subsequently crashed to the ground about twenty feet from Argentum's group. The other two turned to us, knowing exactly where we were. One of the helicopters turned and fired right away. Lucy dropped lifeless next to me with at least eight bullet holes in her. She deserved to be mourned, but right now I needed to live.

I grabbed the discarded rifle before rolling onto one knee as the other two helicopters came toward me. I tried to fire the gun, but it wouldn't fire. Looking at the rifle to see what was going on, I saw it: a bullet hole right in the barrel of the gun. They both fired at me, one sending rockets and the other firing its machine gun. The rocket exploded ten feet to my right, doing little damage, but I could feel the machine gunfire go through my chest and stomach.

Honestly, I thought that it would hurt so much more than it did, but shock had set in almost immediately. The only thing my body felt now was cold. My body was so incredibly cold. It was a scary and terrible feeling, but only one person kept going through my mind: Carmine. Who was going to take care of her, and who was going to nurture her if we made it out of this alive? However, deep inside I knew that Bryce and the others would protect Carmine with their lives.

As they came in to finish it, a giant ball of ice went into the cockpit and through the entire helicopter, destroying it. Not a second later, a giant ball of pure blue flames hit and exploded the other one. Falling back onto my back, I looked at a cloudy sky for a couple of seconds before the faces of Annabeth, Bryce, and Scarlet blocked my view. Shifting my head to the right, I saw Bryce flying toward us. As his head passed over the edge of the cliff, he changed back into a human and landed right next to us with Scarlet on his back. Once he got within five feet of us, a gigantic pyramid of ice formed around us.

As I propped Taylor onto my knees, the only thing going through my head was that I had failed. I had failed Connor in protecting his future, the only thing that really mattered. For the first time in my life, the tears just wouldn't stop flowing. I felt as if I was losing my mom again. Connor was no better, as he balled unashamedly right next to me.

"It'll be all right, Connor. Take care of Carmine for me. It'll be okay, Bryce. I'll be fine. At least I got to die around friends," Taylor said as she barely wheezed the words out.

I could hear Albert, Argentum, and surprisingly Erik start to cry.

"But you were never my friend," I said, starting to cry even harder. "You were my family." I choked out the words.

"You always were sentimental," she said, smiling at me.

The last thing she ever did was take her bloody hands up to Connor's and my faces and stick out two fingers, putting one above each eye. She then slid her fingers down our faces until there was no face left, at which point her hands fell to the ground lifeless, leaving two lines of blood all the way down both our faces.

I reared my head back and released an absolutely deafening roar that would have made a dragon proud.

CHAPTER
55

B ryce had just finished screaming, and along with the rest of us, he
continued to bawl his eyes out. The tears just wouldn't stop. Losing
Taylor felt like I was losing my mother all over again.

A sudden black aura started forming around Bryce. It wasn't like an
EFF, but it was identical to the mist when Argentum had hurt me. It grew
larger and larger around him until it was filling the entire room within
the ice pyramid. As it engulfed me, I could feel pure power from it. Bryce
stood up and exploded with the black aura. The blast was so powerful
that it destroyed the ice pyramid and sent the ice everywhere. Not only
was the blast destructive, but it blasted us with an incredible amount of
power. Five streams of light exploded into the sky. Five of us had just gone
into our EFFs.

An aqua-colored light streamed from Annabeth, a red-colored light
streamed from Jessica, a blue-colored light streamed from Albert, I had
a pink-colored stream of light, and Connor had a dark-blue–colored
stream of light. Finally, Argentum's gray stream of light went into the
sky. Also, Deathwalker was in Argentum's hand, pointed downward
at her side. Those weren't the only things I noticed. Jessica's body had

completely changed, and now she looked like she was made of only blue fire. Everything around us was slowly flowing into Connor, gradually making him bigger and bigger. Annabeth's body looked to be made of pure ice, and half of Argentum's body was covered in silver dragon scales, while the other half was covered in a silver coat of wolf's fur. And the wind was whipping around us so hard that it felt like bullets. The ground cracked like an eggshell.

Bryce turned around to face us, and his appearance was a bit shocking. He no longer had eyes; they were replaced with pure fire. His body was completely covered in jet-black scales, but they looked as if they were about to come off. Turning his head to look at us, he spoke in a voice that was deeper than his dragon's voice.

"This ends now."

He then boomed past everyone through the wind and over the cracks, jumping off the edge of the cliff. He changed into a gigantic dragon with jet-black scales, towering at least three hundred feet over the edge of a seven-hundred-foot cliff. His only features that were not jet black were his eyes, which were red flames, and two lines of what looked like blood from the eyes to the end of the maw.

His gigantic and jet-black wings then stretched out from his back. His wingspan must have been at least a mile long. He lowered one wing so that we could step on it, and all of us except for Erik did; he hoisted his rifle and said he would stay and snipe. Once we were on the wing, we boomed to his back, making it there in under a second. He turned away from the cliff and took off toward the now-retreating mass of soldiers at an incredible speed for his size, creating sonic booms behind us. Within a couple of seconds, we had completely overtaken the soldiers.

He landed in front of the soldiers, and all of us slid down his wings to the ground. Bryce lowered his head toward the lead car, where the general sat. His eyes bored into the general, who could barely withstand the stare, squirming like a dying fish. After a couple of seconds of dead silence, Bryce lifted his head and said to the entirety of the four hundred thousand soldiers, "Die."

Rearing his head back, he sent a herculean-sized jet of white flames into the middle of the army, taking out at least a few hundred. The fire was so hot that the nearby sand turned to a muddy glass. Bryce took off into the sky to face the remaining one hundred helicopters. The downwind force of his wings' movement flattened most of the soldiers around us. We then boomed forward into the army in all different directions. Albert and Argentum went toward the tanks, while Annabeth, Jessica, and I went toward the regular army.

Half the army fired everything they had at me. There must have been at least five hundred thousand bullets in my shields, and every bullet went right back from whence it came. All the soldiers around me continued to fire at me too, as we were constantly in and out of the shade caused by Bryce and Connor.

Then I heard a cry of pain behind me. I turned to see a soldier with a knife in his chest. I assumed he had tried to stab me in the back, but my shield had been up, so it had reflected his thrust. I lifted my pistol to aim at his head, and he saw it and laid his head back on the sand in a way of acceptance.

"You're *untouchable*. It just isn't fair," he said.

Looking at him, I simply pointed my pistol at him and pulled the trigger, not thinking twice. I turned around to face the rest of the soldiers and began walking forward, picking up a dropped machine gun in the first couple of steps. Holding the trigger down, I mowed the soldiers down, as they had nowhere to go. If they fired back at me, it would only make matters worse for them.

CHAPTER
56

The looks the soldiers were giving us were somewhat thrilling and chilling at the same time. They looked scared out of their minds, and it gave me possibly the greatest amount of satisfaction ever. Their pure fear of us in that moment gave them a little taste of what we went through every day for the past three-plus years. It was now time to give it all back to them and make them reap what they'd sown.

Deathwalker said a few simple words as I effortlessly destroyed the soldiers in front of us.

"Let's go after the tanks. Show them how powerful you and I can be."

We exploded out at the soldiers, and I headed straight for the mass of tanks. The closest tank fired almost immediately at me, but it did absolutely nothing to me. It felt like someone flicked me in the chest with their finger, and all it did was create a smoke cloud. I then boomed through the cloud at a speed unknown to me. I was going so fast, but the tank that had been about five hundred feet away from me was now one foot in front of me.

I raised Deathwalker in front of the tank, and it fired again. I brought down Deathwalker at a faster speed than my sprint just now. Not only did Deathwalker split the tank shell in half, but the entire tank was cut in half from the pressure and power of the swing alone. Stepping into the gap between the two halves of the tank, the two survivors looked at me with pure horror. Instead of killing them, I let them live so that they would have something to remember if they ever tried this again. After getting out from between the two halves, both soldiers said, loud enough for me to hear, "A *dragon wolf.*"

"Dragon wolf, huh? I like it" was what I said loud enough for the two soldiers to hear after I walked past the tank.

Then more than half the tanks that were left all fired at me. Only three hit me. They felt like a fly on my body, and the rest missed me, creating a cloud of sand. I had no idea how I looked walking out of that cloud without a scratch, but it must have been terrifying for them. They all fired again with the same result, just five hitting me this time and again not a scratch on me as I walked out of the sand cloud.

I boomed toward the tanks after their second volley of fire, and they were in front of me in two seconds. I stopped right in front of the cannon of the first tank, and it fired at me, but it was easy to dodge. Next, I held Deathwalker to my right with both hands and turned it almost parallel to the ground. I boomed forward, slicing through not only that first tank but three more behind it. The edges that slid off were dripping in blood, staining the sand.

Not a single one of the crew members in any of those tanks survived. Raising my head after the strike to attack more of the tanks, I saw five of the closest tanks explode out of nowhere and then the three right behind those five blow up. I turned my head every which way to find out who did that, and I spotted Albert. He was surrounded by a blue aura, only a couple of feet behind me, covered in sand, and crying. Our eyes met, and he smiled and then jogged over to me as the tank shells either hit us or exploded around us. They did nothing to either of us.

We looked at each other in silent admiration for how far we'd come since meeting almost two and a half years ago. He grew from just five feet to a giant, at six feet five inches, and so did I, growing from four feet seven inches to five feet eleven inches. Our powers also grew from almost nothing to absolutely intense in that time too. It was amazing what could happen in just a little time.

Both of us turned our heads toward the group of twenty tanks that just fired another volley at us, again doing nothing to us. We then looked at each other in a silent agreement to attack the tanks at the same time. As we turned to face them, they fired a third volley at us, putting up another cloud of sand. As it settled, we stood there facing them as they stayed still almost one thousand feet away. I then boomed forward, with Albert giving me cover by exploding the sand in front of me. They were in front of me within three seconds, and Deathwalker was already going through them before they could react. My hands with Deathwalker didn't stop, and neither did the explosions from Albert. Then I stopped moving, sensing no other movement around me. I looked around as the dust settled. Every single one of the twenty tanks that had been there now lay in the sand surrounded by blood, either exploded by Albert or cut in half vertically or horizontally by me.

There was then another volley of cannon fire from another group of twenty tanks. Albert and I locked eyes, and we nodded to each other, silently agreeing to the next course of action. Before we could execute, there was a yell from behind us.

"Albert! Do it!" came the voice.

"What in God's name is that?" came out of my mouth.

CHAPTER
57

"**A**lbert!" I screamed as loud as possible to get his attention.

This was right up his alley. If he could explode the one-hundred-plus-foot pillar of ice, it would be pretty good collateral for us.

As planned, the entire pillar exploded, sending thousands of pieces of ice everywhere. At least a thousand soldiers dropped immediately, and thousands more were injured. Annabeth, Scarlet, Albert, Jessica, and I quickly killed those who were injured. In the minute it took to eliminate the injured, the sand around us was either on fire or frozen. The screams that we heard during that time were the worst of the entire fight. There was no reprieve for us, as there were still over one hundred thousand soldiers left to kill.

For some odd reason when we had finished killing all the injured, we lined up next to each other, shoulder to shoulder. We all shot off in different directions into the tsunami of soldiers—slashing, shooting, burning, and exploding. The soldiers had regained their bearing a little by this time and weren't horribly disorganized, but they were nowhere near being organized. We were still able to pick at them freely without their being able to do anything about it. This was partly possible because of the insane speeds at which we were going, but also because they had no leadership left. Even with them outnumbering us to a tremendous degree, they were nothing without leadership; thus, they were falling.

Most of the platoons, companies, and battalions I came across never really saw me, as they were already dead by the time I was in front of them. They couldn't keep up with our insane speed, and I calculated my exact speed to be just over Mach 7. Seven times the speed of sound was ridiculous for a human, and most of the soldiers who got past me fell to their knees, clutching their ears in pain from the sonic booms going off behind me.

As I was about to finish off the last soldier in the company who had stood in front of me, he exploded in a fiery ball of blue flame. Looking over to my right, I saw Jessica. She was a literal fireball of blue flames with red flames where her eyes should be and a red aura all around her body. She looked as if she was smiling, but it was hard to tell. Just then we heard a giant boom, and the ground shook. A giant fireball of white flame was scorching across the desert through so many soldiers.

CHAPTER
58

Annabeth jerked her head about for a couple of seconds before she saw me. Once she did, she sent a spike of ice at me. It went through me harmlessly, but it was so cold that I could feel the chill from it. Then the ground rumbled, as if there was an earthquake, and not a second later there was a jet of white-hot fire right behind me. Only one person could have that much power. Towering close to one thousand feet above me, with no helicopters in sight, Bryce had destroyed every single one of them—all one-hundred-plus helicopters in less than fifteen minutes. The dragon that had been there the last couple of days was nowhere to be seen, and we would have noticed something that big falling to the ground.

He then reared his head back again and unleashed a godlike roar that announced to the world that we couldn't be broken. We all rallied around him without being told to. Annabeth and I were, of course, the first, followed closely by Argentum and Albert and then finally Scarlet, who walked up to me like it was nothing despite the insane heat surrounding me.

"Looks like you're having a bit too much fun, Flame Princess," she said, coming to stand right in front of me.

All the remaining twenty thousand soldiers started to fire at us, including some rocket launchers that either missed or did absolutely nothing to us.

"That's probably true, but have you seen Erik?" I asked, pointing toward the cliff, where I saw a silhouette of a person standing atop it.

"I can't really tell, to be honest. Just how far away is he?" Scarlet asked.

"He's over two miles away and with a face of stone. He might as well be *faceless*," Bryce said as he leaned his head down right beside us.

A rocket then came out of nowhere and hit Bryce directly in his right nostril. He turned toward all the soldiers and unleashed a jet of pure white flames at them, killing at least a few hundred.

"Finish this now."

At that moment, a shadow enveloped me. Looking up, I saw Connor. He had been like that this entire fight, about half the size of Bryce but towering over all of us and destroying everything in his path.

CHAPTER
59

ill. Kill. Killllllll. Kill them all. They took my woman from me! They will all die!

After raising my gigantic fist, I slammed it into the middle of a battalion of soldiers, killing all but a few of them.

Die! Die! Die!

"Die, you filthy scum! How dare you take her from me!" I roared in an inhuman voice that echoed across the entire mountain range. And I slammed another gigantic hand into more soldiers, killing them. I could feel my sanity sleeping, but I just didn't care.

CHAPTER
60

They all just watched as Connor obliterated the final sixty thousand soldiers, as if it was nothing. Bryce did help a little. But they looked to be at the end of their EFFs, as the light around them was dimming. Bryce and Connor were the only ones who didn't look to be giving out, but Connor was starting to die down in his power, evident that he was beginning to shrink in size. When he finally turned back into a human after finishing off the last of the soldiers, Bryce proceeded to pick everyone up off the desert sand with his giant claws. For how gigantic and sharp his claws were, he picked them up in a smooth and gentle way, so as to pick only them up and not the bodies surrounding them. Once all of them were in his right front claw, he extended his wings and took off.

As he reached the cliff, he hovered above me, sending pounding waves of wind downward, forcing me to my knees. The claw that everyone was in hovered maybe ten feet above me, and one by one everyone slid out of his claw toward the ground. Scarlet stopped about a foot from the ground, as her shields were probably still in effect. Annabeth, Connor, and Argentum thumped against the ground but looked uninjured. Jessica floated down to the ground, as if weightless, her body still only flames. Finally, Albert fell from Bryce's claw and landed on Scarlet, whose shields blocked him and tossed him back up into a tree by Bryce's claw. After that, Bryce softly entered the forest next to the cliff and put his head over us to create shade.

As Albert flew into the tree, Scarlet woke up, but no one else did. Before she could say or do anything, a ferocious roar was heard in the desert. All three of us who were conscious turned to look, and what I saw almost made my hope disappear. It was the form of a black-scaled dragon that rivaled Bryce in size surrounded by at least one hundred Heaven's Justice users in full-blown EFF, every one of them being at least one hundred feet tall.

CHAPTER
61

I t was time to face the music. There was no way that I would be able to defeat them without losing myself to my power and that could not happen. This was the end for me, but I could still buy the others some time to get away.

Turning toward the still-conscious Erik, I said, "Get everyone away from here. As far away and as quickly as possible."

The silent stare we shared told him the reality of the situation. He nodded, accepting it with all his might. Before he went to the others, he saluted me—his sign of ultimate respect.

I turned back toward where the dragon and its comrades were coming from and unleashed a roar to match the other dragon's. Just as my wings outstretched to take off toward them, Scarlet screamed behind me. I turned back toward her, and she yelled at me.

"Don't! There's no way you can win after using all that energy. Please, come with me," she yelled, pleading as tears began to form in her eyes.

"I can't," I said, shaking my head. "If I don't take a stand here, we'll all die. At least this way you'll have a chance to live."

"I don't care about that! I just want to be with you! Please don't try to be the hero! Just come with us!" she screamed as the tears that had been forming now began to fall.

"I'm no hero," I replied. "I'm a protector. I'm sorry that I couldn't fulfill the promise I made to you," I said, taking off from the cliff without another word.

I could still hear her wails even when I was over a mile into the desert, about three thousand feet up and face-to-face with Julie and the clones of the psychotic s00, who were in full EFF and over 150 feet tall. None of us said anything to each other; we only stared each other down. Both of us then nodded to each other to show respect before we got started, but neither of us took our eyes off the other.

Once my head was raised, almost all the clones shot toward me at incredible speeds. It was hard to dodge them, but I managed and dodged most of their strikes. However, four of the ten arrows they shot at me penetrated my scales and went into my body, drawing blood from where the arrows had struck on my right side. As the clones stopped and turned to face me after attacking, I boomed toward them. One was crushed in my mouth, and another was crushed by my right front claw. Once the second one was crushed, at least eight of them jumped onto my back and started to stab me relentlessly. To get them off, I started spinning in midair, and after three full spins, the final one flew off.

All eight of them were hovering not two hundred feet in front of me, still dazed from the spinning. Taking advantage of their confusion and the lack of the rest of the clones attacking, I reared my head back and fired a jet of white flames at them. Three of the eight were instantly vaporized by the heat, and two caught on fire and fell straight to the ground, but the final three escaped back to the main group. I then charged the main group, trying not to give them any chance to regroup the three survivors.

The dragon, meanwhile, had disappeared only to come out of nowhere and slam me into the ground from above. That allowed them to get on top of my back, tear out my right wing, and claw at my back. It wasn't a second after they started that every single clone came down on me, slashing, firing, cutting, and stabbing me everywhere. I was able to spin my body right side up, crushing around five clones on the way. The other dragon was too slow getting away, and I bit down on her neck and tossed her around a bit. However, she got away before I got to her wings with the help of the clones and some rail gun cannons that hadn't been destroyed yet.

She now hovered about two thousand feet up in front of me as the clones surrounded me. She let out a tremendous roar at me, and my only response was to roar back just as loud. All the clones then attacked from every side. Whipping my tail around, I hit some of those attacking from behind, but it didn't kill them, as they were still able to attack my back. They again jumped onto every available inch of my body and continued attacking me.

I spun and stretched my neck as far as it would go to attack the clones. The first attempt was successful, as two made it into my mouth and were torn to pieces. On the second try, only one made it into my mouth. They caught on after that, as the third, fourth, and fifth attempts failed to get anything. As a last resort, I jumped up off the ground and used my only wing to propel me sideways onto my back, crushing only one, as the others had seen it coming. This did more harm than good, as the landing had broken my wing, leaving me almost immobile, and they took advantage of this.

They were toying with me. They knew that they had won, and their attacks continued but not as frontal assaults. They were small assaults from one or two from the sides or back that would swoop down and slash at my legs and claws, hoping to immobilize me completely. They would successfully immobilize both my back and front right claw and legs. Because of this, I was lying on my right side, kicking, breathing fire, and flipping myself if they attacked from behind.

Julie hadn't done anything for the past five minutes; she just watched from a distance. I didn't know where she was now, because she had disappeared, and that was exactly what she wanted. She never reappeared and instead slammed into me from above, sending me facedown into the desert. I couldn't move anymore, and my world was engulfed in pain. I guessed this was how it felt to lose.

CHAPTER
62

My body lay on the soft desert sand as it changed back into a human form. Standing up, I looked around to see only sand every which way. It was a bit disorienting at first, but I got used to it. That was when it got weird; the cloud of sand in front of me shimmered and formed into a forking road with a well-dressed man on the road going left.

The deaths of everyone in my group then flashed before my eyes—Shane dead in the house, Charlie and Regius in the tank, Marie in the explosion, Lucy riddled with bullets from the helicopter, and Taylor dying in my arms. All their deaths were my fault and mine alone. If I had just been more aware, if I had helped, if I was quicker, if I had stopped her, if I was smarter, and if I had been there, they could still be alive. We could still be together.

The man standing on the left side of the forked road then spoke to me in a very relaxing voice. He said, "Peace," he said motioning to the side of the road he was on. "Or Hardship," he said gesturing to the other road. Peace sounded so nice right now. No more fighting, no more death. Only serenity. So that was the path I chose.

I was a mere foot from him when my body stopped and my life flashed before me, but it wasn't my past; it was my future and everything that I could have. I saw myself at Argentum and Albert's wedding. I was there at Annabeth and Jessica's wedding. I saw the school that I had envisioned being opened to everyone, magical or not. I saw the graves of everyone who had died, memorialized and untouched, and the same went for the house in which Shane died. I saw my kids, a boy and a girl, going to the school. I saw them steadily growing up before my eyes and transforming into young adults. I even saw myself die; I was in bed next to my wife, holding her hand as we slept and passed away together. And through it all, the only one to be next to me every time was her, my wife. She had given me noise in my everlasting silence, she had given me light in my eternal darkness, she had fixed me when I was broken beyond repair, and she was the only one who had ever been able to truly feel my heart. It was for those reasons that Scarlet was my everything. It would be the ultimate betrayal if I just gave up here.

These images flashed over and over in my mind until it felt like an eternity had gone by. As they ended, I snapped out of the haze to find myself still in front of the man. I moved to face the other side of the road, as if someone was calling out to me from that direction, all the while tears were streaming down my face, around the blood that Taylor had left there. Then I saw them; they all were standing there in one big group as they held the hands of their other halves—my mom and dad, Regius, Shane and Lucy, Charlie and Marie, and Taylor. They were smiling at me, as if it was the happiest moment in their lives. They all seemed to be saying something, but it was inaudible to me, so I willed my body to walk over to them on their side of the fork.

As I got closer to them, their words became clearer and clearer. Once they were within three feet of me, I could hear what they were saying.

"Don't give up. You're not done yet," they all said over and over and over.

The tears flowed even faster now. They still believed in me even though I had failed to protect them. Every one of them came up to hug me, one at a time, until only my mother was left. She came up to me, hugged me, and said, "You are the *hope* for your friends. Now show everyone who's hopeless that there's still *hope*."

All of them disappeared in front of me, leaving only the man on the left side of the road and the road itself. He looked at me, nodded, and then disappeared. I then turned and walked on the side of the road on which my family had just been.

The road then ended in front of me, and I was right back where I had started. The only difference was that the sand cloud was beginning to disappear. I had a sudden realization. I had almost given up and sacrificed everything that we had worked for. I had almost thrown away our chance at a new life. What type of man was I to do that to them? Saving them was more important than staying.

I released everything that I could control; my rage at myself for almost giving up, and my pure will and determination, giving me the ability to control more than ever before. A white light then shot up into the sky, but it wasn't just a stream of light. It was a mountain of immeasurable size as bright as a diamond, made even brighter by the desert sun. My scales then formed on my body. First, they were red surrounded by red flames, then they were blue surrounded by blue flames, and finally they turned white as I was surrounded by pure white flames.

The ground within two thousand feet of me cracked, as if there was an earthquake. All the sand within one thousand feet of me instantly turned to glass and shattered along with the earth. The wind started whipping around me at over half the speed of sound. All my excess energy that was bubbling at the surface of my skin shot off me as lightning bolts that went straight up into the sky. The pain of all this was so excruciating that all my pain went out of me as a deafening scream.

At the end of it all, I was left looking at my hands, with my fingers turned into razor-sharp talons. The power that came with this was not only overwhelming, but it felt like a two-ton truck was off my shoulders. It felt good. In fact, it was the best feeling ever. At this moment, the only thought going through my head was that I should do this more often.

CHAPTER
63

My God. The heat emanating off him was enough to slightly scorch my scales even with the distance between us. The clones weren't faring any better, as they were about a mile away from him and still cringing from the heat. However, we still couldn't see him, as the sand hadn't settled yet, but what I could feel scared me to death. The sheer amount of power in front of me was both visible and invisible and almost fifty times the size of the mountain behind the town. It was far more power than the tests showed he had ability for. He was on a completely different plane of existence from me; I had originally thought he was just barely stronger than me, but now there was no way I could believe that.

The sand settled in front of me, and there he stood, in the middle of where he had been defeated. He was his normal human size and looked like the devil incarnate. He was covered in scales that were white with the slightest hint of black. His feet had changed to resemble the claws he had in his dragon form. His hands were a completely different story from his feet. Every single finger had changed to resemble razor-sharp talons. He then raised his head, which had been facing down at the ground, and that was the scariest sight of all. His eyes were pure glowing white that burned with an unknown passion. Right below his eyes were the same blood marks going down his face that had been there while he was in his dragon form. Every fiber of my being screamed to run after I saw that.

I could feel his eyes bore into mine, as if he were gouging them out with a spoon. He shifted his body to his left and right side, as if he was testing his mobility. The air around him changed, and I could feel that he was going to do something. That was when his entire body disappeared and then reappeared in the blink of an eye. I thought that it was just the desert heat haze playing tricks on me, but I was dead wrong.

A gigantic boom went off in my ears and everywhere around me. It was so loud that it felt like an uncountable number of lightning strikes were happening in my ears. Not only was the sound horrifically loud, but the wind that followed it was so powerful that it sent me every which way, tossing me about like a rag doll. The pain from the sound in my ears and the dizziness caused by the thrashing of the wind caused me to lose myself and fall all three thousand feet to the ground.

With a gigantic crash, I landed in the desert. The sand cloud caused by the crash allowed me enough time to regain my composure in dragon form. As the cloud dissipated, Bryce was right in front of me, and he was still in the same position and place he was before, but he had the slightest hint of a smile on his face. He gestured with his hands, sweeping them backward from his chest, as if to say, "Look around." I did just that, and what I saw petrified me.

The bodies of every single clone and the shell of every vehicle that housed a rail gun were in front of me. They were cut into so many pieces that it was hard to tell what belonged to whom. Every single cut looked as if a professional had performed it. The parts were strewn everywhere the eye could see, and they stained the sand red. It looked as if I had stumbled into a slaughterhouse.

I immediately took off from the ground, flying straight up at Mach 18 for about thirty seconds. Stopping about a mile above the desert, I looked down at Bryce still standing there, not moving an inch. I then plunged straight down toward him at a speed close to Mach 20. This was a do-or-die play, but it should work. Nothing should be able to stop a million tons of dragon coming straight at them, and knowing Bryce, he'd take it head-on.

All he did in response was raise his right index finger. He didn't move at all the closer I got to him. When I made contact, the sand around us exploded outward, leaving only the space around our heads untouched. The sight was unbelievable. He had stopped me with the same finger he had raised earlier. He had stopped over one million tons coming at him at Mach 20 with one finger. He then put his middle finger and thumb together and flicked my head where he had stopped me. It shattered the scales around my face and head, exposing the muscles, and sent me flying back up to where my attack had started. Before I even got there, he was waiting for me. Punching my underbelly, he sent me flying back toward the ground at a speed that was faster than lightning itself.

Landing at that speed shattered all my scales and broke several of my bones. I somehow survived, but I was reverted into my human body. Surrounded by an ever-flowing cloud of sand, my body just wouldn't move. My entire body felt broken. I tried to get up several times, but neither my legs nor my arms would hold me up for more than a second. It looked like I had failed in my mission to kill him.

As the sand cleared, Bryce stood right in front of me, looking down at me, but his face didn't show anger or pity. It showed curiosity. I was barely holding myself up on my knees, and I could feel him looking my naked body up and down, surveying me as if I were an alien, even though I couldn't see him. He got down on one knee, put one of his talons up under my throat, and edged my head upward to face him. Our eyes locked, and there was only silence between us as he held me dead to rights but didn't kill me right away. He just kept staring into my eyes, and after a minute or so I couldn't restrain myself.

"Are you going to kill me or not?"

"I'm deciding that right now," he said in a regular-sounding voice, still surveying me. "You've changed. You found something, didn't you? Something to protect," he said to me after he looked me up and down for another twenty seconds.

All I could do was stare at him in confusion until he continued.

"I can see it in your eyes. They've changed," he said, looking straight at me with his glowing eyes. He got up from his squat and walked away, leaving me naked in the middle of the desert. As he got about ten steps away from me, he turned around and said, "You can come to our camp once you've regained your strength. Just go to the village, and we'll get you."

As he continued to walk away, something seemed off. He got about fifty feet away from me before he started to limp on his left leg but continued to walk with the limp getting worse and worse. Once he was about 150 feet away, he stopped, fell to his knees, and clutched his head. That was when he started to scream. The blast of power that came from him was less intense than when he had fought me, but it was still enough to toss me back almost one hundred feet. If it wasn't for my scales that came out instinctively, I would have died from the heat. The heat that he had subdued was now back, and it took all my willpower not to be incinerated and to keep my scales up. Then came another blast of power, sending me back another one hundred feet. Not staying around for a third blast, I took off toward the village.

CHAPTER

64

W here in God's name was I, and why did I have clothes on? Everything around me was white. However, it wasn't an endless existence of white, as there were walls only visible because of three thin black lines that outlined them. The room wasn't completely barren either, as about one hundred feet in front of me, a rectangular table sat with the long side facing me. Two regular-size chairs were on either side of the table, along with a man who looked hauntingly like myself, but he was well dressed in the chair on the left side of the table.

He looked over at me, making eye contact. We did nothing but look at each other for a couple of seconds. Then he raised his right hand and gestured for me to come over. Our gazes never left each other the whole time I was walking over; we were sizing each other up. Once I got to the table, the chair moved out for me to sit in all by itself. Once we were both sitting down, there was an eerie silence between us as we continued to silently analyze each other.

"You know who I am, I presume?" he asked.

"My Prime," I guessed.

"And you know what I want too?"

"You want to kill everyone."

"Not just everyone but everything. The multiverse is an unfathomably large place, and what better to destroy it with than a person containing unfathomable power."

Absolute maliciousness emanated from him. There was no way I would allow him to do what he wanted.

"Shall we get this started then?" I asked, getting up from my chair.

"Let's," he said, getting up from his chair, taking off his blazer, and putting it on the back of his chair.

We both moved about twenty-five feet back from the table. Both of us set up ten feet from the other, staring each other down. He got into a position that resembled a judo stance but with a slightly different placement of his hands and feet. I then got into my own stance, and we began to slowly circle each other before attacking.

We were evenly matched as we fought, neither of us gaining the upper hand but each of us landing solid hits on the other. Every hit that connected against the other sent shock waves throughout the area. As we continued to fight, he slowly gained the upper hand against me. He eventually caught my arm and threw me over his shoulder and onto the ground, knocking the air out of my lungs.

As much as I wanted to say that the man got lucky, he didn't. He just straight up beat me. He was the first person to ever do that without my making a mistake. It was disconcerting, and as he stood above me, I knew that it wouldn't be long before he killed me and went to kill the others. However, if that was fated to happen, it wouldn't happen without resistance from me.

"I wish this had been a better fight, but you were really dumb when you powered yourself up earlier in the real world. Too many stray emotions for you to stay in control, and that's why you're having the headaches. As for this," he stated with his foot on my neck, gesturing with his head toward the black ball of energy, "it's unknown to me as to why we can do this, but this is antimatter that we can create."

As cheesy as it sounds, that was when the fight turned around. I could hear a song—the same song from all those months ago at the river. She was here fighting alongside me, fighting for me. I didn't deserve any of this, but it calmed my body down. It wasn't just me who was hearing it either, as my Prime lifted his head and knew exactly what was going on.

He thrust the black ball of antimatter at my head in desperation, but I dodged it, and it exploded the floor out from under us. As we were falling, the entire room inverted, and we were now standing up on what had been the roof of the room.

He lay only a couple of feet away from me, still dazed, with his right foot closest to me. I got up, grabbed his ankle, and twisted it until it broke. Just as his ankle broke, he kicked me with his other foot, sending me tumbling back almost ten feet. Both of us got up, ready to start anew.

I faced him, staring him down with the intent to end this, and his face gave away his fear, as he was hobbling on his left leg. He made a desperate attempt at an attack, jumping at me, landing on his left foot, and swinging with his right hand. I easily dodged it, as it was child's play. I shot behind him and straight kicked him in the back. I sent him flying into the wall, creating spiderweb cracks where he hit.

I walked up to him as he lay in front of the wall. He looked up at me as I approached and said, "I'm your bottled-up feelings, Bryce. There will come a day when you'll need to make peace with me one way or another. I just hope you can see me as an ally when that day comes."

He then disappeared into nothingness, and the world around me became incredibly bright and then pitch-black.

I opened my eyes to see the radiant glare of the desert sun, with Scarlet maybe ten feet in front of me. She was in her own little bubble of clear glass, and everything else was either smoldering or shattered from the extreme heat I had given off. She opened her eyes and looked at me with a smile that was as bright as the sun. She whistled the same tune as she walked over to me and hugged me.

"You okay?" was all she said.

"Yeah" was my only response as we continued to hug each other, basking in the warmth of each other's embrace.

"Then let's go home. Everyone's waiting," she said, getting up and extending her hand out to me, and I took it.

"We can't stay long."

"Why not?" she asked, audibly angered and visibly distraught.

"Don't worry. I just have to make sure this never happens again," I said to her.

"You can't kill them all," she said.

"I know that. I'm just going to scare the hell out of them and free who needs to be freed," I explained.

"Okay," she said, looking defeated but knowing that I was right. "But you better come back, or I'll kill you," she said, regaining her usual stance.

"You're coming with us, along with Connor."

"Why?" she asked.

"Because I'll need you to be there. You two are the strongest, and the people who we free will need to see that," I said to her with the most conviction I could muster.

"Okay, but if we're going there, shouldn't we get some clothes for you and Connor?" she asked.

"Yeah, that's a good idea," I replied.

As we made it back to the camp, we were both greeted with smiles and hugs from everyone, except for Julie, who was tied up against a tree. That didn't really matter to me though. Everyone was getting emotional as we were realizing that we had won. We had gained our freedom. However, the mood couldn't last, and after a couple of minutes, everyone calmed down, and the same question was on all their minds.

"Uh … what now?" Albert asked, being the first to voice this.

"We finish this," I said. "Connor, Scarlet, and I will be going first to the prison camp, where we will free everyone. Connor will then lead all the prisoners back here, while Scarlet and I will take the fight right to their headquarters and have a nice little chat with all the generals. Once that is done, we should be able to meet up with Connor."

"I'm all for this plan, but how are we supposed to find this place again? And what about finding the prison and the headquarters?" Connor asked.

"She knows the coordinates for the prison and this place," I said, lifting a finger toward Julie. "As for their headquarters, I know where that is."

It didn't take long before Julie was giving us the coordinates. Her telling us so quickly was all due to Erik. The man didn't even have to interrogate her. He just looked at her straight in the face before leaning in and whispering something in her ear. She simply looked down and told us the coordinates.

With that being settled, we said our goodbyes to everyone and headed to the cliff. I gave my clothes to Scarlet and changed into my red dragon form to carry them. Both of them got on once I was even with the edge of the cliff. I detached myself from the edge, turned toward the prison, and boomed toward it at roughly Mach 2. And since the prison was only about one thousand miles away, we were there within the hour, making it at four thirty in the afternoon, and we were back with the others at two thirty.

We landed at the front gate of the prison, which was on the outside of one city whose name was unknown to me. The two soldiers who stood in front of us as the ground shook from me landing looked as if they were going to soil their pants. As soon as I changed and stood in front of them with Connor and Scarlet, who looked as if they were in their EFF, the soldiers dropped their guns and sprinted away toward the city. It looked as if Connor wanted to run them down, but I stopped the ten-foot-tall monster by outstretching my hand in front of him. As he visibly calmed down, Scarlet handed me my clothes.

Once I put on my clothes, we walked to the front gate, which Connor subsequently shattered. He punched both sides at the same time, sending the gate into the prison wall almost two hundred feet away. We entered the prison and were met with ten soldiers whom I took care of in less than a second. All the soldiers we passed gave us a wide berth and didn't even attempt to attack or confront us. One soldier even guided us to the control room when we asked. Once there, all the soldiers in there left, except for the prison commander, who was the same man who oversaw my torture. We waited in silence for the other soldiers to evacuate.

"How has the past year treated you?" I asked him as he hung his head at the control panel.

"You killed my son when you escaped, and my family's never been the same. So I haven't really had a good time," he said, still hanging his head at the control panel.

"Well, there's nothing you can do about it now, so why don't you turn on the PA?" I asked.

He didn't respond. All he did was hit the PA button and hand me the microphone. I then tapped it a couple of times to make sure it was on. Satisfied, I began talking.

"Hello, everyone. Some of you may remember me, but if you don't, this is who I am. My name is Bryce Ceribri, also known as the Devil Dragon."

There was an uproar of shouts and cheers that quickly died down.

"As you could guess, today will be the day you all get out of here, all two thousand plus of you. Once your cell doors are opened, I urge you all to go out the front gate, where you will meet Connor, who will be highly noticeable given his power. He will guide you back to camp near the desert. I will join you shortly after, but I will be going to meet the generals to discuss certain things. That aside, trust me when I say this. The long road we've all been on these past couple of years is now over. We are free."

With that, I turned off the PA and hit the button that opened all the cell doors. For the next few minutes, only cheering could be heard, and only tears and hugs could be seen.

Connor then separated from us so that he could lead those free back to our city. Once he was gone, Scarlet and I got to the roof and then went to the military HQ. We encountered no resistance on the way there, and when we got there no one even bothered to try to get in our way. We literally just walked inside the base and got to the elevators. When we got to the one hundredth floor, the doors opened. Two guards in full tactical gear were waiting outside the elevator with their guns raised at us.

Before they could do anything, I noticed a patch on their shoulders. It was the same patch that my father had in his war case. They were not the people who should be caught in the cross fire, but judging by the way Scarlet was getting ready to fight, she might make that decision for them. However, she never did anything, as I put my hand on her shoulder and shook my head. She looked confused for a brief second, but the expression disappeared quickly. I looked around at the soldiers and said.

"I am of the few who don't walk the road but conquer it," I saw their eyes widen under their masks before they lowered their weapons and let us pass. That was a saying my dad told me to say if I ever found people with the same patch as him.

Scarlet turned to me, looking for an explanation, but she got none as I walked away without uttering a word, looking for the conference room. We found it a couple of minutes later after getting turned around a couple of times from the confusing signs. Before we went in, I changed back into my regular human form, and Scarlet gave me my clothes. Both of us walked through the doors, and we were met with stares from every general and even their assistants. They were sitting around an oval-shaped table, with windows on the right and two empty chairs in the corner. Water glasses and water were in the middle of the table, and that was it in the room; it was rather plain, considering the amount of money the country had.

Scarlet went to the corner where the chairs were, grabbed one of them, tossed it to me, and then came over to me and stood with her hands on my shoulders as I sat down. Dead silence fell between all of us for over five minutes as we just sat there looking at each other. My gaze started on the left, where the head of the world's navy was, and slowly went to the middle, where the head of the world's army was directly opposite from me, and finally on the right, where the head of the world's air force was. In the back of the room, a man was standing alone, and he was the head of the Släve, the group that had been haunting us since day one and the group that had replaced the marines. Judging by the way Scarlet's grip had tightened on my shoulders, she had noticed him and had realized whom he was. I reached up with my right hand and put it on her hand. It seemed to calm her, but she leaned down and whispered into my ear, "I'm going to kill that man."

She left the room, only to come back a minute later with a rifle, probably from one of the soldiers from earlier. After walking into the room, she shouldered the rifle and fired three shots at the man behind the generals, all three hitting him in the chest. He fell over backward, and she walked up to him as he was still breathing and fired another shot, hitting him in the head. She continued to pull the trigger until it clicked empty. I got up and walked over to her. She was beginning to tear up, but just my putting my hands on her made her stop. We both walked back to the chair at the edge of the table, and I sat her down, put my hands on her shoulders, and started to massage them to calm her down.

"What you just saw is only a small example of what's happened to us, and I sincerely hope you realize what you've done to all of us. You took us from our homes, killed our families and friends, destroyed our lives, and threw us into prison. And why? Because of the actions of people thirty years ago and because the people called for it? When was the last time the government, let alone the military itself, ever listened to the people? The worst part of all this is all the pain and suffering you've caused not only us but all the soldiers you sent at us who died. Was it worth it? They died for nothing more than politics, trying to get a vote. Do they or their families really deserve that little? You obviously can't change the past though, so listen to the words I have to say here and now.

"I have felt the pain of all those who have been broken by you and your men, and I will fix them so that they can live again! I can see the darkness that envelops everyone you imprisoned, and I will give them light so that they can walk out of the dark! And I can hear the silence of all those who have lost their faith, and I will give them noise so that they can reclaim their lost faith! You will never hunt us. You will never hurt us, and so help me God if you can't follow those simple rules, it won't just be the soldiers you send that I kill. I will destroy your entire military, and then I will destroy the government you so blindly follow and then send your world back into the Dark Ages!"

CHAPTER
65

During the speech, my grandson got increasingly louder. By the end of it he was shouting at us. All his points were dead-on, but what really caught my attention wasn't him or the speech but what was behind him. At the beginning of the speech, a white dragon appeared behind him. Its eyes were black, and on its face were three black sixes. It did nothing after it appeared other than snarl at all of us as my grandson continued through his speech. However, as soon as the speech was over, it was gone, and so were Bryce and the girl who left out the door through which they had come. We stayed in complete silence for about a minute before the naval general spoke up.

"Damn. Your grandson has some serious game. That girl was one of the hottest women I've ever seen," he said.

"You're a pervert. Did you completely miss what he said?" the air force assistant said.

"No, I didn't. I just thought I could break the ice a little, because we all know that our worst fears came to light. We all saw the power readings the satellite picked up from him in the desert. If we exploded every nuclear bomb we have, which, bear in mind, is enough to blow up the world fifty times over, the amount of energy they would create would still be far lower than what we saw," he said.

"I know," I said, and this shut up everyone else. "We follow the rules he gave us, and we help them rebuild, at least for a while. We don't do it directly, but we give them money and resources to rebuild that city they'll live in. Also, disband the Slăve, and we will publicly oppose any politician who wants the hunt of magic users to continue. And get the president on the phone. We have to abolish the law making magic use illegal. That is what we need to do as fast as possible," I said.

"Why would we do that? I completely agree, but what will the politicians say? We can't just overthrow the government by ourselves," the air force general said.

"Because there is no doubt in my mind—and I know there's none in yours—that if we don't do what I just said and we go against what he said not to do, he will kill us all and then take what he needs."

"I don't know if that's enough to gain support from others, but you have my backing," the naval general said, and his agreement was quickly followed by his assistant's and then by everyone else's in the room.

CHAPTER
66

B y now we had already caught up to the caravan of military transport cars, easily numbering into the hundreds. There were also at least five semitrucks with full tankards of gasoline. Getting in front of the cars, I landed over one thousand feet in front of the caravan and changed back into human form with Scarlet in my arms. This gave them plenty of time to stop. Before they could get to us, however, my world faded into darkness. Scarlet's frantic yelling was the last thing that I heard. That was when I found myself in a completely new plane of existence.

The first dream was in the same room that I had fought my Prime, but everything was repaired. Even the table and chairs were back where they had been. This time, however, my Prime wasn't there. Instead, it was a woman. She had cocoa colored skin and beautiful emerald eyes that shined like the sun. Long, gracefully flowing black hair that accentuated her every feature. Her skin was flawless and the gown she wore really showcased her supple thighs and mouthwatering bosom. Not too big and not too small, the perfect size, and when she walked to the other side of the table to let me sit down she swayed her hips every step of the way. Showing off her perfect butt. The best part about her though was her face, it was if she had been graced by the god of beauty. She outclassed every other woman I had ever seen in my life and Scarlet, Taylor, and Annabeth put world class models to shame. This woman though, was in a league of her own and at a standard that no one will ever be able to reach. Still, looking at her I felt that she couldn't really be trusted.

"So you're him? Huh, I expected you to be a bit taller and maybe a bit bigger in stature." That was the first thing out of her mouth after she looked me up and down.

"Well, I don't know who you are, so you can shove it up—"

"Now, now, no need to get hostile. I'm just here to talk briefly. Then I'll be out of your hair," she said.

I looked her up and down again and nodded for her to continue, not letting my guard down for a second.

"A storm's coming, and it's something you'll either weather and become stronger because of, or it will destroy you and everything you know and love. I know you have no grounds to trust me, but if you can't weather the storm, then everything will die."

"And why should I believe you?" I retorted.

"You shouldn't. This sounds ridiculous even to me, but I know you can tell that we are extremely similar. You don't have to believe me, but you should be ready just in case."

The woman disappeared, and the room faded into darkness. That was where I would float for most of the time. There was nothing around me and no one to talk to; it was an endless void of nothingness. There was nothing for me to do in there except twiddle my thumbs for what seemed like the longest time until there was a voice—a gruff and clogged voice, as if it hadn't talked in an eternity.

"You're rather exquisite, boy. I wonder what you are, as you're not human. No human can harbor that much energy and power," the voice said, but before I could ask who or what they were, they were gone, and everything was becoming light around me.

My eyes opened to light all around me. I was on a bed in some room that was unknown to me. When was the last time I had slept on a bed? An open window was to my left, along with an empty chair and sunlight coming through. An open closet was on my right. It looked to be quite big, but it was hard to tell since there was no angle to see inside of it. In front of me was a door, but it had no handle, and there was just a hole where the handle should have been.

Out of nowhere, I heard banging from the closet, as if someone was hammering a nail into something. Then someone with a hard hat on and a hammer in his hand came out of the closet. He stopped in his tracks when he saw me looking at him. It was someone whom I had never seen before, and when I opened my mouth to speak, it was dry; no words would come out. He noticed this but chose to ignore it.

"You've been asleep for almost three months, so you probably won't be able to speak for a bit. I know you probably have a lot of questions, but I'm not one to answer them. The others in your group can answer them for you. Before I go, your girl only ever left your side to eat. She even slept next to you. I don't know what you did to get something like that from a girl like her, but you're really lucky," the man said before leaving the room.

Exactly two minutes later, Scarlet came rampaging through the door and threw herself on top of me, sending me back down from sitting up in the bed. It seemed like she had waited years and not weeks to see me awake again. She then proceeded to hit me repeatedly until she was fully satisfied. Her mouth opened, as if to say something, but nothing came out of her mouth. There was a knock on the door, and everyone else came in. Connor was the first one to come in with a giggling Carmine in his arms. Albert and Argentum were the second ones in with nothing but giant smiles on their faces. Next came Jessica and Annabeth and finally Erik, all three of whom were more serious than the others, but they were smiling nonetheless.

They didn't let me get a word in before they began to explain everything that was going on. They started by telling me exactly how long I had been out: eighty-four days. Unfortunately, they could only guess that the cause of the sleep was the amount of energy I had used. Then they explained everything around me, from the bed to the outside. It was incredible to hear. Everyone we had saved had been so thankful to us that they were building a house for us on the exact same spot as our camp had been. They were also renovating the entire town, with help from the military.

That part was hard for them to explain, but apparently the military finally said enough to the government. It seemed they were sick of sacrificing soldiers for an unjust cause and finally stood up to the government, though not directly. They couldn't directly help us, but they were doing everything they could by sending us supplies of everything we could possibly need. However, the next bit of information blew me away.

"They're building a school, and of course we'll have to go to school soon. On the plus side, they've already offered us a job after we finish our schooling."

"What did they offer us?" I barely got the words out, but as I did, everyone except for Scarlet left the room.

"Who cares about that now? I missed you so much," she whispered in my ear.

"I missed you too," I responded, barely croaking out the words.

She left for a minute and returned with a bottle of water. As soon as it was gone, she pushed me over and got on top of me.

"You made me wait almost three months to see you awake again. You aren't getting any rest until tomorrow," she said, smiling on top of me, leaning down toward my face.

"What time is it?" I asked.

"Exactly twelve o'clock. You've got twelve hours to go, and consider yourself lucky it's that short," she said, smiling from ear to ear as she kissed me.

"What about the workers?" I asked after being able to pull away for a couple of seconds.

"Jessica's on it," she said, leaning back down.

CHAPTER 67

Since waking up from my three-month impromptu coma, I'd been nothing but sore. At first it was because I had been lying in a bed for three months, but after the night with Scarlet my body was sore for a whole new reason. Getting out of the bed was an effort in and of itself. I looked around the bedroom, and the state it was in didn't surprise me at all. It was a complete mess from the activities of last night, but it was still a nice room all the same. In the bathroom a shower was running ... *Wait. A shower. Oh my God, a shower!*

I went into the bathroom to see Scarlet with a towel on. She was currently doing her hair while the shower ran. In an instant my clothes were off and my body was in the shower. The *warm* cascading water felt like my own little slice of heaven after not having a shower for over a year and a half and only bathing in a river for most of that time. Scarlet must have been amused by my reaction to the shower, as her laugh reached my ears over the bliss of the running water.

"Feels good, doesn't it?" she asked as she stifled her laughter.

"Yessss," I said, intent on emphasizing my visible joy in this shower as much as humanly possible.

"Then you'll need these too," she said, opening the shower door and handing me two bottles of something. I recognized them as body soap and shampoo. God, it had been a long time since I had seen either of these things.

Over the next thirty minutes that shower was my home. It was possibly one of the most comfortable and relaxing moments of my life. I didn't want to get out, but a half hour was a long time.

A towel was hanging on a hook right outside the shower door. I grabbed it and used it to dry myself off, and then I dropped it into a basket by the door of the bathroom. As I walked out of the bathroom and back into my own room, it still felt weird to not see the campfire or tents. It had been less than a day, and that was expected, but getting used to this life would take a long time.

It was surprising to see that the room was completely clean. I didn't know it was possible to pick up that mess in thirty minutes. My guess was that Scarlet had cleaned up. She had done the same thing to my tent when she arrived, but it was still weird to see it on this scale. It made my life easier getting to the dresser and finding out exactly what and whose clothes were in each drawer. By trial and error, I now knew exactly where all of Scarlet's underwear was. I let my perverted side take over for a second, and now those locations were stamped into my mind.

I got fully dressed. My outfit consisted of a plain gray T-shirt that was a little small on me and some baggy but comfortable jeans. The socks were plain, but there were no shoes of any kind in sight. What I did notice, however, was the struggle to walk right. Yesterday definitely had something to do with this, but it was more than that. Being out for almost three months wouldn't go without some type of consequences. As surprising as it was, I suffered no muscle loss from the three-month coma. It was a miracle.

Walking out of the room, I was met with nature and the forest that had surrounded me only three months earlier. I turned back around and looked through the door to see another door on the other side of the room. Sighing, I closed the door, undressed myself, and took off into the forest, intent on getting a little workout in.

CHAPTER

68

The boom that shook through the house and inevitably could be heard throughout the town signaled to everyone that he was back. I, of course, already knew that he was back and standing as well as he could after a three-month coma, but that boom let me know that he was back as his previous self. Those who were with me in our makeshift kitchen heard it too. Jessica, Annabeth, Argentum, Albert, Connor, and even baby Carmine had smiles on their faces when they heard it. I just hoped that the people in the village were okay with it, as there had been some mixed reviews about Bryce.

Their sheer audacity to judge the man who literally saved them from being stuck in a prison cell for the rest of their lives astounded me. However, almost everyone loved or at the very least respected him for doing what they could not. They were still scared of him for his feats of killing, in a sense, but they didn't outright hate him. However, some were trying to undermine what he had done. That was inexcusable, and it was the people who did that who made me want to kill them.

It would have been so much easier for everyone if they were dead, but Connor had stressed to me that we couldn't just go around killing anymore, especially since we had rights now as a "Separate Species." It wasn't perfect by any means, and it was downright disrespectful, but at this point we took what we could get. It also didn't help that protests against this were already making their way around the country like wildfire. Few people were happy to see us have not only rights but a place to be educated, a hospital, and our own trade markets already. It sounded ridiculous to have those things already, but anything could be done in any amount of time with the greatest minds on this side of the world working toward one goal.

I served breakfast to everyone at the table. It was a combination of sausages, eggs, OJ, and water. Carmine got formula, as her teeth weren't even remotely developed enough to eat this meal. We ate in relative silence and peace until someone banged open the door.

We all knew who it was before we heard the voice; it was Brandon Schuyler, a lifelong politician who never had a job before becoming a politician. He had a PhD in philosophy and, as such, felt that he was better than everyone. He was one of the few who openly tried to undermine and discredit Bryce on a regular basis and, as such, was *not* welcome in our house. Unfortunately, none of us could really deal with him, as our powers didn't allow gentle persuasion. Erik, on the other hand, could do whatever he wanted to Brandon, but he wasn't there; he was in the city supervising and helping with the construction of the memorial to those who had died. I was planning to go help him after eating, but it didn't look like that was going to happen.

Few people liked Brandon. All he said was a lie. But some hung onto every word he said. It was starting to become a problem. In the time Bryce had been out, he had gotten about three hundred people to see it his way. He had that many because of this magic: telekinesis. It was easier for people to follow him when they thought they knew his every word divinely. The only reason his followers hadn't figured it out was that they believed he could predict the future. Thankfully, none of those three hundred dared cross anyone in this house, because without us they wouldn't be here.

When we came back inside and went to the kitchen, we got to see Bryce viciously tearing through all our breakfasts, and a giggling Carmine. When he saw us, he stood up from his chair with a giant smile. Although they had seen each other yesterday, it still wasn't enough. Thankfully, he was dressed instead of being naked, which was associated with his use of magic. I wasn't complaining about it, but it was rather indecent, especially since we were officially going back into society.

Everyone went to greet him and officially welcome him back. Argentum and Albert came up to him next and did the same, only they were audibly thankful, unlike Erik, whose smile was enough for him. Jessica did the same as Albert and Argentum. Annabeth, on the other hand, swatted away his hand in favor of bringing him in for a giant bear hug, one that he returned. There were tears in Annabeth's eyes, and I knew why. He had saved her and her sister from starvation when they were younger, and he had never left her side. Never had he let her down, and for him to be alive and well officially was too much for her. Eventually she pulled away, and Connor was the last one left.

Connor and Bryce stared at each other for what felt like eons before they walked toward each other and embraced in the biggest hug imaginable. Those two had quite literally been together since the beginning. They were the best of friends, although it didn't always seem like it. Looking past both their normally cold exteriors, they were teddy bears on the inside— ones who were willing to kill for their family. Pulling away from each other, they both looked extremely happy.

"So, who was that?" came the voice of Bryce as he looked over at all of us.

"A pest," hissed Connor.

It was understandable. Bryce looked taken aback at Connor's response but decided not to push it.

"Someone I should worry about?"

"Maybe. I'll tell you about him later, but right now you need to go into town and mingle," I said, grabbing him and pulling him toward the door. He groaned and resisted but eventually caved. Once we got to the door though he stopped me.

"What's up with Annabeth and Connor? They seem off."

"Annabeth and the others buried Taylor and Lucy while he was away getting the people you freed. He's still mad about it." I couldn't blame him either. If someone buried Bryce without me being there, I would be furious. They were getting better though.

As we opened the door, we were immediately confronted by what must have been hundreds of people right outside our door. There was complete silence as some turned around to face us, but most just stopped what they were doing and stared at Bryce. For the longest time the silence continued, most of them just staring at the man who had quite literally saved them from eternal imprisonment. Just as the silence began to get awkward, we heard a lone clap somewhere in the middle of the group. That lone clap soon turned into thunderous applause that refused to stop.

One by one the people came up to meet Bryce, and one by one he greeted them with as much sincerity as he could muster. So many people and so many faces passed both of us in the next couple of hours that it was dizzying. But my smile only got bigger and brighter with every person passing. Their happiness, sincerity, gratitude, and respect for him washed over me like a tsunami. It was awe-inspiring.

After almost three hours, the group began to dwindle. At one point Mrs. Kline came up to me and told me that they were going to throw a party in two days to celebrate everything that had happened. Mrs. Kline was such a nice old lady. She was one of the few from the first generation of magic users. She'd been around for everything in her ninety-plus years of life, and she was still kicking. The woman was amazing, and I had gotten to know her well in the past three months. She was an absolute wealth of information.

As the group died down, there was only one person left. Standing only a couple of feet in front of us was a man of about six feet. He had short jet-black hair and white skin, and he was wearing a trench coat. Under the trench coat was a plain white T-shirt, and he was wearing blue jeans and military-style boots. He had a rather skinny body, but he emanated an obscene amount of power, and it felt almost identical to Bryce's. However, his seemed to be a lot more volatile, and a lot of it seemed to be coming from his hip, where a jet-black sword handle and sheath could be seen. He rested a gloved hand on the handle, looking ready to pull it out at a moment's notice.

He walked up to both of us with extreme casualness. He held out his hand, and Bryce shook it. An unknown tension existed between the two that seemed to cause sparks between them. Their handshake too seemed to be a fight for dominance. Bryce squeezed just a little too much for the man, who winced and pulled away. The man then turned around, took a couple of steps, and then stopped to turn back to face us.

"I look forward to meeting you again, Bryce."

He began to walk away again, but he got only a couple of steps before Bryce called out to him.

"I never got your name."

"The name's Wick—just Wick," he said, turning around.

I swear to all things holy that when I looked between the two I could see a giant white dragon snarling at a pitch-black bat whose fangs were bared at the dragon. However, as quickly as they appeared, they disappeared. I thought I had just imagined it, but the look on Bryce's face told me otherwise. It was one of pure unadulterated hatred. Whoever this person was, he pissed off Bryce to the absolute extreme.

EPILOGUE

Unknown
Unknown location, unknown time

The originals are finally making themselves known, huh? It looks like things are going to get a lot more interesting in the coming years. Maybe they'll try to kill each other off like they did before. Wouldn't that be a sight to behold now in their worlds?

Either way, it won't be long before we meet again. This time, though, they'll die along with everyone around them.

Printed in the United States
By Bookmasters